HUMBLE INSURRECTION

BOOK 4: ARMOUR OF LIGHT SERIES

DONITA BUNDY

JOURNEY
PRESS

ISBN
Print: 978-0-6486387-0-4
eBook: 978-0-6486387-1-1

Editor: Belinda Pollard
Proofreader: Alix Kwan
Cover design: Donita Bundy

Cover images copyright ©
Character: AlexValent via Bigstock,
Background: Zeferli via iStock and mblach via Envato
Armour: fxquadro via Envato

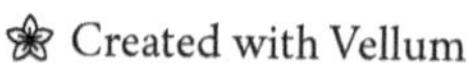 Created with Vellum

For my boys, Sam and Jack,
the apples of my eye and the stars in my sky.

AUTHOR'S NOTE

Dear Reader,

As the story continues, the crew move to the city of Philadelphia—modern day Alaşehir. As well as the letter recorded in Revelation 3:7–13, inspiration for this book comes from actual historical events. For example, in 17 AD an earthquake destroyed this city and ten others. Founded in 140 BC, Philadelphia was still considered a "new city", so the emperor at the time, Tiberius, funded its restoration. Out of gratitude, the citizens renamed Philadelphia to Neo Caesura—*new city of Caesar*—before reverting to its original name, Philadelphia—*brotherly love*.

I have also drawn inspiration from what was happening contextually for the early church at the time the letters of Revelation were written—around 95 AD. At this time, the Roman emperor Domitian was ruling and, unlike most other Roman emperors who were deified after their death, he demanded homage paid, and his deity recognised, whilst he lived.

Needless to say, this book is not historically accurate. It is a work of fiction set in the not-too-distant future. Names, characters, businesses, places, events and incidents are either the products of my imagination or used in a fictitious manner. Any resemblance to actual persons, living or dead is purely coincidental.

My hope is that you will enjoy the story and journey with the growing family who live between the pages. But my prayer is that you are confident that, no matter what lies ahead for the Communities of Light, when you stand in the Light, even if you are only one person, you have the majority. Be encouraged, have faith, and stand strong.

Sincerely,

db

TO THE CHURCH IN PHILADELPHIA

"To the angel of the church in Philadelphia write: These are the words of him who is holy and true, who holds the key of David. What he opens no one can shut, and what he shuts no one can open. I know your deeds. See, I have placed before you an open door that no one can shut. I know that you have little strength, yet you have kept my word and have not denied my name. I will make those who are of the synagogue of Satan, who claim to be Jews though they are not, but are liars—I will make them come and fall down at your feet and acknowledge that I have loved you. Since you have kept my command to endure patiently, I will also keep you from the hour of trial that is going to come on the whole world to test the inhabitants of the earth.

I am coming soon. Hold on to what you have, so that no one will take your crown. The one who is victorious I will make a pillar in the temple of my God. Never again will they leave it. I will write on them the name of my God and the name of the city of my God, the new Jerusalem, which is coming down out of heaven from my God; and I will also write on them my new name. Whoever has ears, let them hear what the Spirit says to the churches."

Revelation 3:7–13 (NIV)

1

———

JONATHAN: FRACTURED

The new year lay before me like an open road fast-tracking to peak-hour congestion. My schedule was already clogged up through autumn. As Overseer of Philadelphia, life was always a juggling act of time, resources, possibilities and sanity. But this year was going to be great. I could feel it like the burst of endorphins at the peak of a run.

Despite it being the middle of summer, the pre-dawn air was fresh. Cool wind blew past my face via the open windows and circled the inside of the car, causing my skin to tighten in gooseflesh. I made a point of not using the heater on chilly mornings, regardless of the season. That way, the cool, damp embrace of the forest wasn't such a shock when I set out.

Turning the lights and ignition off, I just sat for a moment taking in the peace, solitude and breathtaking power of the wilderness in front of me. To have access to this National Park so close to our home was a gift too good not to take advantage of.

Don't get me wrong, I'd prefer not to be a morning person but, with a weighty job, a beautiful wife, four growing sons and a bundle of chaotic joy we called our daughter, I prized a little bit of quality time alone more than an extra couple of hours' sleep.

Just the thought of my family forced a smile from my soul. David would be starting Year Ten when school returned. George was moving into Year Eight. Patrick, desperate to join his brothers at high school, had to finish his last year at Philly Primary. However, Andrew, moving into Year Five, was happy to have at least one of his brothers still at school with him. And our firecracker, Ruby, was convinced she was finally a "big kid" heading off to Prep this year. Our children were growing like magic beanstalks, and I didn't want to miss a moment.

Laura and I laughed at how, finally, she might get room to breathe and have a bit of respite with Ruby off to school. But already she'd been signed up to a whole host of committees and rosters... at both schools. I didn't know how she did it. One day she'd return to teaching, but we all needed her home prioritising us for a little bit longer. Because we both knew there was no way I could do my job of Head Shepherd and Overseer of Philadelphia if she wasn't overseeing our home.

Today on my to-do list was prepping for a conference for the representatives of the Community Alliance to be held next week. Then I had meetings with Sean, Cal and Leah, touching base with my Shepherds of North Philadelphia. There was also a board meeting for CSS—Citizen Support Services. The team there were all volunteers and fully committed to helping families struggling with poverty. It was an honour to work with them. But all in all, it was going to be another exhausting day.

I really must get round to advertising for an assistant. Felix had been strongly suggesting it for a while now... and Laura was nigh on demanding it. She knew me better than anyone and, regardless of what my day held, I knew Laura would be there to hold home—and me—together.

I stretched, limbered up, and set off at a slow jog to warm up and take in the immense beauty that surrounded me. The air was clear and sweet, dew coated every flat surface, and birds welcomed the morning with a chorus. Again, I was tempted to pinch myself. First for my opportunity here in this city. Second for the explosion of blessings raining down on me. And third for the privilege it was to represent and serve the Light at this time, in this place.

Now that my muscles were warm, I stretched out and worked my way up a beaten single-track snaking its way up the side of the mountain. And once again I tried crash tackling the upcoming stress from my mind by pushing myself harder along the trails, relishing the burn, the ache and the exhilaration. Normally I'd aim for at least ten kilometres but, in truth, my distance was dictated by my schedule—which was rapidly closing in around me like one of those shrinking rooms in a B-grade spy film. But I needed to make room for this island of peace and make that goal a habit. It was my mental-health reset.

With the potential for rocks to roll under my feet or a slap in the face from a whippy, wet branch, I found I didn't have to try too hard to focus on my immediate surroundings. I created the rhythm of breathing, running and pumping my arms. It forced everything else out of my mind, which is probably why it took me a while to notice what was happening.

Tremors were a dime a dozen in Philadelphia. Shakes were a little less common. But this was something else altogether.

I was at the turn-around when the quake had me down on my haunches, stabilising myself with hands on the ground. Loud cracks exploded through the hills as rocks broke away from outcroppings. Trees rattled and branches shook. A whirlpool of scents assaulted me —earth, ozone and pine—while my teeth continued rattling from the ongoing quake. Birds shrieked and took to the air and animals bolted through the brush. I followed their lead and ran. The bush is not the best place to be in an earthquake. Although, it was better than the city.

The city.

Laura. The kids.

I had been running for my life. Now I ran for theirs.

* * *

SIRENS, alarms and car horns pierced my eardrums. Geysers shot into the air where burst water pipes divided roads. Billowing clouds of dust and rubble made it impossible to see or breathe. Buildings were down, lights flashed, people ran screaming or walked dazed like grey-coated zombies. Architectural arrogance had preached we could control nature, but I could never understand birthing a city as gateway to three major regions—over a fault line. Right now, however, frustration and fear fuelled my fury and desperation.

Chaos. Everywhere was madness and I couldn't make myself care. I had to get to Laura and the kids.

Lifted asphalt, cars impaled by streetlights, collapsed buildings, hissing live electrical wires blocked all access through the city. I ditched my car and ran, blind to everyone's need but my own. To get to my family. I cut through backyards, scaled ruins, and tried, as the crow flew, to make my way home.

The front of the lower level of our house still stood. Crooked but upright. It looked like a huge hand had swept the top floor into the backyard to rest in a pile of rubble. I forced my heart to quieten and my ears to hear beyond the screams of the street. Was there movement? Life?

I edged closer, scared a mere whisper would bring the rest of the house down. Standing within reach of the lintel of our front door, I held my breath and petitioned the Light.

There it was. A whimper.

"Ruby?"

"Daddy." Her choked sob pulled me into the wreck like a retracting bungy cord.

Crawling through our entrance way, edging under support beams still holding the ceiling off the ground with just enough space for me to squeeze through, I found her. Under the kitchen table held in a nest of arms and broken bodies, my golden-haired angel waited for me.

The rest of our family cradled her. But it was too much to comprehend, too much to digest. Bodies bent at impossible angles. Open, unblinking eyes filled with debris, staring into eternity. Unnaturally stilled, permanently frozen faces.

No. Not possible. Not happening.

My priority was to get Ruby out.

Zebra stripes of light broke through, slicing the space into ribbons of hell. On hands and knees, over shards of the remains of our lives, I inched my way through. Breaking Ruby out of the embrace of our family wasn't the hardest thing I had ever done. Holding her to me and leaving them was.

The space was too small for me to carry her clinging body. Prising her limbs from around me, I forced her screaming and protesting back through the passage ahead of me. Voices called to me from the doorway.

I coughed but managed to choke out, "Stay there. Ruby's coming through." My numb hands and knees were coated with debris and slick with freely flowing blood. My ears rang with the strain of trying to hear any other call, plea, whisper from the house behind me over the increasing groans and creaks of the settling wreck. But I didn't stop, I wouldn't allow myself to stop until Ruby was out.

An ominous crack froze my efforts an instant before the crash. With strength I didn't have, I launched my daughter into waiting hands as I lay pinned under a fractured support beam.

"We've got her," was the last thing I heard before I blacked out.

JONATHAN: APRIL

What did I do wrong?
Tell me and I'll fix it.
Haven't I been faithful, obedient, honourable?
Serving you, serving the Community, serving society?
Serving, serving, fracking serving?
Tell me where I went wrong!
Then fix me, so I can fix… whatever it was.
But don't leave me like this.
Please.
Every fibre of my soul is desperate.
Craving, thirsting, starving for release.
Hear my cry!
Look at me!
Look and hear me!
Don't you turn away from me.
Open your ears.
I know you can hear me.
Why are you ignoring me?
I trusted you.
I trusted your word.

You said you were The Life,
The Truth.
I swallowed it all: hook, line and sinker.
Fully invested and bought the bank.
I put my hope, my life, my… everything in you.
Don't leave me to rot like this.
Do something.
Save me.
Heal me.
Restore me.
Or let me go.
Let me die.
Take me.
Please.

3

JONATHAN: JUNE

Since hearing and smell were now my only real senses, I was aware of it before I heard it. The stench made my eyes water and my nose run. But I lay paralysed and alone. There was nothing I could do to stem the tide of mucus and tears itching heated tracks over my temples and across my cheeks into the pillow. I couldn't wipe my face. I couldn't even sniff as the Dark's minion came by for its daily taunt. "So this"—the reek made it easy to track its presence around my inert body—"is the culmination of your life's work?"

As its captive audience I just focused on breathing. In and out. But I really had no control over that either. The presets in my brain kept my lungs operating, my heart beating and my body functioning in "safe mode".

"What can I say? I'm a fan. Congratulations on a job well done. You've not only lost your job, your reputation and your standing in this city, you've lost your wife and your four boys. All of them, gone. What's the saying? 'You've gone from hero to zero in a day'... a morning was all it took. Seriously, you've pretty much done me out of a job." It came closer and patted my leg. "I didn't have to do a thing, to lift a finger or work out a cunning plan to destroy you. You did it all by yourself. Thank you."

With less and less confidence was I aware that my Guard was also in the room with me. But I neither felt its presence nor heard its voice.

The demon on the other hand was obnoxiously blatant. Its voice travelled around the room then stopped. I heard it inhale. "I'll send flowers as a token of my gratitude. But now, there is really only one more thing for you to do, Jonathan. That is: figure out what your worth is. What you're contributing to society. How you're helping the needy. In what ways are you encouraging and equipping the Community? And how"—it whispered in my ear, a new wave of tears flooding from my eyes from its overwhelming sulphuric fetor—"are you glorifying the Light? You are a burden." Hot, foul breath assaulted my ear and passed over my face. "A waste of a bed, and nothing but work for the people in this good facility. Seriously, the best thing you could do for everyone would be to fall asleep and never wake up. And, since you've gone out of your way to help me, I would like to do the same for you. It sounds so good, doesn't it? To just fall asleep and never wake up. It would all be over." I could hear the grin in its voice. "Now that is something I'd be happy to help you with."

Even after it left, my nose and eyes still soaked my pillow and there wasn't a damn thing I could do about it. The demon was wrong. It wasn't that easy. How could I "just fall asleep and not wake up"? Believe me, I'd tried. And failed. I couldn't even do that.

Apparently, there was nothing wrong with me. Physically. But obviously I was seriously whacked in the head. All my physical wounds had healed but my fully capable body was paralysed. I could hear, smell and feel. But I was blind and locked in a prison of my own making.

Twenty-four times a day, nurses came in to monitor, move, wash, change, roll me or treat bedsores. Tubes brought food and air in, and a tube took waste out. I was a vegetating tunnel, consuming time, resources and oxygen.

Why? I didn't fracking know. All I did know was when I opened the door and remembered Laura... and the boys... Ruby... I black—

* * *

"Aʜ, Dr Nichols, I'm glad we caught you on your rounds. We have a visitor from Laodicea who has shown particular interest in this patient. He is on the board of the esteemed Laodicean Private Hospital. Where, as you know, ground-breaking discoveries, cures and treatments have been developed."

There was a shuffling around my room as my doctor and Jenny, my principle nurse, made room for the newcomers. Great. It wasn't enough that I was an exhibition piece for all training med students and nurses at this hospital. I was now drawing a crowd from further afield. Murmurs and rustling fabric indicated the formalities of the introductions were taking place.

"Dr Nichols, may I inquire as to the cause of your patient's prolonged... hiatus?" I recognised that voice! Felix. I was madly trying to remember if I had known he was on the board of the hospital that had done amazing work curing blindness and deafness, and missed the next part of the conversation. Not that it really mattered, I'd heard it all before.

The instant spark of joy to know he was here was inundated by a storm of frustration as the usual prognosis was rolled out for a new spectator. "We believe it's a psychosomatic coma." As much as I appreciated Felix visiting, I hated being labelled as a nut job to a new audience. "Everything is functioning perfectly. Jonathan even shows signs of being aware—"

I did? I didn't know that. *Hey, Felix, I'm here, I hear you. Hey. Look at me. See me.*

"—it's obviously directly related to what happened in The Quake."
You reckon?

"Ahh. I see." Felix was quiet for a moment, then his hand—cool and dry—vaguely patted my arm. "Is there anything we can do to... assist you with your treatment of this condition?"

My doctor continued. "I'm afraid there is not much we can do apart from care for his physical needs. The rest is up to Jonathan. But, presently, his brain can't cope with the immensity of his loss. His psyche is disassociating with the reality of the horrific deaths of his fam—"

4

____

JONATHAN: AUGUST

Why do you hate me?
What are my crimes that you need to punish me like a
    whipped dog?
I have been preaching you are a god of love?
Of grace?
All powerful, all knowing, all loving?
But the joke is on me now, isn't it.
At least convict me of my crimes so I know why I'm
    suffering.
I can't even blame the world or the Dark for my
    condition.
This is all you.
Only you.
There was no attack or siege, trap or ambush.
Just you.
You used your overwhelming, powerful creation
    against me.
And I am indefensible, incapable, inadequate to
    combat it.
Your victory over me is decisive and complete.

I am nothing.
I am less than nothing.
I am a black hole consuming everything that comes into
    my orbit.
I've lost everything.
Everything but my rage.
Blistering, savage, all-consuming rage.
At you.
Why did you bother to save me from the building's
    collapse?
To make me a laughingstock?
The butt of jokes?
To lie here paralysed and listen; to be forced to hear
    every single thing they say…
every single day.
The pity.
The judgement.
The humiliation.
Better yet, why did you allow me to be born if the sum
    total of my life adds up to this?
Useless.
Worse, a burden.
Well, here I am.
Available,
listening.
Give it to me.
Accuse me of my faults.
At least give me a reason,
a kernel,
a splinter to hang my argument on.
Tell. Me. Why.
What did I do wrong that you would punish me like this?
Answer me!

"Perhaps you should cry louder, Jonathan." It was back. The nauseating gut roll almost had my stomach revolting past the feeding tube. "Your anger is justified. It is… righteous. You are an innocent, merely used as a plaything of the Light. You are nothing to Him. How long have you been waiting now? Seven months? Surely it is time to rest." Its silky, forked tongue whispered temptations in my ear. "You can do it, Jonathan, curse Him. Curse Him and embrace the abyss. Then you will find peace with your loved ones. It isn't hard. I will help you. Here, take my hand." Cold, dead flesh took my hand and gave it a gentle squeeze. "You can do it."

5

DAISY: TROPHIES

"Your father was a good man. One of the quality people lost in The Quake, I miss him."

I really want to hit you. It wouldn't have to be closed-fist. I imagined the sting across my palm and the crack as my hand made contact with his flabby, ignorant cheek.

And I know that's just plain wrong, and I am truly sorry. But you know this guy gives off Creepy Dude feels. Hard-core Creepy Dude feels. So... I sighed, attempting to release some of the pressure of my frustration. *Please forgive me, and help me not to focus on our history and the past. Or say something truly offensive, intentional or otherwise.*

Instead of slapping the guy, I smiled through grinding teeth. What was he saying? Something about my dad? "Yes. Yes, he was." More lies. *Where do you draw the line, Daisy girl?* The woodenness of my voice had the fool doing a double take.

"You must be drowning in grief right now. I understand." He attempted to pull me in for a hug. But the stiffness of my shoulders and the metaphorical metal rod up my spine made it as awkward and uncomfortable as hell.

I tell you what. Let me go and I won't sink my fist into your fat, sweaty gut. Oh, how I'd dreamed over the years of putting my dad's cronies in their place. Maybe now he was dead... maybe I could just give this man an extra strong shove... in the head. *Please? Just the one? Or you could do something? Anything, just make him let me go.*

One... two... The creep put both hands on my shoulders and held me at arm's length, fake sympathy turning his ugly features even more pathetic as he waited for my response. Oh dear Lord, what was he saying? Something about grief? Now the eternal question: tell the truth and offend... and suffer the consequences. Or lie and be socially acceptable? "Yes. Yes, I am." *No, no I'm not. And get your grubby, gropey, grimy hands off me. You do. Not. Touch. Me, Mr Hamilton-Ward. I want you and your mates to stop touching me. No one touches me anymore.*

"If there is anything you need, you make sure you let someone from the Community's High Council know. Your father was one of us and we'll... I'll... make sure to do good by you, Daisy girl."

I need you to leave. And for you and your useless, blind cronies to leave me, leave Tent Village, leave us all the hell alone. For someone who is supposed to represent the Light and the Community, you are a bunch of hypocritical... blind... banal... What I wouldn't have given for a thesaurus right then. Anything to tip my mind away from the pooling vat of wrath I wanted to spew all over him. "So kind." Obviously, my go-to monotone voice finally alerted him—he and his associates were as thick-skinned as they were misogynistic—of my sarcasm.

"Oh, Daisy girl. Still with the thorns? You know your father named you for the innocence and purity of the flower. For the woman he wanted you to grow into." The fool had the arrogance to chuckle. "How he tried to mould you into a girl fit for this world."

Yeah, to play doormat, whore and housekeeper to old, sleazy krets like you. Surely the steam pulsing through my veins was pouring out my eyes by now. *Don't say it, don't do it. Hold your tongue, Daisy. He's not worth it. You can think it, just. Don't. Do. It. Please help me focus on good things, nice things, friends, family... well, family here, my craft... anything.*

He tilted his head and ran his leery eyes over me, stopping at my heaving chest. A grin broke through his mask... until he saw my eyes. I suspect they'd turned red from my murderous thoughts.

So help me, if you don't stop this bloke, I will.

He took an involuntary step back. Looked at his watch, then mumbled some inane excuse about a meeting he was late for.

I focused on breathing slowly and not acting-out my fantasy of wringing his grotesquely flabby neck. My hands probably wouldn't reach the full way around anyway.

"You almost done, Daisy?" Travis, my friend across the path, had been leaning against one of the beams holding the tarp open at the front of his workshop. He'd been watching the whole show. And enjoying himself immensely by the look of it. The kret. But he knew the signs and when enough was enough. He always let me fight my own fights. Travis wouldn't even know the word misogyny.

Useless slug-feature's face fell as he eyed my fellow craftsman across the way. "Oh well, maybe next time."

I grimace-smiled. *Over my dead body.* But then froze as his ever-wandering hand slipped from my shoulder, running very close to my breast. *Or your dead body. Either way, one of us is going to die.* I guess I wasn't very successful at hiding my thoughts. He pulled both hands from me, stood up straight, coughed, then spun on his heel and, praise the eva-lovin'-Light, he left.

I counted to ten. Then twenty. If I could just make myself stand still until he was out of sight, I would be less tempted to run after him and stab him in the eye. Or the groin. I wasn't fussy. I'd be happy to stab him in the back if it was the only target I was given.

Finally, the germ had removed itself from our camp—*thank you*—and I hadn't done anything or said anything the world would consider rude. I started a mad search for something of use, something Travis would need. Or want.

"Got any more of that last batch of mead?" Deep, mellow laughter rolled out from under Travis's awning.

The old coot knew how desperate I was. But a whole bottle? It was November, Patrick would still be harvesting honey up until the end of summer, but... "Maybe I've got a jar left somewhere around here." I honed my search, trying not to reveal the remainder of my stash, and thankfully found a sample in an old honey jar.

He coughed.

I turned.

He held up a small rectangle of silver between his thumb and forefinger.

I sighed. Grabbed a whole bottle and made my way over. It was a seller's market, and he knew it.

Banging the bottle on the trestle table, I reverently held out my hand to receive my prize. Travis—Tea—knew the score. And he knew me. "Furnace is running out the back and all my tools are laid out. Let me know when you're done, and we'll crack this beauty together."

Now, if you wanted to talk about "good men" and "quality people", I could wax lyrical about this man. Regardless of the situation, time of day, or people involved, he was like a soothing cup of tea. The guy had been more of a father-figure than my own, recently deceased dad—who was one of the countless victims of The Quake. But I refused to think about Dad, or his cronies, or anything, as I worked the thin rectangle into a clasp. That was the rule: while I worked, there was to be no thinking apart from the art. The crafting. The wonder of moulding wood—or, this afternoon, metal—into something useful, or beautiful—more beautiful than its natural state—art.

The fury ebbed as I focused on the clip, etching an intricate design into the soft, receptive skin. When at last it was done and moulded, I brought it out to Tea, showing him my work as it perched on the palm of my hand.

"Nice." He laid down his pipe then picked up my work, hooked his glasses from the string around his neck to balance on his nose, and scrutinised my efforts in the glow of the kerosene lamp set on his front bench. "Your file work is improving." His deep, dark eyes considered me over the rim of his glasses. "Where do you want this one?"

I spun my back to him. "Don't care. You pick."

Tea hummed as he inspected my hair. I could taste the potential of a soon-to-be-shared cup of my finest mead. Sunset was filling the camp with liquid gold and the last of my anger seeped out, bleeding into the earth at my feet. This had always been my favourite time of day—*thank you*—and this camp had become my favourite place in the world. Filled with good people. Real, honest, genuine people. Like Tea. My father's world didn't often choose to mix with the likes of us here.

But even now, even after my father had finally gone, they'd still come looking for me. Still wanted things from me. It wasn't enough to serve the needy, the desperate, the helpless, I had been brought up to serve the machine. And that was something I swore, by the eva-lovin'-Light, I would never do again.

For each victory in fighting back the tide, I rewarded myself with a new clip. A prize. A trophy. I hadn't given in to them. And I hadn't succumbed to my anger and resentment. And that was something worth celebrating—*thank you*.

Tea understood. Very gently he picked up one of my dreads and fastened the clip. Then stepped away. Without touching me. Like I said, Tea knew the score. He was the one man I could trust.

6

DAISY: LIE OF THE LAND

"Give it back, Ruby." The quiet adolescent voice cracked, losing some of its street cred. But the little girl under the boy's glare didn't seem to notice. I put down my tools and walked over to the trestle table that showed some of my wares, including the items ready to be picked up by customers at the weekend market.

The two were locals. Who was I kidding, the boy was kind of like royalty. Jet was the grandson and only surviving relative of the winery's owner, Mary. His family had run Knox Hill Winery for generations. Their forbearers may well have been here before the city. But, like all of us, they'd lost people in The Quake. Now it was just the two of them: Mary and Jet… and the rest of us.

After the utter chaos and hell we simply called "The Quake", our city was demolished. It was so devastating it destroyed all the cities in our region. Ten in all. These past twelve months we'd had help to rebuild, and now that the city was all shiny and new again—thanks to the Gerent and his bottomless pockets—we were all expected to move back into the buildings that killed three-quarters of our population? I didn't think so. And the people I lived with in Tent Village agreed. Our original camp in Emperor's Park—in the heart of the city—had been shut down about six months ago. But Mary had invited those who wouldn't… couldn't move back into "civilised" accommodation to set up at her place. Said there was no one left to run the winery anyway and, at fourteen, Jet was too young. So, those who wanted to, upped stumps and resettled in a flat paddock in the front corner of Mary's property once used for grazing cattle.

To be perfectly honest, I could have moved back. My nice little bungalow had been restored to "quake" standard. But I was needed here. Don't get me wrong, it wasn't completely altruistic. I was making a nice little nest-egg from the rent I was pulling. Not that we needed money here, but in the future, one never knew.

The little girl Jet had with her was another story. She was as tragic as Tripod, the three-legged dog who'd adopted me when the dust settled. Or maybe I adopted him? I found him, silent, pinned under a car he'd been hiding under when The Quake hit. With a few helping hands and a helluva lot of physics, we got him out and I took him to the vet. We saved him, but not the leg.

Ruby, the girl—who was about four? five?—still had both her legs, but no family to speak of. Her dad was somewhere but was a no-show… ever. Some guy came by most days to take her away for a while. I didn't know where. I didn't ask. It wasn't my business. But she always came back clean, fed, and quiet. She never said a thing about where she went or what she did. I didn't pry. We all had our secrets. But I did check with Mary to see if the transporter guy—Taxi—was legit. All she told me was that, yes, Ruby was safe with him, but this was her home for as long as she wanted. It had all been arranged.

So, with the minimal details, we kind of adopted her too. She lived up at the house with Mary and Jet but wouldn't go inside. So, we pitched her tent on the front lawn. And every night Jet sacrificed his comfortable bed to camp out with her. To keep her company and make sure she was okay. I tell you, this kid was the real deal—a true prince among men.

Right now, however, Ruby was fiddling with something in her hands, staring at the ground whilst Jet was fuming.

I stepped outside the tarp's shelter and squatted down in front of her. She wouldn't look at me. Jet nudged her shoulder.

Back off, Jet, she's just a kid. Okay, so are you. But still. Chill, dude. Do. Not. Say. That out loud. He'd freak and think I was taking his man card. *Play it cool, Daisy girl. And whatever you do, think before you speak.*

From my squat I could look Ruby in the eye—if she were to look at me, that was. "What you got there, Rube?" She swallowed her lips. Jet tapped her on the shoulder. *Better, dude. We'll get there.*

I rewarded him with a nod. It was obvious he was embarrassed. Not as bad as Ruby though. Eventually she held out a fist. She didn't open her fingers. So, I held my hand out flat under hers. One at a time, she prised her fingers open and a ring, darkened by her sweat, sat in her red palm. A small cube of wood I'd whittled, filed and sanded into a ring, etched with an intricate pattern of vines and flowers.

"You like this one?"

She nodded.

"But she doesn't have anything to barter for it, and she shouldn't have taken it." Jet's voice had settled into his newly acquired baritone, now he was calmer.

I nodded. "Yeah, this one took me a bit of time and a lot of practise. I like it too." I lifted it out of her hand and held it up, the sun glinting off the red stone chips I'd set in the middle of the flowers. I looked at the two of them. Well dressed, well fed, clean, but, like the rest of the people in our "village", still carrying an edge of the haunted. "You've been here long enough to know how it works, yeah?"

She dropped her head and nodded. Jet nudged her shoulder again and she mumbled, "I'm sorry I stole your pretty ring. It was wrong. But it reminds me of my mummy, and it has rubies in it—"

"But stealing is wrong, Ruby," Jet cut her off. "You know that."

"You're right, stealing is wrong. In fact, there's no right about it. But, in another sense, I'm kind of flattered you like my work."

Ruby lifted her head and finally looked at me. Her hazel eyes catching on my tatts and the sleeve that covered my right arm—the girl was fascinated by my artwork and her focus took off like a hunted rabbit down a warren. Before we lost her attention fully, I went on, "You know the way it works here with the locals is bartering. You know what that means?" She nodded. "So, you can either buy this with money—like an outsider—or I'll trade it for something you have that I really like."

Her face dropped and her eyes became glassy. "I don't have any money or anything worth that, Daisy."

"How about"—I pretended to think it over—"art for art. I put heaps of time and practise into this piece. You been doing any drawing lately? Or sewing? Writing stories? What about pottery? You been working with Dori on any nice pots or mugs I might like? Or over at the patch with Callum? Are you growing any flowers you could transplant into a pot that'd make my place look... nice?"

Again, she nodded. "Right then. When you guys have finished your rounds here, you get stuck in to working out something you think I might like, and I'll put this aside for you. When you're ready, come back and we can talk about a trade, okay?"

"Daisy, you know she's only five, right?" Jet was giving off some pretty serious patronisation. *Chill, dude, I'm not an idiot.* However, Ruby didn't pay him any attention at all. When I finished showing her where I was storing the ring for her, she was nodding like one of those awful dogs that people stuck on the dashboards of their cars. Already I could see the wheels in her head smoking. This was going to be good.

"Right." I eyeballed them both. "It's in a safe place, waiting. When you're ready, come back and we'll do a trade." I leaned over the trestle table and met Ruby's gaze head-on. "I want your best work. Don't knock something up this afternoon. This took me months. Take your time, make it worth my while, okay?"

She clutched her hands to her chest and fiercely nodded her head as her little bottom started jiggling all over the place.

* * *

GREAT. Another outsider come to give me grief.

"People are moving back now. Have moved back. Why are you still here? Living in this hovel, Daisy?" This time it was a member of the Council. Beryl? Betty? Bertyl?... something.

Here we go. To be honest and insult her? Or lie and insult myself?

Or I could do what I normally did and take so long to think of how to answer, she'd walk away and no one would have to be insulted. Win, win. *Yeah right. Only that she thinks you're a complete moron and are too dim-witted to answer a simple question.* But it wasn't a simple question. There were layers. *Yeah, yeah. Just like an onion. Seriously, just make something up and say... something. Anything.* "I like it here. The people are... nice. And I like to think I'm helping out." Nice. Default response again. Well, at least word was getting round not to come here for answers... or conversation... or stimulating repartee.

She looked down her imperial nose and shook her head, her perfectly coiffed hair a lacquered, immovable helmet. "Oh, Daisy, your father would be so disappointed. You're not helping, you're enabling. It's time you gave up this ridiculous... experiment"—her snark-eye scanned what she could see of the Village—"as a lost cause and came back to reality."

Condescending twik. You've no freaking idea. At. All. And why should I? What's in it for you?

And then the earth shook. Literally. Screams and pounding feet blocked out everything. Or that could have been my brain trying to determine: fight or flight. Waiting to see what the fallout from this one would be. Bodies raced past in a blur, heading for the clearing. Others turned to statues: white-marble, frozen, panicked statues. Pod came bolting out of my shelter with his tail tucked up under him and tried to climb my body, like he was drowning and I was a life raft. I squatted beside him and rubbed behind his ears, whispering quietly to soothe us both. And waited. And counted. Five. I only got to five. An aftershock. Nothing serious, it didn't even spill my coffee. I counted again. This time to twenty. I waited a beat. Ignored the intruder and kept going to forty.

We were good. It was over. For now. Tonight was going to be rough. Night terrors were going to come riding through our camp and pillage the peace. And we'd all live through it again. I might not be a stimulating conversationalist, but I can tell you this, there is very little privacy behind tent walls.

"Daisy?" Ruby's cry pierced my heart with a soldering iron. She came skidding into my side, wrapped her spaghetti arms around me and Pod, and shook like an autumn leaf in a summer storm, her long, straight hair a wild nest and her face and hands covered in dirt. She must have been on garden rotation. Her smock wasn't looking much better. Somewhere along the way she'd taken her shoes off… again. The kid was like a mountain goat. Climbed anything higher than herself. Said she needed bare feet for grip.

But right now, she was making herself as small as possible, a ball of quivering nerves. We breathed together and I got her to count back from twenty to "help Pod out". When there were still no more tremors, I gave Pod a final face rub and returned to Brenda?… Bertha?… who was squinting her eyes at Ruby. Did she know who the kid was? I edged in front of both my shadows and shifted Bessy's attention. "It's just not that easy for some folk to move back into their homes."

She countered like the ignorant observer she was. "But they've all been rebuilt to the highest specifications."

"Tell me, Betsy—"

"Rebecca."

I just stared at her for a beat. "Becky, where were you in the quake?"

"*Rebecca*," she stressed. "I was in Laodicea on business."

"So, you weren't here. You have no idea what it was like."

"I lost everything, just like a lot of people. I came straight back and helped out. I saw what happened."

"But you. Weren't. Here. You didn't live through it. You didn't survive it." *You don't know what you're talking about, you narrow-minded, mean-spirited, poor-shoe-choice-wearing woman.*

She turned her squinty eyes back to me and tilted her head. "You can't rescue them, Daisy."

I scoffed. "I'm not here to rescue them. These guys don't need saving. Just because we live differently to you, doesn't make it wrong. Or even substandard." *Get off your high horse and stop judging us, you imperious woman. And what gives you the right to think you know me? That you can read me? Puh-lease.*

"Okay then, Daisy. You tell yourself whatever you need to so you can sleep at night." Her beady eyes raked over Ruby, who was now curled up in a ball in the dirt with Pod as they comforted each other— her stroking his back, him licking her face. *Yeah, that's kind of gross guys, but, I guess, whatever gets you through the storm.*

Becky gave me one more once-over, raised her eyebrows at Ruby and turned on her ridiculously high, strappy heels and left. Praise the eva-lovin'-Light.

You have no idea why I'm here, woman. Not that I would tell you anyway. The people who need to know, know.

7

JONATHAN: DECEMBER

"I think it's time we started to accept reality, don't you?"

My visitor spoke quietly. I could hardly hear her over the beeps of the heart monitor and the background bustle of the hospital outside my room. I knew the voice—this one was human—but I could not pull my brain out of the latest fog to pinpoint the owner.

"Time to move on, Overseer... or I should say... Jonathan. Jon. Can I call you Jon?" Cold fingers picked up my dead hand. A small rod... a pen? Was placed between my fingers. "Now, if you can just make your mark here, I'll make sure everything is taken care of." Her hand closed around mine and the pen moved.

"What are you doing here, Rebecca?" A new voice had entered the room. There was shuffling as the newcomer came over and took my other hand with a strong, smooth grasp. He gave it a quick squeeze. "How you going, mate? Still hanging in there?" I'd known this voice most of my life. Alario, or Al—he hated his name, and I can't say I blamed him. I had teased him mercilessly for it as we grew up. Until I'd stopped growing and Al hadn't. When I couldn't take the beatings any longer, I gave up. But despite that, he'd always been my best friend. We'd been the dynamic duo... or terrible two, depending on which perspective you were looking through.

After we managed to survive our early teens, Cissa joined our ranks—first as a welcome intruder, later more permanently as Al's wife. Not many believed they would make it—or understood what the sophisticated, wealthy girl saw in him—but not all teen marriages were destined for failure. Al and Cissa were still joined and making their way. Still skitching off her parents, Mr and Mrs Chalmers—significantly influential people.

"Just coming by to pay my respects to the… Overseer."

"Cripes, he's not dead, just… not well. And I thought you said *Overseer*"—Al stressed the word—"Jonathan should be replaced as he was no longer compos mentis."

"Just because I can see the writing on the wall doesn't mean I don't care."

"Yeah, right. Care enough to—" Al paused. "What's that?"

I heard the rustle of papers, and the pen was removed from my hand. "Nothing."

"Doesn't look like 'nothing' to me, woman. What are you up to?" I knew that tone. I pictured Al's disarmingly plain face taking on a chiselled edge. My friend was up for a fight, and I relaxed. He had my back.

"It appears that I am the only one who really does care. I am making sure Jonathan's daughter is put into proper care."

Ruby?

Al stepped into battle. "You're going to want to hope I didn't hear you properly. Would you mind repeating yourself?"

"That child is running wild."

What the heck?

"She should be with family, or in proper care."

"One, that is none of your business. And two, she won't stay with them." The tiredness in Al's voice washed over me. "Pines for her dad. Which, considering the circumstances, is understandable, wouldn't you say?"

"Then she should be in proper care."

"She is. Ruby's staying with Mary and her grandson over at the winery."

The woman spat, "Winery? It used to be the finest winery in the region, now it's a disgusting... den of miscreants."

"Tent Village?"

The woman spat again, "It's past time those people returned to their homes. They're being completely irrational. The Gerent has funded the repair of our city and the suburbs hit hardest. Their disregard of his help is an insult to his generosity. The Community in Philadelphia is too small and insignificant to withstand the focus of his attention. They should all have moved back into their own properties and had that abomination closed... burned down, so the winery can get back to business. He has mentioned his fondness for Knox Hill Wines. We need to be doing everything we can to make this man happy."

"But the people are scared. Heck, the aftershocks are still enough to shut this whole city down in a communal panic attack. And I believe Mary has the right to say who comes and goes, who stays on her property, and what she does with her family business."

"Mad Mary is barely capable of looking after herself, let alone anyone else in her care."

"You mean her grandson and his inheritance? Listen, Ruby's safe, healthy and happy there. I check on her regularly."

If... when... I got out of this nightmare, I was going to have to figure out how the hell I could ever pay Al back.

Papers rustled. "Not for long. *Overseer* Jonathan has just signed a release making her a ward of the state."

I heard the tiny whimper under my bed. Al and this snake of a woman were fighting over my inert body and Ruby was caught in the crossfire, a casualty of my inability to fight for her myself.

Damn it.

With every cell in my fracked body, I fought the paralysis in my mind. I forced air through my dry throat, around the feeding tube, and moaned. Silently I roared and damn well demanded my hand to move, to drop off the side of the bed. Again, I yelled, this time with everything I had in me to make a noise.

She heard me. Her tiny fingers wrapped around mine. Ruby

climbed out from her hiding place and clambered up beside me. I could feel sweat prickling over my entire body as I forced my arm around her and, with atrophied muscles, pinned her to my side. I was breathing heavily and on the verge of passing out again. But one thing I was absolutely sure of. No kret was taking my last surviving child from me.

8

JONATHAN: JANUARY

I. Hate. You.
I wish I could hate you.
But I can't.
I've tried.
And you know I've had the time to work on it.
You engineered it.
But against my best efforts I just can't.
I love you.
Despite it all, in my heart I know you are good.
I know you are faithful.
I know you.
I know you love me.
You are my shield.
I just don't understand.
Help me understand.
Help me…
Just, please, help me.
Please, just…

9

DAISY: WELL-EARNED REWARD

Tea and I waited until the last of the visitors from the market had vacated the premises then shut the gate. It was the end of another successful day selling produce and products to the wider community, and we'd once again earned enough to pay rent to Mary and turn a tidy profit. I hadn't picked the position closest to the gate so I could be the first port of call for the punters—I just wanted to keep an eye on who came and went.

Having a whole horde of hustling shoppers wash through our home each Saturday was taxing. It was good for our livelihood, but it drained the eva-lovin' life right out of me. I had to retreat to my cave for the rest of the day to recover. But not this afternoon. I'd have to be three parts dead not to know something was up. Something good.

Ruby had been a bundle of nerves, jiggling, wriggling and giggling all over the place like a puppy. I knew she'd been working on her barter assignment for about four months. Of course, the project was supposed to be a secret. But seriously, we live in a fishbowl. I knew she'd crafted something with Dori who'd helped with shaping, glazing and firing. Then she'd asked Callum for a lavender cutting, which he'd shown her how to grow in a space in the garden.

Every day Ruby visited it and tended it until Callum assured her it had taken. Together they transplanted the shoot into the pot. I thought at that point I'd be getting the trade for her ring, but no. She waited and kept tending the plant until it filled out a bit. She waited and watered, but not too much. Jet had told me how she'd freaked out when he went to "help". "No!" she'd screamed. "They don't like too much water, only a little, every Thursday."

Callum had also told her the plant needed to have some sun every day. So, with ill-attempted subtlety, Ruby had scoped out my workshop and found the place she thought the pot should live, deeming it had just the right amount of light. She quietly cleared a space. Never said a word, but of course I knew what she was doing. I'd rattle her chain sometimes by purposefully putting something in the cleared space, which I'd find moved shortly after.

A while later I'd forgotten about the gift. I thought something must have happened to it. But I kept her ring wrapped and ready. Right after we'd made the deal, I'd cleaned it and bundled it in soft, lightweight cloth and put it in a little wooden box I'd made especially. Then I folded the box in some more fabric and tied it all together with two palm fronds I'd plucked from one of the trees around Mary's house. Over time, whilst Ruby was working away at her barter, the palm fronds had dried, paled and locked into place, sealing everything tight.

But today was the day, I just knew it. Jet brought her down the hill. The buzzing around Tent Village had given me the heads-up. I walked out to the carpark where I could see around the outside of the village up to the main house, and watched them descend the driveway. Slowly. Ruby was carrying her project. When I lost sight of them behind the tents, I moved back into the main entrance of our camp and waited in my workshop.

As the chatter grew louder, I stepped onto the pathway and was genuinely shocked to see a crowd had gathered behind her, essentially forming a parade. Mary had joined Jet on their trek down the hill and, as they made their way through the village, others followed. Not just Dori and Callum, everyone. Word had spread, of course, about what she'd been doing. And when she arrived it was at the head of a huge group. In her little hands she held a wonky little pot, with a healthy little lavender bush, with one little flower. And my heart turned to mush. Squatting down in front of her, I put my hands out to receive it. But no. She hugged it to her chest. "This is not for you, Daisy. This is for Travis."

"Me?" He almost fell out of his chair. "What did I do to deserve such a grand gift?"

"I wanted to say thank you for being here at the gate. For helping Daisy when she needs a new clip and for being super special."

Seemed I wasn't the only one whose heart had been mashed. I swear I saw an extra glimmer of shine in the old man's eyes.

Tea took the pot in one hand and wrapped the girl in his spare arm. Hauling her in and kissing the top of her head. "This is beautiful, Ruby. Thank you." His warm-treacle voice hummed.

The kid blushed and stepped back as Travis turned to put it in pride of place on his work bench.

"This is for you, Daisy."

The crowd parted and I froze. Jet came through carrying a huge pot glazed in amber swirls with gold and white highlights. In it sat a massive, flowering lavender bush, its petals several shades of purple but a perfect contrast to the pot. A hand squeezed my heart so hard it forced tears out my eyes. I couldn't breathe. It was simply beautiful. I looked to Dori.

"She did it all herself. She said she wanted to copy the style of your left sleeve. Said she wasn't good enough to attempt any of your other ink. I showed her how, and she practised. Lots. But was adamant. No one could help. She had to do it all."

By this stage, Ruby was jiggling with glee. Her hands in a ball under her chin, her little body bouncing as she giggled. Everybody was laughing, they were all in on it. Jet threw his arm over Ruby's shoulder, keeping her from flying away. "Yeah, the little one was a decoy."

"Hey," Tea grunted.

I ignored both Tea and the murmur of love waltzing through the group; all my attention was on Ruby. Squatting on my haunches, I hugged that kid silly. "That is the most beautiful plant and pot I have ever seen. Ever. In my whole life." She squealed and wriggled till I let her go. "So, do you still want to trade this amazing creation for a ring?"

She went very still and solemn, and nodded her head slowly with owl eyes.

When I handed the parcel to her, she sat in the dust in the middle of the path, dirty, bare feet stretched out as she held the box on her palm. For ages she just sat there looking at it, gently turning it around in her hands. Then, ever so slowly, she cracked the dried bow, and gently unfolded the fabric wrapping. With the greatest of care, she worked the lid free and, with thumb and finger, lifted the inner package out. She passed the box and outer wrapping to Jet with strict instructions to, "Keep them safe."

Then, slowly, she folded back the inner fabric to reveal the wooden ring carved into a flowering vine. The lights of people's torches assisted dusk's fade to catch the chips of polished red glass in the centre of the flowers. I sat in the dirt next to my little shadow and hugged her as she rocked and remembered her family. Her mum.

She didn't cry.

I did. Silently.

But not Ruby.

10

JONATHAN: THE CHAIR

I was like a toddler—loving and hating something equally at the same time. I loved the chair because it meant freedom and progression from the bed. But I hated it because it was the halfway point... the point I'd been stuck at for months. It had taken me a whole year to break the chains of the coma but, with three months of physio, surely I should be strong enough to walk again? Surely my muscles should be restored by now. Once again—for the millionth time—I'd been assured my brain was fully functioning and my body had no defects... well, none that should stop me from getting back to life...

Life.

What was that supposed to be like, now? What was that going to look like? How could I start over, without Laura... without the boys? How could I be a dad to Ru—

"Jonathan? Oh dear, you were doing so well. Come on, let's get you back to bed." Back inside my comatose prison, I heard the sigh. I knew Karen, my physio, wasn't upset *with* me, just disappointed *for* me. It had been weeks since I'd blacked out. No doubt she'd be booking me in for another session with my psych as soon as I was "taken care of".

"Luke, come and give me a hand getting Jonathan back to his room, would you?"

I waited till Luke, an orderly—my orderly—came. His strong, calloused hands gently lifted me like a child and, like normal, instead of following procedure and placing me on a gurney, he carried me back to my bed and made me comfortable.

Since Al had swooped in in the nick of time and alerted me to Rebecca's plan to make my daughter a ward of the state, Ruby had been officially, with my consent, a resident of Tent Village. It had all been signed off and squared away before Lightmas. Mary told me they had all tried to make it an extra-special celebration.

I really couldn't be too angry with Rebecca. I truly believed she had been looking out for my girl. And it had been the kick up the rear end that forced me to break out of my self-made isolation. Seriously, Rebecca had served me the—literal—wake-up call I'd needed to get my act together.

Al still brought Ruby in most days after school, which was run onsite. Luke's dad, Travis, lived at Tent Village with Mary and Jet, thereby serving as another pair of eyes for me, watching over my girl when I couldn't. For this and so many other reasons, I'd grown close to both Luke and Karen. They'd become like family. Both patiently and stoically riding the storms of my tantrums, celebrating my small victories, and generously sharing the humour when I had grown and healed enough to learn to laugh at myself. Both were unsung heroes, in my book. I loved them both dearly, but I thought I might love them even more when I wasn't quite so dependent on them.

A deep alto voice tickled my ear. "Just so you know, been talking with Dad. Ruby's doing real fine and Al's bringing her up later today after schooling. So, you have your rest now, then do what you have to do to wake up. Don't want to bore her to tears having to sit here and stare at your sleeping butt for a couple hours." He squeezed my hand, buzzed for the nurse and silently left the room.

Moments later Jenny came in, checked my vitals, scratched notes in my file, straightened the blankets, patted my leg, then she too silently left me to myself and the demon sitting in the corner of my room. No, I couldn't see it, but the funk of sulphur was coming from that direction.

"So, here we are again, *Overseer*." It laughed at the irony of my title, and I just died a little more. "What is it now? Two steps forward… five steps back? You know, if you ever get out of here, it will be into assisted living. There is no way you'll ever live independently again. Ever take care of Ruby again. And seriously, why should you? You were supposed to be caring for Laura and the boys. And look what happened to them. If you hadn't been so selfish wanting time to yourself, you could have been there. You could have saved them. Or better still, you could have died with them. Then you wouldn't have to endure this… humiliation."

Its voice came closer. "Being carried like a baby. A grown man of forty. How utterly pathetic. I don't understand why you don't just curse the Light and die. He's obviously skitched at you. After all you've done for Him in this city. Waving the flag like a good, badge-wearing member of the Light. Such a *good* boy. And this is how He repays you?" Its voice changed direction, probably looking out the window. "At least, if you were dead, you could see your precious family again. And you wouldn't have to worry about Ruby. She's doing real well without you, by the way. Happy as a lark, running free and wild over at Tent Village. No, you'd probably be doing her a favour too if you ended it all. Cut the ties. Then at least she could move on and stop pining over you, watching her hero fade into… dust."

It squeezed my hand in a parody of Luke, then left me drowning and paralysed in corrosive darkness.

I was on the verge of my self-pity canyon, ready to dive into another spell of self-loathing, self-serving, gratuitous grief when warmth cloaked the left-hand side of my body. At first, I didn't notice the smell. All I could register was the absence of sulphur. But there was a purity… a clarity in the air. A presence neared. Silently it leaned over me and lifted both my hands to rest on my stomach. A Light weight pressed warmth in a length down my torso from my chest to my knees. Two warm hands closed my fingers around the hilt of my sword.

Tears flooded down the sides of my face, my temples becoming waterfalls once again, soaking my pillow. A warm, soft cloth cleaned and refreshed my face, and two warm hands took hold of my cheeks. I could feel the presence invade my personal space. I couldn't pull back or turn away. Soft, dry lips kissed my forehead. And the words, "Time to fight, my beloved. I am here. I am with you, always. Now it is time to make a choice," formed in my mind.

Focusing all my might, straining every muscle, I forced my hands to tighten and grip that sword like my life depended on it. Because it did. This was the point of no return. Step into oblivion for good or turn the hell around and fight like the soldier I was created to be. Internally I roared and forced the crushing weight of the paralysis away. In my mind I formed a fortress—an impenetrable wall—and pushed. Millimetre by millimetre I forced the darkness back. I pulled on the strength of my armour and allowed the Light to infuse not only it but me with the full force of His power.

No more. It was time to move, to leave this place and start living again.

11

JONATHAN: RESET

How could I ever truly know the vastness of Your power.
Your wisdom.
Your intentions.
You are Creator. Sustainer. Provider.
For all the earth, for all creation.
You are.
I am a locust.
Here today, consuming. Gone tomorrow.
But you are eternal.
The architect who designed the plans.
The builder who constructed the universe.
The author who wrote the plot.
I am clay.
Dead… dormant, until you give me life. Purpose.
You hung the stars in the sky.
Placed the planets within their orbits.
Flung the galaxies into existence.
I am a blade of grass.
Fragile, temporary, indistinguishable among the
    multitudes.

You are the ticking of the clock,
the life in the air,
the beating of the heart.
You formed the earth, from the quarks to the
    atmosphere...
You are.
I am Yours.
Still confused, still hurting, still ignorant, chosen, loved.
Constantly humbled.

12

JONATHAN: FLOODGATES

I was being engulfed by a bear and an octopus with two steel bands that were doing their best to split me in half, whilst bird feathers were stroking my arms. Marcus had arrived with his family.

Felix told me the Light was bringing them here, and it was good to see him and Marcus again. I'd been out of action these past sixteen months since The Quake, and not been to the monthly Alliance meetings chaired by my good friend. But Al had been keeping me up to speed. Felix, the administrative head of the Laodicean Community, had answered my call for help in the early days of establishing my place as Overseer here in Philadelphia. His then-driver, Marcus, had brought him for a visit and proceeded to set up our Community with resources and insight, financial advice and grants, as well as constant support and genuine friendship. He had gone on from there to extend his work, creating the Alliance of the Seven Cities so that the larger, more financial Communities could help support and shadow the smaller, newer Communities from the Gerent's unwanted attention.

Since my hospitalisation sixteen months ago, Felix had dropped in regularly to visit, but I knew he didn't handle my situation well. I had a feeling "socially awkward" was Felix's middle name.

But Marcus was a different story altogether. Where Felix was hands-off, Marcus was all systems go. Squeezing my head up through the scrum I was currently engulfed in, I saw he'd brought his whole family. I hadn't met any of them yet but I had heard so much about each of them, I felt I knew them intimately. And my tiny assisted-living unit was currently bursting at the seams hosting them.

Luke had brought them over—everyone needed a guide the first few times they visited the care facility. Heck, I still needed a guide to get me to the dining hall. Luke stood at the door, grinning like a loon at me in my bound and awkward state. "Well then, I'll leave you to it. I'll be back to get you for lunch."

I tried to acknowledge him, but my arms were still pinned to my sides. He didn't even attempt to help free me as he nodded to my guests before shutting the door behind him.

"Breaks me heart like a kettle of fish to hear your story." Eventually Marcus released me and I looked to the dark head that was pushing into my stomach. Marcus's son, Raph. He was twelve. Just like George... had been... would forever be. Because he was dead. Gone. Crushed by the house.

"Sariah," barked a stoic woman encased in indigo armour, and the bird feathers turned into claws and gripped my shoulders.

The black storm assaulting my consciousness stilled. It didn't dissolve, but its onslaught halted. A trickle of peace seeped through the cracks of my wall, and warmth... comfort? followed hot on its heels. I didn't pass out like normal. I felt a bit woozy, but the two kids and now Marcus, once again, held me upright.

"Marcus," Val barked again. She must have given a wordless command because I felt myself being lowered to the couch. But still, I didn't black out. I was still conscious—not steady by any means, but I was still in control of my body. I forced myself to look at the boy's head and to remember. To allow the memories, the grief and the pain to surface. And like a fractured window holding back a dam, the wall plinked, chinked, then splintered. Tears erupted followed by sobbing and wailing. My heart literally exploded from the shattered glass of my demolished fortress, piercing every nerve fibre, every sense, the very essence of my being.

My default retreat to the cave was barred. I could see it, just out of reach, but I was pinned under the weight of my grief. Frozen in place by the iron bands that had started out under the guise of peace and comfort. I was forced to confront my reality, my loss, and flounder in an ocean of my pain. It was the first time I had cried since…

Oh God, no, it was real. They were gone. I'd failed them. Devastation like a black hole swallowed my soul. I was a bottomless pit of anguish. I couldn't escape it. I tried desperately to claw my way into my self-created oblivion. But no, I was a prisoner of the truth and I felt it tear and render my spirit as my new reality of loss. My soul mate, my other half, was gone. *Oh Laura. I'm so sorry. How can I possibly go on?*

Once again, I was swamped by rage and grief. I yelled at the Light. I yelled at life. I screamed and cursed my fate. Why? Why give me so fracking much, then take it all away? All of it. My heart ruptured like a severed artery and my life was pulsing, gushing, flooding out of me. And all the while I railed against my lot, Marcus sat by me, his boy held me, and his daughter gripped my shoulders like a vice.

In silence they all sat vigil with me as the storm of my anger, grief and despair consumed me from the inside out. At last, at long last, the storm ebbed and I lay wrung out, a husk, half on the couch, half in Marcus's arms. A cool washer bathed my face, and a glass of iced water was put in my hand. Then taken away as it started to spill onto my chest. It was the shock I'd needed to bring me back to the here and now.

A woman squatted down in front of me. Indigo armour. Val? Warm steel braced my knee. My swollen, gritty eyes tracked a path from her fingers to her face. She spoke.

I stared.

She repeated herself. "Jonathan."

I gave my head a brief shake and made an effort to listen. Pulling myself upright on the couch I took the cloth Kaitlyn handed me and wiped my face with it again, then switched it for the glass of water she handed me. *Right. Pull yourself together man.*

"Jonathan." Val called me again and this time with clearer focus. I responded with a nod. "You survived." She halted and pinned me with twin laser beams. "Finally, you have confronted your path in The Way and come out the other side."

A shorter woman encased in green armour, Kait? brought a chair over and helped Val stand. It was then I really noticed her and the knives. All the knife hilts stuck to her body at every joint. And then I realised they weren't just hilts. The blade of every knife was embedded into each of her joints. It was a gruesome image I couldn't disentangle my eyes from. But then she quietly groaned and I looked to her face. She could barely move. Pain carved deep creases into her face as she attempted to manoeuvre her body from squatting to sitting in the chair. From the strain on Kait's face, I knew she was working hard to support this wounded woman.

"Jonathan." Whether it was pain or impatience that roughened her voice I couldn't say, but she had my attention once again. "You have taken your first step to acknowledging and owning your suffering."

Initially, my mind baulked. How dare she speak to me about suffering? She had no idea… Then, of course, I realised how childish I was being. She had every idea. I couldn't help my eyes from travelling over her thick, intricately ornate armour, encrusted with knives. When I came back to her face, she lifted one perfect eyebrow like she knew exactly what I'd been thinking. I felt the heat of shame rise from my chest to my neck. I dropped her gaze and considered my hands as she continued.

"What happened to you happened with the Light's permission."

Again, I baulked and the heat of shame went up a notch as anger took hold. She pinned me with her eyes. *You know it's true.*

Damn it, she was right. Wasn't that part of the problem? The root of the pain? That despite my life dedicated to serving, loving and living in the Light, He had allowed this to happen to me. Instead of reward, He had exacted the greatest cost. My family. I had thought I had dealt with this truth as I lay comatose in hospital. But here, in the light of day, conscious, confronted by another, the truth was undeniable.

"And it's not over," Val continued. "There is more to come, more to pay, more to suffer." She waited a beat for that to settle in.

More? Is she serious? Is that true? What more of me could You want? What more do I have to give?

Inevitable as death and taxes, she ploughed on. "You have laid aside your mantle for long enough. Your time is up. Make a decision: Curse the Light and die, or embrace Him, His truth and The Way and re-join the battle. You hold the key to the Light's plan for His people in this city. You are needed. But if you are not going to accept the challenge, step aside and let someone else lead His people through the gateway."

Fire sparked and my anger leapt to rage. "I will not step aside. I will not be left on the sidelines."

Very calmly, the one eyebrow lifted as her head tilted slightly.

Damn it again. Hiding. I had been a coward in hiding. Unable… unwilling to face my loss, when so many of my people had also lost everything. But whilst the rest of the world had moved on, faced their loss and made a go of recovery, I had been stuck in the past. Worse, running in retreat. My body deflated as my unrighteous anger fled.

I am so very sorry. I have dropped the ball and not been Your faithful servant to Your beloved people. Forgive me. Please show me where I go from here. How do I serve You in this changing, wounded city? How in my broken-ness can I be any good to anyone, most of all You?

"The Community may have revoked your position as Overseer, but it was the Light who commissioned you as Shepherd. The battle is coming and the faithful will be greatly tested. He has opened a door to safety for his beloved children along the narrow, rocky path. Your job is to show The Way—leading from the front, guiding from the sides and ushering from behind." Val's words ignited a fire inside my soul and sparks along the engravings of my armour.

Thank you.

"Now, finish your recovery and get back in the game. You are needed and sorely missed." This was said by a woman who now required both Kait and Marcus to help her stand as they made their move to leave. For once in a long time, my focus was forced away from myself and my woes; how I would love to know her story.

13

KAITLYN: SURE AS HOUSES

It was a beautiful house, make no mistake. But it was with a punch bowl of swirling emotions we'd set up our new "home". Such a small and powerful word. All our lives, the Light had seen to it that we had a place to come home to. And now, as we started our lives in this recovering city, we were gifted with this beautiful, new house. And even though it wasn't as big as our first house we'd been gifted—or mausoleum as Dan called it—in Laodicea two years ago, it was still big enough for us to spread out again.

But there was a blanket of sadness cloaking everything here. Even though the house was brand new, it was Jonathan's property. Whilst we were so very grateful to have use of it, it was hard not to remember what had happened here. The man had lost his family. He'd crawled through the wreckage and rescued his daughter. Then been pinned under a beam and spent nigh on one-and-a-half years in hospital and assisted living.

It could have been so much worse. Onlookers say it was a miracle. Rather than the top floor falling flat onto the second, it was like a huge hand had pushed the top floor into the backyard. This had not only saved Ruby, it had enabled enough room and light to break through the wreckage for Jonathan to find her.

She wouldn't come back here, and I doubted Jonathan would either. He'd been advised to sell it, but at this point in time he couldn't bring himself to let it go. So, in the interim, it was ours until we learned otherwise... and what our role was, here in Philadelphia. I was confident, in His time, the Light would make that clear.

"He is here," Raph called from the front door as Felix—well, Felix's driver, Arty—drew up to the curb. Since he began his work petitioning for and establishing the Alliance of the Seven Cities, he had come to know the Council here in Philadelphia. As our dear friend and colleague from our time in Laodicea, Felix was going to make our formal introduction to the High Council. Of course, Marcus knew them too, but Felix had offered to make it official in the hope of demonstrating a strong union with Laodicea. Jonathan obviously would have been the one to do it, but he was still convalescing at the assisted living rabbit warren.

"He has someone with him," Raph announced. By this stage we had all gathered by the door ready to welcome our dear friend. Our boy waited until Felix was in range before launching himself at the man and wrapping him in an embrace. We all knew how much Raph loved hugging, but I suspect he was on a mission with Felix—to break some of his aversion to physical contact by immersion.

"Ahh. Yes. Raphael." Felix's hand patted Raph's shoulder woodenly.

Val's voice shot out from behind me. "You'll have to do better than that."

Felix grimaced then slowly placed two hands around Raph's shoulders and made an attempt at an awkward squeeze. He must have passed the test, because Raph released him, and he was allowed into the house where he tolerated the rest of us giving him less enthusiastic embraces.

"Felix, me man, don't leave your drivers in the car. Invite them in." Marcus still had his eye on the street where three cars had pulled up. Yes, three.

"They will join us momentarily. I suspect they are making arrangements for their return trip."

"What's going on and why are Clyde and Clair here?" My husband voiced the question pushing at my own lips.

"My team will be returning to Laodicea presently, after they have seen to the handover of the vehicle." Felix looked Marcus square in the eye and we caught a glimpse of the negotiating businessman behind the stoic mask. "I understand the… monstrosity you drive has merit, but it is… ungainly, and fossil fuel is becoming harder to source and more expensive to purchase. Not to mention the strain on the environment. We are currently upgrading our fleet to hydro auto-drives, and… experimenting with Air Borne Pod Carriers. Therefore, I asked Clair to pick a reliable electric seven-seater from our fleet, which is more economical and is safer for transporting people than your… current mode of transportation." His lips pursed to the side. "And may I suggest… significantly more practical?"

I was surprised my husband—all fuss and bluster—was capable of holding back his tirade until Felix had finished his critique. "Now, you just park your purse for a moment. That, there, is far too much this time, Felix. I can't accept something so grand."

"You don't have to. It's not for you." He tilted his head at Marcus and gave him the best of his beady, crow-eye glare. "It is an engage-ment present for Daniel and Contessa." Our dear friend Felix just kept talking right over the gasp exploding from Dan and the cry erupting from Tessa. "Now, if you're ready, Clair will do the handover, then she and Clyde will begin their return trip to Laodicea."

Felix had survived the hug from Raph because he had been under-going hug treatment for a few months now. But I suspect the smoth-ering from Tessa and hearty back slaps from Dan were in completely uncharted territory or perhaps an entirely different atlas to his comfort zone.

Everyone tumbled out of the house to inspect the beautiful new addition to our family: a gleaming, dark-grey four-wheel drive, with—as promised—seven seats. The grin on Dan's face was bright enough to be seen from space and Tessa was already sitting in the front passenger seat trying to look at all the knobs and switches and inspecting every drawer, cabinet and nook, but her tears were making it too hard for her to see. In the end she just sat and stroked the seat cover, overcome with emotion.

"Dear girl, let me remind you it is second-hand… three years old… a used, fleet car… it is not the latest mod—"

"It's beautiful, thank you so much. How can we thank you? I mean, we *do* thank you. But we can't thank you enough. It's too much. We should give it back. But I don't want to because I love it too much." Dan pried Tessa's arms from around Felix's neck before he passed out from discomfort whilst everyone else was climbing through the car, exploring. The twins had already unfolded the back two seats and were buckled in, Marcus was under the hood with Clair, and Val brought up the rear slowly, manoeuvring herself—without her walking sticks—giving Felix squint-eye in an attempt not to reveal her own, almost visible, emotions.

Felix turned to her. "Do you think this might be more… comfortable for you to be transported in?"

She shook her head and pretended to brush stray hairs back into her ponytail. But I didn't miss the surreptitious wiping of her glistening eyes. She hobbled over, got up on her toes and gently kissed him on the cheek. "Thank you, Felix."

He blushed and a few pennies started dropping into place. Felix, the cunning fox, knew how to get around my husband in order to assist my sister. "It is nothing really. And, after all you have done for me…"

Val growled and the subject was dropped.

In the end, Marcus and Val drove with Felix in his town car, and the kids and I tested out the new toy. Dan drove carefully… very carefully… a few times the lead car had to pull over to wait for us. But eventually we made it to the building the Community of Philadelphia were using for their main Soteria house.

I thought we might have to use a crowbar to get Dan and Tessa out, but soon enough we were following Felix through a side entrance and down a hallway, Tessa skipping every step of the way.

As we neared an open door we heard terse conversation, and when we entered, we walked into a crackling atmosphere. A wiry man was pacing in front of the windows; a woman stood next to a table set with water jugs, glasses and a pod-coffee machine. She was wringing her hands.

"Felix, have you heard?" The wiry man did not acknowledge us. I'm sure he noticed us… the seven of us… standing behind our friend who was here to make a formal introduction. Of course, they all knew Marcus from his time driving Felix and the Overseer… ex-Overseer around the Seven Cities, wheeling and dealing to get this alliance rolling.

"Dennis, I have heard a great many things. Which, in particular, are you referring to?" Before Dennis could answer, Felix turned to us with an outstretched arm, inviting us to take a seat around the large table in the centre of the room. Five other people were present: three were sitting; one looked relaxed.

"The Gerent, Felix. The Gerent is coming to Philadelphia to inspect his handiwork *and* receive homage."

"Ahh, yes. I had heard, Dennis. That is a particularly… prickly problem I have been doing everything in my power to alleviate." Felix took Val by the elbow to help her. Now, that wasn't the most shocking thing I had ever seen. But Val, letting him help her, was. Before I could wrap my head around it, Felix continued. "By being vocal about the unity of the Community of Light in the Seven Cities, I am hoping the smaller Communities such as in Philadelphia and Sardis can hide under the wings of Laodicea and Ephesus. But I have not quite had two years yet and have encountered… hindrances along the way."

"Yes, well, he's out of the picture now." By "he", I believed Dennis was referring to the ex-Overseer of Laodicea—not Jonathan, the Overseer of Philadelphia. "But what are *we* going to do? Philadelphia is too small and under the Gerent's thumb."

A woman, seated at the table with perfectly styled, lacquered black hair, spoke up. "We need to have someone stand in Jonathan's stead until he is back on deck. Someone who can advise us on what we should do."

"We've just been to see him. Is he aware of the situation? I am sure he could still give advice or at least make comment on the state of play." The room froze and stared at Marcus. I had to keep reminding myself that they all knew him, and he hadn't really spoken out of turn… much.

"He already has." The relaxed man swung his chair to face us, the first real recognition we had received since entering the room. "He advised us not to bend the knee."

"Kait, what does that mean?" Raph tried to whisper, but it was like a cannonball through the fragile atmosphere.

Dennis's climbing hysteria beat me to the punch. "It means, young man, that the Gerent believes he is a god and expects everyone to pay homage—to… bend the knee and worship him."

"Does he do miracles like the Light?"

Quick to respond, Dennis didn't hide his snarl. "Only the one. Financing exorbitant schemes that hold the world hostage to his will. Any who do not pay homage are sent to The Games."

Raph, bless him, stepped forward and tried to calm the overexcited man who had not yet stopped pacing. "That does not sound so bad. We used to play games at the Factory in Laodicea. We could teach you how to play, if that would help?"

Dennis's breathing became shallow and his pale face turned a nasty shade of blue. But he had enough oxygen in his rapidly fluttering lungs to turn on our boy. "The Games, you ignorant child, are the Gerent's new entertainment for the masses." The tension in the room tightened as Raph slipped back under my wing and our family amped up a level. Dennis, however, did not notice as his breathing devolved into wheezing and his pupils dilated into the whites of his eyes. "All who displease him are sent to the arena as fodder for the gangs who are currently overcrowding the prisons of the Seven Cities."

And that there, folks, was the straw that gave the camel an aneurysm. With both hands clutched to his chest, his mouth opening and closing like permanently triggered automatic doors, Dennis bowed out of the conversation.

The room burst into action. Someone grabbed pills from the pocket inside Dennis's jacket, another loosened his tie, a third guided him to a seat. The woman who had been near the drinks table sloshed water into a glass and stretched across with it. Obviously, this was not the first time Dennis had suffered a heart episode. One of the men drank the water as another placed a pill under Dennis's tongue where it would be the most effective.

Within moments, calm returned, and it seemed to be business as usual. The shock that paralysed the rest of us broke when Dennis croaked out another of his fears. "Jonathan will not bend the knee, compromise at all, or even consider closing Tent Village down. The Community here is doomed. We are all doomed."

"Come now, Dennis." The anxious water-pourer fluttered her hand on his back. "That's enough for one day. Margery's on her way to take you home."

Once Dennis, in a slightly healthier shade of lavender, had been handed over to his wife, Marcus got back on topic. "What's this Tent Village he's on about and what's wrong with it?"

Well. For the response he got, my darling husband may as well have asked if anyone wanted kitten pie. Horror, shock and extreme distaste. Except the calm man.

I don't know if it occurred to anyone that we hadn't actually been introduced yet. We were all—except for Val—still standing, for crying out loud. It was becoming more than a little awkward. How on earth could we lend a hand or dip our oar in the water if we were left on the bank, capable yet sidelined, flies on the wall.

So, I broke the spell.

"Hello, I'm Kait, and it's a *pleasure* to meet you all." I made my way to the calm man with my hand extended. "And this is my family."

He stood, shook my hand, and said, "Charlie," then smiled and addressed us all. "Welcome to Philadelphia."

14

DAISY: KEEPING THE GATE

Oh goodie. Looked like the Community's latest round of butt-kickers had arrived. Interesting to see they were mixing things up and using clandestine tactics... or at least trying to. When would they come to realise this was private property and not some down and out collection of no-hopers they needed to help or evict? We were doing just fine without them... and their "help".

Two young Hispanic kids were at the head of the pack. But once their eyes locked on the garden, they were a lost cause. They made a beeline to the space and disappeared from view, either unaware or unconcerned they were on private property. A sunshiny dryad had trouble leaving their vehicle and... had she just patted the car? A mean-looking wild cat grabbed her by the hand and pinned her to his side. Next to them walked hot cocoa—spiced with chilli—and a fierce mountain man. And bringing up the rear was the biggest contradiction I had ever seen. A warrior carrying her weapons on the inside, being assisted by a dapper musketeer. All—as in, each and every one of them, even the kids—kitted out in totally audacious, abundant... artistic? armour. I didn't want to be intrigued, but I couldn't help it.

I was so wrapped up in trying to unravel their mystery I almost forgot to sound the alarm. "Batter up! Company."

My little shadow took off from the corner where she'd been playing with my carving tools. With Pod at her heels, Ruby carried whispers throughout the village.

Tea gave me a nod as we both downed tools to "keep the gate". With my friend and fellow gatekeeper behind my right shoulder I gave them the special welcome reserved for Community intruders: feet planted, arms crossed, chin up, eyes narrow, very still and… silent. *You think you can come in here and intimidate us? Push us around? Well, not on my watch. And I'm* always *on watch, people.*

I'd let the two kids go through to the keeper, but this lot could give a "please explain" before entering our home. I was so freaking sick of the Community and their little yappy dogs. Not that this lot looked little… or yappy.

The first four parted and waited for the Warrior to approach. Good choice. I'd do the same. Even if she was a cripple, she carried an edge. Before she came to a stop, Wild Cat whistled. Credit to him, it was a good one; sharp, shrill and striking as a bell. I'd always wanted to whistle like that.

Musketeer dropped the Warrior's elbow and stepped to one side as she spoke. "Good morning, Daisy. It is a pleasure to meet you"—her eyes flicked over my shoulder to Tea—"both. Forgive the twins for barging into your home uninvited." At that, two red-faced kids came to heel beside Hot Cocoa and Mountain Man. "We have heard a little bit about what you've achieved here and were wondering if we may have permission to visit with you and see for ourselves. We understand this may not be a good time and are happy to come back at a time that is suitable."

Well, fancy that. A member of the Philadelphian Community demonstrating respect and common decency. I uncrossed my arms and put my hands on my hips. "To what end?"

"Pardon?"

"Why do you want to come in here to, 'see for yourselves'? To see what? To what end? To throw us out? Make our lives hell? To send reports to… who knows where, this time, to have us shut down? This is private property and we have been invited to be here and you and your preachy… poncy… peacock friends back in the Community can go take a flying leap off a short, sharp… sh…" *Dammit, what I wouldn't do for a thesaurus.* "Sh…"

"Shack?" Tea murmured behind me.

The corner of the Warrior's mouth hitched, and she gave Travis a nod. Mountain Man's face broke into a fully-fledged grin. He went to move forward but Hot Cocoa grabbed him by the back of the shirt and pulled him into line. He wrapped his arm around her shoulders but didn't wipe the smile.

Wild Cat protested, "Never been called a poncy peacock before."

"Dear boy, poncy leans towards… compassionate, compared to what I have been accused of."

That I could believe, Musketeer.

The Warrior growled and her crew shut up. "We have only just arrived from Laodicea—"

"That's no better. They're just as bad. Worse."

"Daisy, just let 'em speak." Tea's caramel—yet edging towards exasperated—voice helped soothe the sparking wires in my brain.

"We spent over a year living in a community a bit like this and we're interested in learning from you. Maybe we can send some hints and tips back to our family there."

Tea stepped forward. "Were you lot with the Silverscales?"

I turned and gaped at my friend. What the freaky freaks was he doing?

He must have read my face. "Al told Luke that some bloke from Laodicea comes to visit Ruby's dad pretty regularly at the hospice where Luke works."

My friend could be so longwinded. Comes with age I guess, but come on. "Get on with it, Tea."

The kret just paused and smiled at me before he continued waltzing around the freaking block with his story. "Well, this guy told Al and Luke there had been some pretty crazy action going on in the Community there. Seems a group of Greyscales who'd been living in hiding met the Light, turned to Silverscales, then took down the

Temple of Ashera with a crew of…" His head turned and he considered the people who wanted access to our home. "Misfits?"

Wild Cat muttered, "Well I guess that's better than a poncy peacock."

One of the kids—the Colt—started bouncing. "Yes. That was us."

"And a couple of kids took on a gigantor…" The Filly beamed and the Colt buzzed with electricity. My right-hand-man looked back to me and gave the slightest of nods. *They're good people, Daisy, give them a pass.* "I reckon now's as good a time as any to call smoko."

I knew Luke, Tea's son, had his finger on the pulse and was pretty tight with the Big O in this city: Ruby's dad. And I knew Luke was as good a man as Tea, whom I trusted with my life. So, I stood down and notched this one up as another loss to my mentor.

We led our visitors to the Meeting Place—a big tarpaulin tent in the centre of the garden. Folks stopped what they were doing and stared as we passed. It wasn't that we didn't like visitors. Heck, we opened ourselves up for the markets every Saturday. It's just we didn't trust them… easily. I was sick of the Community's tactics to sabotage, scare and or… scurry? us away. Not going to happen.

I was kind of swimming in the bog of my unhappy memories when a high-pitched scream had me and everyone else on high alert. "Ruby! What is it?"

She was a statue, her eyes locked on our guests. Then knock me down if she didn't do the weirdest thing. She semi-squatted and raised her hands like claws and growled. Yep, the kid was imitating a cat, or a bear, or some feral animal. Even Pod backed up a step or two. But nothing prepared me for the roar that emanated from the Mountain at my back.

I swung around ready for a fight with my knife palmed. And blow me down if the big man wasn't doing exactly the same thing. I stepped back so I could see the both of them in my peripheral vision, but still very much on edge. "What the freak—"

The bloke's primal roar and surprising burst of speed cut me off.

Ruby squealed and ran. I went to block the guy. He dodged me. Tea tried to grab him from behind. He weaved. Ruby dashed off between the tents with the Mountain hot on her heels.

"Someone stop that guy." *Bleeding Community and their freaking tactics. When would they leave us the bleeding heck alone?* "Now."

"Actually, if you don't mind me interrupting." The Musketeer stepped over. "They—"

Ruby's screams interrupted the bloke before she broke into peals of laughter over the top of… raspberries? The guy came back carrying Ruby in his arms. Or should I say, wearing Ruby. The kid clung so tight to the guy's neck, her legs squeezing his waist, he started to go red.

The Musketeer continued, "—know each other."

Well, that was a story I was looking forward to hearing. But by the look of it, it wouldn't be from the Mountain. If we didn't disengage Ruby soon, he'd be out for the count.

But then, for the second… third? time in about five minutes you could have knocked me over with a breeze. Ruby was crying. Ruby never cried. Or I should say, in all the time I'd known her, I'd never seen… or heard… or heard of her crying. I mean really crying. But she clung to this fella and her little heart overflowed into her eyes and washed her face.

Tea gave me a nudge from behind and got me moving with his wisdom, along with the whole gobsmacked crowd. "How about we pop the kettle on and give these folks a seat in the shade whilst Ruby gets reacquainted with her friend."

We ushered everyone into the cool of the Meeting Place, and allowed the scents from the herbs, flowers and honey to weave their medicinal, mending… marvels on our little girl. The Mountain gave me a nod as I held out a chair for him and tried to encourage Ruby to ease her grip just a little. Nothing we did helped, but Pod, who was beside himself seeing his mate upset, was fretting and sticking his cold, wet nose on her leg. It did the trick. For a bit. She released her hold long enough to scoop Pod up in her arms. Then she was trying to figure out how she could hold the dog and the Mountain without strangling the dog or falling off the Mountain's lap and out of his chair.

Hot Cocoa came to the Mountain's aid. She put a seat right next to the flailing group and, knock me down… again, managed to persuade Ruby to release her death-grip on Pod and slid my dog onto her lap without batting an eyelid. Ruby maintained a vice hold on the Mountain while she told them all her woes. At this point we were all very, very… very quiet. Because none of us had yet heard her woes. Don't get me wrong. We knew she had them. We all had them. But I gotta say, this kid probably had more than most.

I had to give it to the couple, they knew their stuff. Neither of them flinched, frowned or lost focus as the guy's shirt became increasingly drenched in snot and tears. And believe me, eighteen months of pent-up grief produces a lot of snot and tears. But they just sat, crooned, and… petted. Yep. Petted. The Mountain stroked her knotted, golden hair and Hot Cocoa stroked Pod.

The others, aware something special was going on, just quietly took a seat. At one point the Colt and Filly made to go over, but Hot Cocoa held up her hand and they paused, but didn't return to their seats. Just waited as if they were on call.

I felt about a skyrise out of my depth, and constantly flicked my eyes between Tea and the little quartet. My mentor just took a seat, puffed on his pipe and waited, nodding that I should do the same. So, I did.

Eventually some words became discernible and, I have to tell you, it was a hard task keeping the tears from my own eyes. On repeat, Rube just kept saying, "They were crushed and broken, and everything was broken, and Daddy came and the house fell on him and now he's broken too. They're all broken. Crushed and broken. Everything is crushed and broken." Then she'd have a spell of sobbing.

"Mummy said she loved me. She said we should sing a song to the Light and He would make sure everything was alright. But it's not alright. I miss Mummy. I miss the boys. I miss my Daddy. It's not alright. Everyone is crushed and broken. And gone. They are all gone. Crushed and broken."

And what can you say to that? Nothing, really. You think you're having a skratty day. You think things are a bit rough. That the Community and their sucky attitude are a pain in the butt. That people constantly breaking into your home is not okay. Then you hear a little girl's litany about how her family died trying to protect her and you realise, you got nothing to complain about. I might have scars. I may have lost family. But I did not have to live through everything in my world being crushed and broken.

After a while, Hot Cocoa motioned for the twins to join her. And yep, you guessed it, I was bowled over again as both laid their hands on Rube. The little group closed around my girl and hugged her, wept with her. Wild Cat and Sunshine Dryad joined them, and the group encircled her.

In that moment I kind of had a blinding flash of realisation. From what I'd heard of it, this was kind of how she'd been found. Wrapped in the arms of her family. Her dead, crushed and broken family. But instead of freaking her out, it kind of settled her. Her sobbing eased, her breathing calmed and, as someone started humming and as the Dryad shifted position, I had a glimpse of my girl cradled in the Mountain's arms as her eyes grew heavy. In a matter of moments, she was out like a light.

In the last year or so that Ruby had been with us, she had never, and when I say never, I mean not once, ever, slept so quickly or peacefully. I know crying does that to a soul, but not like this.

I didn't want to say it, but... speechless, I was completely lost for words. Who were these people? And should I start worrying now, or wait for the next fallout to gauge my response?

15

MARCUS: CIRCUS ACT

"Who do you think you are, coming in here telling us what we should do and how we should do it?"

This particular crowd were as welcoming as a briar patch at bedtime. For two and a half months, we'd been travelling to the different gatherings of the Community within the city and surrounding regions of Philadelphia, on the coat-tails of the official edict from the High Council, to "bend the knee".

We couldn't believe it. Jonathan had told them it was non-negotiable, inconceivable and unacceptable. Sadly, he'd passed out shortly afterwards so wasn't "present" for his own defrocking. Had to wait till he came round to hear the news he was out of a job.

The Community was divided. And I was as shocked as a newborn slapped on the butt as a welcome to the outside world that it was roughly eighty-twenty in support of bending the knee.

Felix didn't endorse the motion and, as a visual sign of his vote of no-confidence, came with us on our campaign to tout the truth, whenever he was in town and able to. At first, we all went in support of Val, who discussed the ramifications of the decision and then debated The Way with them. Some were open to "dialoguing" with her. Others, like this mob, were as closed tight as a bank on a feast day.

"Open your eyes while you still have the sight to see." Val didn't so much yell as project her voice, launching to her feet and holding her hands out from her sides. I knew the gesture cost her, the unseen knives piercing her flesh and joints, but the slight clenching of her jaw and flinch in her right eye was all that gave it away. "My armour is my testimony to my experience and place in the Light."

"Yeah, well, if you're so special, why does the Light *bless* you with all the knives? Surely that's a sign of judgement. Of ill-will."

Ya ignorant son of a wild, hairy boar. You wouldn't know blessed if it came up and slapped you in the face.

An alarmed hiss, "Marcus!" from me beautiful wife informed me that, contrary to me best intentions, that thought had made its way to the outside world. However, judging by the lack of response from the group that confronted us, I don't think they heard me. Sariah on the other hand, who had turned her head into me side and was jiggling slightly, may have.

Val dropped her arms and her head, exhaling the heat of her annoyance in a cloud of frustrated acceptance. Another lot of believers who didn't have the collective sense of a single goose. I could see some folk I'd come across in me time working with Felix. Even now, their armour was dimming. They were well on the way to being as lost as a ball in high weeds. It made me so angry I just wanted to yell, or hit something really, really hard.

A middle-aged man with overly white teeth and a shmick suit stood up. He too lifted his arms out to the side in a placating manner, manipulating their strings masterfully, and within moments, the crowd quietened. He then turned to Val. "We really do appreciate your efforts and intentions to come and speak with us today. But we have been thinking over the advice from the High Council, and some of us can see reason in what they are saying. The Gerent has power to shut us down. If our doors are shut, we can no longer minister to the needy or support those who fall through the cracks of society." He waved his hand to indicate a young woman with a baby and toddler. "For us to stay effective and open, and continue ministering to the poor, on behalf of the Light, we need to work with the government. Don't you see? We are called to obey the law of the land and bring love, peace and joy to a troubled world. How can we do that if our doors are shut, we are maligned and are only known for being a public nuisance?" The guy was slick, and he had the gathering under his spell. He was preaching comfort and alignment with the enemy —the slimy and slippery path of the highway commonly followed. He looked around the room, his eyes taking in the calm and agreeing members, then came back to Val with a condescending, patronising shake of his head, his slicked-back hair not shifting. "Your heart is in the right place, but you just don't understand how it works in the real world."

I subconsciously moved me chair back. The only reason I knew I'd done it was the scraping of its legs on the floor. I was not going to be within reach of Val—wounded, disabled, or unwell—when she responded to that ignorant kret.

First, there was silence that stretched time and space to within an inch of its life. Goosebumps crawled up me arms. I think me heart may have stilled, just so it wouldn't miss a thing. Then Val responded. "Your words flow smoothly from your forked tongue and your sheep's cloak does its job well. Yet if you don't have the ears or the intelligence to heed a watchman's warning, your blood is on your own head. But worse, the blood of these under your thrall is on your hands."

There was a beat. Just the one. Wasn't even long enough to exhale before a wrinkled rake stood and gave his mindless response. "Listen here, girly, why don't you and your family go back to where you came from, and you get that fella there to see if he can find you a good man to settle down with and fill you with babies. That'll give you something to keep your hands busy and your nose out of our business."

At this last comment, the crowd broke out into jeers and laughter. Despite his age and frailty, he looked like a good candidate for relieving some of me pent up stress via dishing out physical harm. But it was pointless carrying on. What more could we do?

Val turned to look at us and shook her head. Water off a duck's back to her. The insults, that was—not the refusal to see sense. That broke her heart. What we were fighting was a cocktail of fear, ignorance and lies which could only be cured by a dose of rude awakening... or direct intervention by the Light.

We corralled the kids and headed out to our car. Dan's car. At first, Dan and Tessa had come with us on our trips. But after the first few where they felt as useful as a marble in a game of chess, they had asked permission from Tent Village to be an extra pair of hands there. We'd suggested the twins go with Dan and Tessa to start meeting the local kids and make friends. But they were adamant they were coming with us. And since the three of us couldn't find a good reason to say no, we agreed.

"Excuse me." A quiet voice brought us all to a standstill halfway through helping a pained Val into the car. "I just wanted to say thank you." A mousy woman—the one used as an example of "the poor" by the wolf with the forked tongue—stood with a baby fussing in her arms and a toddler attached to her legs. "I know it was hard to stand up and bring the truth to my... family. I don't understand their reaction and acceptance of the edict. Fear, I guess. I-I just don't know." Her focus and attention left us for a moment, one hand buried in the blond curls of the lad at her knee.

But then she came back with a vengeance. "I don't agree." At our disappointed response, she continued, "With them. I agree with you. I... I just find it hard to stand up to them." She planted a gentle kiss on the head of her babe in arms. "You see, I lost my husband in The Quake. I was just on twelve weeks pregnant. It was a miracle Nasya survived. And these people, my Community... my family, saved me. I couldn't have done it without them." Tears sparkled in her eyes and a frog stole her voice. "They are beautiful, compassionate people. I don't understand their behaviour or their choice. But I just wanted you to know, I appreciate you coming all this way and speaking as you did."

"Lisa, you out here? I'm heading out if you want a—" The speaker transformed from congenial provider to prickly heat in a ticker's beat. "What are you doing with these people? Come away. Now. Or I'll leave without you."

Lisa started to turn. "I have to go." But she dropped her head and whispered, "Thank you," before she was out of earshot.

Her guard dog gave a good, but ineffective attempt at being menacing until Lisa had walked past him with her toddler in tow, then shot his final command. "And don't come back."

And for the first time that morning, we were in agreement.

Thank the Light not all Communities had been like this. Some had been receptive... respectful even. Some were in agreement, but sadly too many were not. Val had been invited back by some to open The Way at gatherings. To teach and encourage. Truth be, troubled times were coming and we all needed as much encouraging and fortifying as possible.

Don't get me wrong, I knew making a stand against the world wasn't easy. But that was The Way of it. I had learned the lesson though; it was harder when the fight came at you from family. The enemy was easy... easier to confront. But it sure did strip to the quick and still the will when opposition came from within—your own brothers and sisters.

Even though fruit had been scarce on the ground, it was there for the picking. Those wanting to take the narrow path now knew they weren't alone. And, praise be, the folk at Tent Village were on the side of wisdom, knowing truth was not in the way of the world. Those who needed refuge from their *family* and the war about them, knew they were welcome there.

16

DANIEL: TENT REPLACER

I guess it didn't come as a surprise to anyone that we moved into Sanctuary—the new name for Tent Village. The main surprise was that it took us three months. We'd met as a group a couple of times with the Community's head honchos here in Philadelphia, but that was a complete waste of energy and electricity. Although, I still got a kick out of driving my—our—new car. It was a ridiculously delicious, sweet ride.

Another gold lining was the "fuel" card in the glove compartment. Even though the car was electric and charging was a fraction of the price of fuel, Felix insisted we charge it to the business card. He had taken me aside and explained how he'd had his people set it up. He saw us as an extension of the work on the ground here in Philadelphia that his team were keen to support. Knowing we were here gave him and his crew peace of mind. So, giving us transport and a means to keep it on the road, the charge card was part of the package. Thus giving us ties back to the Community in Laodicea—or Felix, really—if trouble arose. Whatever. I just reckoned he was a wily dude and was trying to make an epic gift look like a work expense.

I would not admit it to any living soul, but it hurt, and I mean literally hurt, to hand the keys over to Marcus for their first trip—adults only—to meet with the High Council. It didn't bode well that Tessa and I were left to watch the twins whilst they waded into battle. I guess they knew it wasn't going to be pretty—or successful—from the get-go. I think it was the final meeting of the brains trust and an inevitable parting of the ways; their last-ditch effort to convince the High Council to stay strong in the Light, not to cave into fear and imagination. It made sense not to take Old Faithful—the truck. I got that. Didn't mean it didn't hurt. What hurt more, though, was the evil gleam in Marcus's eye when he realised what it cost me.

Anyway, things travelled from bad to worse—not with the car, with the Council. Seems that they were so freaked out about the Gerent dude coming and, as far as they were concerned, their imminent ticket to The Games, they were sweating all kinds of bullets. Not having their Overseer on hand to calm their overactive imaginations didn't help. Val tried speaking with them about tactics and strategies. Marcus tried talking to them about their history and foundations. I think Kait just went to keep the other two calm when they couldn't get through to any of them.

The Council had voted. As a Community, they would bend the knee. Their reasoning? When the Gerent came to inspect his new playpen—the rebuilt city—and his new toys—the population—they would pay homage "in words only". Like that made a difference.

They were bat-skrat scared. So much so, they started making life awkward for members who didn't agree with them. Dissenters were silenced at meetings, made to sit at the back of Soteria houses for gatherings, and had their positions of leadership revoked. Soon, only those in agreement with the High Council held any power or had any say as far as the official Community went in Philadelphia. Everyone else was walking the highway.

After doing their bit to encourage—debate vigorously with—different gatherings of the Community of Light in and around the city of Philadelphia, the official word was, our family was persona non grata. The harder the door hit on our way out, the better.

Jonathan made it very clear we were welcome to keep using his place, but since Tessa and I had been spending most of our time helping the crew out at Sanctuary whilst the rest of our family were crossing swords with the Community gatherings, we decided to stop giving Felix's charge card a beating and asked permission to move in.

The kids were pretty excited to be living in tents. Tessa, not so much. She tried to pretend to be happy about it. Gave a good attempt at nonchalance. But she wasn't fooling anyone. Least of all me. But then, those stolen moments of privacy with my fiancé—frackle, that still sounded so good—when she clung to me weeping, were a dead giveaway. So, despite accusations to the contrary, I was sympathetic. And discreetly—yes, I did know what that word meant—spoke to Marcus about a plan I had come up with.

It was mid-morning... for us. Our crew had already done sets, workouts, I'd gone for a run—we were not too far from the seriously sweet chunk of forest with hills, trails and single track I was having a ball exploring. We'd had showers and breakfast. The rest of the camp was awakening and emerging from their shells and getting ready for the day. Winter was on her way out, but it was still crisp and fresh in the morning light. Mist rose off the dams in the wet paddocks and there was a reverent hush that all of nature observed. Even the birds. They started bursting their lungs before light, but as the sun set sail across the sky, they too seemed to be in silenced awe for a few moments. Then they, and the rest of Sanctuary, stepped into the day.

We gathered in the centre of camp at the Meeting Place, a large tarp held up by massive poles, with sides that could be rolled up or down. There was an urn on a table in one corner with cups, a jug of milk, and jars filled with tea bags, sugar and instant coffee. The general babble increased as caffeine was imbibed, dissolving the remnants of sleep fog. But once again a hush settled as the old girl, Mary, and her grandson, Jet, made their way down the hill to officially kick off the day. She did a mini meet and greet until Len, the farm manager, arrived and told everyone where he needed help on the farm.

For generations, Mary's family had produced wine and beef. But mainly wine. And from what I'd heard, it was pretty good. The best even. But after she lost all her family—and most of her marbles—she and Jet just pottered at tending vines and keeping a minimal herd. They'd not produced a drop of wine since The Quake. Her heart and head just weren't in it anymore.

After Len had pulled the help he needed, Callum, the head gardener, stepped up and called his crew out. Then, each of the artisans who had onsite workshops put out their requests for help. Since our lot weren't skilled working with any of the arts and had trouble telling one end of a cow from the other, we tended to be put on mindless manual labour. Not that I was complaining.... Yeah, I was complaining. Just like Tessa couldn't cope living in a tent, I was going spare with the boredom.

I'd tried to work my way in with Daisy and her woodwork, and Travis with his metalwork. But it didn't take too long to see the truth of it, especially about Daisy. She didn't share her space with anyone, day or night, helper or friend. Except for Ruby and Pod. For everyone else, her workshop was out of bounds. And Travis? He just didn't need help.

Next, I tried Caspian and Indrila; nice couple who were electricians. They were the ones responsible for all the solar panels and ensuring each family's plot and the Meeting Place had some modicum of power. They also did other stuff I hadn't asked about, like channelling a decent amount of energy to the work hut of February and October, who not only needed power for all their tech, but to keep their gear from overheating. Even in winter. The electricians had told me at this point in time I'd be more of a spectator than anything else. Reading between the lines: a hindrance.

The aforementioned twins were my age, in their mid-twenties, and a couple of ridiculously superior computer gurus. And from what I could make out, members of an elite tech society or something. They were partly responsible for "Drone Wars"—a reinvention of the old-school homing/carrier pigeon concept, but on steroids. Backed by seriously hardcore AI and programming. As far as I could make out, Drone Wars was "capture the flag"... to the death... of the drones. It did my head in, trying to follow what the hell they were talking about, but I was seriously impressed by the footage that came in via the onboard cameras. The machines themselves were pretty intimidating and came with a strictly "touch with your eyes only or die" policy. And only then if you passed their intense security check. They were paranoid about their innovations being leaked or hacked. I think we were deemed safe because we didn't speak Programmer. Needless to say, they never asked for help from the masses at the morning meetings.

There was an... interesting lady, Miriam, often dubbed "the goat lady", who'd been quickly adopted by Riah. Just as Callum, the head gardener, had drawn Raph. I wouldn't have minded spending time with Joshua, a carpenter, who seemed pretty cool. But he had little to do in a village of Tents and was often left standing toward the end of roll call, much like Marcus and me.

One guy I made a point to stay away from was the retired teacher, Mr Berry. There was nothing wrong with the guy, but I was not keen on helping out with the fifteen or so kids he tried to wrangle for a couple of hours of school each day. I knew he wanted help, daily, but I always made sure I was looking the other way when he was asking for volunteers. Don't worry, he always had a few kind-hearted souls help him out. Kait and he were getting on great guns.

After these positions were filled, the uninitiated were sent off to the tip... on bicycles and trolleys, to scavenge for skrat to be recycled into useful items or... art? It was a good system that had been working just fine for the past twelve months or so. But I knew I wasn't going to last the distance if something didn't change soon.

An idea had been working away in my brain and wouldn't let go. It all started when we offered to lend Old Faithful for the tip runs. They helped pay for fuel with money from their markets, and Marcus and I piled kids and others not needed for the morning's duties in the back.

The blokes who ran the tip had been busy and industrious. Since the destruction of the city, they had collected a lot of materials and put on extra staff to sort everything into a kind of seconds store. They sold everything. Including recycled building materials.

This morning, Marcus and I stood beside Joshua, the carpenter I'd met earlier, and Tim, a builder, as they did their daily drool over the treasure, mesmerised by the acres of stacked timber, sheeting and roofing. Prompted by my intense boredom, I took a chance and shared my idea.

Marcus looked at me and grunted. It wasn't an impatient sound; I could actually see the wheels of his brain spinning before I finished explaining. "We'd have to pass it by Daisy and Travis first," he said. "And Mary, of course. But I can't see why it would be a problem."

We both looked to Tim and Joshua, whose eyes were wide and not seeing the tip around them. I suspect they were both visualising their own version of my idea and, with their experience, weighing up if it were a plausible reality. Joshua's head slowly started nodding. But Tim was giving the idea some serious squint-eye.

"Do you think the people who aren't confident about going back inside buildings, like Ruby, might be okay with a lighter structure, like a hut?" As far as I could see it was the only real sticking point. "I mean, we could try doing something like those glamping tents or yurts for them? Solid floor, thicker walls… but the huts shouldn't be too much of a step up from that."

We stood in a line weighing up the sea of possibilities that stretched before us. I also started nodding. Then almost lost my breath as other ideas crushed me with their enthusiasm to be acknowledged. "You know, if we built simple huts, we could install more than one solar panel on each roof. And connect rainwater tanks."

Marcus chimed in. "And it would give me something to do other than picking caterpillars off tomatoes. Not that I mind mucking in, I can tell you. But feeling like a nub teat on a bull's udder is not me idea of being useful."

I kind of thought this may have been the final selling point. The concept of not being sidelined or feeling completely useless had the other two signing on. After that it was hard not to rush the picking crew to get on with their job so we could go back and start negotiations and making plans.

As soon as we'd pulled up back at the camp, the four of us made a beeline to Daisy and Travis's workshops, where we had a meeting of the minds. The two leaders of Sanctuary were all in, but we would wait until Daisy could have a word to Mary... and Jet. The kid was only fifteen, but he was the potential owner of the property and had to be consulted.

For the first time since we'd arrived in Philadelphia, I started to feel the excitement of finding my purpose. Whilst folk here appreciated music, they couldn't pay for it. The markets open to the public only happened on Saturdays, so I had limited opportunity to earn money for my family. Not that money had much of a place here. And as much as I wasn't proud to admit it, fetching wood to burn, scrap metal to buff and snipping shoots off vines just wasn't doing it for me.

But building a village? That I could do.

17

CONTESSA: SEWING UP A STORM

I love him. I mean, I seriously love him. He is absolutely wonderful and…

I.

Love.

Him.

Gushing much?

I know.

I was in my workshop because Marcus had had enough of me and kept sending me away until I could "get the nettle out of me petal". I mean I kind of understood. He was old and had forgotten what love felt like. But I was in the middle of it and I hadn't. Seriously, I couldn't stop singing and dancing… unless I saw Daisy. Then I was very good at hiding in the shadows.

Oh. My. Word.

I thought Amina—head of security at the Factory in Laodicea, one of the original Silverscales and ex-Mother, high priestess of the Temple of Ashera—was scary. And she was. Don't get me wrong, even in the end when the Light chiselled off some of her razor edges, she still carried her "scary girl" card. Of course, Val didn't need a "scary girl" card. She was the flopping queen.

But Daisy? Daisy'd be the princess in waiting. Thank the Light she wore thick armour, because otherwise I'd be thinking she was "in waiting" to stab you when you weren't looking... or if you were. I don't think she'd mind either way if you watched her or didn't as she tore you to pieces. I just kept reminding myself we were on the same team. I was in the Light. She was in the Light. And the Light loved me just as much as He loved her. And so did Dan... loved me that is, not Daisy.

And we were going to get married. I still couldn't believe it. I kept getting snagged on the beauty of the creation perched, as in locked onto, my finger—nothing was taking this baby off. It was so. Flopping. Beautiful. And it was the ring Abbot's dad gave his mum, and then Abbot gave it to Dan to give to me. Well, I thought he did. He really was a cunning old fox. I was sure he had known how things were going to work out. Which made me even happier. I seriously thought I might burst. I hadn't sung this much in like... forever.

"Will you please keep it down in there? I am trying to get my baby to sleep."

"Sorry." Eeeks. I kept forgetting how thin tent walls were, because... I wasn't living in one anymore. "Yay."

"Please." I think the woman may have been close to tears. I didn't think it was my singing, but I could never be too sure, because... you know... family are too nice. Well, not all families. But mine was and they wouldn't tell me if my singing was awful. Actually, Marcus would.

"I'm so sorry, I promise. No more singing." So, why was I singing? Apart from having the love of my life want to marry me and having THE most gorgeous ring? Well, I was no longer living in a tent. Dan built me a house. Well, he had some help. A couple of guys, Joshua and Tim who were builders by trade, and Marcus, and a few other people. But it was Dan's idea. So now I got to live in a cabin. My very own cabin. I mean, I shared it with Val and Sariah. But apart from them, I had it all to myself. I felt so very blessed, I could sing. But I wouldn't, because of the poor lady who moved in next door. I mean, if I were inside my house I could, it was insulated. Yes. Insulated. And you'd never believe how. Obviously with insulation. But what I mean is, how we got the insulation.

Audette.

Yes. Audette.

And Felix.

They showed up here in Felix's fancy hydro-auto-drivo car thingy one day, on the pretext of visiting everyone and catching us up on the gossip of the Factory's refurbishment and Iza's baby. Well, her pregnancy. She was due in two months. Eight weeks. I'd been sewing madly for her too. Anyway, soon after Audette and Felix's visit, huge trucks arrived with pallets of insulation and water tanks. Narrow ones that sat along the side of the cabin walls. So now I had water. In. My. Cabin. Seriously, I had to pinch myself to stop from singing. Well, when I was in my workshop out the back of my cabin. Because, you know, not soundproof.

Anyway, I didn't know how to feel about Audette helping us out. Audette was Izabel's mum. Long story short, she and Felix had bought the run-down Factory Iza and Indy, Dan's childhood friend, had been hiding in to keep them safe from the Temple of Asher and Iza's dad. Iza was at war with her mum for allowing her to be donated to the Temple when she was a baby. But they had sorted through that horrible situation and were well on the way to making amends. Anyway, it turned out that she was not only Iza's mum, but a skilled surgeon and significantly well off. And seriously generous.

Just like Felix. Not that he was a surgeon. But a very successful businessman and seriously generous. I'm a bit ashamed to say I had come to expect receiving gifts—like a car—from Felix. I needed to work at not taking him for granted. Maybe I should make him something, too. Anyway, it seemed that since we'd become part of the Factory family in Laodicea, we'd become part of Audette's family, and she had a tendency to throw vital resources at family. Which we learned and experienced for the last one and half years when we were living with the Silverscales. But seriously, I—along with everyone else —almost choked when the trucks arrived. But they had to get past Daisy and Travis first.

Just like on the first day. The girl… woman, stepped out in front of the mega vehicles and stood her ground with her arms crossed. They had to explain what they had on board, who they were from and, most importantly, what was required in response. The poor driver. The guy was a bit of a mess trying to explain, but it seemed he had a letter. If only he'd handed it over first it would have been a lot simpler. It was from Felix, explaining. Apparently now that Daisy knew Felix, and had caught up on the goss, like how amazing he was, she accepted him as part of the growing Sanctuary community. She didn't know he was the guy who'd been behind the bulk of the funding to set the place up and supporting the crew here. See, when he'd first heard about how the Council didn't approve of Tent Village, the place where his friend Jonathan's little girl, Ruby, lived, he'd done everything to support Mary to establish this place so they could stand on their own feet without help from the city or the Gerent.

When she, Daisy, put two and two together after we first got here, it was a different matter altogether. I'm surprised the name didn't change to Felixtown. Anyway, when Daisy and Travis learned that the gifts were from him and Audette, it was all systems go. Yay.

Especially since Val had done the rounds, sticking her verbal boot into everyone's metaphorical butt, there had been a bit of a division in the Community here in Philadelphia. Apparently, if you didn't agree with the Council, you were being asked to leave. And by that, I mean, if your house was one of the ones restored or repaired with the Gerent's funds, it turned out it was no longer your property. But the saddest thing of all was that the Council was pre-empting the Gerent's visit and culling the Community of those who were likely to "displease" him by not acknowledging the guy was a god. I mean seriously, how delusional can a person be? Thank the Light his visit had been delayed because he got sick. Hospital sick.

Anyway, people have been coming to Sanctuary—the new name for Tent Village because, you know… no more tents. Well, for me anyway. "Yay."

"I'm begging you, please keep your voice down."

"Sorry." Well, in time there wouldn't be any more tents. My cabin was the prototype. Then all permanent residents—those with the greatest need first—would get a cabin. I was making the furnishings. Yes. I got to make curtains, cushions, tablecloths… all things to make the places feel more like home.

I had made the mistake of taking some furnishings next door to my new neighbour, Lisa, and her two adorable children. But, since her cabin wasn't ready, I had kind of jumped the gun and she had nowhere to store them and it kind of made things worse because it kind of made her remember all the things she'd lost—as well as her husband—in The Quake.

And I made a real mess of things when I called her little girl, Nasya, a boy. The trouble was, she was so poor, she was dressing her daughter in hand-me-downs and what she could scrounge from her little boy's clothes. So, I was trying really hard to make up for being a noisy, foot-in-mouth neighbour and making a wardrobe for Nasya from off-cuts from my sewing projects. Cute little patch-work designs so that no one would confuse her for a boy again. Now that it was almost summer, I was making her the most adorable little pinafores and frilly pants to go over her nappy. So cute.

I thought her cabin would be next, and I suspected she would want it a bit further away from mine. But that was okay. At least then I could sing while I worked and I wouldn't be troubling anyone. And we were closer to the laundry here. Yes. I know. I still got excited about laundries. This one was part of the toilet-shower monstrosity. There were three old laundromat washing machines installed. They were coin operated, but the couple who were electricians rigged it up so that the coin dropped in, then fell straight back into the little catchy-box thing at the bottom. There was a huge bank of solar panels on the roof. So, we did the washing while the sun shone and all was good. And these machines were humungo. We could do our whole family's wash in one some days. Dan and Marcus put the load on, on their way to work, and I went over with the twins a little bit later to hang it out in the field of lines out the back.

So, all things considered things were, "A-may-zing."

"Please."

"Sorry." Except I hadn't seen Dan in a very long while. And we were supposed to be getting married. But I didn't know when, or how, or… when. He'd been working so hard building cabins and wooden walkways around the Village, so that in all the rain we could stay above the mud. He really was doing a fantastic job. All of them were. But he was gone from sunup to after sunset and he was exhausted. And I missed him.

18

RAPHAEL: CAT AMONG THE CHICKENS

We were like two new chickens being introduced to the coop. Sorting out the pecking order was my least favourite part of a move. It had been my experience that, just like chickens, children could be very mean spirited. Even those wearing armour. When we first arrived in Laodicea, we were made to go to the Community's school where hardly anyone was wearing any. It had been the second worst experience of my life. Here at Sanctuary, most of the people were encased in the Light's colours and some of the children had faint dustings of it. But not everyone. And not all of it was thick and healthy. Mostly people were welcoming. Just not all the kids.

It made my heart so heavy. I missed my friends back home at the Factory. Although, it was fun living in a tent. It was exciting that they had a healthy, vibrant vegetable garden with a huge compost system and chickens and worms. Riah was almost beside herself because there were cattle and, finally, some goats. The cows were for meat, but the goats were for milk, cheese and soap. She tried very hard not to show how she felt. Especially since we were among new people and she was busy keeping her wall up.

I was ashamed to admit it, but I just didn't feel like being oil to her choppy water this time around. If she wanted to fight people, and they wanted to fight her, maybe it was the best way to get the pecking order problem out of the way as soon as possible. Then we could all just get on with life and try to figure out what the Light wanted us here for.

It was a bit unnerving to have a constant gathering of demon spies. They did not do anything but watch us. Always. Small groups wandering throughout the camp, around the clock. But I found I couldn't really raise a care for them. I had a hard time getting excited about anything. Because I missed... everything. I missed Kazi, Joko and Hiro. I missed cooking for everyone with Vashti and Aiko. I missed spending time with Val everyday, going into the city to visit with Felix. I missed him too. And I missed playing my drum with Dan for Missy and her customers at Serendipity.

I just wanted to go home. So, I did the next best thing. I spent time in the garden where I could not see anyone working away in their own little bubbles, or the tents spread out like a checkerboard across the dusty paddock, or the workshops constantly banging and buzzing along to their own unique hum, or the storage sheds, or the cows and goats grazing in the pasture, or the vines strung out along their clothes lines. Just the calming, beautiful green of seedlings growing into mature plants, producing glorious fruit and vegetables.

The weight of my sadness made me feel like a snail. Small, slow and useless. I turned a bucket over and sat, letting the soft hands of the tomato leaves soothe me with their scent. A gentle breeze brought hints of mint, pineapple sage, and broccoli. Shutting my eyes, I lifted my face to the sky.

Where are you? I am undone. Heavy. Lost. Wet, dark-grey sand on a stormy winter beach. A jagged rock lost in the undergrowth at the bottom of a dark ravine. What are we doing here? Please help me to.... Just... help please.

I jumped a mile when a small paw batted my ankle. I looked down and saw a kitten whose face was dominated by two very large, reflective black pools. A little mouth opened, and two rows of sharp teeth buried themselves into my ankle. "Hey. Stop that." Four paws full of needles attacked. The front two held fast whilst the back two pummelled my boot. After my initial shock, the pain set in. I grabbed the little tiger by the scruff of its neck and lifted it so I could look it in the eye. At arm's length. It just hung in the air, limp, regarding me with its curious eyes. "Hello, little one." I pulled the baby cat into my lap and scratched it behind its tiny ears: two little sails swivelling toward me to catch my voice. It purred, then exposed its belly. So, I gave it a scratch there as well. My hand covered most of its body, so I gently rubbed its ribby stomach with the tips of my fingers, mesmerised by the soft, warm fur and the roar of its purr.

The sudden hissing and spitting of my new little friend as the scent of sulphur invaded my bubble of peace made me cranky. A humanoid demon manifested a bucket, similar but bigger than mine, and took a seat beside me.

"Don't be like that. I just came to keep you compan—"

The intruder screamed as I laid my hand on its thigh and gave thanks to the Light for reminding me we had work to do here. We were here on His business. The box where I kept my memories of the Factory still smouldered with loss and loneliness. But at least I was reminded to look at what we had been given to do here.

Footsteps came running. A burly boy, Craig, who had not gone out of his way to make us feel welcome—but neither had he bullied or picked on us—approached me from the path leading to the Meeting Place. His eyes madly flashed left and right. "I thought I heard something."

"Do not worry, it is gone now."

His wide eyes dropped to me sitting awkwardly on the little bucket, my knees near my shoulders and Tiger in my lap. "Great. You found one of the pests."

"Why is he a pest? Surely it is good for him to catch the mice. And to have as a pet? There are dogs here."

"Yeah, but these kill birds and wildlife and breed fleas and… more cats." He stood over me like a giant, his eyes following my fingers as they continued to trace circles in the kitten's—once again exposed— soft belly. Its head back, four legs flung wide, at peace with the world and apparently with me. After a while Craig shook his head. "School's about to start." Then he turned and left.

The expectation I would follow was a non-negotiable—as Val would say. And my feelings on the matter were irrelevant—another one of Val's favourite words. Thinking about her made me smile. But then remembering how different she was with her knives back made me sad. And without any conscious thought, I found myself meandering down the path to the Meeting Place with Tiger curled up in the crook of my left arm, whilst the fingers on my right hand still found comfort stroking his warm, bony little body.

I took a seat at the back, in the corner, and watched while I waited. Jethro, Mary's grandson, told us that originally this place was a lot fuller when people who had no homes migrated here after The Quake. Then, when the Gerent repaired the city, family by family they returned to their old lives in their new homes. Numbers dropped to about fifty people. Now, only those who decided they didn't trust any building made of something heavier than canvas—and those who enjoyed the different style and flow of life—had decided to take Mary up on her invitation to stay.

Mary was so funny. And lovely. When we first arrived, every day she would come down the hill with Jethro and Ruby to greet everyone, seeing they had all that they needed, and greet us as newcomers. "And who do we have here?" she'd say. "Jet, looks like you've got a couple of wonderful new helpers for your crew," she'd say. "Welcome to Tent Village. You are welcome as long as you need a place to say," she'd finish.

And Jet would smile at his grandma and say, "Yes, Nanna-May, another couple of pairs of hands are going to come in handy." Every day for a couple of weeks. Until she'd look at Riah and me, tilt her head and smile. "Well, it does my heart glad to see my two new friends this morning." She never remembered our names. But then there were only a few she did. "Have you asked Jet for a job to do? I am sure he could use a couple of pairs of helpful hands like yours."

And we'd say, "Yes, Nanna-May,"—because she said we could call her that, all the kids did—"Jethro has put us on rotation." Then Jethro would wink at us and smile, and Nanna-May would walk on to greet her other guests, both of them encased in the most vivid, intricate armour: hers mauve, his forest green.

Jethro wasn't the biggest or the oldest kid here. But this had been his home for fifteen years and he had grown up learning about producing wine and growing cattle. And we were as much his guests as we were Nanna-May's. None of the other kids gave him trouble. But then they would not want to, because Daisy and Travis were his very good friends. And Daisy was almost as scary as Val.

I was happy that, even though I was sad and missed our home at the Factory, this was not as bad as the school we had been forced to go to when we first arrived in Laodicea. Whilst we still had to work out where we sat on the perch in the coop, at least we were not picked on… much, or bullied. And while I did not understand why I had to learn about some of the things we learned at "school" here, it was definitely more interesting than school there.

Here, it was for everyone. Because the day started early, so too did lunch break. People would leave their workshops late morning and gather at the Meeting Place. Someone would have put the urn on and there were water jugs as well as bowls of fruit and freshly picked salad vegetables to snack on. Then someone shared something they knew something about. Yesterday, the goat lady, Miriam, gave us a lesson on milking goats and udder care. Today a lady, Indrila, with a little baby, Cyan, stood at the front with her husband, Caspian, behind her. Normally they worked with electricity, but today they stood at a table with a big tub of water in front of them.

After the first lesson of the day, someone else would stand and share something about The Way. And after lunch, there was regular school for the kids. A retired science teacher, Mr Berry, lived in the Village and he taught us kids what he remembered from his years teaching in Ephesus.

This morning, people had seen us training and doing sets at sunrise. It was suggested it should be an option for everyone and something our family could do to contribute to the wellbeing of the whole group. Marcus did not mind. So, I guess, tomorrow even that would change. More and more I felt I was losing my family again like I did when we first arrived in Laodicea, and then later again at the Factory. I was so very grateful for Riah. I felt in my bones that I would always have her as my soul nest.

As I hid at the back of the Meeting Place waiting for my sister to spot me, I looked around the space. It was really a tent roof in the middle of the sea of vegetable gardens and fruit trees. Three big poles held each side and one in the middle took the weight of the roof. Today, all four walls were rolled up and the gentle, late-spring breeze had been cooled and scented on its way through the vegetables, herbs and citrus on its journey to us. Bees buzzed, birds chirped, and Tiger purred. It really was a lovely location, and for a while I could enjoy the peace. It lifted a bit of the sadness weighing me down to see most of the people left living in Sanctuary, in armour. Knowing that most of the people here were journeying the same path, heading to the same location and treasuring the same truths as me and my family, helped.

But right now, my attention was bearing down on Sariah. She was sitting next to Miriam, her eyes constantly scouring the shelter. But instantly, like a magnet pulled to North, she swivelled to face me. Her chin hitched and she patted the space next to her. But she became a statue when she saw I was holding something. Her curiosity was worse than the cat's. Like a rubber band it pulled her to me. When she reached me, she dropped to her knees and tried to take the baby away from my embrace. I should not have resisted. I should have shared. But I felt he was special. He found *me*. He had picked *me*.

Her tugging woke him up and he hissed at her, striking at her hand and drawing a faint line of blood. She snatched her hand back and accused me with her eyes and a flurry of hand movement. I shrugged and rolled my lips to hide my smile. I should not have been happy. "Can you help me, Riah? He is just a baby and needs food. Do you think Miriam would help us by sharing some goat's milk with us?"

She looked at her hand then gave Tiger a dose of squint-eye. He did not care, he just rolled over and purred at her. I rubbed a finger behind his satellite-disc ears. His eyes closed and his chin lifted. Riah took another chance and gently scratched the exposed fur. The kitten purred louder. She was now officially inducted onto Team Tiger. Her help was guaranteed.

The meeting started, so we quietly snuck our way through the group and took the seats Riah had saved for us. When we reached her, Miriam looked at Tiger, raised an eyebrow and ducked her chin in acknowledgement. Normally, Indrila was confident—quiet but, from what I had seen, sure of herself. Much like Caspian. Normally one of them would be working with a baby pouch on their back. But today, as they stood in front of the group, they looked nervous. Cyan was in front of them on the table playing in a tub of water. It might have been helpful to somebody in the group to learn how to bathe a baby, but I was not sure how or why. When their short talk ended, it was time for my favourite part of school; Val took the stand and opened The Way for us. Then, finally, it was lunch.

Miriam had agreed to exchange some goat milk every day for an extra hand cleaning stalls. Now all I had to do was work out what cats ate and figure out how to supply that. So far all I had seen Tiger eat were grasshoppers—apart from the sharp pointy bits, he didn't like those bits—little lizards, and my ankles.

19

RAPHAEL: FIGHT CLUB

Kait gave me an extra squeeze before she released me and we headed out for sets and training. I should not have been surprised or upset that so many showed an interest in joining us. It was selfish. I should be glad that we could help so many people be better prepared for battle, and help them learn new ways to get closer to the Light.

But I was struggling not to think about myself and yet another thing I had lost in this move to Philadelphia. Morning sessions were my special time with my family. The one thing that was my anchor, the thing that did not change no matter where we went or what we did. Sometimes, some family members could not be with us, and sometimes we had a few extra, but always we worked as a family. And it was one of the main things I used to keep the Dragon at bay. But today and, I felt, for the future, it would all change. The red haze crept into my periphery. I tried not to give it my attention. Instead, I breathed deeply, Light in… two… three. Out… two… three. Over and over. In and out. I was trying to focus on the Light, but my attention was becoming snagged on the needles sinking into my ankle. I scooped up Tiger and let him chew on my finger. I learned this too was a good distraction from the red haze.

After Marcus had led the crowd for sets, there was a quick survey of skills under Val's eagle eye. Marcus, Kait and Val put everyone who had shown up into groups, and assigned them a leader. It was no surprise that Riah and I were to tutor the kids. The older teenagers and young adults had been put with Dan and Tessa and were all bursting with enthusiasm. Unlike some in our group who were oozing cynicism. There were three girls, Ruby, Jayne—the bee-keeper's daughter, and Lucy—the builder's daughter. They were quiet and reserved. Opposite to the five boys.

An extra weight wrapped itself around me. So, I held Tiger a bit tighter. Not too tight. But just enough to send his purring through my palm straight to my heart. I did not feel confident teaching others to fight. But I could help them understand Riah who was eager to teach, and I could show some of the younger children how to do self-defence. I guessed it was a good thing we had had practise teaching different people different skills at the Factory.

Sariah marched off toward a clearing while the kids just stared at me. I looked at my sister and tried to muster enthusiasm for the inevitable. I sighed. "You kids are with us. So could you please follow my sister, and we will begin."

The biggest of the group tried to make himself look bigger. Yes, it was exactly like chickens. A boy called Rory fluffed his feathers and puffed out his chest. "What if we don't want to go with you and your sister?"

I did not reply by saying what I felt, instead I sighed again and tried to muster some enthusiasm. "She really is very good at this, and you could learn a lot from her."

The rooster crowed. "She's just a girl."

A feminine snarl exploded behind me. Perhaps I should have felt sorry for Rory, but he had made the mistake of saying that in the hearing of Tessa, who did not attempt to contain her disgust. "I beg your pardon. What did you say?"

Dan came up beside me and threw his arm around my shoulders, like a hot water bottle for my blue soul, and whispered, "Oh boy, is he about to have a rude awakening."

"I said"—the boy clucked and ruffled his feathers some more, bringing him up to about the same size as Tessa—"she is just a girl and I think we would learn more from him." He pointed his finger at Dan.

Before Tessa or Riah could manage a retort, Dan stepped in. "Okay, I'll do you a deal. Anyone who can defeat Riah, and by that, I mean, pin her to the ground for the count of three or until she taps out, can train with me… and Tessa."

The rooster swivelled his imperious head to rake his judgey eyes over my twin from her head to her toes and back. Then turned to take in Tessa. He was about to do the same when Dan stepped in front of him. Very quietly he corrected the uneducated child. "Do not push your luck, boy."

The deflated rooster gulped, and our two groups merged and went to join Sariah. Of course, she had heard the bargain. Her eyes were glinting, her armour was flashing and she may have even been salivating. Strange girl. But at least I would have a quiet time of the session this morning as I was not really required, and have another opportunity to marvel at my sister's skill and give thanks for her character, personality and hunger.

I should not have had the kick of excitement as a circle formed around her. Clutching Tiger to my chest, I raced to stand in front of Sariah to make sure I could tell everyone her rules. I already knew what to expect and what she would want. But I wanted to give her time to settle and make sure she was okay. Riah's hand indicated the growing crowd, then with two fingers she tapped the back of her left arm and amended the deal. "Are you sure?"

She cast her eyes around the group. *There are so many, it will take too long otherwise. I want to get to the goats this morning.*

"Okay." I turned to face the group. "Sariah says she will not take on more than two at a time and if they can pin her to the ground, or survive in the ring with her longer than three minutes, they can train with Tessa and Dan."

Dan whistled. "Nice one, Riah. Deal."

Tessa dashed in and hugged her. "You've so got this sweetheart. But don't hurt them too badly, we have to live with their parents."

One of the children who chose to stay hidden called out. "Hey, why can't she talk?"

"Sariah can. She just chooses not to," I answered.

"Why not?"

I searched the crowd until I saw the short boy who was asking. I think his name was Eddie, the youngest of three brothers. I stared at him. I looked around the group. Maybe I should have been more charitable. But I could not find it in me today. "Why should I lay our pearls in the mud at your feet?"

The accuser scrunched his face. But Jethro and a few of the older kids laughed. "Nice one."

My face heated and I turned to see that the melding of our two groups, and the cheering and scoffing at Riah's challenge, had brought a larger crowd. Marcus, Kait and Val made their way over, and behind them came the parents and others. Daisy shouldered her way to the front to stand next to Val. Val eyeballed Riah with her laser-beam eyes, then nodded once. Riah stood tall, chin high, shoulders back and returned the nod.

I grabbed a stick and drew a circle in the dust. Then asked my family to stand around the outside. I knew they would not let anyone in. I then clarified to everyone: this challenge was for our group only. Riah gave me a nudge in the back. So, I turned on her. "No. Do not get above yourself. This is not about you. This is about us helping these people and teaching these kids how to defend themselves against the attack that is coming." I pointed to the edges of the circle formed around us where a growing crowd of demons had come to watch the spectacle, and insert their toxins to create fissures and trouble within our community. "Do not turn this into a show. Use your head and stay focused." I gave her my own version of laser-eye and waited till she dropped her head and nodded. "For the glory of the Light, Riah. Not yours."

And so, we began.

Unsurprisingly, the Rooster lasted less than thirty seconds. And even less the second time round. Each person who had been assigned to our group came forward, except the smart ones. I made note of who they were and felt a ray of hope that they would be good students. These, I could teach.

2 O

DANIEL: PAINFUL INSPIRATION

Man, it felt good to tick another cabin off the list. Well, it would. Not much to do now, just a few bits and pieces of trim to finish off, then a general tidy-up and put-away before starting the next one. Marcus, and some people on rotation—as well as Josh's tweens, Oliver and Lucy—had already started marking out the dimensions. Caspian and Indrila would take less than a day to link this one up to solar and it would be good to go.

The salvage crew had been to the tip and gathered another round of supplies. We were on such a good wicket there. We sent boxes of veggies, cartons of eggs and a bottle or two of Daisy's mead, and the guys at the tip let our team pick through the salvaged materials to find suitable building supplies. Once they'd brought back another load we'd be onto the next, and then another family would be out of the dust, and I would be one step closer to making my and Tessa's home.

The first I had made for her was basically us—Marcus, Josh, Tim and me—finding out a system and how we worked together. As well as trying to sell the idea to Mary, Daisy and Travis with our prototype. We did the best we could, but I knew that by the end of this adventure we would be doing even better.

It had taken me a while to recover from Josh's bombshell. "Since this is all your idea, you're in charge." When I almost fainted, he laughed. "Tim and I will show you what to do and we'll teach you guys what we can. But you're calling the shots."

Frigity, fragrity, frogs.

The learning curve had been a crumbling cliff face. But it was starting to level out to a steep incline. To try to be as fair as possible to the folk here at Sanctuary, after our prototype—which Tessa, Val and Riah now occupied—we were building cabins for the neediest families first. Everybody else went into a ballot. As we neared the end of one cabin, we negotiated with the next on the list. That person or family'd tell us what they'd like, and Josh'd give them the truth about what they could have. We tried to meet in the middle or get Tim to talk them round. He was good with that kind of thing. Had a real knack at making people see his way of thinking.

I'd purposefully left my name out of the hat because I wanted to leave it till last. I wanted to make it the best I possibly could, learn from my mistakes, figure out what was possible, and then, when I couldn't do any better, I'd present it to Tessa as a wedding gift. Our first home together, for just the two of us, that I had built all by myself... with a lot of help. But to be honest, it wouldn't feel right moving into a cabin when others had been roughing it in tents for much longer than us.

We were moving along at a cracking pace. With some of the teens coming on rotation with us, we were finishing a cabin per month, roughly speaking. Josh and Tim had set up the extra helpers to make the wooden walkways around the camp, and the basic preparations for the builds. I was trying to keep up with everything going on here at Sanctuary, remember names, routines, and roles and, most importantly, what I was being taught. But I had to confess, with my dreams railroading my sleep, I felt like I was operating with half a brain. But Josh and Tim were patient and great at teaching us all the basics. The teenagers who had a flair for carpentry came on board as apprentices. A kid called Craig was a natural, as was a slip of a girl, Kelly. Where he swamped her with his bulk, she came to the fore with her quick wit and flair for problem solving.

It was getting hard to see my way around the worksite now that the sun had fallen behind the mountains to the west, but I just had to tidy up and make a list of any new materials we needed to scout for on our next trip to the tip. I might try to get one in tomorrow, so we'd be ready to go on number five the day after. There was no doubt Tessa's and my car was the best ever, but I had to admit, once again Old Faithful had come in handy. The stuff we could get into that truck defied reason, especially with Marcus's mad Tetris skills.

"Daniel?" My whole name issuing from my fiancé's lips was never a good omen. I was in trouble for something, and no doubt was about to find out what.

"Yes, Contessa?" Two could play at that game.

She paused. Then it began. "When were you planning on packing up and coming home?" In the warm glow from the hut I was finishing, I could see predator bird had come out to play. "Like everybody else?"

"I just have to tidy up and then I—"

"For someone who is pathologically messy and can't see a dirty plate or filthy laundry on the floor, I want to know why and how?"

"How? Why? What?"

"First, how can you see this mess and none at home. And why do *you* 'just have to tidy up'. Why not everyone else? Together?"

"Because they've gone home to..." *oh skrat* "...be with their families?"

"Exactly. So why aren't you? With *your* family. Why are *you* still out here working?"

"Listen, Tessa, honey, can't you see? I'm doing all of this for us. For you."

The predator bird morphed into an owl. Eyes wide and mouth fallen open in shock. "Are you flopping serious right now?"

Rhetorical or not rhetorical. The eternal question. Perhaps silence was best.

With the squint-eye and hands on hips, predator bird came swooping in for the kill. "Are you seriously using my words against me? Are you mocking me Dan-iel?"

Oh skrat, oh skrat, oh skrat. "No?"

"I cannot believe you are doing the very thing you accused me of doing when we arrived in Laodicea." With puckered lips—which was a serious skill, because to flay someone's flesh from their bones in a tongue lashing, with your lips pursed, could not have been easy—"Well, how do you like this, Mr Pot-Kettle."

"I think you mea—"

"Shut up." Oh, dear lord, the head wobble. Tessa had started doing this thing, like a cobra rising out of its basket, her head waving from side to side as she unleashed her anger. It was a skill she learned from Lily at the Factory in Laodicea, who was the Cobra-head-wobble, hand-on-hip queen. "Did you ever think to ask me what I wanted? I would have told you, I'd rather live in a tent"—she froze and gave me a hard case of laser-eye because we both knew how much she hated living in a tent—"in the dust, with you in my life, than in a perfect little cabin all by myself."

Then the walls came tumbling down. *Fraggle.* "Oh, Tessa, I am so sorry." She had me. One hundred percent. I was doing exactly what she had done when we first arrived in Laodicea. She had gone out to work around the clock so we could live in a fancy house with fancy clothes in a fake fancy-land. And here, shortly after we had arrived in Philadelphia, I had left her to go to work so she could have a beautiful place to live so she didn't have to live in the tent. But I had effectively removed myself from her life. However, she had the gonads to confront me on it up front—using my words back at me. Unlike me, who went off in a sulk for about a year. "Tell me what I can do?"

"What do you mean, Daniel? It's not that hard to figure out."

Friggle. Now here was the perfect opportunity to end up floating down dog-house creek in a barbed-wire canoe and no paddle. *Please help me.* "Okay. I could…"

She ran out of patience and jumped the gun. Which I was kind of hoping she would. "Well, Mr Black—"

"Don't you mea—"

"Shut up. Mr. Bl-a-ck." She enunciated the word into three syllables. The final K had its own special kick. "You could leave when the others do. To go home to their wives. It's probably why *they've* all been married forever and you're not *ever* going to be." She punctuated this bombshell by crossing her arms with a little cobra head-wobble to top it off.

"What? What are you saying? Don't you want to marry me anymore?"

She glared at me.

"Tessa?"

"We are never going to get around to getting married if you are never around to talk about it, plan it, or invest in your relationship with your fi-an-cé." Again, she broke the word into three distinct syllables.

"But don't you see? That's why I'm racing to finish all the cabins. I figure when they're all done and I've finished ours, we'll get married and move in."

"When do you plan on that happening and when did you plan on telling me?"

"Well, I figure I've just told you now, and Indy and Iza needed about three days max to plan their wedding. In the end, they took about half an hour. The longest thing was finding a Shepherd of Light in the hospital. I figured when all the others were done, and we started planning ours, I'd let you know to give you a heads-up."

The owl was back, and I was completely lost. "Dan." Thank the Light it was just one syllable. "Where are we going to get married? Here, or Laodicea? Who are we going to invite? How are we going to feed them all? We need to make a plan and figure a few things out first. So, a bit of time together. To work out a plan. Would be good. Also, I kind of miss you. I feel like when you're racing toward your end goal and leaving me behind, we will end up married strangers. Just like we were at the beginning of last year. I don't want to go back there, Dan. I couldn't." Her eyes softened and her voice soothed. "I see what you are doing for everyone, and I am so proud of you. I'm not asking you to be chained to my side, we just need to remember to schedule in some quality time. Maybe go on the occasional date. Like Kait and Marcus do."

"Point." Once I acknowledged she was right, we were back on level ground and the predator bird flew home to roost. Tessa really was a very competitive woman. Or maybe it was just with me. But I had to admit she had me on this one. "Hey, I'm heading back to the tip tomorrow, and I'm taking Raph. The kid's really struggling, so I figured some quality time might help him out. Do you wanna come and make it a date?"

She froze. And just like that I was back in the barbed-wire canoe. "Are you trying to tell me that your idea of a date and quality time with the love of your life is a trip to the dump? With Raph? To help him feel better?" With every question mark, her voice rose an octave.

But since she put it like that... "Point." *And clarity, thanks for that.* "How about tomorrow we take a long lunch and I drive you and me into Philadelphia... in our car... and we check it out. Maybe find a nice place to have a meal?" Then inspiration struck. "How about we look for some charity shops? I still have a bit of money left over. Would you like to look for some clothes to work your ways with?" Her gasp signalled: point to me.

"Maybe I could look for some material to start working out a wedding dress... I could really use Kerm's help with this." And just like that she was lost to me, making new trails of rabbit warren into her world of design.

And this time it almost hurt when inspiration hit me upside the head. Mainly because it was something I really wanted, too. "Hey, Tessa." I had to shake her free of the rabbits. "Laodicea isn't that far away, you know. Hour-fifteen. And we have a car. And a charge-ca—"

Her scream and body wrapped around me like a wetsuit, signalling game, set and match to me.

Thank you!

21

DAISY: SHAME-FACED

Alario's costly... carbon-free car cruised into the carpark. This was nothing new. He came pretty much every day to collect Ruby. But today he didn't get out of the car. *What are you up to, Mr Intruder, and who have you brought into our home?*

Alario always came alone. He'd stop at the gate, have a chat and chew the fat with Tea, wait for Ruby to get ready, then off they'd go. I never had much to do with him. Had no need to. All I was interested in was making sure our girl was ready to go, and that he brought her home again each day in one piece. As far as I was concerned, the guy was a taxi service. And today he'd delivered an unwanted stranger.

I didn't alert Ruby just yet that it was time to go. I wanted to see who was in the car and if they were safe. By the looks of it, the two occupants were having a heated conversation—if their hand gestures were anything to go by. In the end the driver, Alario—Taxi—gripped the wheel with both hands and stared straight ahead. His passenger, still facing him, gesticulated some more, placed a hand on Taxi's shoulder, stilled, then got out of the car. Taxi didn't even look at him or anyone as he took off out of the carpark, leaving a cloud of dust and grit in his wake, obviously not a happy camper.

I then gave my full attention to the old codger making his way

96

over, leaning heavily on a cane and swimming in his Sunday best: collared shirt and pressed slacks. If you wanted a look that summed up the establishment, i.e. the Community, there it was, stumbling his way to our doorstep.

Why, for all that's good in the world, did you have to create so many fools? And why for freaky-freak's sake can't they leave us the bleeding heck alone?

I'd had enough of these guys coming in here trying to convince us to shut down and move on. Aside from the fact it was none of their business, we were on private property, and we were doing no harm. But I wasn't going to let any of them in to discourage and demean any of our community. "Batter up! We've got company… of the wrong kind."

Ruby shot off from her space in my workshop with Pod hot on her heels. Reinforcements would be here soon enough. Not that I'd need them for one old geezer. I went out to meet him before he got to the gate. "Listen here. You are not welcome. So you can get your mate to come back in his gaudy, gloomy, … g— g—…"

"Gizmo?"

"Thank you, that works." Turns out he wasn't as old as I had originally thought, and nowhere near as put out as I'd hoped. The realisation that I knew him—or who he was at least—hit me like a fist in the gut. As a kid, he'd been my Young Light leader, an underling of my dad's. So, I tripled my efforts, upped the snark, pulled down all barriers and did my absolute best to get him out of here ASAP. "And now you can turn around, call your mate in his *gizmo* back and get the hell out of here. You and your kind are significantly unwanted, and your harassment is bordering on illegal. I'm tempted to call the cops on the lot of you."

The quirk at the corner of his mouth and the twinkle of humour in his eye got my hackles up real good. Enough for me to bring out my pointer finger. I hated pointing at people. As much as I hadn't had the best relationship with my father—if you could even call it that—he did have some truth about him. He often said, "She who is reduced to personal insults and finger pointing first, loses the argument." He said a lot of things my dad, some of which were useful. But nothing got me riled faster than someone who didn't take me seriously. So, out came the pointer to demonstrate how he—point—could take himself back to the carpark—point—and wait for his friend—point.

Would you believe he actually laughed. He looked me in the eye and the twinkle turned into starburst. Damn it. "Listen here you bent, buckled, b—"

"Daddy." A scream split the air like lightning riding a summer storm. With finger raised mid-point, I turned to see Ruby riding on the Mountain's shoulders.

"Sweetheart." In seconds she'd disembarked, and the two of them had clashed in a mess of arms and a tangle of legs. And like an old oak in a cleared forest the two of them went down. Hard.

A whirlwind materialised out of nowhere and the two were being attended to by the Mountain and Hot Cocoa. *For freaky's sake, the guy just fell over.* Significant case of overreacting if you asked me.

Ruby gasped and froze, and the Mountain dropped to a knee and gently spoke to the guy. "Jonathan, can you hear me?" Hot Cocoa had his wrist and was measuring his pulse.

"Ow." The three of them exhaled as Jonathan slowly sat up with the help of the other two. And Ruby, not so much. "It's okay, sweetheart, I'm not hurt." He took our girl's sobbing, shaking body onto his lap and he comforted her. In fact, all of them sat in the dirt, on the driveway, and had a chat, like they were at a cafe on High Street.

"Princess!" It was just a murmur, but Tea heard me, nonetheless.

"Pretty sure that's a 'P' word not 'B'." He bumped my shoulder on the way past and nodded at my still-raised finger. "Teapot." Then went and joined the reunion. In the dirt.

It was only then I realised I was looking rather like a teapot with one hand up with my finger still mid-point, my other on my hip, and my lips still rolled waiting for the perfect "b" word to land itself in my brain. "Barnacle?" Okay, so it didn't work, but no one was listening so, what the hey. I shook myself out and went to join the party. But I would not sit in the dirt. Not that I had a problem with dirt. I loved the stuff. But I would not meet this person from my past, who happened to be my girl's dad—making him also a big part of my present—where he was at. He would have to get up and meet me face to face.

Show no weakness, Daisy girl, you can do this. He has the upper hand and holds all the cards, but you can do this. You are a rock, paper and scissors.

"So, you're Ruby's dad. Head of the snake who's been striking us every which way to Sunday." The little group stopped and stared at me like *I* was the odd one out. He was the enemy. Not me.

"Yes, to the first and not so sure about the second."

"You're the head of the Community. Where you lead, they follow. And from what I can see you've led them down to the depths of weak-willed… watery… ways."

One of his eyebrows lifted. "Well, as it turns out, when I was side-lined others stepped in. I didn't realise I wasn't leading until I turned around and found no one following. So, I guess that makes me a… bodiless snake? Which would ultimately be a no, to the second."

Wait, what? I didn't call him a snake. Did I? For freaky's sake, first with the finger pointing and now with the name calling. I could not only hear my dad growling from the grave, I could see him in my mind's eye: lips pursed, head shaking and his miasma of disappoint-ment marinating through me. I shook the all-too-familiar image out of my head and addressed the prone… problematic… princess. "Well then, what are you doing here? What do you want? We're not leaving." *You can't have her. I mean, I know she's legally yours. But she's ours too.*

"First, I'm glad to hear it. Second, I would like to say thank you for taking such good care of my girl." He dropped a kiss onto Ruby's head and she dug deeper into his embrace.

You can't have her. You can't take her. You won't take her. "Took you long enough to visit her—see if she was okay. Real father-of-the-year material right there. How long has it been? Just over two years before you decide to drop in?" It was like I had thrown rocks at an injured puppy from the looks I was getting from the little group.

Ruby launched to her feet and stood in front of me. She'd had one of the mums plait her bird's-nest hair into millions of tiny braids.

However, instead of looking like my auburn dreads, her hair looked like rows of winter-bleached grass lit by pale-gold sunrise. The bits and pieces she'd started collecting to decorate it, however, and the pictures she was forever drawing on her arms to imitate my ink, were spot on. Dryad had made her a cute little A-frame overall-y dress kind of thing in a ruby red to match her name, and the overall effect was button-cute. The fire in her eyes made me proud. She stood defiant, hands on hips, feet apart, chin up, giving me as good as she could. "He's been sick. Don't you be mean."

"Mean? Me? I'm not the one who abandoned you. Decided you were fine being looked after by the nanny while your dad's been… 'sidelined'."

"He did not abandon me. He came for me. He climbed through our broken house for me. He rescued me. He got hurt because of me. He almost died because of me. And now he is getting better, and he is here, and you are being very mean and very rude. And I don't think I like you very much anymore."

And just like that, I wasn't feeling quite so proud of myself either at that point in time.

She pulled at the leather cord around her neck—the one that held the ring she'd bartered for almost two years ago—and she threw it in the dirt at my feet. She ran off into the village. Even Pod stopped to glare at me over his shoulder before he loped off behind her.

And… game over. I was set adrift on a raft of brokenness. All I could do was stare at the ring at my feet. Didn't she understand, I'd been standing-in to bat for her. Fight her cause. Watch her back.

Movement from the corner of my eye stole my attention and a quiet voice stabbed me in the heart. "I would've been here to take care of Ruby, but I've been in hospital, first in a coma then in rehab. I'm afraid it's been a long journey. As I believe you know, her mother and the rest of her family were killed in The Quake." He stopped and swayed on his feet. As the others raced to support him, he held out a hand, stopping them in their tracks.

He took a slow, deep breath and continued. "It has had an interesting"—his eyes twinkled again—"effect on me. When I try to move past it, or if I recall it, I pass out—fall back into mini-comas. I am improving. But you're right, I should have come by earlier. Just because I was still recovering didn't mean I couldn't have visited."

"She never said. Never spoke a word about you or what happened." Not that I asked her, mind you. Actually, made a point of *not* asking. Didn't want to know in case there was a timeline… a deadline for when she'd be taken away. "She only really opened up with Mountain when he arrived with his family." He tilted his head at the use of the name. I nodded at Marcus.

Jonathan lifted his head and smiled. But then looked to the ring on the ground between us. "You've changed so much, Daisy." I think we were both transported back to the days of my youth when the chip on my shoulder was as big as a forest. "I owe you so very much. You mean the world to my girl. I feel we're already reacquainted from all the stories I've heard. And believe me, I've heard them all many, many times over. When I was in my coma, I could hear but not move. Every day Al brought her in, Ruby would curl up in the bed next to me and tell me stories of Tent Village, of Jet and Mary, Travis, Dori, Callum… then recently about Marcus and his family—Raph especially—and everyone and everything going on here. But most of all, she told me about you." He bent down and picked up the ring. I thought he'd give it to me, but he blew the dust off it then slowly closed it in his fist. "Please forgive me for not making it sooner."

"Why are you here? Now. What do you want? Are you taking her?" I was ashamed of the fear that wrapped its barbs into my words. If she left…

"And take her where?"

"Away?" The barbs pierced my soul and tears tore their way through the fissures.

Jonathan reached his hand out and touched me. He touched me and my heart did not freeze. My mind did not revolt. My fists did not clench, and I did not have thoughts of how he would suffer at my hand. His bony thumb brushed a stray tear away. In romance novels —*yes, I read romance, but if you ever tell anyone, alive or dead, I will personally torture you to within an inch of your life and deny everything—*

they talk about a spark. This was no spark. It was a mule's kick to the chest. Not that I actually knew what that was like, but… I'd heard the saying and knew what a mule looked like. And stubborn? It was front and centre on my family's coat of arms. The punch stole my breath and hurt like hell. It caved my chest in on its way through to knocking a six-inch hole through my wall. It was big enough to expose my lone-liness. And it was permanent enough to let his loneliness in.

Connection. He looked into me and all I felt was understanding. Like he saw me. The real me. He stripped all my defences, broke my walls and before him I was exposed… vulnerable… naked.

"I have nowhere to go. I have nothing to offer. I have been evicted and stand in all I own." He looked down at what he was wearing and laughed. "That's not actually true. I don't even own these clothes. Al brought them round when he picked me up. Seems not only have they reclaimed my property, but my stay at the assisted living—which was funded by my work insurance—has been revoked. Somehow, along the line somewhere, I seem to have also lost my car. There was nothing wrong with it when I left it in the street. Literally, I have nothing. I am still frail, I still tend to fall over"—another quick quirk of the lips and a tilt of his head to the ground behind him—"but, if you will have me, I'm here to do what I can to help. Word around town is, this is the place for strays, refugees and"—the twinkle rolled with laughter—"bodiless snakes."

How could he be so bleeding calm when he was so helpless, home-less, hopeless? I looked him over. Dark, sunken circles rimmed his eyes. Lank, long locks fell over his face. He was a frail skeleton that came nowhere close to filling out the ridiculous clothes he stood… wavered in. But, now that I took the time to consider it, I was drawn to his thick, dark, vibrant, vivid… vivacious? armour wrapped around him like a second skin. It was beautiful, dark, bordering on indigo, but not quite, like it wanted to make a statement, but stopped short of jumping out of violet into blue. Intricate pattens were a testament to his favour. It declared to the world—those who could See—"this one is cherished". Just looking at it made me want to climb closer to the Light. No, he was not hopeless.

I sniffed and wiped my face on my shoulder. When I looked back, the twinkle in his eye was a starburst again. His eyes roved my face. Freaky freaks, I bet I was now covered in streaks of snot, tears and sawdust. *Great.* I nodded.

"Thank you." He exhaled and lost some of the stiffness in his shoulders. "I appreciate you looking out for Ruby and what's best for her. Believe me"—his brown eyes bored through my conscience—"I really appreciate it."

Double growl. Why did he have to be so nice after I had been an utter twik? It always made things worse. Don't ask me why, it just did. "Okay, well then, welcome to Sanctuary. Peg out a space, and we'll pop up a cabin. But I'm not too sure how you're going to go with Ruby. She won't stay in a hut, and definitely not sleep in one. She's getting a bit better, but she'll still only sleep in a tent on Mary's front lawn. Jet might be happy to have someone else share with her, but you'll have to work that one out with the two of them. I think I've done enough damage for one day." I turned and, with not a shred of pride left, took my smeared face, shattered soul and shamed… self, back to my workshop to hide till lunch.

22

DANIEL: THE REMEMBERING

It had started again. And it was doing my head in. Every night I was being plagued by dreams. Or more accurately, the memories… snippets of past dreams. I knew I had a job to do. I just didn't know what it was or how I was supposed to do it. Not the building of huts and raising the walkways. In comparison, that was easy.

When we had defeated the Dark in Laodicea, or, I should say, heaven's legions and the Star of Laodicea had annihilated the enemy in the end game at the Temple of Ashera, I had been given a message, "Remember your dream".

This would be fine if I'd only had one. Unfortunately, I had multiple "Light" dreams that all meant different things, or so said Abbot, the old monk who'd been part of the crew when we first met up in Sodom. He'd been the coolest old guy I'd ever known, apart from my grandpa. He'd always been calm, wise, and—with his badge of Sensing—on point. We'd had many talks, but he'd been the one, with Val, to sit down and hear me out as I walked the torturous tightrope back through all of the dreams. He'd helped me find the meaning behind them and the way forward out of them. But now I was supposed to remember a specific dream because it was key for this "arduous journey" we were on. So now, each night, my sleep was plagued by a patchwork quilt of terrors.

It wasn't helping that, with the arrival of Jonathan, the demon activity had upped several gears. The blighters were everywhere and in everything. Most of the people here had armour and we all had helmets that helped block the incessant skrat dribbling from their toxic mouths. But you couldn't swing Tiger—not that I would—without hitting one. We all had work to do, and having a plague of them under our feet was not helping matters one bit.

It kind of reminded me of Sodom. Well, the everyday life in Sodom, not the end battle. It wasn't a full-on, in-your-face battle here, swing, slash and fight for your life every moment of every day… yet. I mean, we still had our guards who were very attentive. But every hour, in everything we did, they—the enemy—were just there. Lurking. Watching. Picking through things, wandering around things, getting under our feet and generally making a nuisance of themselves.

I learned my lesson in Laodicea. Whenever one started to focus in on me and target a personal attack, I would quote The Way, or jab it with my sword. Then they'd back off and give me some space, but they didn't leave. Most of my time in Sodom, I'd not had the sight. In fact, it was only the last few weeks I was there—after I had met this lot—that I had any knowledge of the Light at all. But back then, the place had been riddled with the enemy. When we'd taken trips into the city, I watched them move, whisper, tinker, and get their grubby fingers and venomous words into everything and everyone. What had been almost as hard to get my head around as discovering the truth about their existence, was watching how they worked around those who couldn't see. Their victims were blind puppets.

And now they were everywhere, here. And I was supposed to learn to live with that, and do my job, and get ready to get married, and remember a particular dream I'd had. Actually, that wasn't the hard part. Every dream that I'd ever had—every "Light dream"—was so different to any normal dream. I could feel, taste, hear and see in colour in those dreams. They weren't just vague, hazy experiences. It was like I was awake and living in an alternate, but very real… reality.

Each one I'd had multiple times, and each time they changed depending on my actions. Totally understandable how every one of them was burned into my memory.

Although the one I'd had about riding horses—I know, don't go there. I have not, nor could I ever see myself riding a plains pony—never changed. In that one we were surrounded by the enemy and since we were outnumbered, I would sheathe my sword and unleash the double-headed battle axe that lived in a harness on my back. My companions would move to the outer edge of the fight, and I'd draw most attention to me as I stood alone in the middle of the mess and basically started disassembling the opposition. Yeah, I know, gruesome. Well, for everyday life it was. But when you were surrounded and outnumbered by the enemy, the song this axe would sing as I swung it through the air, still sent shivers of excitement through my soul. Abbot suggested this dream revealed my badge for Battle.

I'd had another one where I stood on a beach. Again, don't ask me where I got the inspiration for this one either. I had been to the beach as many times as I'd ridden a horse. However, I stood on a large hill of sand looking over a stretch of beach that reached to the horizon either side of me. The frigid wind whipped sand into every millimetre of exposed skin and salt peppered my eyes and coated my tongue. My role in this dream was to stand, wait and watch. Eventually a line of people—about seven—in cowls would appear and walk along the water's edge. For years I had this dream. I knew I wouldn't be released or be allowed to wake up until they had made their way past me. The last time I'd had this dream, the person on the end of the line looked up and her piercing grey eyes nailed me.

I know, weird right? But what can I say… dreams. Abbot suggested this one was to help me believe sooner, rather than later, that I belonged to something bigger than myself. Apparently, it was to help me move from being a loner to a team-player on short notice. Of course, there had been the dream of the black-and-white girl literally doing my head in almost every night for six months. Until thankfully we found her… them… at the Factory in Laodicea.

Another dream I had was pretty brutal… even for our standards of gruesome warfare. I tried very hard *not* to remember that one, as it did very scary things to my sanity. But I had to acknowledge it had saved my butt in the showdown at Sodom. In the middle of the epic battle in Ebony's library, before the city dissolved into a ball of flames, I had found my place fighting between Tessa and Riah. We had formed a spearhead and forged our way through the enemy to turn the tide of the battle. The three of us had aligned into what had become our natural? comfortable? logical? fighting formation. It was hard to describe, but it was right, and it was good. Much like Val, Marcus and Kait. And, come to think of it, like Felix, Marlene and Fleur.

Anyway, I was now tasked with finding the right dream to remember and figure out what it was that was important to remember and how it was going to help us here and now. If only I could get some space to think.

A bit of help with this would be greatly appreciated, thanks. It's so hard to keep our eyes on You and the task at hand when we're surrounded by the enemy. I know You can see that we're literally swimming in them at the moment. So, please, a bit of Light would be great.

I had learned the hard way that the enemy doesn't like it when we quote The Way or stick them with the Light's sword. Every day we are studying The Way, and training with our swords and armour. But for everyone we dispatch, ten more fill their space. It really was hampering progress and getting us all down.

If only I could remember my frolking dream, then maybe we could get somewhere and kick these krets to the curb.

23

KAITLYN: WHAT'S IN A NAME

It was Dan who first gave me the name, Mamma Bear. And I had heard Daisy refer to me as Hot Cocoa; Hot *Chilli* Cocoa. And I had to say, I had a liking for both of them. After my significant absence of sanity for a snap at Laodicea, which, quite frankly, I'd rather not revisit, I was determined to live up to both of my given names—old and new. To the world I wanted to present as the protective shield of a mother bear to my family, my chicks. For my kids to know that they were safe with me standing in the gap and on the front line for them. But to my family I wanted to present as a cup of hot cocoa. The warm, soothing, comforting brew of chocolatey paradise that lifted spirits and healed the soul. And the Chilli Cocoa?—let me clarify that is spelt with an "I" on the end not a "Y"—that was for my husband.

However, the straight up hot chilli, well, that was for the enemy, or anyone who wanted to harm my family. Any member of my family. Just thinking about harm coming to them or any who wanted to hurt them was enough to make my blood boil. Oh, dear Lord, what my fool-hearted children did back at the Temple in Laodicea was enough to age me twenty-five years. I still don't think I've recovered from seeing them fight a gigantor. Dan and Indy, bare chested and ineffective against the mammoth beast. Tessa lying unconscious and so terribly vulnerable. And, oh my word, when Raph and Riah scaled that thing's back and attacked it head on? I will not ever recover from the fear of it. I could have tanned all their hides… many times over. If they ever… ever… tried a stunt like that again, I swear, I'd… I'd… probably do exactly what I did this time—cry a river and explode with pride. I just had to keep telling myself: it was in the past, we all survived, what's done is done. The kids were in the Light and He could protect them far more effectively than I ever could. Philadelphia was a new city, with a new adventure waiting.

But it didn't matter how much I wanted to leave the past in the past, I still had to make sure I brought the lessons learned into the present, so it did not wreak havoc with my future. And that meant using eagle-bear eyes to watch over my family. Which at Sanctuary wasn't too hard. Marcus and I shared one tent. Our names were in the ballot for a cabin, but I suspected we would quietly ask for a redraw if we were pulled too soon. There were many worse off and who were less suited to living in these conditions. Dan and Raph shared another tent—their names weren't in the ballot. And Tessa, Riah and Val shared the two-bedroom "proof" cabin Dan built to sell the idea to the good folk we were living amongst. It was a bit hard communicating to those still fearful of another quake that they would be safe. And if the cabins did fall, the materials were so light, they wouldn't do a lot of damage. So, Mary had given permission for a trial.

The Light was gracious with timing. Between the frequent rain and still fairly-common aftershocks, Dan and his team raised the prototype, and the "proof" was in the pudding. Our girls were living out of the mud, with simple cooking facilities, a gravity shower and a compost toilet *inside* their dwelling. And after it didn't fall or fracture in the settling of The Quake's wrath, hands went up and names went in to be drawn in due time.

They were making great progress with the ingenuity and experience of Josh and Tim, the endless resources at the city tip, and the cavity in the back of Old Faithful. It literally meant the sky, and their imaginations, were the limit to what they could create.

Marcus was busy, useful, productive, and therefore happy and content. Just like one of those cows across the paddock lolling in prime pasture. He'd invited Josh and Tim to join him and Dan for regular "Secret Men's Business" meetings, just like he'd done in Laodicea. Dan had invited Jet and a young man who'd joined their building team, Craig. And both Marcus and Dan had insisted Raph join them. Along with Josh's son Oliver. It was a non-negotiable. Whatever they were doing or from whatever corner they had each been working in, they both knocked off work in time for early dinner on Tuesday nights. Then hauled our boy away with them to touch base and keep a close eye on him.

Dan was blossoming in his new role. I was so grateful to Josh and Tim for pushing him out the front. Teaching him how to lead. Forcing him to reveal his strength of character and stunning intelligence. He was so busy building a nest for Tessa, he'd forgotten to make time for her. But my beautiful girl had also brought her lessons from the past into her present. There was no way he was going to get away with that rubbish. I was confident they'd be just fine. Especially since her star was shining brightly here. She had skills and Badges she was using to build up this community and it gave her back her joy.

Sariah? Well, my other dear girl was also swimming in joy because she was using her Badge to teach others how to battle. However, she was not her brother, and it wasn't the teaching that gave her joy. It was the battle. And I tell you what, if it wasn't one hundred percent impossible, I would swear the child was of the same genetics as Val, my dear sister.

Val was trying so hard not to show just how much she was hurting. Praise the Light, these folk knew a good thing when it came to visit. She had been invited to use her Badge to unlock The Way for the good people here every day. Yes, every day. Can you imagine the hunger that warranted that? It may also be partly due to Val's particular way of serving up that glorious honey. But it gave me joy to watch, and learn, with everyone else. I had always known she was something special. But as Marcus would say, in this place she had the opportunity to prove she was no one-trick pony. Her mastery of The Way and understanding of the Light blessed all who had the ears to hear.

But my sweet boy Raph was drowning in grief and still struggling to find his place. Eight months ago, when we'd first made Sanctuary home, he'd found a little friend, and whilst some of our family were not the biggest fans of cats, we all saw how important it was for Raph to have a purpose and someone to care for. I think that may have been part of the problem. He had always seen himself—pulled himself out of the red haze—by acknowledging and fulfilling his love of caring for others. It's how he pulled his oar. And here, there wasn't that space.

It was hard for him to cook for us, or even contribute to meals, because all the prep was done in the girls' tiny cabin. Since Marcus and I were still living in a tent, and Dan and Raph were in another, we would join the girls at—outside—their cabin for meals in good weather. The kitchenette wasn't huge, but better than the compact little gas stove we had. And with Val, Tessa and Riah all trying to live in a tiny two-bedroom cabin, Raph felt another body would just be in the way. And that's why we needed music.

It started off with just our family winding down the way we used to in Sodom. Offering our praise and relaxing to the gift of music at the end of the day. Touching base and seeing how everyone was travelling, as well as checking in and giving thanks to the Light. But, as you can imagine, in a world without solid walls, the sweet scent of Badge-inspired music travelled. Others with a similar Badge were the first to make contact. Then all the others with a heartbeat came next.

Now, on Friday evenings—and any other night when the weather was fine—we gathered at the Meeting Place, and it was a time to shine. It was wonderful for everyone to see another side of our girls too. Not only did Sariah play her guitar, Tessa had been encouraged by Dan and Raph to join in with leading the singing. And I do declare, it had been pretty hard to hold back my own—somewhat imperfect— voice from the fray.

Even now as we cleared the dishes and leftovers from our meals, I could hear the beating of two feet making their way down the hill. I was almost bowled over by a little mite as she crashed into my body. "Ms Kait-a-lyn, does Raph have his drum? Is Raph coming tonight?"

"Ruby. I am standing right here." The girl jumped at Raph's words.

He'd been coming back out of the cabin after clearing plates. "And I always play. And I always have my drum."

My poor boy did not understand what it was to be in the spotlight of someone's awe. While Ruby's heart was full to overflowing with love for… pretty much everyone here, her eyes took on a particular shade of sparkle when she saw our boy Raph.

"Do you want me to carry it for you? I can help." Every night it was the same. To start with, she had to come to terms with Raph's love for his drum; even family weren't allowed to carry it. But eventually she wore him down. The girl had just had her seventh birthday and now that she was no longer a "baby"—Raph and Ruby's word, not mine— things had changed.

He sighed. "Sure, Ruby. But only when I am ready, and I will walk with you. Okay? And no running."

She beamed. So, turns out this little one was a cunning fox. Well, good luck to her. She had managed to secure Raph's company and undivided attention as she carried something he treasured. Smart little cookie.

To speed things up, we put Ruby—and Jet who was never far away —to work helping to pack up, then headed over to the Meeting Place. Tessa came out carrying a comfortable fold-up chair and Riah followed carrying a blanket in one arm and her guitar in the other. I brought up the rear walking with, but not touching, my sister. The cooler autumn weather was not her friend. But there was no way she'd miss out on this golden time with family, and no one would dare suggest she take the easy way out.

Marcus and Dan set up the space and the girls had prepared a place for Val near a brazier. And finally, Ruby, taking baby-steps, reverently handed Raph's drum over and the music began.

Thank you for this incredible gift. Thank you for our growing family. Thank you for this opportunity to bless and be blessed in this beautiful place with these truly beautiful people.

24

JONATHAN: THE MANTLE

The way I saw it, Overseer was not a job. It wasn't even really a "calling", a word so many in the Community liked to bandy about and slather over everything. To me, my role of Overseer—and, equally so, Head Shepherd—were an identity. It wasn't merely what I did, it was who I was. Appointed by the Light to care for His people. It literally was the air I breathed. *Great, now I'm a cliche.* So when I was defrocked by my flock—*and a poet?*—it didn't change how I felt, or how I saw my people. Even though they had abandoned me, I had not abandoned them. It broke my heart that they had forsaken their journey in the Light. But each of us walks our own path. When Al had brought me here, it lifted my soul to see the faithful. My people. So many I already knew, others I was excited to get to know.

Al was furious. He wanted to take me home to his place. So he could care for me. But he didn't understand that would be the death of me. I needed to start standing on my own feet... literally, and start working... to put the boot on the other foot. I needed to be among my people. But that wasn't the real issue. My thanks to my best, lifelong friend was forcing... begging him to leave. To leave me, Ruby and Philadelphia. Trouble was coming and we needed friends on the outside, in other cities.

I knew we had Felix, based in Laodicea, heading up the Alliance. I hadn't yet been able to catch up on how that fared under the Gerent's gauntlet. But, with Al and Cissa's business, Black and Light Architectural Designs, having bases throughout the Seven Cities, Al had places he could go. To move to a different city was nothing for him. I had hoped he might join Cissa at her main and preferred base in Sardis. That it might be an excuse for them to live under the same roof for a while. And maybe reconnect?

I seriously didn't know how they did it: Cissa, always on the move; Al, with fingers in all the pies. I believed the two mainly communicated through their PAs, Freyer and Charlotte. When I tried to explain the phenomenon that was Al and Cissa to Laura, she just shook her head and said it wasn't right. I had to agree, but it was their marriage, not mine. At times I was compelled to confess my concerns to Al, but he just assured me all was good.

Al had confided years ago the only reason he was Black and Light's representative in Philly, was because we were here. But I needed him away, to be ears and eyes on the outside. And be safe. He'd argued, of course, and, even after he reluctantly agreed, still maintained radio silence. He'd not returned my emails, texts or calls. I just petitioned the Light that he was safe. Skitched-off, I could handle. One more death, I could not.

But life here at Sanctuary was blissfully busy. I knew a good number of folk who had gravitated here. Of course, there was Mary. As always, a pillar we could cling to in a storm. The woman radiated irrepressible joy and generosity. There was nothing she owned she wouldn't give to a person in need. I'd had several serious chats with her in the past about the possibility of giving away a bit too much? That perhaps stewardship—being responsible for the blessings in her hands—might involve hanging on to them so she could continue to bless in the future, and ensure her family continued to have a home?

She'd always sat, listened, nodded and when I had finished, she'd shake her head and pat my cheek. "You're a good boy, Jonathan. One day you will understand that the Light gives to us so we can give to others."

Of course, I agreed with her... to a point. But it was always a useless argument; we'd travel in circles. Her son would be tearing his hair out for all their possessions she'd given away. Things he'd needed to run the winery. Things Kylie, his wife, needed for the cattle. But today we all had somewhere to live, a Sanctuary, because of her worldview and generosity.

Josh and Tim were still mentoring and bringing on youngsters. They couldn't help themselves. Both of them inherent teachers and encouragers. It was only natural they would find a kindred spirit in Marcus. What they were doing here was incredible. I was immediately impressed by the young man Daniel and the potential bursting from his seams.

It was great to see February and October had made their way here. My heart warmed with joy when I saw them. Such gifted, wonderfully unique, charming human beings. That they had stuck to their guns and not been swept away in the Community's division was a testament to their substance. I had enjoyed catching up with them and learning how they had adapted. Never ones to be too focused on material belongings—except their computers and drones, of course— they were two very happy campers at Sanctuary. I noticed they were wearing new clothes, adapted to fit their tall, willowy figures. And October had started wearing her thick, glossy black hair in a braid. "It keeps the hair out of my eyes, and I don't have to brush it in the mornings," she explained. "That new girl comes by every couple of days and does it for me."

"Tessa," February filled in.

"You aren't interested in having your hair braided?" I'd asked October's twin.

"It helps people tell us apart."

This was very insightful and socially aware for February... or October, for that matter. I'd suggested another style perhaps? February had looked up from her screen, tilted her head, nodded and I was dismissed. I wasn't insulted. I knew how the girls thought and worked. I was just so glad to see them here.

Their parents were university professors, originally from Ephesus but moved here to help establish the science department of our newer campus—an extension of Ephesus University. To be honest, I suspected not only did they not plan for February and October, they didn't know what to do with them when they arrived. One baby would have been shocking enough, but two? So, from the earliest possible age, the girls had been dropped off at every Young Light activity and holiday camp we had run. Not only had we grown to love and metaphorically adopt the girls, they had grown to love the Light. And now they were here, and we were doubly blessed.

Apart from the regulars, it was great to meet the newcomers and of course Marcus's family. On my first day I sat under Valarie's teaching and was greatly impressed. Such a gift to be encouraged in The Way by another long-distance runner. We now took turns and I hoped, in the same way, I could bless her when I shared from my knowledge.

And so it was, every morning, I'd come down with Mary, Jet and Ruby and walk through my flock and connect with them all. By the end of the day, after several power naps along the way, I made a point of ending my rounds with Travis—my old friend and father of my new friend, Luke—and I would catch up with the bigger picture of Sanctuary. Of course, I was even more delighted when Luke occasionally dropped by after work to join us.

I made a point of inviting Daisy. Sometimes we met in the shade of her shelter, sometimes in Travis's. But when Val and Marcus joined us, we ended up sitting right in the middle of the wide wooden path under the stars at the gateway to Sanctuary. Daisy, the girl I had once known, had changed so much over the years. I'd been an acquaintance of her father. A hard man from the old stock who believed in "not sparing the rod" and the "school of hard knocks". Told me he wanted to make sure his kids grew up knowing how to save themselves *and* everybody else. Just like he could. You see, Carl believed he, too, like Mary, had been given blessings to share. Any time, any place, any reason—if someone needed saving, Carl was the man to go to. He'd rescue you, guaranteed. Milly'd cook that meal, Jared would fix those railings, Daisy would babysit your kids. No matter what, Carl had what you needed. Whether or not his family were available, tied up or just plain exhausted, Carl would see to it they'd come by and sort things out. Then he'd follow up afterwards to make sure his "blessings" had done the job well. And to bask in the gratitude.

He hadn't always been that way. Well, mostly not. Milly, Daisy's mum, had dulled his edge so it sat under a thin veneer. But after she died... maybe he just didn't have the energy? The desire to try anymore? He became harder, fiercer and far more unyielding.

I knew it drove his son, Jared, away. Then Daisy was left to bear the brunt of *his* worldview. Even though I could see Carl's edge upon her, I knew they weren't close. I never could work out why she stayed. But it made me laugh—privately of course—when she got her first tattoo. Carl almost had a coronary. She was so pleased with the result, she invested most of her savings into ink. They were beautiful images, but Carl hated them. Eventually she'd moved out of home to learn her trade. Another thing Carl hated. He'd wanted her to settle down and produce male heirs for her husband, "like any decent girl would". Goodness knows he tried hard enough, pushing all sorts of unsuitable men at her. It was most likely why she'd left home as soon as she was financially able to.

I lost touch with her over the following years, and Carl never mentioned her. To say I was shocked to see her here, in full amber armour, was an understatement. Pleased? Yes. I was glad she'd found her niche and that she was blossoming. She made me laugh. It was all I could do not to explode with joy when I heard she was still taking the advice of Jake, a Young Light Leader. Daisy has always been... blunt. Always spoken her mind with brutal honesty. She welcomed that from others and was frustrated when she didn't receive it. On top of that, she couldn't understand how she offended people. Making people cry was a gift Daisy'd had from the time she learned to talk. So, Jake suggested she stop and think of three things starting with the same letter, to say before she answered. It worked to engage her incredibly intelligent brain and slow down her stinging mouth.

Being at Sanctuary, reconnecting to the folk here, and especially Daisy, made me truly laugh like I hadn't since I lost... I lost Laura and the boys. Daisy never reached out to catch me when I stumbled. She made a point of stepping over me if I did fall and threw a commentary or a score over her shoulder as she moved on, not waiting. "I'd only give that one a six, Shep. But come along, keep up, we've got work to do."

She never made life easy for me. She never treated me like an invalid or made excuses. There was no pity. Compassion? Yes. Despite her best efforts to hide it, it was there. But pity? No. And of course there was that weird connection I'd felt. I don't know if it was the same for her. It wasn't sexual or romantic—she was still a child—but I'd felt a bond. She knew… understood… lived in the same void of lost-ness. Sounds crazy, and maybe I am, but it was there. We both had the Light, but there was an… absence where we dwelt.

But apart from that, Daisy was completely refreshing because she treated me like a normal human being. And I found I could breathe in the evenings in her company… in *their* company: Travis, Marcus, Val and Daisy.

25

DAISY: SET IN STONE

The guy was an anomaly. He was the Overseer of the Community of Light in this city. And because the Community wasn't particularly big, he was also Head Shepherd. But you'd never know to look at him; he didn't look like anything much except a skinny, sunken skeleton. Well, he had when he first arrived. During his time here, under Mountain Man's ministrations, spending time in the sun working with Callum, alongside Josh and Tim, and under Miriam's instructions, he had developed a bit of colour and filled in some of his frame. I'd even seen him occasionally attempt a bit of a run with the Wild Cat.

Hot Cocoa had tamed that mass of dark, unruly hair with scissors. Which turned out to be dangerous. That man was not as defenceless as he seemed. Not that I was saying he was dodgy, deceitful or devious. He really was *that* weak. But those eyes. They were CT scanners, they saw every person, every need, every thorn, every stumbling block. When he turned those weapons on you, you were defenceless. He was a man who not only saw things, he took the time to unwrap them.

It was the end of the day and he'd made his way from his afternoon nap to join us for the close of play debrief when it struck me. Shep reminded me of Ruby the day I had given her the ring she'd worked so hard to earn.

That day I sat in the dirt next to my little shadow as she so carefully, delicately peeled away every loop, leaf and layer to reveal the treasure within the package. When it rested in the palm of her hand, she regarded it like it was the most precious jewel. I stayed with her and hugged her as she rocked and remembered her family. Her mum especially.

And that's just how her dad was. He took the time to sit in the dirt and unwrap the treasure buried in each one of us. I had never known a person to care so much. To give so much of themselves. It didn't surprise me that even after two months of care, exercise and healthy living here at Sanctuary, the guy was still a skeleton, still exhausted. He was so generous giving himself away to everyone, he never seemed to have enough to fill himself.

Watching him care for all of us here in his very limited capacity, the realisation hit me like a boulder. Jonathan was not "just like" Ruby. She was a dim reflection of him. His love was real. And it was reciprocated. Like sunflowers turned their faces to follow the sun, the people of Sanctuary turned their hearts to follow Jonathan.

"Batter up! We've got company." Tea broke into my thoughts with his warning.

The five of us, Shepherd, Tea, Warrior, Mountain and I, sat in folding chairs on the boardwalk between Tea's cabin and mine, plumb middle of the gateway whilst Ruby played in the opening of my workshop with Pod. In the carpark, four suits—two men and two women—climbed out of an expensive town car and formed a scrum. Ruby froze and her eyes locked onto mine. I gave her the nod and she hustled, dashing around the circle of cabins giving the warning that something was up.

Things had changed so much since the Laodicean crew had arrived. For the better. Before, we had been a gathering of haphazard tents with add-ons and make-dos as more and more people came in and went out. But for the past few months or so, we'd settled. And with Wild Cat and his team building up a storm, our people were being housed in unique, totally funky cabins forming a ring around our huge veggie patch and orchard. The heart of which was still the Meeting Place.

At one end was the amenities block, which was getting less and less use as more folk had facilities built into their tiny homes. And at this end was the gate; it was also where those of us who had noisy sports for a living were grouped. Travis's and my cabins sat either side of the main gate leading to the carpark, driveway and road. Everyone's workshops were on the outer perimeter, essentially building an extra layer of privacy.

The four from the city had obviously settled on a battle plan as they turned and made their way over. My heart dipped and my hope sank. It was team Head Honcho… Horrible? of the Community come to give us grief. Beside me, Jonathan groaned and Travis glared. This couldn't be good.

All five of us stood but the team waited for me to kick off. I decided to serve the ball in silence and not pre-empt their purpose. Not that I felt particularly welcoming, nonetheless. Maybe they weren't used to silence. The four of them stood facing us. It reminded me of an old western I'd seen on the telly as a kid. This was effectively an old-school face off. But there was no way I was going to speak first. I was enjoying their discomfort too much.

Dennis was the first to crack. "Good evening."

I stood slightly in front of Travis and Jonathan, so I couldn't see what they did, but I gave him exactly one nod in return.

"We were wondering if we might speak with you." His head twitched side to side indicating his wingman, and women.

Again, I gave him just the one nod.

"We think it only fair."

I didn't think that warranted a nod.

He then lifted his voice and threw it over my head to the growing crowd behind me. "We feel it only fair that you all get to hear. You all have the right not to be kept in the dark by these"—he actually sneered at the three of us—"…three."

It was my turn to flick my eyes over my shoulder to Tea and Jonathan. *What the hey? Is this dude for real?*

Tea addressed the invaders. "We have no problem with people hearing what you've got to say. People here are free to come and go as they please. Listen or not listen as they wish."

Yeah, you crazy person, stop trying to make us out to be... crazy people.

Ruby made her way through the crowd and wrapped one arm around her dad's leg and the other around mine and peered out around my hip. Now I knew where she was and that she was safe, I was ready to move aside. I looked to Tea and tilted my head to the Meeting Place. *You go ahead, I'll bring up the rear.* Then looked at my watch. *Let's make this quick.*

Little solar-powered lights lit the raised walkway through the garden into our heart: the Meeting Place. A string of solar-powered lights hung around the perimeter of the huge tarpaulin and wrapped around each pole. It wasn't overly bright, but it was enough to see clearly. Even though I wasn't a fan of these people, I was grateful they had come at the end of the day and not interrupted work. But, believe me, I was not happy they were killing my end-of-day buzz.

Tea indicated the "front" of our Meeting Place and arranged four chairs for them to sit. I stood at the edge and waited until all our people had filed past me. I noted not everyone was here, but every family had at least one representative.

Once those present sat and settled, Dennis, who'd been too nervous to sit, began. "Thank—"

"Wait." I cut across his opening speech. "Mary's not here yet." I knew Ruby would have raced up to the house to tell them and Jet would bring our matriarch down in due course. Since it was "only fair" that everyone heard their message, then it was "only fair" we wait for everyone to arrive. And so, we did. The whole gathering sat silently facing the four on the stage area built by Wild Cat and his team. The instruments were neatly stacked to either side and a couple of tables were pushed up against the back flap. And stuck right in the middle, like insects under an oppressively silent magnifying glass, our four "guests" waited. From their previous harassments... I mean, visits, I knew them to be Dennis, Becky, Niccola and Stuart.

Jonathan surprised me by calling out from beside me. "Where's Charlie?"

Dennis fidgeted then squared his shoulders. "He decided he could no longer abide by Community guidelines and recommendations, and so we decided it was best he stepped down from the High Council."

Jonathan whispered in my ear. "He was always quality. A good man. I miss him." Then to Dennis he asked, "Is he still in town?"

Dennis's fidgeting increased and red climbed his neck. "Ah, no. He decided that life would be easier with his family in Thyatira."

"Right. So, you 'reclaimed' his possessions, too, did you?"

"He forfeited the right to his belongings when he refused to give thanks to the man who restored them." The red in Dennis's neck had darkened as it encompassed his face.

"Ahh. When Mary gets here, could you please explain how when a property is restored *for* the original owner, it is no longer the property *of* the original owner? And perhaps you could enlighten us on the difference between showing gratitude and giving glory?"

"What's all the hullaballoo about?" Mary and Jet had arrived. Mary in a bit of a bluster, Jet as cool as ever. "Oh look, Jet, we've got visitors. Go pop the kettle on, sweetheart."

Jet arranged her in her chair near the front where someone had set up one of the braziers, then went over to check that the urn had been turned on. He then came to stand at the back of the group where Warrior, Mountain, Hot Cocoa, Wild Cat, Dryad and their twins had joined us. A few of the others also stood around the outside. I nodded to Josh, Tim, Craig and Kelly on one side, Callum, Caspian and Dori on the other. We were ready. So, I turned my attention to Dennis. "We're all here now."

26

DAISY: SHOWDOWN

Dennis continued to be as unsettled as a new-born calf on the side of a steep hill. I can't say I was upset. The amount of trouble this man and his cronies had caused us made me officially not a fan.

"First, we wanted to encourage you as a Community of Light to come back into the fold and turn away from your errant ways and thinking. It is only fair that you, the flock, hear the truth and not be misguided by the wolves in sheep's clothing who wish to lead you astray. I have heard reports about this group of people you have welcomed into your midst. They have caused trouble in Sodom, in Laodicea, and now they are here. It was their actions"—he looked directly to Warrior—"that caused a major split in the Community in Laodicea. We know she"—at least he was finally direct with his accusations—"accosted and threatened the Laodicean Overseer, and together raised a band of miscreants to destroy the Temple of Ashera, who had been working peacefully in the city for years alongside the Temple of Light."

At this, Dryad and Wild Cat bristled. Mountain was moving and Hot Cocoa, for once, was not stopping him. But Warrior did. She halted them all with two words. "Stand down." In a quieter voice she continued, "This is not our fight."

Dennis continued his monologue. "The Light has planted us in Philadelphia to work alongside, throughout and from within the culture. How can we do that if we make ourselves an enemy of the State? Listen my friends... family, The Way of the Light is peace, love, humility and grace. What part of setting yourselves up as a thorn in the Gerent's side is fulfilling any of those commands? No, you are defying the calling of the Light and you are an embarrassment to the true Community in Philadelphia."

Jonathan stepped into the light of the overhead string illuminating the aisle. "What exactly is your message, Dennis? Get to the point. We know where we stand in the Light, and now, we know where we stand with you. We are walking different paths, ours a bit narrower, rockier and straighter than yours, by the sounds of it. But surely that is not why you're here."

"Right, well. We had hoped you, or I should say, those under your spell, would appreciate hearing the truth. And I must say"—his eyes scanned the dimly lit tent until he picked out his targets—"I had thought more of you, Carol, Callum and Timothy... These others may be naive and easily led astray, but you?"

Tea surprised me by showing hints of impatience. "Get on with it, or if that's all you've got to say, time's up."

"We just felt that it was only fair to let you know how things stood in the outside world." He looked around the Meeting Place and almost didn't wrinkle his nose. "The Gerent had always planned to visit Philadelphia and inspect the results of his generosity. However, he was delayed due to illness. He has now recovered and has scheduled his visit for a few months' time." Dennis's Adam's apple bobbed away, apparently struggling to continue. "Unfortunately, since taking the seat of power, our new Gerent has claimed the ancient right of Deity. His reasoning"—Dennis raced on over the gasps sweeping through the tent—"that his ascension to leadership and extreme wealth are both evidence of blessings of favour from the gods... therefore his adoption by the gods is obvious, thereby making him a god."

Dennis's hand clutched his chest and Becky gently pushed him into a chair and took over. "Due to his outstanding generosity to us after The Quake, the Gerent now sees Philadelphia as his personal city, bought and paid for in full. As a symbol of our gratitude the Mayor and his council have agreed to rename Philadelphia to Domination, at the Gerent's… request, in honour of his grace and generosity. On his arrival he will officially change the name in a ceremony to be televised throughout the Seven Cities." More gasps were released. "He is also expecting the citizens of *his* city to pay him homage. To bend the knee and worship him. He is funding a new temple to be built in his honour."

We knew this was the case. It was why our numbers had swelled. The Community made life impossible for people who didn't see eye to eye with their submission. But I guess having them come into our home, reminding us of the devil lurking, made the reality even more unpalatable.

Betsy continued spouting bad news. "Any who do not offer him 'god status' will be sent to The Games. Which, as you know, he has restarted as a way to free up room and lower the costs of the penitentiary system. The Games are growing in popularity, and he is now looking wider afield for 'contenders' to entertain their growing audience. None of us are immune." At this, Becky's pale face dropped a shade or two into grey.

In true tag-team fashion, Niccola stood to speak as Becky collapsed into her chair. "When he comes to Domination, he wants to visit Sanctuary. He's scheduled a visit to meet with you specifically and discuss your response."

I jumped again as Jonathan spoke out. "How does he know about Sanctuary? Or our response? We have no significance to the city. We are on the outskirts of town within private property. Mary has had this parcel of land rezoned to allow us to live here. We have no political, social or economic leverage. And more importantly, we have not voiced our opinion publicly. Why is he interested in us?" It was an accusation, a laying of blame at the feet of the guilty, more than a question, and Niccola knew it. They all did. Eyes flicking to the floor, to the darkness cloaking the Meeting Place, to the corners of the tent... everywhere but at us or Jonathan. "Why did you do it?"

Dennis shot to his feet. "He was grilling us. He knew the Community only bows to the Light. He knew we would pose a problem, so he challenged us personally. Wanting to know if we would give him any trouble. He bullied and overrode us." By this stage Dennis was panting, his lips mottling to blue from the lack of oxygen. "He threatened us"—his arm shot to the side indicating the other three—"personally. Holding us responsible for every member of the Community. Said we were the head. If any didn't follow, he'd find a new head; one that was aligned with his theology. What were we to do? I told him that on the whole, most of the Community were compliant, but there was a small group who chose to defy him."

"Did you get your thirty pieces of silver?" Jonathan's accusation was a growl that was picked up by the crowd.

"Oh, for crying out loud, Jonathan. Get off your high, self-righteous horse. How dare you stand there and accuse me... us of weakness. Where were you when we needed you? When the city was in ruins? When we were lost and without direction? We can't all just run and hide in a safe little cave, and have everyone spend all their time and resources because"—he threw his hand to his forehead in mock despair—"I can't possibly cope. We all lost people, homes, relationships in The Quake. For pity's sake, even your daughter lost as much as you, and *she*"—he spat the word—"didn't check out. So don't stand there and judge me... us for making choices for the whole Community. And right now? Where are you when we need you most?" Phlegm shot out of his mouth at this last tirade. At least it had brought a bit of colour to his face. He looked around, disgust leaching through every inch of body language. "Hiding. Hiding in an unrealistic, impractical joke of a... a... hovel. Snap out of it, Jonathan. The world is moving on and disaster is rushing toward us. It is time you man up and start taking responsibility."

"Freaky-freaks, Dennis, don't hold back. Tell us how you really feel." It was meant to be my inside voice—a murmur at most. But at the ripple of laughter and the wry smile Shep threw my way, I knew it was out there for human digestion and judgement.

"Regretting the decision to evict me from leadership, Dennis? The weight of being 'head' a bit top-heavy?"

Dennis burred and stared daggers at Jonathan.

The Shepherd merely replaced his mild-mannered mask and reflected Dennis's stare before engaging. "What? You want me to argue with you? We all know you're right." Again, gasps raced around the tent and Jonathan raised his hand. "Mostly. I did drop the ball. I did let my daughter, my Community and my team down. But I have made my confessions to the Light and am at peace with Him. I am doing all I can to make it up to my daughter, and since I no longer hold a position with the Community at large, I am doing my best to be who I am called to be to this colony of the… faithful… in the Light… here, at Sanctuary."

Jonathan stopped, took a breath and waited a beat before continuing. "I am not perfect. I was truly unaware I was a captive of my own making. I am still, to this day and likely for the rest of my life, carrying the scars of that situation." Then, from within that frail tent of a body, Jonathan stood tall and invoked all the power of the Light that was his to call upon; he went from meek to mammoth in a moment. Sparks flew from his flashing, dark-violet armour. "But do not ever make the mistake of maligning the people of the Light, the apple of His eye. You stand on shaky ground. Yes, war is coming, and we are preparing. And when the Dark arrives, we will be ready—standing in the Light, bowing to Him and Him alone. What will you be standing on, Dennis?"

The man countered, but a bit of his fire had dimmed. "The law of the land and the grace of the Light. That is why we are here. To warn you. And to hand out these." He reached into the bag at his feet and pulled out a sheaf of papers. "Census guides. Every family is to fill one out online by tomorrow evening. Everything you need to know is written on these." Again, he waved the papers. "Then, he is coming. Here. To punish all who do not pay homage; those who do not acknowledge him as a god on the census, who do not accurately fill in the information. All who do not comply, he will punish. And if you are members of the Community of Light, he will punish us." This time both arms shot out to incorporate his colleagues either side of him. "We will be the first sent to The Games. Then, he will find a head who is better equipped to 'manage' the Community." Dennis clutched his heart and swayed. "Your decision doesn't just impact you"—he looked around the tent—"or your elderly... or your children. It directly impacts us. If you don't change your mind and bend the knee, you will be responsible for your own deaths and for ou—"

He couldn't go on. Something was happening to his heart and Becky had her hand inside his jacket retrieving a vial of tablets from an inner pocket.

Stuart finally stood and finished the sell. "So, we thought it only fair that you knew what was coming. And now that you know, your blood... and ours... will be on your hands." And with that, the three bundled Dennis up and, in an island of panicked hostility, made their own way out. At this point I didn't care if they got lost. As long as they didn't do any damage along the way. The krets had sold us out. And they were wrong. Their blood... and ours... was on their own hands.

JONATHAN DREW me and Tea aside. "Someone needs to speak to the group." His head flicked between the two of us. Genuine concern lit his face.

I looked to Tea, he looked to Jonathan, so I spoke. "Would you do it?"

Jonathan squeezed my shoulder, smiled a sad smile and shuffled his way to the front of the group. "Friends... family." The irony of him addressing us the same way Dennis had, was not lost. But the honesty and affection in the greeting went a long way to calm the atmosphere. He took the time to make eye contact with everyone in the tent. "It looks like we are in for some hard... harder times." He paused, looked to Hot Cocoa and she nodded. Apparently, she had a direct line to the Boss and got Words from him. Handy.

Jonathan pursed his lips, creating a dimple in his left cheek. "We can work out a plan and details later. Tonight, I want each of you to consider whether you want to stay at Sanctuary. As each one of us already knows, the persecution is real. But the trial has only just begun."

Ruby walked down the aisle through the heart of the gathering and Jonathan picked her up. She laid her head on his shoulder and he stroked her hair as he continued. "I, for one, believe we have made the right choice. I believe the Light is faithful to his people; He is able to, and will, protect us. And I believe life is going to get far worse before it gets any better; I am confident there will be casualties. If any of you have families or other places outside of Philadelphia you can go, even short-term until this storm passes, consider whether that is the right option for your family. No one will think badly of you for leaving." This was said with a force similar to that he had used to put Dennis in his place. He was laying down a law to his flock. "Times are getting harder for those of us who live in the Light. But the High Council have just put a target on our foreheads."

The silence after his speech was deafening. The truth tore and tortured our souls. Our own people had set us up to take their fall.

"Let's petition the Light," Jonathan continued, then guided us into a time of giving thanks and asking for continued protection, wisdom and guidance. Then dismissed us to our homes for a night of troubled tossing and turning. Because *I* believed no one was going to sleep tonight.

27

RAPHAEL: CARPARK PROTEST

When we first started our garden at the Factory in Laodicea, we had to use second-hand equipment because we did not have money. To water our garden, we used to sneak out at night to fill buckets from the canal that ran along our northern border. A lot of our buckets had holes or cracks. It meant that we not only had to run and become clumsy with our loads, it also meant we spent all our time trying to plug the holes. It took our focus away from how much water was needed in the garden and where it was most needed. Instead, we just dumped what we could where we could.

I felt it had become just like that in Philadelphia. Lately, every night there was some new kind of damage to Sanctuary. At first it was tunnels and furrows throughout our vegetable gardens. We had thought some animal had found a way to climb into the raised gardens. But, as Mary told us—many times—in all her years here, she had never come across this kind of activity in the vines, the improved pasture, or their own personal vegetable garden up at the house. We lost a whole rotation of crops. It meant we went without food and had nothing to sell at the Saturday markets.

After that, some wild animals had accidentally been locked in the supply shed. Feed bags, fertiliser, poisons, hay and whatever else was stored in there had been ripped to shreds and rendered useless. By the time people had been alerted by Pod's barking, everything had been blended into a soup of chaos that the critters had feasted on and enjoyed ravaging. It took the whole garden team plus extra help to clean it up. Not only had it pulled people away from their daily tasks, it also cost Sanctuary dearly. Supplies were not cheap. Most of the people here lived by bartering. Earning money from the Saturday markets held in the carpark was a slow process.

Daisy and Travis had explained that each store holder paid a percentage of their takings to the kitty, and the rest they used to buy the supplies they needed to create the items they sold. The money raised in the kitty went to paying rent to Mary to help cover the costs of rates, and expenses like the septic system and electricity to run the bore water that kept the Village alive. It was a tight few months to make back what was lost from the sacking of the storage sheds.

The next hole in the water bucket was when someone made the mistake of filling the bug spray with water and the fertiliser with poison. If Callum hadn't been on the ball and smelled the difference, it would have resulted in the total decimation of one harvest and the collective heart of our village. We had only just recovered from the last lot of garden decimation.

Obviously, timelines were backtracked and the people on duty turned themselves inside out trying to figure out how they had made such a terrible mistake. If it had been in isolation, we would have been casting a sceptical net over the individuals involved. But since it was one of many—multiples of many—events, that net was stretched to breaking over the whole situation.

It was not just me, there was an agreement in the wind that we were being targeted. I could not understand why. I could not figure out who. We were out of the way. Not hurting anyone. On the contrary, we were providing care and housing for the lost and broken. We paid our way and contributed to the wider community. I do not know how we were upsetting anyone. I was worried that as the incidents increased it would not just be a financial burden. What if someone got hurt? We were fighting an unknown enemy we could not see. And I would not be surprised if we learned they were being aided by the Dark.

But for now, we managed, due to Callum's diligence and everybody's hard work, to divert absolute disaster and we were on track for another Saturday morning market. It was similar to the ones we had in Laodicea, except here, everyone had their own stall, so it was a lot larger. Since the Community had made it their business to shut Sanctuary down, Travis and Daisy moved the markets into the large area at the entrance to the property. It was fenced off and people had no reason to be climbing through the paddock's barbed wire fences to get in and among our homes.

The day had started with the usual bustle and buzz, with bodies running back and forwards to the carpark with trestle tables, chairs, canopies, tablecloths, stands and produce. Winter's chill had settled across Sanctuary, adding extra incentive to move quickly. We joined the mass of movement with our instruments and chairs, making our way to our own plot marked out next to Tessa's stall where Dan, Riah and I would play music like we used to do at Serendipity for Missy. Just thinking of her and how much I missed her made my heart sad. But a flurry in my periphery pulled me out of my self-pity.

"Jet, darling." Miriam, the goat lady, was running around like a sloshy bucket. Layers of clothing, wisps of hair and her hands were flying every which way. But she was straining to sound calm and collected. "Have any of your cheeky cherubs been playing around my workshop?"

Jethro was herding the younger children to the carpark carrying extra supplies and equipment needed for the stallholders. He reminded me of a character Abbot once told me about. A man who played a whistle and all the children followed him. Blindly. The children here collected in Jethro's wake. A bit like the way Jethro followed Dan—and Craig followed Marcus. Jethro was subtle about it. But wherever Dan was, Jethro's starry eyes followed. He stood taller and broader when Dan was around.

But for now, Jethro called and his flock followed him to the back of Miriam's workshop.

"My poor girls have done the work and now they won't get the rewards." Miriam knotted her fingers and worked very hard to breathe deep and talk calmly, but her voice was at least an octave higher than normal. "Some tricky little monster has pulled my tent pegs out and the collapsed tarpaulin has damaged all my stock. I don't know what I'm going to do. I need my takings to pay for grain. And"—she looked at me—"we need to keep Tiger fed, don't we, Raph, my lad?"

I followed her into her workshop and saw the devastation. Not only had the pegs been pulled, the poles had fallen and the tarp had collapsed and tipped the tables. Pretty packages of soap and freezer boxes of cheese were upturned, spilled out and ruined.

"Oh, Miriam." Jethro's voice was a whisper. "No one has been here. We've been prepping the carpark and helping to take stock down." We all stood and took in the catastrophe. Miriam tried to pretend there was a silver lining, but none of us could see it quite yet. Jethro rallied the troops and we all pitched in to help. "Come on team, let's see what we can do."

An army of industrious children—there were about ten of us—set to, to see what we could salvage. Riah stood next to Miriam with her arm wrapped around the woman's waist. I suspect there might be a bit of Badge action going on as Miriam sighed and her hands stopped wringing and knotting.

We set a table up and started salvaging. There was enough for Miriam to have something to sell at her stall, but still the mystery was how it had happened. Or more likely, who would have done this. Craig came by with Kelly and a cart they normally used for building. On Saturdays we used it for transporting supplies. We loaded what we could of Miriam's stock on board. Half of the group headed to the carpark, while we stayed with the other half who helped Miriam put her workshop back in order.

To be honest, I did not think it was a person who did this. I think Dan may have agreed. He came by after hearing the news. "Anything I can do to help?" His eyes cast around the shadow of the workshop. His eyes narrowed and his nose scrunched. His eyes darted to me and

Riah. He smelled it too. Over the top of the soap's natural-oil perfume, there was a stronger than normal hint of sulphur. It seemed like it wasn't just the Community's fear ranged against us. As always, where the Light was working, the enemy undermined. I would have to talk to Val.

Once everything had been put back in as much order as possible, the four of us, Dan, Riah, Miriam and me, made our way to the marketplace. Miriam was calm enough to take over from Kelly and Craig who had volunteered to stand in for her till she could get there. Riah, Dan and I left her to set up. We were a bit late, but that was okay. It was more important to help Miriam. Over the past few weeks we had raised enough money playing music at the markets to restock our personal kitty... my share went into a fund to feed Tiger. It's as if thinking about him made him appear. He head butted my leg in his normal greeting, and I reached down and pulled him into my arms before he could resort to climbing my leg with his needle-claws. He showed his approval by rubbing his face against mine.

As we approached the markets, we heard yelling and chanting. The carpark was empty of anyone apart from the residents of Sanctuary. Barring the entrance, rows of people walked back and forward with placards. I could not see what was written on them, but I could hear their yelling. "Dan? Why do they want to shut us down? And what is an insurgent?"

With his arm around my shoulders, but his focus on the chaos, he answered, "A rebel. Someone who fights, or rebels against the government."

"But that is not who we are. We are living in peace... obeying the law. We are not fighting the government, or anyone. Except the enemy."

"If the government makes it illegal to be in the Light, we are."

"But that is silly. How is us being in the Light bad? How can it be against the law? We help people... who want to be helped. We do not make life difficult for anyone. Why is it illegal?" I could feel my pulse beating and my focus narrowing. A buzzing was building in my ears. I tried to focus on the weight and warmth, the soft, vibrating fur of Tiger.

"I don't think it's personal, mate. Look at the enemy now."

I tried to remember my breathing and clutched Tiger a bit tighter. Not too tight. But I let my focus wander over the two main crowds. Our visitors gridlocked by the roadblock, and those who were causing it. Then I looked to the perimeter. An audience of demons laughed and pointed out individuals who were acting out their frustration. Others weaved in and out of both groups, whispering their encouragement and fanning the anger. The ones protesting against us being insurgents were blocking the path of those stuck in the long snake of cars wanting to come in to buy their weekly produce.

A good number of people who lived on the southern side of the city used our markets as a staple part of their grocery shopping. And you had to get here early to get eggs. They went quickly. The other stalls, like Daisy's woodworking, Travis's metalsmithing, Dori's pottery and Miriam's soaps and cheeses were also well patronised. Even Tessa had made a good turnover of her sewing stock. And not just clothes. Some extra house furnishings, like cushions, or bags made from offcuts, were really popular.

But now there was an angry line of people blocking the entrance, and an angrier group of people who could not do their shopping. And right at the back of the line there was a siren and flashing lights. Someone had called the police, but they could not get through because none of the cars could move. It was chaos.

If I could not make any money, and if Miriam couldn't sell any of her produce, I would not be able to feed Tiger. I could feel the red haze rising. I tried harder to breathe slower.

What are we going to do? How can I provide for him? Where am I going to get food for him? Oh dear, oh dear, oh dear. Please help. Please do something.

I held Tiger to my chest and tucked his little body under my chin. Breathe the Light in, hold. Breathe the angst out, hold. Soft, vibrating fur tufted between my fingers. His little head butted under my chin and four paws full of needles flexed in and out of my chest. The prickly pain helped anchor me in the here and now. I focused on the pain and his purr and my breathing. And gradually the haze dissolved.

When I came back to the carpark, I felt the weight of Dan's arm still around my shoulders and Riah's arm threaded through mine. Whilst the police were speaking with the angry protesters and the placards were stacked up like dominoes against the fence, visitors had left their cars and snuck in to do their shopping.

It looked like we were going to make some money today, but sadly it wasn't a music kind of morning anymore.

28

DAISY: A NEW NORM

So, it turned out that Hot Cocoa's badge was Hearing Words from the Light. Which turned out to be a bleedingly… blessed… boon for us. Yesterday's market had been a debacle. All day, talk around Sanctuary had been discouraging and doomsday-ish. Shepherd had spent time with everyone, hearing woes and petitioning the Light with them. Tea and I had a pretty unproductive day as there had been a constant trickle of people coming by, just wanting to "chat". To see what we thought, to sound us out and to make sure we were all going to be okay. I didn't lie. Told them straight up I didn't know.

But it turned out Hot Cocoa did. In the frigid chill of the evening, we sat rugged up around a brazier in the gateway for our daily debrief when she approached. Tea, Shepherd, Warrior, Mountain and I usually chewed the fat and made plans for keeping Sanctuary running smoothly, succinctly and safe. Funny thing, initially… and regularly, she was invited to join us—the woman had crazy insight—but she declined every time, saying her main focus here at Sanctuary was caring for her kids, and that wasn't just the Colt and Filly, but Dryad and Wild Cat as well. Especially since those two were speeding down the highway to marriage.

But at times like this evening, when she had something to say, she came by, normally with the younger two in tow. And we all made a point of sitting up and listening. "Yesterday was just the beginning." I'm not sure if she noticed, but her hands reached out and made contact with one of the twins standing either side of her. They leaned in and both ended up tucked in and wrapped up in an arm. One each. "The Council's warning is genuine. The Gerent will come. But that will be later. Between now and then, there will be trouble. We are on the cusp of significant trial." She looked to Warrior and Mountain. "The 'arduous journey' has begun and it is time to prepare"—she locked eyes with Warrior for several beats and spoke an essay none of us could hear, then looked back to the Shepherd—"and sift out those who, in the end, will not stand. If we are going to survive, we need to weed the weak-of-will." She then looked to Mountain, and even I could read her unspoken message of love, tinted with fear. The way she clutched those kids, I was putting my money on the fact it wasn't for herself.

The Shepherd spoke up beside me. "I agree. It's been coming and we've been slow. This last attack has done more damage to the spirits of those who are here, and I suspect when it comes to"—he looked to Hot Cocoa—"'weeding', the hard work has been done for us. Those who can't stand under what we have faced so far will not stand under what's to come." He paused and looked into the shadows of my workshop. It was like his attention called to our girl. Like I said, he was the sunshine to our sunflower hearts.

Ruby looked up and accepted the invitation of his outstretched arms. As she snuggled in his lap, he kissed her head and stroked her hair. Since our chairs were arm to arm, Ruby reached out a gloved hand to me and I took it and kissed her fingers.

Her dad spoke into the moment. "We all need to make the same decision. Before we take it to the people, we each need to count the cost and decide what is best for our family."

Silence settled over us, slick with nauseating fear. Who here would go? He wouldn't leave, would he? The Colt and Filly turned and were fully hugging Hot Cocoa, and she was squeezing them back. Her eyes were locked on the Mountain. Then they both looked to Warrior.

I looked to Tea, then exhaled as he smiled at me. *We're going to be okay, Daisy my girl.* He tapped his pipe to empty it, and winked. *You're going to be just fine.*

I held my breath as I looked at the Shepherd and my heart kind of broke as I watched him hold my shadow. Without conscious thought my hand was on her back and I leaned over and laid my own kiss on her head. Jonathan released one arm from around Ruby and pulled me into an easy, three-way embrace. Right then, I was a coward. I'll admit it. And I will confess it shamed me. But I couldn't look at him. With my chin tucked to my chest, I asked, "What will *you* do?" Fear stole my voice so that it was only a whisper.

Oh, for freaky-freak's sake. You are an absolute embarrassment. Toughen the frack up, Daisy. You lived perfectly well before he arrived. Before Ruby arrived. You don't need anyone. You are an island. And anyway, you have Tea and Mary and Jet... and a whole community of family here. Sit up. Get off him. Look around. Even the Filly is tougher than you.

Ruby clenched me tighter as I eased myself away from the two of them, and I sensed everyone else freeze. He'd been the last to arrive and, even though many knew him from his days as Overseer and Head Shepherd, since he'd got here he had worked his way into everyone's heart. The Light was our purpose, love and goal. Every person here, no matter how odd or quirky... or prickly, were family. But Jonathan was the pulse that brought us closer and held us tighter.

He turned to me and waited till I looked him in the face. The fireworks exploded in his espresso-brown eyes and warmth infused his words. "Daisy girl, as I said before, where would I go?"

The use of my childhood name didn't raise my hackles, but it did kick me in the guts. *See, you are behaving like a child. You are supposed to be a leader here. Have responsibility. Help call the shots. Grow the frack up before you start being relegated to the playpen. You have worked too hard to give it all away in a moment of weakness.* I straightened. "You know the Musketeer would find a place for you and Ruby"—her little fist was bunching in my shirt like a noose tightening, waiting for her sentencing—"if you couldn't use one of your multiple contacts in another city. I'm sure you have friends who could help you both."

He shifted Ruby on his lap and held her little body that had curled into a ball. One of her hands still clenched my shirt and a bit of skin. And to be honest, it hurt. But not as much as the thought he'd take her away.

"Yes, I have contacts and Felix would help me…"—he looked around the group—"would help any of us if we wanted to go." His eyes came back to me and sparkled with joy. I don't know how he did it. In the midst of all that was going on, the guy still oozed joy… exhaustion, but joy too. "But my heart, and my girl, are here."

"It won't be safe for her. Maybe it would be best." Despite my best efforts to think of the bigger picture, my bravado was tinny and hollow. *But at least you said it. You showed them you don't need them. Ruby's safety is paramount.*

As a result, however, our girl squeaked and burrowed deeper into her dad's chest.

By the limited light given off by the brazier, he looked around the group and into Sanctuary. "Considering our journey to get here, what we have all been through to make it, I think it best for me and my girl if we stay. I feel… strongly that this is where the Light wants me. And as I said before, no one will take my family from me ever again."

Was it wrong that there was a tingle of excitement throughout my whole body when he said this. *Yes. Yes, it was.* It was stupid. He was a dad fighting for his kid. I wasn't even in his family. But the strength and the conviction of his words, spoken after years of living his testimony, was as powerful as setting a seal on his words. The word "truth" rang in my mind.

I settled back in my chair and stroked Ruby's arm.

Warrior spoke from beside me. "What about you, Daisy?"

I snorted. Yep, a genuine, full of class, ruin the moment, snort. But enough of the cosy skrat, I sat up and took my place back in the circle. "Like I'd leave. They'll bury me here. I've picked a spot over in the next paddock on a slope under the old gum looking out across the countryside. I must remember to tell Jet."

Warrior smiled at me. Now *she* was my kind of people. I mean, they all were.

I'd had my doubts about Dryad to start with. But the chick was cool. What she was doing for folks here. The secret gifts she left on everybody's doorstep. She tried to make it anonymous, but she was the only one with a sewing machine, for crying out loud. But we didn't want to ruin her treat, so no one thanked her verbally, but we all made a point of showing everyone what we had received and how grateful we were. And, believe me, there was no faking our enthusiasm. The chick was good at what she did and what she created. She was good people.

Each week she and Wild Cat went out for a coffee date, which entailed them scouting Charity Shops for clothing, household goods for new cabins, fabrics and books. Wild Cat loved to read, and he was building a library in the Meeting Place. And I can't even begin to express my gratitude for what he'd done... inspired... led... here with the cabins and boardwalk. He literally lifted us out of the mud and gave us our sense of humanity back. Individually, they were quality. Together, they were a force. They were just like most of the others here at Sanctuary, which is why they fit in so well with the rest of their family.

Time to move on and get this show sorted before we took it to the people. "Tea, what about you, old man?"

He made an effort to look mock-offended. All he said was, "Silly girl." And went back to puffing on his pipe.

"Hot Cocoa, Mountain, Warrior?"

Again, they did the silent speak thing, and it was Warrior who spoke for the group. "The Light brought us here, to Sanctuary, for this very purpose. To stand beside you in the trials, and to lend our swords for the battle. This is what we do." The glint of enthusiasm that shot out of her eyes when she mentioned battle was a little bit crazy. Like I said, she was my kind of people. When I grow up, I'm gonna be just like her. I did wonder though, how she did any good in a fight, stuck like a porcupine with all those blades.

Nevertheless, with these people... good people around me, I knew with confidence it was going to be okay. It would get ugly. But in the Light, we would be okay.

29

DAISY: TIRESOME, TENACIOUS TRESPASSERS

So, the protest against our markets wasn't a one-off. The following week the same thing happened. Our customers were getting cranky, and our people were getting nervous. Right or wrong, we needed the income. And it was a healthy and important opportunity to meet and mix with the wider community. We weren't a secret commune. We were just a group of people who were doing life a bit differently, and doing the best we could after The Quake, finding our new norm. We didn't want to be secluded or cut off. We still wanted to contribute and have a positive impact. So this protesting lark was causing us more than financial distress.

That's when Tim's wife stepped into the fray and saved our butts, on the evening of the second failed markets. Gemma, a woman in her mid-fifties, was quietly spoken but solid in nature—evidenced by how she'd, alongside Tim, raised three riotous boys into steadfast men, now living in nearby cities. Gemma and Tim had joined our community like everyone else after The Quake. They'd not accepted the invitation to return to their home once the Gerent had repaired it, because one or both of them—I still didn't know which—wasn't comfortable moving back into a solid building. But they had stayed on because they had fallen in love with the people of Sanctuary, and found the different pace of life here really suited them.

This evening, as we sat around debriefing and discussing what to do about our markets, Gemma approached with February and October to offer up their idea. Once we'd arranged seats, October—I could tell it was October because Dryad had been helping them with their hair and she now wore hers in braids—laid it out for us. "Drones."

We all just sat and stared at her. Waiting. For something… anything… more.

I looked to February—her hair now styled in a bob—who graced me with a rare smile. Then to Gemma who gave her head a little shake and threw us a lifeline. "I was thinking, we are not in a position to tackle this problem head on. It's not going to help anyone if we try to stop or fight the protestors. We need a way to side-step this opposition. So, I came up with an idea and went to ask these wonderful young ladies if it was possible."

This time February—bobbed haircut—reiterated, "Drones."

Understanding started evolving. Mountain must have been on the same trajectory as me. "How do we chase the cat out of the bag?"

When February and October sat back and looked to Gemma, she took the floor. "We put together a simple website. Each week we put up lists of what produce is available. We could put up images of what goods each crafter has to sell. And then take orders. Sanctuary already has a bank account. People pay directly into the account and then"—a victorious smile lit up her face—"at night, we send the deliveries out via drones."

Jonathan said, "I can understand the need for… stealth, and going at night is a great idea, it's all brilliant, ladies, but won't the darkness make it difficult for finding the locations? And how do we set up the timing and get information out about the exchange?"

Both February and October scoffed at him. It made me really glad he'd asked and not me. I actually thought they were good questions.

October—braids—answered. "GPS."

Again, we waited. And Gemma intervened. "February and October are involved in 'Drone Wars', as you all know, and they suggested that night-time is no obstacle." Gemma froze then looked to Braids and Bob. "Do you think your friends might help us?"

The twins looked at each other and mind-spoke. Bob answered, "Yes."

Gemma obviously had learned not to wait for more. "Okay, so this is what I was thinking. I have a camera, not very classy, but good eno—"

"We have cameras," Braids interrupted.

Gemma smiled warmly at her then continued, "We take photos of what's on offer for the week. Put it up by Wednesday. Take orders by Friday. Deliver on the weekend nights, at a time that suits the buyer that they can select. If February and October's friends will help, we could get all our deliveries out on Friday, Saturday and Sunday evenings so people could have their food for the week. Depending on how well it works, once we iron out the wrinkles there would be no reason why we couldn't extend the delivery times to other nights of the week."

I was just about to ask how we would let people know when Gemma answered that for me. "This week we make up heaps of small flyers. Small, because we don't want to make them obvious, and we don't want to waste resources if we don't have to. I will do what I can to get our online presence up and running. Next Saturday, we make it look like it's a normal market, but we send the kids to each of our customers and down the line of cars along the road to hand out our cards with the web address on it. It will be pretty self-explanatory once they go on and check it out.

"When they sign up, we can send out a weekly email and explain that if they would like to continue to buy from us, we would love to keep in touch and supply their needs. But considering how there is growing antagonism toward us, we would appreciate it if they kept it to themselves or to those who are our regulars."

She sat back in her chair and looked to each of us. I was gobsmacked. It was brilliant. Sounded too good to be true, and I had absolutely no idea how any of it would work. I had a basic understanding of the internet, but that was about it. "Do you really think you can do all that?"

This time Braids, Bob and Gemma all scoffed, and I couldn't hold back my smile.

Just maybe we would be okay.

* * *

"GET OUT. GET OUT. GET OUT." The gravelly screaming—*I know, gravelly screaming?* seriously you had to hear it to believe it—was so obnoxious I could hear it over the top of my hammering. Downing tools, I stepped out to the gate to see what all the commotion was about this beautiful winter morning.

A classy looking woman—apart from her mouth that was—stood in the carpark ranting at... no one in particular. She thrust her fist in the air and raved and raged like she had a swarm of bitey insects in her underwear. Her face was twisted in fury and her coiffed hair was giving its styling products a run for their money.

She didn't actually approach so I met with Tea and we stood shoulder to shoulder at the gate, watching the performance. It wasn't like she was asking for an invitation to come in or anything, so we just watched and waited for the second act.

Thing was, though, not only was her tirade in heels totally bizarro, there was a crazy shimmering about her. Not armour shimmer on the outside, but dark shimmer on the inside. I'd not come across it before, and since she wasn't approaching, I took the time to try to figure her out as spiders walked up my spine sending shivers through my brain. There was something definitely off about the whole thing.

The woman had a disgusting mouth on her which was at total odds with her polished appearance. If she didn't put a cork in it soon, I would have to intervene. It wasn't good for my girl Ruby hearing language like that. But as the thought was forming, Warrior marched past me and went to interact with our vocal, vitriolic visitor.

"You think you can stop us, Valarie? Mighty Warrior?" She stopped to spit. Like I said, classy. "Do you think you can stem the Dark tide coming for you? You are nothi—"

Without stopping or slowing her stride, Warrior drew her sword and slayed the shrew on the spot. Mid-rant. There was an ear-piercing screech and the woman dropped to her knees. Then, after sheathing her sword, Warrior bent down and helped the woman stand up. Yep. The strike had slain something, but not the woman. She shook her head and looked around, lost and in a daze. But praise the eva-lovin'-Light, the noise had stopped.

Even though she spoke quietly, we—the crowd that'd formed at the spectacle—could hear Warrior's voice. "You have made a poor choice, but it is not irreversible. However, your time is running out. Once that line is crossed for good there is no going back, and the consequences are eternal."

The woman shook herself and gave Warrior's jeans, work boots, and scruffy button-down the once-over with a sneer. Then straightened her skirt, flicked her hair and strutted back to her car. And with a quiet hum of her electric engine and a spit of gravel, she was gone.

"Interesting." I addressed Warrior as she came back to me.

She smiled. "She was a Host."

"What? Like a party planner?"

At this, Warrior actually chuckled. "No, a Host to the Dark." She looked around the group and continued in a louder voice so everyone could hear. "Not all Hosts are willing, but the Dark will use anyone who has dabbled in his territory and who is not filled with the Light. He and his minions don't care about the body they take, but when it suits their purpose, they can control the Host's actions."

Someone called out from the back of the group, it may have been Craig. "Didn't seem too much of a problem."

Warrior's smile was sad. "For us, no." She sighed. "That one was testing the waters. The Host was alone, in broad daylight, and up front. You may want to ask yourself, what was going on behind the scenes when we were all up here focusing on her. I would suggest you all go back to your homes and workplaces and check everything is okay. Our enemy loves the shadows. More than likely, this was a decoy."

Her cheery lesson in Hosts had everyone spinning on their heels and hurrying home to check under the bed and in the closets, no doubt.

* * *

"For freaky-freak's sake, can you give it a rest? You people are a pain in my butt. And you're on private property."

The Host replied, "I'm not here just to give you a message, Daisy, daughter of Mildred. I am here to warn the Great Warrior, her soldiers and the rest of your insurgents. You are all going to suffer. You are all going to go down to hades. You are all going to have to eat your own excrement and drink your own uri—"

An indigo blade sliced through the man, dissecting him from the right-hand side of his pop-rock T-shirt collar through to the left-hand side of his designer jeans. He dropped to his knees intact. Then he did the whole "confused wet dog" routine. Warrior helped him stand. Gave him the "Good Choices, Bad Choices" spiel, and saw him off the property.

But before we could brush our hands off and go back to our cups of tea, another car sped into the carpark, kicking up clouds of dust and gravel. This one was a hippy-chick in a rainbow tie-died skirt. She launched out of her beat-up hatchback and picked up from where the other left off "...excrement and drink your own urine."

For crying out loud, a crowd was forming to watch the latest spectacle. But as fun as it was, it was becoming tedious. "Alright. Alright. I get the doomsday message. You actually have me looking forward to it. Maybe then you'll shut up." I'd had enough of these "messengers" from hell. But did that stop her? Of course not. She wasn't here to engage in rational conversation. She, like all the rest of them, was here to deliver a message. And drive us freaking-freaky mad. Jonathan unsheathed his sword and went to deal with our latest messenger. But

I put my hand on his arm. "Maybe if we let them get it off their chest, they might give us a break?"

He nodded, and leaned on his sword as we all turned back to the woman's rant. "All within the walls of Sanctuary, hear the word of the Dark Lord and his agent. This is what the Darkness says: 'Do not let the Shepherd and Warrior deceive you. They cannot deliver you from my hand. Do not let your Gate Keepers persuade you to trust in the Light when they say, "The Light will surely deliver us; Sanctuary will not be given into the hand of the Dark's Agent."'

"Do not listen to your leaders. This is what the Dark says: 'Make peace with me and come out to me. Then each of you will eat fruit from your own vine and fig tree and drink water from your own well, until I come and take you to a land like your own—a land of grain and new wine, a land of bread and vineyards, a land of olive trees and honey. Choose life and not death!'

"Do not listen to your guides, for they are misleading you when they say, 'The Light will deliver us.' Has the god of any nation ever delivered his land from the hand of the Dark? Where are the gods of..."

She kept up her prattling, but I turned to the group behind me. "I think we've heard enough now, don't you?" Mostly people shrugged and nodded. So, I turned to Jonathan who went to meet with our "guest".

"...who of all the gods of these countries has been able to save his land from me? How then can the Light deliver this insignificant gathering of insignificant people from my ha—"

And down she went. Jonathan helped her up and blah, blah, blah. You know the drill. I won't bore you with the details.

However, I was surprised they never fought back. Why didn't the demons possessing these Hosts ever fight back? Were they minor spirits sent to mock us and entertain the growing demonic crowd around our perimeter? I had no idea. I just hoped the racket would stop for a while and give us some peace.

30

ANONYMOUS: STRENGTH IN NUMBERS

Dear Brothers and Sisters,

I just wanted to reach out and make contact.

I am in the Light and am still gathering with the Community I have been a member of for fifteen years. The only reason I am still here is because my home was not significantly damaged in The Quake, and I was able to repair it myself, thereby maintaining ownership of my property.

I will not bow to the Gerent. And I suspect I will shortly bear the consequences as I've declared my stand in the Census. I am sure I will be routed soon.

Be encouraged the care packages you are sending out via drones are being well received. Word is spreading of your service and care. If you have the resources, attached is a list of families who are currently doing it tough and would also benefit from your provisions.

I guess I just wanted to let you know, you are not alone. There are a few of us, but we are keeping a low profile. Please accept this small token of support we have gathered to enable you to purchase those things that can't be grown or produced within your home.

You are not alone.

Stay true and strong and He will see us through.

Your friend on the outside,
Anonymous

31

CONTESSA: ABOUT TIME

I was squished in the front seat of our—seriously, that would never get old—car. I had gifts for everyone crammed all around me and taking up every spare centimetre in the footwell. Why was I not using the boot space? Or the back seat? Because it was raining. Well, that and because word had got out that we were heading back to the Factory in Laodicea for a visit, and everyone…

Every.

One.

Wanted to come with us.

I couldn't complain. Well, actually I could, but I wouldn't. Dan had spoiled me on one of our weekly—yep, weekly—date days. Well, they were more like coffee or lunch trips into the city when he could take a break from building the cabins. We didn't have a set day or time, but we made sure we went once a week. We did the banking for Mary and for the Village too. Even though we didn't use money in the Village, Mary still had to pay bills and people who had stalls liked to keep topping up their savings accounts.

Oh, and you'll never guess what. Val, Marcus and Kait strongly suggested Dan and I start an account of our own too. That way we could put a little bit of our earnings away and start saving some money. I thought maybe we'd just put it in the kitty, but they said no. "You guys need to start building a nest egg." For nesting, I guess.

Well, if that didn't send my mind racing.

Nesting.

Eggs.

People-eggs… babies.

Now that thought was all kinds of scary… well it used to be, but now?

Not quite so much.

Mary came with us into the city, once. She had to see the City Council about property zoning and wanted to speak to her solicitor to do something to her will. Val, Kait and Marcus strongly suggested we do that too—make a will. Dan and I laughed. A will? To leave what to whom? Marcus pointed out that we had a car now, and we were about to get married and perhaps there might be some things we wanted sorted if something were to happen to us.

And that just made me think about that horrible night several weeks ago when the High Council came with their nasty news. Things had been pretty bad in Sodom, where we were constantly under attack and targeted every time we raised our heads, purely because we were in the Light. They weren't that bad here yet. The tide had turned, but we were still able to go out and about without drawing attack. But it made me think that we just didn't know what was coming and that I did want to make sure everything, all my interests, were taken care of.

It also made me want to hurry up and marry Dan. I know. I was telling him he had to take time out to be with me, but he also had to get on with it and finish the huts. Mixed messages, much? Although we'd had one happy outcome. After the Council had come and frightened the pants off everyone, we… and by we, I mean Daisy, Jonathan and Val, had spoken to Lisa, my neighbour with the babies, and strongly encouraged her to move to the Factory at Laodicea. She fit their profile really well. The kids would have other kids to play with and Lisa would have more support. And they would be safe.

The extra good news was that one of the families in the ballot could take her cabin. Therefore, we were one step closer to getting married.

So now, would you believe, we were down to the last few to be built. I was just so excited. "Yay."

"Tessa," Marcus growled from the back. He didn't like it when he had to sit in the back seat and Dan drove.

"Sorry." I tried to tone down my happy, but seriously, like that was going to happen. Once our cabin was built, we would get married.

I'd started a dress. I loved it. It was whitish, a soft, delicate cream. And I'd found the most beautiful, aged, white lace in a charity shop over the top of a ghastly puce gown. Somewhere in the tangle of parcels at my feet and on my lap were my designs I was going to show Kerm, Iza and Carley.

That was another reason why we were going to the Factory today. Mary, Daisy and Travis had insisted we have the wedding at Sanctuary, and Mary declared she would provide the meat. Obviously, the gardens would provide the rest of the food. But the other great news was that we had arranged that, for a week before the wedding, Raph, Riah, Kait and I would stay at the Factory to prepare. Raph was on cloud nine because he was in charge of baking the cake and lots of bread and other goodies. Vashti and Aiko couldn't wait to have him back.

And Riah? She'd volunteered to be on wash-up duty for the week. I know. Strange girl. Anyway, no one complained. And Kait had insisted that where her kids went, she went. Just as well, really. There was no way I was going to have a week preparing for my wedding without her.

Oh. My. Word. I was so flopping happy I could just sing. "Yay."

"Tessa." Marcus's bark was growing growlier.

Dan reached over and laid his hand on my leg. Well, he tried to. It was covered with parcels. But in the end, I managed to free one of my hands and laid it on his leg instead. He smiled at me and… gah.

So. Flopping. Happy.

"We are here. I can see it," Raph squeaked from the back seat. He was squished in with his drum and Tiger. Considering all the drama we'd been going through at Sanctuary, he'd insisted on bringing them both with him. And believe me, I got it. As much as everyone tried to keep a lookout, guarding their house and family, we still couldn't be sure things were safe.

I swear the car floated into the carpark of the Factory, considering the happy vibe pumping from within.

We were home.

And there was squealing.

There was always squealing.

Then there was growling. "Keep it down, yeh? I've only just got Grace to sleep?" Indy whisper-growled from their cabin in the middle of the carpark. The redesign and rebuild of the Factory were coming along beautifully. The apartments at the western end were finished and occupied. The garden in Warehouse Two was now out in the open. There was a protective shield of shade cloth around two sides, and it incorporated a play area with equipment and everything.

I couldn't wait to hold my little Light-daughter again, but considering the look on Indy's face, I would. Wait, that is. Just until she woke up. Then I would be in there like a bullet.

The whole Factory family had insisted Iza and Indy move into the first unit block, since Iza had been heavily pregnant with Gracie. But they vehemently declined. They would not move into a completed apartment until all the women and kids we'd rescued from the Temple were housed, and our sisters were settled into their permanent residences. Only then, after everyone else, would they leave their little house.

I kind of think it had something to do with their hut holding so many memories for them. And the fact that it was originally a Soteria house. Not that they had known that, until we arrived. But it felt safe… because it was. I suspect, as Grace began to grow, they would be grateful for the extra space. However, I had witnessed, and experienced first-hand, just how stubborn Iza could be. I knew, without a shadow of a doubt, they would stick to their guns.

For now, the demountables and Warehouse One still stood, and our old living quarters had been completely remodelled. The internal offices where we once slept had been replaced with a licensed industrial kitchen. The rest of the area was divided up into artisan workspaces. I was very happy to see that a sewing shop, with banks of machines and shelves of fabric, had been given pride of place under a huge skylight.

32

ANONYMOUS: CHANGE IS HERE

*D*ear Brothers and Sisters,

We are counting down the moments. Surely the day of our demise is not long off. Talk around town is hushed and furtive. People are scared: scared of being reported; scared of being accused; scared of the Dark. The walls are closing in.

Trust is a currency that holds no weight.

Hope is a shadow of its former self.

Love is a wage that takes its toll.

Please accept our latest offering for your needs. You are not alone. Whilst one of us still stands, within the Light we have the majority.

Stay true to your faith, for the glory of the Light,

Anonymous

33

MARCUS: RIGHT ROYAL RUCKUS

"For the love of all that's good in the world, what the bleeding heck is all that racket about?" I just wanted one night of sleep. I was tired to the bone. Building huts and walkways and cracking the whip with training and sets for the world and his dog. But no. Between crying babies—who, thank the Light, were now safe and making a new life with their mum at the Factory in Laodicea—and this bleeding ruckus—led, no doubt, by that three-legged mutt, Pod—there was no rest for the wicked and even less for those of us in the Light. Me ears followed the progress of the dog's caterwauling, the crash and bash of equipment and who knows what other madness around and throughout the village.

"Earth to Marcus." Kait's tap on me shoulder almost had me landed on me rump. I was so lost in thought, I paused with me leg halfway in me trousers. She now stood fully dressed, hands on hips, face set in question. "If you're too occupied doing something else? Or too tired?" —she eyeballed me half-dressed state—"or possibly... too scared? I could go and check it out alon—"

It took exactly one half of one second for me to get both me legs into me trousers, and have me disrespecting, belligerent wife pinned to her camp cot, hands either side of her head, giving her me undivided, fully awake, fearless attention. The early spring moonlight cast a soft blue glow across her stunning face, and I growled at her. "Scared?"

Not only was I not scared, I obviously wasn't scary. Not that that was me intention, but Kait giggled and pulled me in for a quick kiss. "Come on now, Bear, put a shirt on or you'll be frightening the wildlife and innocents, and have all the fair maidens swooning." She pushed me aside and I rolled the short distance to the floor. She stepped over me and I was a tangle of shirt sleeves as I scrambled to follow her out. No way was me wife going to beat me onto the battlefield, even if I had to tie me laces when I got there.

I didn't think it needed saying, but I was not in me best frame of mind when I got to the Meeting Place and found a score of others with torches and… garden implements?

"What's going on? And will someone shut those bleeding mutts u—" Pod's scream of pain had us all bolting in the direction of the outer work sheds. His whimpering gave us a target and we narrowed in like buzzards to a carcass. Bad reference; the pup was still alive. Daisy led the charge, swinging a jimmy bar looking for blood. But we all froze when we smelled smoke. Except Daisy—she ran on and swooped down on her dog. Kait pushed past, and the two of them tended the casualty.

Val hobbled to the front of the group and faced us. The full moon gave off enough light to see what was what, and who was who. "Spread out, find the smoke. Some go door to door to check everyone's okay. We don't want to get caught out by a diversion. Marcus, Kait: go check on Mary and Jonathan. They'll be vulnerable up there on their own."

"Right you are, Val," I threw over me shoulder as I high-tailed it up the hill. The clear night and the full moon revealed a beautiful, crisp, still night. It didn't take too long or require too many of me senses to realise I was not alone. Pounding footsteps and heavy puffing trailed hot on me heels. I smelled me wife's lavender and rose, and the other person—I had to turn to check—Daisy. Turned out I didn't have to waste me time checking. In seconds she'd flown past me and burst through the little wooden gate leading into the house paddock on the hill. She made a beeline to the silhouetted tent on the front lawn and disappeared from view as she dived inside. Me heart broke with her scream of anguish. "Ruby? Jet?"

The night's light made her profile clear. Standing outside the tent, her head scanning the hill. She cried again, "Jet? Ruby?" Next, she was banging on the door. "Mary. Mary, wake up."

Deaf to the world, Mary stayed silent and sleeping. That is, if the old girl were still there. We didn't have time to wait. Abandoning the door, the three of us darted to the garden bushes to inspect a low, quiet groaning.

Jet lay on the ground holding his head. Kait squatted down next to him to check him over. Mary still hadn't come to the door, but we heard a faint call from the back of the house. Daisy and I left Kait to tend to Jet, and bolted. Jonathan lay on the ground in a ball.

Daisy was beside herself, energy sparking out of her. "Ruby!" It was a scream, a wail and a shattered heart all in one.

"Here. She's here." Jonathan was panting, clinging for all his worth to a limp little body. He was wrapped around her, like a macadamia shell around its soft, sweet kernel. "Alive. Breathing." His lungs wheezed like partially perished bellows. "Unconscious. Drugged… I think."

Daisy didn't break the stride of her run. Rather than helping the man up, she merely skidded along the ground like sliding into home base, coming to a stop next to me friend and his babe. Her body wrapped around the front of his so her hands could caress the little tyke. Tears wove their way through her whisper. "Ruby? Sweetheart?"

"I think," Jonathan panted and wheezed, "she's okay." Daisy broke down and wept. Jonathan lifted his arm over her and hugged them both.

"What about you, mate? You don't sound too chipper."

"It was Jet's nigh—" Jonathan jerked his head up. "Jet? Is he okay?" Panic pushed the wheeze aside.

"He's fine." Kait came around the house, her arm around Jet's slumped shoulders with the moon lighting up their fronts. The lad's hands were covering his head.

They stumble-walked over to us. "Is Ruby okay?" His voice broke and he took a moment to recover before he continued. "They came in and tried to put something over my mouth. I fought them off, like Dan and Tessa had taught me. But the guy hit me over the head and the other one took Ruby." He looked down at the knot of bodies on the ground. "I am so sorry. I tried to fight them off." Emotion choked his words.

Jonathan eased himself out of the scrum still lying on the ground and pulled Ruby up onto his lap. His wheezing returned. I leant down and took the treasure from him so he could climb to his feet with Daisy's help. When he was righted, he addressed Jet. "Mate, you saved her. If I hadn't heard you putting up a fight, I would never have known there was trouble." Just to make sure Jet heard him, he looked the boy in the eye. "You saved her."

I'm not too sure Daisy realised one arm was still wrapped around Jonathan as she leaned over, her other hand stroking Ruby's sleeping head as it lay on me shoulder.

Me wife put on her nurse's voice, which brooked no argument. "Okay everyone, let's go inside so I can give you all a proper going over."

Just as we turned to make our trek across the back lawn, we were blinded by spotlights coming from the house. "Hello? Who's out there?" Finally, Mary was awake.

"It's alright Nanna-May, it's just us, we're coming in now." Daisy had enough wherewithal to answer the woman calmly. We didn't need any more panic if we could help it.

"Alright, dear, I'll get Jet to pop the kettle on." Seems Mary was not only as gentle as goose down, she was as sharp as a marble. All she knew was there were people coming to her house and Jet should make some tea. She turned back into the house calling, "Jet, honey, we've got guests."

The boy groaned from beside me. Kait still had an arm wrapped around his middle and he had one hand still on his head. "Nanna, I'm out here." Pain evident in his voice.

The old woman froze. She may have been a roo or two short of a deck, but she was keen-witted enough to know there was trouble with her boy. She turned her gaze back to the garden, her hands clutched to her nightie as she watched us emerge from the shadows.

"Everyone alright?" Val had arrived with Dan, Tessa and the twins.

Mary flinched at the voice, but her eyes didn't leave her grandson.

"I'll be fine, Nanna-May, they just hit me in the head. Kait said it didn't look too bad, but she'd check me over and keep an eye on me. But they got Ruby." His voice caught on her name and his head dropped into both his hands.

With a gasp, Mary became like a skittle: paper-white and slowly rolling on its base, halfway between standing and falling. Dan and Tessa raced to catch her as Jonathan tried to give the woman reassurance. "She's right here, Mary. She'll be fine." The man's voice was not as solid as it could've been. The shock taking over as the fear made its way out.

We reached the back door and with trembling hands Mary inspected Jet first, then gingerly caressed Ruby's face. The girl's breathing was slow, deep and normal for sleep.

"Any other casualties?" Val had her bossy battle-pants on and assumed leadership. Thank the Light.

"No."

"Yes."

Both Jonathan and Daisy spoke over each other. His face a twisted mask of confusion. Hers defiant. Daisy turned to address Val. "Jonathan. He took off after the abductors. Caught them. Rescued Ruby. But he's... he's..." She stopped and seemed to realise she was hanging onto him. And that whilst he had his arm around her, he wasn't leaning on her. His breathing had returned to normal. For all intents and purposes, he looked fine. She looked at his calm face, turned red, dropped her arm and finished her sentence. "...fine. Thanks for asking."

"Right." Val assessed the group. Then turned to Mary. She gently laid a hand on the woman's bony shoulder and called her name. Then used both hands to physically turn the elderly woman away from the scene of her worst nightmare—something hurting her last remaining kids. In a gentle voice I often forgot she owned, Val spoke. "Mary, do you mind if Tessa and Dan make tea for everyone? Give Jet the night off?" She smiled.

Mary looked at her, took a while to digest her words. Then slowly nodded. Val then put her blade-enthrusted arm around Mary's shoulders and gently led her into the house. But to us she gave her bossy eyes and pointer chin. *Dan, Tessa, kitchen.* Obviously, Kait was taking care of Jet and I was carrying Ruby, so there were no commands at us. I grinned at her discomfort and not being able to boss us around. She shot me with her laser-eyes, but they bounced off me superior armour.

"Stop it, you two. We have bigger issues here," Kait scolded the both of us as we filed into Mary's house. "Raph, Riah, go help."

Good ole Tessa had found some throw rugs from somewhere and she placed one around Mary, another around Ruby. And there were enough for Jet, Jonathan and Daisy. Daisy insisted she didn't need one, but clung to it around her shoulders, nonetheless.

Once we all had cups of soothing tea, the debrief began.

"The fire was a decoy. Just smouldering grass. It was too damp with dew to catch or do real damage. On a drier night, though, we'd have been in trouble." Val looked at Daisy. "Pod's okay." And just to confirm the news there was whining at the back door. The girl shot out of her seat and let her dog into the house. Once they'd each given the other a check, the mutt came over and put his cold, wet nose on Ruby's leg. Though still unconscious, she flinched, giving us all a huge bolster of relief. "What happened up here?"

Jet began. "I was having trouble sleeping, thinking about all the stuff that's been going on round here lately. I wasn't wide awake but stuck in that roll between dozing and dreaming. It took me a while to realise what was happening and that it was actually happening when I felt a bump on my leg and the cloth over my mouth." He stopped and shivered. "I struck out and tried to use some of the moves you guys taught me." His gaze went to Tessa and Dan who were leaning against the sink. "It was enough to scare him off, but I was tangled in my sleeping bag. One took Ruby out and the other one followed. I ripped the zip and flew out of the tent, yelling as I took off after them. One was waiting for me behind the hedge. I didn't think. I just bolted after the figure carrying Ruby. As I ran past, he hit me in the head and my knees gave out." His fingers skimmed over the side of his head.

"I woke because I heard your yelling." Jonathan picked up the telling of the tale. "Ever since they tried to take her from me at the hospital, I guess I've been more alert." He reached out to me, and I handed the girl to her dad. "I figured they'd go down the back of the hill, not wanting to travel through Sanctuary. So, I bolted out the back door and saw him. I literally flew with energy and strength I didn't know I possessed and launched myself at the guy. Tackled him to the ground and pulled Ruby into me like I was back playing rugby, protecting the ball."

He gave a rueful smile as he looked down at his golden-haired girl. She nestled closer into his chest and sighed in her sleep. "The other one came by, so I curled around her and locked in, ready for the raking of the studs that didn't come. The bloke stood over me, heard you lot bashing at Mary's door and took off after his mate." He looked up to me. "Next thing I know, Daisy's sliding into the maul and you're standing over me." He smiled fully then. "And all I could do was cling to Ruby and wonder if I was ever going to get enough air back in my lungs." He laughed then. "Bit out of training, I am."

I clapped him on the back, trying to disguise me tears of relief. Everyone was going to be okay, and they'd saved our little treasure.

"Right." I jumped. I'd almost forgotten Val was still here. "We need to make a plan. And"—she looked to Ruby—"I'm afraid it might be best if she moves down into Sanctuary. Even if we put her tent up down there. In the middle somewhere. What's to say they won't try again? They obviously see the power of that kind of leverage over you, Jonathan. And we are all aware of your leverage over the Community

—here, and wider afield." She squinted her eyes and nodded her head, thinking.

But we all jumped a mile when Dan blurted, out of the blue, stars bursting with excitement in his eyes, "I've got it. I remember. We build a wall."

34

DANIEL: HARD AS NAILS

One could never accuse Val of being slow off the mark. Or of being soft. Especially when it came to defending. Or offending, for that matter. True to her word, the next day she sat us down and served us a dose of reality. Hot off the press.

The enemy, human and Unseen, had crossed a line and it was past time to do something about it. Once again, I was overwhelmingly grateful to be standing beside her and not on the other side of that line. The fierce she was giving off in response to their latest attack made me, for one, feel a bit more secure.

I don't think there had been any real thought or logistics behind the initial layout of Tent Village. When we first arrived, it was a bit of a shanty town with tents roughly placed wherever. When we started planning the layout of the boardwalk and huts, it just seemed natural to set it all up around the food source. And that the Meeting Place would be established in the heart of the Village, which also just happened to be in the cool of the greenery. The noisy workshops were toward one end of the circle—near the entry gate, convenient for deliveries of raw materials not produced on the property. The toilets, laundry, and shower block were at the other end of the oval, backing into the other paddocks, closer to the bore-water pump.

When we'd pegged out the walkways and the potential plots, we offered families a similar location to where they'd initially established their tent, or an opening on another side of the perimeter. I was quietly relieved when a couple of families took Jonathan's advice and shipped out. One, because I was genuinely worried about what was coming. Not for me, but for the babies, and the elderly. I didn't think I was being cocky, but I felt confident the Light would get me and my family through. I was confident we were doing what we could to be as prepared as we could in the Light, in our training and in our study of The Way. But I wasn't so sure about some of the others.

I was also a bit relieved that when folks left and vacated their cabins, we could move others in and shorten the waiting list in the ballot. Every family or person housed, was one step closer to me building my own house for Tessa and me. And one step closer to sealing the deal and starting the rest of our lives together. We were on the final run and, I will admit, any hold-ups to my schedule were becoming more and more tiresome and harder to be polite about.

But I could understand why a general meeting had been called this morning. An invitation had been issued with the expectation that every remaining member of Sanctuary would attend. No excuses. We had completed our sets and an easy session of training earlier this morning, then after showers and a light breakfast, the twins had run around letting people know they were expected front and centre. Tessa, Kait and I set up coffee, tea and juice for everyone in the Meeting Place, and Marcus, Val, Jonathan, Daisy and Travis had a bit of a meeting about how things would run.

Mary had given her blessing but was too distressed from the events last night to offer much input, apart from being wrapped in her blanket, positioned in her chair with her eyes constantly pulled toward Jet who was on guard duty. His focus was locked and loaded on Ruby who was wrapped in her own blanket, laid out on a stretcher in the corner of the Meeting Place. Pod had scrambled up and curled into a ball on the cot next to her. Kait had been monitoring both her and Jet throughout the night. The girl had woken to go to the loo, had a drink, then gone back to sleep. Kait was pretty sure when she woke this morning, she'd be on her way back to normal. Her body just needed time to work its way through whatever they'd used to knock her out.

"Thank you for joining us this morning." Standing to the front of the leadership group, Jonathan kicked off proceedings. He looked frailer and paler than normal, but his voice was strong. "We wanted to fill you in on what happened last night and how we feel best to proceed."

Jonathan then handed over to Val, who gave a brief and factual account of the decoy fire and the attempted abduction of Ruby. Before a riot broke out, she went on to explain that Ruby, Jet and Pod were all well and would recover. "Exhibit A" were present and accounted for. And, since everyone could see them, the hostility drained a notch or two.

She then continued with the plan that had been hatched over coffee, late last night. "We are under attack. It will only get worse. Again, please know that if you feel there is somewhere else you can go to be safe; if you are fearful of what lies ahead; if you have any doubts about your decision to stay and defend your position in the Light: Then you are welcome to leave with our blessing."

Then in true Val style, she sunk the boot in. "Because we can't afford to have any weak links here." She nodded toward Kait, who stood with both twins tucked under her wings.

Kait, grim-faced, nodded back. "We have received Word that things are going to become very difficult… arduous, here. Harder than I think any of us can imagine. If you think you are not going to be able to stand, or if in your heart you don't really want to, we will help you relocate. We have contacts in other cities."

Val half-turned and lifted her chin at Jonathan. She waited for his nod of agreement before continuing. "There is no shame in leaving now. However, know this: if the Light lives in your heart, if your life is in the Light, we will face the same end, no matter where we go, what we do. In the end there is no grey. There is Light and there is Dark. The choice is yours."

She paused.

The Meeting Place froze. Everyone waited. No one breathed. Val scanned the tent. I suspect she was attempting to read everyone in her sphere of vision and put them under the test of her Knowledge. Not many could stand up to her laser-eyes if they had something to hide. I was surprised when she pinned me down as well. "What the frolk, Val?"

"What makes you any different to the others here, Dan? You are about to be married. You and Tessa need to consider what lies ahead for you. And whether you want to stay."

Tessa, who happened to be pinned under one of my arms, bristled. And even though I couldn't see Tessa's face, I suspected Val was getting a good dose of the predator bird right now.

Val smiled and the room sighed. "I would suggest all families go to their cabins, petition the Light, count the cost. Then come and speak with us at the gate when you have made your decision. Yes or no. We want to hear from you before lunch." She eyeballed me and Tessa again. Then led us all in a time of petitioning the Light.

* * *

"How dare she think that we would leave." Tessa was ropeable. We'd gone for a walk through the goat pens and into the cattle paddocks beyond. It was mid-spring and the regular rain had ensured lush, green paddocks, drunk bees and perfect temperature. But I suspected Tessa wasn't taking in the surroundings. Her fists pumped at her sides and her head kept shaking in the motion of "no".

However, once I had got over my own shock, I'd thought Val was onto something. Not that we should leave, but that we should think about it. "She has a point, you know."

Tessa turned on me, her face awash with rage. "How can you say that?"

"She's offering us the opportunity to make the decision for ourselves. We're part of the family, Tessa, but we're not kids." I reached out and stroked her wild hair. "You and me, Tessa. You and I need to decide for ourselves if we stay or if we go. We're part of their family, but we're also our own family now, too. Don't you see?"

She softened into my hand, and I cupped her cheek. She then moved into my embrace, and we just stood like that for ages. In the middle of the paddock, surrounded by cattle softly chewing the cud in the shade of an ancient gum. The peace was almost overwhelming.

Tessa murmured into my chest, "I know if we wanted to, we could go back to the Factory. They'd have us there."

I didn't panic at her words; I locked my knees so they didn't jerk into this sensitive conversation and set off a riot. I was learning to wait. And I was actually proud of the fact that I was able to keep my hand circling her back as she pressed into me. I even managed a reply. "Yes, they would."

"But I don't want to go, Dan. I can't. I mean, I couldn't live with myself if we did."

The relief almost crushed me. "Me neither, Tessa. Me neither."

"What? You couldn't live with me, if I left?"

"What? No. What are you saying?" Panic grabbed my heart and thrust it into my throat. My knees were twitchy and it was all I could do not to say something I knew I would regret or would get me in deeper water. How could she think that? I could hardly breathe or swallow.

She hit me. "Calm down. I was joking."

Bleeding heck. "Oh. I knew that."

"Liar."

True. "I don't want to leave either. How could I set you and me up safe somewhere when our family… Raph and Riah are here… struggling, fighting a battle that we have the skills to help fight. And what's to say life is going to be safer anywhere else in the long run? You heard Val. She's right. This isn't a one-show wonder."

All levity left her posture and she sank back into me. "Then we are agreed. We stay."

"I love you, Tessa."

"And you are my home, Dan."

Thank the Light for that.

It was such a beautiful morning, instead of going straight back to the gate with our response, we took the long way round and picked a path through the paddocks populated with clumps of flowering clover, then came back through the grapevines. New shoots were unfurling and blooms were giving off a faint, sweet scent. Turning left down the driveway that led up to Mary's house, we made our way back into Sanctuary. From this vantage point I could see the almost-full circle of cabins we had made. Here and there, hints of the dark-wood boardwalk connecting everything showed through the gaps. There was a sea of green in the centre of the circle and right at the heart was the Meeting Place.

I was stopped in my tracks by a wall of… pride? A sense of accomplishment? Gratification? Gratitude. That I was permitted and equipped to be part of something so amazing. Something that had improved people's lives. I'd helped make a difference. We had literally lifted people off the ground and put them in more permanent, comfortable homes. Given them a sense of stability, ownership and place. They weren't dregs, discarded or forgotten. We were a community of citizens who not only supported ourselves, we provided for and positively impacted the environment and people around us. And the Light had brought us here to not only help equip, but to help defend and fight for them—for who we were and who we served.

A fire started burning deep inside me. Not an inferno, but a slow boil. I think Raph would call it a simmer. Maybe because of all of that, or maybe because I had had a vision to build and help the families here, a sense of belonging and purpose rocked me to my core. And it made me pretty mad that someone wanted to harm our home. That they were doing it because we wouldn't bend the knee to some self-inflated, self-obsessed, self-appointed god made me downright angry.

By the time we made it to the gate, I was fairly riled and ready for a fight. Not with the gatekeepers, but with the world that wanted us to turn away from the Light. So, I let Tessa speak. I let her know by squeezing her shoulder that was under my left arm and nudging her forward to face the five. "Where's Kait?" Tessa looked around.

Val responded, "She and the twins are helping put together a combined lunch. We were just waiting for you two to come in with your answer." Once again, the woman stunned me with her gentle-warm. I should not have been shocked. I had been a recipient of it on many an occasion. But I had been on the receiving end of the hard nails more often.

Tessa came back with her classic, "Oh." When I realised that was all she was going to say and I suspected she was currently travelling through some rabbit warren of her own making, I nudged her again. She turned to me, *what?*

Tell them our answer.

"Oh, yeah." She smiled at me, then turned to the group. "We're staying. But you knew that already. Didn't you?"

This time it was Daisy who spoke. "I thought you might, but when you took so long to come in..."

"Oh. Sorry, we thought we had till lunch so we went for a walk. It's so beautiful here."

"Bleeding heck, Tessa. You coulda come and told us, then gone for a walk."

"Marcus." I couldn't hold in my shock. "Did you really think we wouldn't stay?"

He turned red and looked at the ground. "No." Val laid a hand on his arm. There was more to this, obviously, but now wasn't the time to push.

Tessa moved us into safer territory. "Is anyone else leaving?"

"Yes. Just the one family. Phil and Kerry are taking their kids." Jonathan gave the good news. Not good news that they were leaving, but... Actually, yes it was. I hated to think of inexperienced kids in a battle. I was glad they would be safe somewhere else. And also, that was one cabin left to build. Ours.

I didn't even think. I just grabbed Tessa from behind, pulled her in and kissed the top of her head. Joy instantly deleted all previous anger and indignation. Relief washed through me as I exhaled into her hair. "Not long now."

Marcus understood. "We'll start the build tomorrow, son."

"All hands on deck." This from the old guy, Travis.

I gave Tessa an extra squeeze and gave my thanks to all of them. Feeling ten-foot tall and bulletproof, I took my life into my hands and entered the lion's den; I offered to help Val up from her chair and assist her, walking to the Meeting Place for lunch. My heart burst with warmth when she let me. She didn't really need my help. But leaned on me nonetheless. Marcus walked in front of us with Tessa wrapped under one of his arms. How could I possibly even think of leaving the family the Light had given me.

But all cosy thoughts flew out of my head when I heard screaming coming from the veggie patch.

35

RAPHAEL: SNAKES

Tiger hissed and spat, and Ruby screamed. I froze and looked up to see a snake. A giant, black, slithering snake winding its way through our veggie patch. Ruby had awoken a while ago but was still recovering from her horrible night. She had been sitting in the garden keeping me company whilst I worked and waited for people to make their minds up if they were staying or not. Tiger had been playing under the leaves, batting us with his paws when we came near his ever-moving hideout. But now his hair stood on end, his back arched, and he growled intermittently between fizzing hatred at the huge, unnaturally large creature. But then like a bullet he flew up a trellis and put as much distance as he could between him and the ground.

Screams and yells rose from all around me. But no one came to help us. It seemed everyone was too busy defending themselves against other creatures invading our home. I pushed Ruby up onto the garden bed behind me and stood between the growing, swelling snake and her. She was still weak from the poison in her system. I knew it was the right thing to do but I was very, very scared. The snake stopped two metres in front of me. Its body was now as thick as mine and, when it raised its head and drew it back, its black eyes looked directly into mine. All the while, its tongue flicked and licked the air, smelling my fear.

After my first battle in Sodom, I was feeling ashamed and weak for freezing in the midst of the fight. I had not only not helped my family who were under attack, my inactions had made matters worse. In the aftermath, the Light came to me and helped me see my future and intensified my gift of healing. From that day, I made a promise to the Light that I would not be responsible for taking the life of anyone or anything—seen or unseen. I would defend myself and others, but no more. As a sign of confirmation of my vow, the Light had shattered my blade. I was not defenceless—on the contrary, the power the Light had infused into my hands caused great pain and suffering to the enemy. But today, for the first time in three years, I drew my broken sword because I was confident I could not lay my hands on this enemy before it hurt me.

Please help. Please help. Please help.

I tried to breathe through my fear. I tried to remember my training. I tried to focus on the Light.

Its neck kept extending and its head kept rising and rising until I was looking up into its opened jaws. Its head swayed from side to side, never releasing my gaze. My shaking increased and my palms were slick with sweat. Rivers ran into my eyes. I did not dare to wipe them on my shoulder or lose eye contact for a moment.

Please help. Please help. Please help.

Then everything happened at once. It lunged. I stabbed. Ruby screamed.

As the jagged edge of my sword made contact with its neck, its progress stopped but it hissed and spat venom in my face. I dropped to the ground and tried not to rub my eyes. They burned but I did not think rubbing them would be a good thing to do.

I could not think of much else because my ears were filled with Ruby's screams. But then, like someone pressed mute, it stopped. Then pounding feet raced toward us. They kept time with my heart. Rough hands shook my shoulders. "Sweetheart, what happened?" Kait gently lifted me.

"My eyes. The snake spat in my eyes."

Big, solid hands picked me up and carried me at a run to a tap. I was held sideways, and cool water gushed across my face. It still burned but it was a relief.

"Darling boy. You need to try to open your eyes for me so we can flush everything out. Can you do that sweetheart? Try to blink your eyes… open and closed, under the water." Kait stroked my head while Marcus held me.

I tried to be brave. I tried not to whimper. But I was also trying to hold back the red haze that had been swamping me since I first saw the snake. Tremors shook my body; I could not get rid of the image of the huge black snake weaving its massive head above me.

A small hand took mine and squeezed it twice. I tried to breathe deeply, but water gushed into my mouth and up my nose, almost choking me. Marcus sat me up, bent me over, and gently patted me on the back as I tried once again to breathe and calm down.

Riah still held my hand, and I knew she would be lending me her Badge. I just had to open the doors and let the Peace flood in. But the red haze kept fighting me, surrounding me in a wall, keeping her out. The Dragon was trying to steal me away. And a steady, all-consuming shaking wracked my body.

A warm, calloused hand stroked my cheek. I sensed a body in front of me. Val. "Hey, Raph. You did really well. You defeated the snake"—I could hear the truth in her voice—"and you didn't kill it. You have kept your vow. You put yourself between Ruby and the enemy, you were very brave. Receive the Light's peace Riah is sending you." Her voice was melodic, and her calming cadence broke the haze's back. It thinned enough for Riah to get through. Gentle blue waves ebbed and flowed and washed the remnants away. My eyes still stung but as my body relaxed back into Marcus's embrace, Kait finished cleaning my face. After my eyes were flushed thoroughly, a cool, soothing balm was slathered on my burnt skin and eyelids, then they were bandaged.

"Hey, mate, found this little guy and he's a bit upset. Reckon you could help him out a bit?" Someone wrapped me in a blanket and Dan laid a soft ball of fur with sixteen needle claws into my hands. I clutched Tiger to my chest and did my best to soothe him until he purred, which helped soothe me.

36

DANIEL: INTERESTING TIMES

"Regardless of shape or size, you all have a shield." Val began her instruction in the Meeting Place, addressing those of us who had decided to stay.

We had taken the afternoon to see to the kids; Kait treated them and the rest of us generally made a nuisance of ourselves getting underfoot trying to comfort them. After lunch, we helped the last family who had decided to leave to pack and organise places to go. Before they departed, Jonathan petitioned the Light for a blessing on them, their family and their new home.

Now, as evening made its way in, Val held centrestage. "Not all of us carry it on us all the time, but we all have one." She looked around at the remaining members of Sanctuary. Those who had decided they were here for the whole nine yards. The bond of camaraderie was ridiculously strong; I could feel my connection with every person who had decided to stay and fight for our right to live in peace in the Light.

Val brought her shield into sight and held it in front of her so we could all see it. Not surprisingly, it was small and could have fit in a Laodicean lady's carry-all... even with the token dog in there as well. I couldn't ever imagine her using it... the shield, that is. Or the carry-all for that matter. It would get in the way of her swords and knives.

Val was definitely an ambidextrous kind of gal when it came to fighting.

But sit me down and shut me up if she didn't just make that thing grow. It swelled to become about the width of a sheet of roofing iron, and about a metre or so taller than her. We could see through its indigo light, so she just kept talking and explaining. "I will show you all how to increase the size of your shield." She lifted her arms with a grimace and thrust that thing into the earth. After a moment's pause, she carefully rolled her shoulders and limped around to stand beside it. "Don't panic, you will still have access to your shield." In the blink of an eye, she brought her small, round shield back into existence whilst her indigo, roofing-iron shield stood in place behind her.

"Each of us will plant our shields behind our houses and link them up. Everyone will be responsible for maintaining the strength and vibrancy of their part of the wall, every moment of every day." There was an audible gulp, which Val rode roughshod right over the top of. "And to assist you we will be setting up a new schedule for life here at Sanctuary. Until the heat passes. Hear me, brothers and sisters. You have each made a commitment to stand apart from the world so as to live in the Light. He has seen you and cherishes every one of you. You have counted the cost and have weighed Him to be of greater value than all the world has to offer.

"But do not be mistaken; the toll will be great. We will sustain loss and injury. Of this we can be sure. Things will only get worse and harder from this time on. But He is the Light of our lives and love of our hearts, He will guide, protect and strengthen us in the battle. May our blades be sharp, our armour thick and our wills aligned with His."

Like an exclamation mark to her speech, a burst of light exploded like a spear from heaven and smashed into Val, piercing her whole body. An almighty cry burst from her lungs and brought us all to our feet. The Light pulsing into her was too strong to be contained by her mortal body. A bright aura of incandescent light lit her up from the inside out, surrounding her with a blinding halo. Her body formed a rigid cross. With her head thrown back and her arms thrust wide, her mouth was open, continuing her scream in silence. As one, each of her knives dropped to the ground just before Val collapsed in a heap among them.

Our family had seen this before and raced to pull her to her feet and wrap her in a scrum. There were tears and emotional murmurings, there was indiscriminate hugging and backslapping, and there was a truckload of joy. Relief. Not just for Val: I know I harboured my fair share. She was free. She could move. She could fight. We were going to be okay.

But then an ice bucket of reality hit. The last time I had seen this happen was just before the skrat came to town in Sodom. I started frantically scanning the shadows as they crept in past the edges of the Meeting Place. "Are they coming? Now? Are they on their way?"

At my words, an invisible cold hand of fear spread like mist throughout the tent. Unified by fear, everyone shuffled closer to the centre and turned to attempt to see into the darkness. As much as I tried to strain my ears to hear, the only sound I could make out was the pumping of my blood, the croaking of frogs and the song of cicadas. I loosened my shoulders, then, without looking, took Tessa's hand.

"Relax everyone." I don't think I had ever been so grateful to hear the soothing alto of Kait's voice. "We have time. The Light has blessed us with the gift of Val's help in preparation for the battle, which will not happen tonight." Like steam escaping from an overheated radiator, tension fled, until she spoke again. "But we cannot drop our guard completely. Stay vigilant. Stay focused on the Light, watch for the enemy's attempt to break in, and watch each other's backs. Tonight, we build our wall and start our watch."

"Okay, so… business as usual?" My quip did the job and lightened the mood.

By this time, Riah had raced around and retrieved all of Val's blades with the help of Jayne, Lucy and Eddie, some of the kids she'd been training. They stood holding them and handing them to her one by one as Val inserted them into the many… many sheaths all over her armour. Kait came in and gave her sister a last, fierce embrace, brushed her hands over Val's cheeks to clear the remaining tears, then pulled her down and kissed her forehead. And Val let her.

After allowing Val her moment of shared celebration, Jonathan came forward, side-stepped Val's wall-shield, smiled at her then took the lead. "Every morning, for our own good and security, we will start the day with sets led by Marcus. After breakfast we will cycle through chores and battle training led by Val, Marcus, Kait, Dan, Tessa, Sariah and Raphael—when he is back to health. This is mandatory. Everyone here will do battle training, both for the Unseen and the Seen." Another audible gulp did the rounds of the tent. "We will continue with our routine of journeying in The Way, after lunch each day." The man still looked exhausted, but he smiled at his flock, his eyes alive and energised with an internal spark.

"Things are going to be tough. We are now at war. But we are in the Light. We are His people, and He will protect us. Have faith and continue to trust in Him. He is with us. Can you feel that? His presence is so strong, His love for us is palpable. People… family… we are blessed to live in interesting times."

37

RAPHAEL: SOUL POISON

"Get out. I do not want *you* here. Leave me alone." Ruby was inconsolable. Well, when it came to Daisy, that was.

Every time Daisy tried to visit, Ruby screamed and threw an epic tantrum. I did not understand. I knew Ruby loved Daisy. Thankfully, she did not have a problem with her dad being here. He was here as much as he could be. Holding her hand, helping to care for her, to dim her constant moaning.

We had been put into the same cabin so Kait could keep an eye on us. My eyes still burned under the bandages, but I had not been bitten like Ruby had. Whilst I had been held captive, focusing on the snake in front of us, I had not seen what was coming up from behind. Both snakes had attacked at the same time. But I had had a sword—even though it was broken—to defend myself. Ruby had nothing.

It was not her fault. She was only seven. I am sure she knew the Light and loved him, but was it just that she had not really grown into her armour yet? And now she spent most of the day lying in bed, groaning. Very loudly. I understood she was in pain. She could not eat or drink much at all. Every time she tried, she was sick. Kait made her special ice blocks from fruit juice and salts. She was so unwell, she did not mind that she was inside a cabin, all day, every day. We even had a small tremor yesterday and she did not notice. But when she was not asleep, Ruby made a lot of noise, incessant and exhausting. Kait had tried to move me out because I could not sleep or rest. I was almost in tears from my own pain and lack of sleep. But when Kait went to move me into another cabin, Ruby screamed and fought everyone. She would not settle and was uncontrollable until I came back. It was the same reaction she had when Daisy came in to visit. It was so bad, it had been decided I had to stay and Daisy had to go.

I still could not see, but I could hear the sadness in Daisy's voice. I think because my eyes were covered, people thought I could not hear. They talked in front of me, or just outside the door. And it seemed that this latest attack, straight after the attempt to abduct Ruby, had torn our community in two. Throughout our home there was murmuring and gossiping, and it made my heart sad. Could they not see what the Dark was doing?

"What is wrong with her, Kait?" Jonathan's voice was heavy with distress.

"I don't know. I have tried everything. She has no marks on her, she doesn't have a temperature. She just can't eat or drink. And she's obviously in pain. I just don't know why or what. But I have an idea I'd like to run past you. After we see to Raph, I'd like your help." Kait's voice disappeared down the boardwalk, taking Jonathan with her.

* * *

IT WAS the third day since the attack. Thankfully, Ruby had finally exhausted herself into a stupor.

Kait was back and I could hear her quietly moving around the cabin, preparing for my release. Finally, it was time for the bandages to come off and for me to get back outside, back to my life in the garden and caring for Tiger.

She quietly finished preparing for the unveiling as new footsteps scuffed the wooden floor. My bed dipped several times. Chair legs protested as they were pulled up close. The door latch fell into place. A rattle and slide, rattle slide, rattle slide told me the blinds were shut.

A small body I had known my whole life climbed over the person sitting on my right and squeezed between my back and the wall. A firm hand flicked my legs to move them aside, then another body sat on my left. A large, firm hand gripped my knee. Tiger sat in my lap, purring under my constant stroking.

My whole family were here for the unveiling. Everyone was in place.

Kait's hands gently brushed my hair back before she peeled the tape and started unwrapping the bandage. Slowly, red light broke through my eyelids. "Gently does it, sweetheart. Keep your fingers on the pads and keep your eyes shut for a while." Riah reached around and took Tiger so I could follow Kait's instructions. Kait stepped away and I listened as she moved things around on the nearby bench. Everyone was silent. Thankfully, so too was Ruby from the bed on the other side of the room. By the sound of her breathing, she was still asleep.

Kait returned and squatted down in front of me—I could feel her breath on my face. "Okay, darling, very gently." She pulled one hand away and peeled back the pad over one eye, then the other. "When you're ready, slowly open your eyes."

The room held its breath.

The red light through my lids burst into bright, tear-inducing light in the dim room. I looked around into all of their wavering faces. Water cascading from my overwhelmed eyes made it hard to see.

"Well? Do we need to get you a seeing eye dog to go with your crazy-butt cat?" I grinned at Marcus as Kait slapped his shoulder.

"Sweetheart? Can you see?"

I looked to Marcus and shook my head, then looked to Kait and nodded.

"What? What does that mean?" Marcus was nearly jumping out of his skin.

"Shhh, don't wake Ruby?" It was a plea on the verge of tears. Kait and I were in agreement.

"No, I do not need a dog, and yes, I can see. Of course, I can see. Why did you think I could not s—"

Everyone exhaled at once and I fell under a forest of hugs. No one had told me my eyesight was in danger. The thought made me ill. I was glad when Val pulled everyone's attention away from me. That I could have been blind was going to take some time to come to terms with.

"Right." Val's hushed but authoritative tone put everyone on guard. "Now it's Ruby's turn. Kait, glasses. Jonathan?" Kait handed me a pair of sunglasses before Jonathan opened the door and came in. "It's time we dealt with this."

From Ruby's bed, a snarling, gravelly voice I did not recognise sent shivers down my spine. "I would not do that if I were you."

My family and Jonathan circled Ruby's bed.

The snarl raised to a shriek. "I would not do that if I were you." Ruby's face twisted into a mask of fury.

"Dan, Tessa, get ready." Val gave her covert orders, nodded to Jonathan, then turned back to Ruby. Everybody else laid their hands on Ruby's legs or arms, in some way making contact with her. Except me. I sat on my bed, agog, as they all dropped their heads and closed their eyes. Except Tessa and Dan. They kept their eyes open and stood in the doorway.

Jonathan took over. "By the power of the Light, I command you to leave my daughter and not return. She is a child of the Light and you have no dominion here. I name you and expel you from my daughter never to return. Go back to those who sent you. Lord of Light, I ask that you fill your daughter, Ruby, with your Light and encase her inside and out."

Even with sunglasses on, I saw Ruby's little body give a shake. A black, vaporous snake lifted from her body and fled from the room.

Dan and Tessa bolted out the door, following its lead. I couldn't see anything after that as the light from the outside burst into my eyes, blinding me for real.

"The hills to the west," Dan called back through the door after a short minute.

"Right. Let's see if February and October can get a drone up there to check it out."

* * *

I HAD ALWAYS loved music evenings. Tonight, I loved it even more because of the dim glow—I was still adjusting to the light—but also because I felt I could play my drum and sing, and people were not looking at me. I had been told I would have a few new scars. These ones, on my face. Dan said they would match the ones on my legs and hands. "But not to worry, chicks dig scars, hey, Tessa?" She had scoffed, then kissed his cheek.

In the quiet, everyone's attention was back on the gentle music Dan and Riah led us in. The darkness gave me freedom to play and sing invisibly. The day's discovery governed the tone of the night. There was a group of people petitioning the Dark against us. And despite all the things we had survived, this knowledge made me feel small.

I knew we were at war. Getting hurt in the fallout was nothing new. But in the past, whilst other people had made our lives difficult and had been used by the Dark to stop us or hurt us, they had never actually petitioned the Dark against us… that I knew of. February and October's drone had discovered evidence of a clearing and activity in the hills west of us.

Val, Jonathan, Daisy, Marcus and Dan drove over and searched the area on foot and found the place had been deserted quickly. Val said, when Jonathan refuted the curse that had been cast at us, it returned to those who sent it. It would have given them a fright and maybe done some damage. This also made me sad. I did not have a problem fighting the Dark, or defending myself against people, but I did not like the thought of attacking or hurting people. But then I thought of what they had done to Ruby, and I was angry. And confused. But everyone else seemed disheartened.

The sombre mood in the Meeting Place led us all to finish early. People drifted off to bed, but Daisy came and sat next to Jonathan, who was playing a beautiful acoustic bass guitar alongside Dan and Riah. Ruby climbed into Daisy's lap a totally different person. Before, she was a hissing, spitting cat when Daisy came round; now she was almost purring in her lap with no memory of what had passed just days before.

Daisy stroked Ruby's hair, as she spoke to the gathering in general. "Well, that was a successful attack."

I put down my drum and picked up Tiger who had been chewing my boot laces. "What happened to Ruby? And why did it not happen to anyone else? Why did it not bite me?"

Jonathan answered my questions. "The Dark knows our weaknesses and that's where he will strike. He knows how valuable our children are and how much we love them. So, he will use them as pawns in the war. We would do anything to protect them."

"Well, we all know that isn't true." A woman came to a stop at the edge of our group, dragging two suitcases on wheels. She planted them like an exclamation mark when she stopped.

I think Jonathan must have been very tired and worried, because it was the first time I heard tension in his voice. "I have been trying to tell you for some time, Carol, we are at war. Can't you understand? This is serious."

"But the children? The children are in danger. How can you stay here and endanger your child?"

"What part of war are children exempt from? What enemy gives a free pass to innocents, or the elderly, or the frail, or the sick? On the contrary, the enemy will target them because he knows they are our weakness. They hold the key. Every day that we front up to battle, we have to lay everything down… everything… before the Light and trust that He will protect them, watch over them."

"Well He did a great job with your family"—she paused for a beat and let that barb sink deep—"and a right royal job looking after these two." She flicked her eyes between Ruby and me. "I would have thought you'd have been a bit more careful with your only remaining child. Especially after the attempt on her life."

Oh dear, oh dear, oh dear. Please do something.

Silence screamed like a death knell.

All the oxygen was sucked from the air in an instant. In its place was ice.

In a low tone I could barely hear, Jonathan responded. "As always, you are free to take your children and leave. I believe there are still safe havens in neighbouring cities. I don't know how long that will be the case. But you are free to go at any time."

Time stood on a fulcrum, balanced perfectly on the head of a pin. Frozen. Then it tipped as Carol responded. "Don't worry, I'm not staying in a place where our supposed leaders are happy to put their children in danger. Because I will not." She looked around at my family in disgust, her eyes finally resting on Kait and Marcus. "And you. I've seen the videos on the web, I've seen the news footage. How irresponsible"—this one word carried an ocean of loathing—"to let your children go into battle the way you did. No wonder the Light has not let you have children of your own. Surely that was warning enough, but to steal street urchins? And endanger them? Just because they don't have real parents, doesn't mean the Light loves them any less. You are responsible. You need to think of them first. You don't deserve children."

Jonathan's face went red. Kait went white. But Marcus turned purple.

Her words were so vile and vicious, it could not be normal. Maybe it was like Ruby with Daisy? I thought it was best to check. "Did you get bitten by a snake too?"

Carol looked at me, eyes wide and her brow crinkling into her fringe. "What?"

"You are speaking to your friends and people you love like Ruby spoke to Daisy."

Val chuckled. "No mate." She then stood to face Carol.

But before she could speak, Carol fired her venom at Val. "And you are no better. Going out of your way to be obnoxious… a stench in the nose of the Community. Look at you!" Carol's eyes accused every inch of Val as she stood in front of her. "You dress and act like a man—it's abnormal. You encourage others to be antagonistic and belligerent. Dennis is right, we are supposed to be messengers of peace, but you? You are a warmongering battle-whore who wouldn't know the meaning of grace or love if you tripped over them."

The atmosphere dropped from cool to arctic in a fraction of a second. I could not breathe… or move… or think. All I was aware of was the stand-off between these two women: Val's chest rising and falling indicating her slow, deep breathing, in contrast to the shaking of Carol's rage.

Then out of the void, Val spoke. "It is healthy to be scared, it shows you are neither an idiot nor ignorant. We are facing difficult trials. Every day, we need to make a decision whether we stand in and for the Light. Or if we fade into the shadows. But do not let your fear be a weapon *for* the enemy. If you have made the choice to leave, then do so. If you want to stay and fight, then do so. But do not"—at this point thunder from heaven filled Val's words—"hide behind empty excuses and baseless insults. Have the backbone and integrity to own and confess *your* truth and back it up with actions." She looked Carol in the eye with her laser beams and did not snarl, but I think it was clear Val was not a fan of what the woman had said to and about her family.

Without responding, Carol turned to her two sons, Craig and Rory, who stood in the shadows. "Come on boys, we're going." She picked up the bags at her feet and started to walk away. But was pulled up short when Craig didn't move.

"I'm not going, Mum. My place is here. And I choose to stay. To keep working. And to fight." His eyes flicked first to Marcus, then to the corner of the tent where a small crowd was building in response to Carol's hostility. He nodded once then looked back at his mum.

"I beg your pardon, young man. You are coming with me. This instant."

Rory stood between his hero and his mum, his head turning from one to the other. He had always tried to mimic his big brother, Craig, but now he looked as frail as Tiger—small, helpless and lost.

Craig didn't respond. But he didn't move either. Carol narrowed her eyes and pursed her lips. I guessed she knew how stubborn her son could be; it was genetic. Craig was seventeen and I think that maybe his mum could not tell him what to do anymore, because with one more accusatory glance at Val, Marcus and Jonathan, Carol grabbed Rory's hand and stormed off.

I had never really liked Rory. From that very first day he joined us for training, he was the rooster, always challenging me and everything I said. But right now I felt sorry for him and there was nothing I could do to help.

But You can. Please make them be okay. Watch over them.

"Bit more room at your place now, Craig?" Even though it sounded like an attempt at lightening the mood, Dan was also obviously upset. Probably just as well Carol decided to leave.

38

ANONYMOUS: SLUR CAMPAIGN

Dear Brothers and Sisters,

I debated long and hard as to whether to send this letter. I do not in any way wish to discourage you or been seen to feed and power the rumour mill. But the slur campaign against our esteemed leader, Head Shepherd and Overseer, Jonathan, has begun. I do not wish to go into the details but suffice it to say his integrity has been brought into question.

The few of us who are still able to quietly and subtly influence whilst remaining under the radar will do what we can to refute the slander. Not for a moment do we believe any of the lies. But be aware you may expect visitors and reporters to come to Sanctuary to "hear your side of the story".

May the Light give you wisdom, guide, encourage and sustain you.

Fight the good fight and stay strong in the Light,

Anonymous

PS: Oh, please also find our early Lightmas gift for you to use as you need.

39

JONATHAN: WEARING AWAY

The building of the wall only seemed to increase the attack. Well, from the outside, that was. The demonic had, largely, been evicted from within. But now, the gathering of demons around the perimeter of Sanctuary was slowly growing in size and hostility. We were now facing a sustained attack on every side. Even though we had our shields up, and we worked at maintaining our armour at full force, still the enemy's lies trickled in like an icy breeze, seeping through the doorjambs in a constant stream of insults. "You call this a wall? A mouse could climb it and bring the whole thing down." "Pathetic excuse for a shield. It has gaps all over."

The ongoing put downs. "Your garden can't support you all and your precious supplies will dwindle. You are going to starve in there. All because you choose to cling to the Light. And where is He? How is He helping?" "You cannot possibly stand. The only question is: how many will survive and what pitiful state will you be in when you surrender?"

But perhaps the worst of all was the persistent undermining. "Did you know Phil isn't pulling his weight? Too busy watching out for his daughter, Jayne. He's having second thoughts. Thinking about how he should get her out of here." "Did you see Miriam and Indrila whispering? They're planning on leaving. Caspian is almost convinced. Of course, Cyan has just turned one. They're going to run, and reveal everything to the Council." "Everyone is tiring of you as a leader. You're still weak and constantly tied down with fatigue. You need more daily naps than Cyan. How can you fight? What are you going to do when the skrat hits the fan? Call timeout so you can have a little lie down? People here thought they were prepared to follow you into hell, but apparently now they're here, they've changed their minds. They don't love you, they resent you. They are beginning to hate you. They are planning a mutiny." "They're coming for you. There's a target on your head and the Gerent, led by the High Council, is gunning for you. You have enemies both sides of this pathetic wall." "Ruby will be hurt... more hurt than she already has been, in all of this. You failed Laura and the boys, but that was in The Quake, which you had no control over. But this is different. You are intentionally allowing her to be hurt, to be used as a weapon against you. You are arrogant to think you can lead this group and make it out the other side."

Funnily enough, I no longer wavered or came close to blacking out when the memories of Laura and the boys were provoked. I hadn't stopped missing them. Or grieving for them. Or hurting like my soul had been ripped in two. But I no longer ran to the embrace of the abyss. I had come to accept that the Light was offering me a choice: an ultimatum. "Accept Me and My way—regardless of whether you understand, like or approve of it—or leave."

There was only one choice in all that confronted me. Stay or go? Light or Dark?

There was nothing else. No negotiating terms of agreement. No bending of the rules. No loopholes in the contract. Living in the Light was a package deal. He'd never promised easy, safe or pain-free. He'd only ever guaranteed relationship, protection, provision, purpose and eternity. But it was so easy when things were good. Maybe too easy. I had been lured by a false sense of... not luxury or prosperity, but perhaps... safety? I had not accepted that war with the world was a matter of life and death. That it was costly. And the Light was challenging me to count that cost. Light or Dark? Stay or go?

I was being forced to accept that the Light could have saved Laura and the boys. But he didn't. He saved me and Ruby. He could have made me whole again after my injuries. Physically, I was. But I still lived under the permanent chains of fatigue—never-ending, soul-crushing fatigue. But always there was a bigger picture. Regardless of the decisions I made day in and day out, I had no control over the long game. I wasn't able to save anyone. Not even myself, without His help. Could I keep Ruby safe here? No. Could I keep Ruby safe anywhere? No. But He could. So, for me and my family the only choice was to stay in the Light, at His mercy, in His purpose for me.

Therefore, with a renewed effort I did my rounds of Sanctuary, touching base with all who remained. Encouraging, shoring up the gaps, challenging others with the same knowledge He'd given me. Offering them the same choice He'd given me: Stay or go? Light or Dark?

Ruby's call interrupted my musings in the garden as I worked alongside the others, weeding and feeding our main food source. "Daddy, Daddy, a new letter has arrived." She barrelled into me with Raph hot on her heels.

Trying to brush the dirt off my hands before muddying the crisp, clean paper Ruby was attempting to thrust into my face, I stood and created a bit of distance. To say we were encouraged by the mail we'd been receiving from "Anonymous" was an understatement. I didn't blame them for hiding, but I was grateful for their support and information. However, one quick glance at this letter and I knew it was trouble.

I gave my daughter a quick kiss and thanked her and Raph—our self-designated mail sorters and deliverers—for being so quick off the mark to get the mail out to everyone as soon as it arrived after their "school" with Mr Berry and Kait.

But then my heart shrank a bit at the contents. It was from the Gerent's office in Ephesus, informing me he was sending an intermediary who would like to meet with me in Laodicea. Interesting.

I didn't think for one moment it was for mutual gratification and sharing of terms. In fact, I suspected he wanted to remove me from my support base and isolate me from Sanctuary. In a way, I was honoured he saw me as that much of a threat. But was I being arrogant in my assumptions? Maybe I wasn't a threat; perhaps I was more of a gnat they wanted to annihilate. Which they could eradicate so easily. And not just me, but my community… my people.

Ruby watched me read the letter, as did the others around me, waiting to see what Anonymous had to say today. I slipped the letter into my back pocket and with my hand on Ruby's shoulder informed them all. "Not from Anonymous today, just a bit of junk mail." I wasn't fooling anyone who'd seen the quality of the paper. But they all understood the message. *Not open for discussion here and now.*

What to do? Should I meet with them or keep my distance? Was it a trap or a real opportunity to explain our situation and belie their fears?

I know You are the answer and know the path I should follow. I know with everything in me that You have our best interests at heart, but I don't know what to do. What's best for Sanctuary? What's best for Ruby? Staying here, staying quiet… is it the right thing? Will I ever be able to defend myself against the claims of fraud, of marital infidelity, of scandal and anything else they can come up with?

You know my heart. You know the truth. Can't You vindicate me in front of them, so people know it's all lies and slander? I am not a bad shepherd. I love Your people as if they were my own. I loved my wife—and only my wife —for our whole marriage. Every day the lies go unanswered, are they going deeper? Do people believe the slander? Just show me what to do. Where to go? And how to get there.

"Come on Rube—"

Raph's attempt to move Ruby on to deliver the rest of the mail was cut off when a tremor shook the ground. Panic washed through Sanctuary like an electric charge. We were all tangled in a net of fight or flight. But freeze won out. "It's okay, Ruby." I attempted to calm my daughter. Her skin was glistening white, and her eyes were buckets of fear darting every which way. "Remember what to do? Let's count." I petitioned the Light that she wouldn't hear the fear in my voice over the rumble of the earth. "One… two… three… four… five."

With her arms spread wide and her legs bent she looked like she could be riding a surfboard. I continued the drill. "Deep breathing, one… two… three… four… five…"

By this stage, the electrical current had eased to a tingling. In my periphery I noted some of my fellow workers were moving about again after the cessation of the earth's grumble. But Ruby wasn't ready yet. So, I squatted in front of her. "It's stopped, my darling. How about we count to five again just to be sure."

Her darting eyes, still huge and unseeing, came to land on me. I gently took one of her hands and I started counting again. Each time to five, and then wait, listen, assess. Five deep breaths, wait, listen, assess. By our fourth time through the cycle, her little body drew in a full breath and exhaled the tension. Her shoulders dropped from next to her ears and tears welled in her eyes. "It's okay, my darling. We're all okay. Would you and Raph like to come with me and check in with everyone and make sure it's all okay for them too?"

I had learned early on, Ruby couldn't settle after a tremor unless she could see for herself that there had been no injuries or damage. We even had to check on the goats, cattle, chickens, bees and Tiger, but it was worth it to give her peace of mind. And to be perfectly honest, it helped me too. She nodded and, with her free hand in Raph's, we started out on our rounds, cabin by cabin.

By the time we had made full circle, Ruby was almost back to normal and starting to think about afternoon tea, which was perfect because we pulled up to Kait and Marcus's new home. They had almost finished the process of cleaning out and moving into Phil and Kerry's old cabin. They had invited Raph to move in with them, but he had chosen to stay with Dan until Dan moved in with Tessa. What had seemed like utter chaos at the time had settled into a balanced new normal. Accommodation-wise, anyway. The only cabin left to be finished was Dan and Tessa's. Their impending wedding was a spark of light in a season of trial.

"Kait-a-lyn, are you okay? Is your cabin okay? Were you hurt?" Ruby went through her litany but all the while her eyes were tracking

Sariah as she was putting food out on the table outside the cabin she shared with Val and Tessa.

Kait didn't answer with words straight away. Instead, she knelt down and embraced my daughter, then leaned back and stroked her cheek. "You, dear girl, are a beautiful soul whose richness goes far beyond your name's sake. Thank you for asking. We are all well."

Raph's twin was still an enigma to me, but she too came over and hugged Ruby, then led her away to feed her. Knowing Ruby was in safe hands and her mind was at ease, I was about to head out to see about getting myself something to eat when Kait stood and placed a hand on my arm. She didn't say a thing for a while, she just looked into my soul and read my deepest fears.

Slowly she nodded her head and said, "I see an image of a tree, standing firm, standing strong. Its branches are wide and its roots are deep"—her alto voice deepened with the Word—"tapping into the bottomless pool of refreshing, sustaining water. Across the land a savage, dry wind is whipping the moisture and life out of everything in its path. Behind it is death and devastation. But the tree with deep roots stands tall, bearing fruit, a sentinel… a watchman guarding the flock, providing shade and revealing the way and the door to the source of life."

A smile that reminded me of sunshine, laughter and joy broke across Kait's face. "Does that help?"

I chuckled. "Maybe. I'll have to think about it. But thank you."

"Don't thank me, I'm just the messenger. Now, come join us for afternoon tea before Ruby eats it all."

Kait linked her arm through mine and led me to their picnic table, where I lost all sense of time and my surroundings as I basked in the image she had given me.

40

CONTESSA: THIS IS IT

This was it.

I was crazy excited.

And a bit scared.

But mainly excited.

Once again, we were heading back to Laodicea. All of us. Dan had pretty much finished our cabin, and we had set a date to get married.

One week. In one week, we would get married. So, Dan, Val and Marcus were dropping Kait, me and the twins at the Factory for seven days to get prepared. Raph was going to bake up a storm with Aiko and Vashti. Sariah still insisted she was on chore duty—anything that needed doing, she would do it. I know, crazy. Kait wanted to help me get ready. The others also wanted to come for the day to hang out with everyone and catch up. But they weren't staying. Marcus and Val, without her blades—I was still getting used to it, it made me so very happy—were going to help Dan prepare while Dan made the final touches to our house.

Our. House.

I could barely contain my excitement and internal zinging. Never in a million years had I thought I would ever have a house.

Or a car.

Or a husband.

Oh. My. Word. I couldn't focus on a jolly thing, my brain kept firing all over the shop. A warm weight rested on my leg and the jumping stopped. I didn't even know I had been jiggling. I looked at Dan's hand and smiled. "We're going to be married soon."

He kept his eyes on the road as we came into the city of Laodicea. "I know."

"The next time I see you is when we're going to be married."

"I know."

"I love you so very much."

"I know."

And I knew he knew. Because I told him every day. We had been working on communicating and telling each other how we felt and whether we were skitching the other off. And how. But we were good. I felt good about where we were and where we were going.

Marriage.

Just as well the gates of the Factory came into view. I just don't think I could have sat still any longer. As soon as we pulled into the carpark, I leaned over and kissed Dan's cheek, then exploded from the car. They didn't know we were coming, but they knew to expect us. And at this point in the process, they all knew what it meant. The grapevine was activated with calls, yells and screams and it wasn't too long before we were engulfed. It wasn't only Iza who was crying now. We all were. Not just because of the reunion, but because of what this visit meant, and the memories of their wedding and all that had happened during that crazy, heart-breaking, wonderful time leading up to Iza and Indy's wedding.

Please, please, please don't let our wedding be like theirs. I just don't think I have their strength.

Since our last visit, the demountables that had been home to the Silverscales for years had been transformed into an extended carpark. With all the new structures and the serious face lift the Factory had seen, the little cabin where it had all started, Indy and Iza's home, looked a little lost and out of place. I figured since the original crew had been moved, it wouldn't be long before Indy, Iza and Grace were forced to follow suit.

* * *

Once everyone broke away and Aiko and Vashti led the twins to show them the latest happenings in the kitchen and garden, Dan, Marcus, Kait and I started unloading our baggage from the roof racks. Iza insisted we take a three-bedroom apartment that had just been finished. It didn't take a genius to realise it was being set up for them. Even though we fought the idea, it was inevitable. I had a sneaking suspicion that as we were here to prepare for a new chapter in my life, they were taking the opportunity to farewell a chapter of theirs.

We had only just deposited our luggage into the beautiful, bright and open apartment and made our way to meet up with the twins, when a dark town car pulled into the carpark. Without waiting for his driver, Arty, to open the door for him, Felix was out and making his way to meet us at the veggie patch. "Friends, how... wonderful to see you." His scrutinising crow eyes took us all in, but snagged when he came to Val. "What? When? Why did I not know? Why do you refuse to use the phones I have provided for you?" He made his way to Val and walked around her, inspecting her fully.

"Ah, Felix?" Marcus coughed. "Are you checking me sister out?"

"Well, yes, Marcus. I have noted that she is without her..." He stopped, looked at the group smiling at him, then at Val. A crimson wave swallowed him whole. "No. Not at all. I mean... that is to say... I am... ecstatic for you, Valarie." He stepped back, almost tripping over himself in his haste to put distance between them.

Val glared at Marcus, shook her head, then turned to face Felix. "It's okay. Yes, they've gone. After a nasty message from the High Council in Philadelphia, we realised we were in for a tough time. As we were making plans on how to proceed"—she lifted her arms and slowly spun, and when she had done a full circle, a grin ate her face— "this happened."

"Well, that is... fortuitous. I am sorry I have not been to visit with you all. However, the Gerent's ridiculous god-complex, and the fires Philadelphia's High Council's decision has caused, I have been… occupied with the other five cities, trying to speak reason and make plans ourselves. We are deliberating how best to support you through the… extraordinarily complicated and dangerous times ahead. Who knows when… where and… how this insanity will end. And how far the cancer will spread before it does."

On that sobering note all laughter died—and I mean dead. Silence snaked around us until Kait brought us through to the other side. "However, that is not why we are here. We are here for a week to help prepare for the marriage of our two wonderful children." She went over and tugged Dan's face down to kiss his cheek then came and put her arm around me. "We are here to get ready, celebrate and catch up with family. Enough talk of the Gerent for now."

We spun at the gurgling noise behind us, and all logical thought and sensible conversation dissolved in baby drool as Indy arrived with Grace.

* * *

AFTER DINNER it was a sad farewell as Dan, Val and Marcus left.

I would miss him.

Seriously and achingly so.

I would miss them all.

It was then I first realised that I would also kind of miss Sanctuary. I guessed one of the disadvantages to always moving around was leaving family. And one of the advantages of always moving around? Was growing more family. I knew it was only for a week. But it was for a whole week. Last time we were that long apart it was during the nightmare of my working for Kari. I knew we were in a better place now, but still, I had grown used to having Dan around.

It started me spiralling down into memories of all the things we'd been through, all the things we'd survived, all the things that had happened and, all of a sudden, a week seemed far too long.

I wanted to call you back.

To stop you.
Demand that we just get married now.
Right now.

But with extraordinary effort I planted my feet and leaned into Kait's side as the car's tail-lights were absorbed into the night. I had a terrible sense of certainty: *I will never see you again.*

* * *

A WAVE of nausea washed over me like the plague, dragging me to the depths of despair from which I was confident I would never see the light of day again.

How could this have happened?

When could this have happened?

Who could have done this?

Why?

My tunnel vision almost blocked the chorus of gasps and cries as we all stood around staring at my wedding dress.

I'd finished it weeks…? Months ago. So excited to be ready for when Dan finished building our house. I didn't want anything I did to be the cause of a delay. I didn't want him to have to wait for me to be ready. For this, I wanted to be on time.

I had worked hours into the night in the little workshop they had built for me out the back of the cabin. This was my special project so I wouldn't let it interfere with my work for our new family. I received such joy making gifts for everyone. I had hoped a few little furnishings and some home-made, personally styled clothes would make people feel special. That they were cared for, and they had somewhere special to go home to every night. Especially since they had lost everything in The Quake. And had to live for far too long in those ghastly tents. Just the thought of it made me shudder.

But the night-time had been for me to work on my project. My gift for Dan, in a sense. I wanted him to know that marrying him was the most amazing thing that had ever happened to me, so I wanted my dress to sing to his soul in a way my mediocre voice never could. I know, seriously cliché and gag-inducing sentiment. But I admit it was how I felt. I knew I brought nothing to this marriage. I had no material belongings or guaranteed income, just a truckload of baggage and hand luggage of awkward. So, my dress was going to be perfect.

And when I'd finished, it was. It was a dream. It was the evidence of my fairytale come to life. Once it was completed and I was one hundred percent satisfied, I zipped it up in a special bag I bought from a charity shop. The same one I'd bought the dresses that were going to be reborn into something far more marvellous than they'd started out in life to be. No one was allowed to see it. It was my special surprise to everyone. I had explained the details and shown drawings to Kerm, Iza and Carley, but no one else.

And now we all stood around and stared. It was still clipped to the hanger. But the body, the sheath and the train, were ripped to shreds. I spun on my heel and barely made it to the toilet in time before I was violently ill.

On my knees in front of the bowl. My head in my hands. My body violently shaking,

Again, the carousel of questions circled through my mind.

Who?

How?

Why?

I felt a hand on my shoulder. It could have been any one of a million people, considering we were back at the Factory, but the subtle hint of lavender and rose gave it away. Kait handed me a cool, wet washer to wipe my face, then wordlessly embraced me with the comfort, strength and love only a mother could give.

"It is going to be alright, my darling girl. The Light has us and will watch over us. I am so very sorry for the devastation of your dress. The time and effort you put into it. What it meant to you. And what a special surprise it was going to be for us all." She pulled me back so she could kiss both of my cheeks. Then pulled me tight again. "You know, even though it was destroyed, I can see it was so far beyond and better than the dress I wore." She laughed as she led me out of the toilets and into the fresh air around the garden. "Marcus and I had no money. I was a student nurse. He was an apprentice mechanic." She shook her head. "I bought my dress the same place you bought yours." At my quizzical look she explained. "A charity shop. But even if I had owned a sewing machine, I didn't have the skills to make one, let alone the flair to design one... from other dresses." She pulled me tighter into her side. "You really are the most wonderful treasure. And I am so very proud that you have asked me to be one of the ones to walk with you down the aisle."

Each moment in her embrace, the nausea and shock retreated. I wasn't ready to speak yet, but I was so grateful for her... insight? Wisdom? Love? For her. I had missed her so much when we first came to Laodicea from Sodom. After the first week of shopping heaven, we had each been absorbed into our new worlds. Kait had managed to still fit family in. I had not.

Later, when we moved to the Factory, I had been hoping to reconnect, but Kait fell under Dawn's spell. Her mother, Genni, suffered with post-natal depression and wasn't capable of looking after her baby. Once again, Kait and I orbited around different suns. But before the fall of the Temple, she'd come back to us. To me. And she'd been a significant part of my life ever since.

I had loved my mum when I was growing up. When I lost her and my dad, my world disintegrated. But in the Light, I had not only received new parents, but a solar system of family.

I would miss Dan until he was in my sights again, but I was really grateful for this opportunity to connect on a new and deeper level with Kait.

* * *

I WAS NOT ALLOWED at the sewing station in Warehouse One for the rest of the week. Kerm took the tattered remains of my dress, and closeted himself away with Carley, and Iza when she was free. I was kept busy reacquainting myself with my sisters, and Lisa and the kids, Nasya and Tommy. Lisa was a lot happier and not so teary, now that she had landed on her feet and was well entrenched in the serious wonderfulness that was Factory life and community. The kids were doing well.

Since Iza had nominated herself to be a critical member of the "Save Tessa's Wedding" team, I was given extra quality time with my Light-daughter, Grace. Kait was a bit stiff and distanced at first, but at my insistence she joined me. The three of us also spent time catching up with Genni, who was doing so much better now. Dawn was three years old and still an angel who was very proud to be a big sister to the only other Silverscale girl born onsite. She was partial to Nasya, but she was big sister to Grace.

When I wasn't spending time with the babies, I was being spoiled.

Rotten.

I was being inflicted with every pampering known to humankind. It was almost enough to take my mind off Dan.

And my dress.

Would someone at Sanctuary have done it? Was it the Community? A demon?

"Tessa. Enough." Iza gave my toe a tweak as a very successful way to stop my spiralling.

"What?"

"I know what you are thinking, and you need to stop. Turning yourself inside out is not going to solve the problem, or help you prepare for your wedding."

* * *

I WAS WOKEN by all my sisters as well as Raph, Riah and Kait crowding into my room with hugs, kisses and coffee. Which was just as well. They would not have wanted to wake me this early without some kind of peace offering. But, today, even without it—the peace offering of caffeine, that is—my heart exploded with joy. This was it. I'd made it. Today was the day I got to marry Dan.

The morning was spent in pampering, preening, and being pinned into place—well, my hair at least. I wasn't allowed to see my dress until we were back in Sanctuary and I finished getting ready.

Felix came by with a small fleet of cars to transport us all.

And the food.

And the flowers.

"Not long now, Contessa. How do you feel?" The question came out woodenly, like he had been practising. Someone had been schooling him in conversation. And it turned my heart to marshmallow that he was doing this for us. All of it.

I covered the ground between us in three steps and very slowly lifted my arms and gently wrapped them around him. "Thank you, Felix. I feel much better knowing that you are there to help us when we need it. And I promise, when I get home I will make a point of remembering to take my phone with me wherever I go." I gently laid a kiss on his cheek and silently congratulated Raph on his work at breaking down Felix's barriers, conditioning him to receive our love and affection. Felix didn't flinch and only stiffened to reinforced cardboard, rather than his usual state of steel, at the physical contact. I then very slowly stepped away.

Then it was all systems go. At his request, Raph, Riah, Kait and I travelled with Felix, and we led the way. Only one hour and fifteen minutes till we were there. If the traffic was flowing.

41

KAITLYN: OVER MY DEAD BODY

Well, that turned out to be a pickle. As we approached Philadelphia, the traffic slowed to a carpark. Felix had warned us that traffic into and through Philadelphia was always tricky and it was important to get the timing just right. Definitely plan to travel either side of or diametrically opposed to peak-hour. Which we had. But as we approached the city, cars, trucks and buses stretched out in a long line of linguine. I could see Tessa trying to stay calm. A couple of times I gave Riah the nod to work some Peace her way.

Eventually we crawled along, three lanes merging to two, two squished into one, one stop-starting through a checkpoint. A man in uniform—not a local enforcer's uniform—stepped in front of our car with his hand up, causing our driver to stop. Arty wound down his window and spoke to the guard.

I jumped a mile when someone tapped the glass beside me. I then realised there was someone at everyone's door. We powered down our windows and were addressed by the man standing beside Arty.

"What is your purpose for entering Domination?"

As one we responded like silent, still statues. Raph, bless the boy, spoke first. "Isn't this Philadelphia?"

"Not anymore, boy. What is the purpose for entering Domination?" the guard repeated, gravel making its way to the surface of his voice.

I jumped in before Raph could get him, or us, into trouble. "We are returning home after a week away."

"Where do you live?"

"Sanctuary. I mean, Knox Hill Winery… Knox Hill… Just outside of the city." The man just stared at me; he was frozen like a cheap cardboard pizza. He then looked over the roof of the car. I suspected he was meeting all the other guards' eyes, as they too had stood up straight at this information. Then they all tapped madly at their tablets. Our initial guard looked back through our driver's window and eyeballed everyone. "All of you?"

"Ah… no." Felix spoke up. "My driver and I are travelling with our friends. We are from Laodicea and are just visiting." This was also recorded on the man's device.

"How long do you intend to be here and where do you intend to stay?"

I did not like the way he stressed the word "intend". As if what we *thought* we'd be doing was not necessarily what we *would* be doing.

Felix answered the man's questions. "We are only staying for the day and attending a function at Sanctuary… Knox Hill Winery."

Again, there was a communal eye-meeting above the car, then this was all added into their devices.

"We won't hold you up much longer, we just need all of you to turn to your windows for registration."

"I beg your pardon?" I tried to follow Felix's lead, and my own common sense, not to anger these people, but an icy chill crawled under my skin at his words.

Straight-faced and monotoned, he replied, "It does not hurt. You will be on your way shortly." He spoke like I was an imbecile. That I didn't understand their technology. It wasn't that at all. It just so happened I had a basic understanding, and therefore a very healthy fear of their technology. We were trapped in the car and there was nothing we could do but comply. Arty, Felix and I all received a healthy beep from their reading. Raph, Riah and Tessa, however, did not.

"Could you three please step out of the car." The man said "please" but let me tell you there was not one iota of politeness in his manner. He had gone from frightful to enforcer in a tick.

"What is going on here?" I leaned forward and stretched my hand out to Raph's shoulder sitting in the seat next to Arty, and another on Tessa sitting next to me, holding them in place. If I'd had a third, I would have snaked it around Riah in the back seat and pinned her to my side.

"Please calm down. You will be free to go once these three non-citizens leave the vehicle."

"Calm down? How dare you tell me to calm down." I was fighting with my seatbelt, trying to hold my children and climb out of the car to tear a piece off this fool who thought he could separate me from my children, whilst telling me to "calm down". The fact that I had not already laid him out flat was indication that I was still mildly rational. I finally freed myself from the tangle of restraints and made to launch myself from the car.

"Please remain in the vehicle, ma'am. We only require the three non-citizens to vacate the car."

"Well, I am sor—" The man standing at my door physically pushed me back into my seat. He had me at a distinct disadvantage, standing over me as he was.

"Stay. In your vehicle. Everybody. Put your hands where they can be clearly seen."

"Kaitlyn." Felix laid a heavy hand on my shoulder.

I turned to snap him in half when I caught what he was indicating with his chin. Armed soldiers, all of whom had shouldered their rifles, now stood fully focused on us.

Sitting on the edge of my seat, I wrapped an arm around Raph in the seat in front. He was the most vulnerable. Flight and freeze had fled the building and I was left with non-negotiable fight. So, it was just as well Felix took over the negotiations. "My apologies, there seems to be some sort of mistake. Could you please let us know why these people have been deemed… non-citizens?"

The lead guard took his time to answer. I suspect he was weighing up the cost of a fight over the time of an explanation. "There are no records for these people on file. We know nothing about them and therefore the Gerent has deemed them non-citizens. They will be sent to the labour camps and trained for service, or for The Games."

Raph squeaked as I squeezed him a bit too hard. I eased my death grip and started my not so calm reply to this nonsense. "If you think that I am going to let yo—"

Felix spoke through his open window to the head guard whilst reaching over and grasping my thigh in a grip that would, I suspect, leave permanent bruising. "I am confident there has been a mistake. All of these people have documents and are previous citizens of Laodicea."

The guard looked down at his device, checked Felix's face, then back to his device. "Even if that is the case, they are not showing up here. Therefore, they are deemed non-citizens. Please allow them to vacate the vehicle."

The gunmen surrounding us had not lowered their weapons. The demons walking around them had not stopped fuelling the fire with their forked, lying tongues.

Felix's eyes travelled the perimeter. "Where will you take them?"

I gasped and galled at his agreement to allow them to take my children. He spoke right over the top of me and dug his fingers even deeper into my thigh. "And how may I retrieve them when I have sorted out this… irregularity?"

"A camp has been established on the outskirts of town. Now. I will not ask you again. Allow the three non-citizens to vacate the car." All the guards immediately around the car slipped their devices into thigh pockets, stepped back and unholstered their handguns. The soldiers surrounding us dropped their eyes to their sights. A wild bear roared and raged inside of me. But I was trapped. Bound. Clawless. There was nothing I could do.

"Kait." Tessa took my face in both her hands and forced me to look into her eyes. Fire blazed. "I will take care of them. I will defend them with my life. We are in the Light and we are His." She forced me to focus on her unblinking, burning eyes until I nodded. "Good. Now, let us go before anyone gets hurt. And Kait?" I blinked. "Tell Dan I love him, and he better bleeding well wait for me, or I will kick his buttooshie." She tried valiantly to hide the shake in her voice. She was making a supreme effort for me and the twins.

Oh dear Lord, I was going to be sick. My body was shaking, sweating, frozen and shutting down all at the same time. I couldn't move. My brain was telling me I had to let them go. But my heart was screaming, *Over my dead body.*

"Felix?" Tessa looked to him as he slowly undid his seatbelt, then put his hands in the air and asked if he could exit the car to let the others out.

Riah climbed over the back seat, embraced me fiercely, kissed my cheek and I felt the words, "I love you, Mum," permeate the miasma of panic. I couldn't seem to force my arms to release her. She pulled back and let Raph climb through the front seats to give me a quick hug before they threatened to physically pull him from the car. He thrust Tiger into my arms. "Take care of him for me. Please." His voice faltered.

Felix climbed back in, still with his hands in the air, and we were ordered to leave the checkpoint under the intense focus of a multitude of eyes staring at us through rifle sights.

As soon as we were clear, Felix was on his phone making multiple phone calls. All I heard was, "Turn around, go back."

"Turn around, go back."

"Turn around, go back."

Oh, how I wish I could turn around and go back to this morning when I was blissfully ignorant in my joy. What kind of world did we live in that took children from their mothers?

But then I remembered the demons. And their laughter. And their taunting. And their vulgar innuendo. And I was consumed by a rage that devoured all rational thought. I, too, wanted to turn around and go back. I wanted to reach into the heavens and pull down the stars.

With the sun in one hand and the moon in the other, I wanted to wreak havoc and destroy this city and everything that stood between me and my children.

I hated everything and everyone who had brought me to this place. I turned to face Felix who was still on the phone. I wanted to rip that blasted thing from his hand and shove it down his throat.

"…then check Daniel's. Make sure his records are watertight. After that, go through and create records for all the children at the Factory. We don't know how far this will spread."

His mention of Daniel's name broke through the fire. Then I realised what he was doing. Feeling the heat of my glare, eventually Felix hung up and turned to face me. We stared at each other for a millennium. I don't know what was going through his mind, but mine had run out of gas and I was lost. Adrift. My soul torn and shredded by rage, grief, and my absolute inability to save my kids. I was utterly and completely powerless.

He broke the silence. "I am sorry for… hurting your leg."

At his mention of it, I became aware of the throbbing pain in my thigh, just above my knee.

He continued. "I think I can… rectify this situation. I believe I might be able to, through my contacts, pass this off as a mistake, a… glitch in the system." He paused again and his beady crow-eyes narrowed. "But if you had been allowed to assault a guard, if you had been imprisoned or shot, if you had caused anyone else to be imprisoned or shot, I would not be able to… rectify that."

Everything boiling away inside me broke out in an endless, bottomless tsunami of wracking sobs. Nothing registered until rough hands gently pulled me from the car and I disappeared behind the wall of Marcus's shared rage.

42

DANIEL: BIRD'S EYE ON HELL

It was done. Finally, all the people of Sanctuary were housed, and we'd finished Tessa's and my cabin. Actually, it had been completed shortly after she left for Laodicea. But there had been enough materials for us to continue building shells of cabins to close the gap between ours and the first—the one I'd built for Tessa fifteen months ago. With everyone helping out, we had one cabin that had four walls, a roof, and a floor. It was insulated and had the solar panels on the roof and the water tanks connected. The other one still needed to have the walls finished, but it had a roof, solar and the tank in place.

In the week before she'd gone, Tessa and I had done our last shop for stuff to kit our place out. She'd been sewing up a storm making "soft furnishings" as she called them, the stuff that gave the place colour: cushions, curtains, chair covers. She really was pretty amazing with that kind of thing.

I stood inside our cabin and couldn't keep the grin off my face or the pride and anticipation from swelling in my heart. If you had asked me when we'd first arrived in Philadelphia, nineteen months ago, if I'd be standing in a house I'd helped build, furnished by the woman I was going to marry, I'd have laughed myself silly. And probably run for the hills. There was no way I could ever have seen myself being able to achieve what we had in our time here.

"Proud of you, son." Marcus clapped me on the back. Val joined us and linked her arm through mine. I pinned it to my side as the three of us stood in the sitting room. Everything was scrubbed and polished. The three of us had already moved Tessa's and my belongings in and later today the two of us would move in. Up until last night I'd stayed in my tent. I wanted us to move in together.

I looked to them both, standing either side of me. "Do we know what time they're going to be here?"

"Kait said they'd planned to rise at sparrow's, get our girl ready then hit the road. So, I expect not too long. Mid-morning at latest." Marcus moved to stand in front of me and look me over. "You ready?"

"Yep. Can't wait."

"No. I mean, are you ready to greet guests and stand in front of a crowd to receive the woman you're going to commit the rest of your life to? A woman who will probably have spent hours preparing... and being prepared, wearing a dress that took days... weeks to design and make?

"Yep. Good to go."

"So, you don't think it might be worth having a wash and a shave and get your clothes ready."

I looked down at what I was wearing: holey jeans, ripped T-shirt, a stained long-sleeved flannel over the top, and paint-splattered work boots. I'd grabbed everything out of the clean clothes basket. There weren't too many holes. And not too much paint. "Should I change my shirt?"

"She'll skin him alive." Val half chuckled, half sighed in despair. "I would have thought Tessa might have helped find something for you to wear for the ceremony today?" When she said "helped" we all knew Val meant "Tessa picked out something for me to wear today".

"Oh. Yeah. I'd forgotten." I hadn't really. But I was going to feel like a goose wearing that get-up.

Val and Marcus looked at each other and then back at me. He said, "Where'd you stash it, lad? We'd best see if we can make a bride's pride from a pig's breakfast before Tessa decides to wear your guts for her garters."

Because I flatly refused to use our cabin to get ready in, I was hustled into the shell of the cabin next door, with my suit. It did look a bit crumpled. Women were called in from all over Sanctuary. Men stood around and watched the show. I suspected all of them were exceedingly grateful it wasn't them. But it was Jet who came to the rescue. "Nanna-May has an iron." The kid looked me over. "And a shower. And soap. I have a razor."

I didn't mind too much being the punchline of everyone's light-hearted joke. It meant I was family. Plus, nothing could dampen my spirits today.

Thank the Light, Gemma came and took my suit, and me—not quite so keen on that, one motherly-type in my life was enough, thanks all the same—and marched me up to Mary's. Jet had explained the situation to her and she insisted we all have a cup of tea. So, with Val, Marcus, Jet, Ruby, Jonathan, Travis, Daisy, Josh, Tim, Gemma and Craig sitting around Mary's cavernous kitchen drinking tea, I went in to have one of the most luxurious showers I'd had since the Mausoleum in Laodicea. I had almost forgotten what good water pressure and steaming hot water felt like.

I mean, we had water and the option of making it hot. But with the little pumps and bore water, and minimal heating, it was nothing like this. I may have taken a bit longer than I needed. But it was the perfect opportunity to step away from the crowd and really take stock, to thank the Light for what He'd done and for what was in store for us today. He really had turned my life around and showered me with countless blessings.

I was mildly ashamed when Marcus knocked on the door to see if I was okay, or if I needed rescuing. "Time to get moving, lad. Mary's cooked you some breakfast and poured you another cup of tea."

I emerged from the bathroom wrinkled. Shaved and dressed in a cleaner version of my regular attire: jeans, T-shirt and flannelette shirt over the top. The suit would wait till just before the ceremony. Thank the Light.

And thank Mary. It turned out to be a great time of sharing and laughter and I was able to relax and think about other things apart from the now-daunting reality that was rapidly approaching. I really wanted to marry Tessa but, all of a sudden, it was kind of hitting home that it was forever. And forever was a long time. And what if I stuffed up? And what if I couldn't make it for forever? What if Tessa decided I wasn't good enough for forever? What if…

"Breathe, lad. You'll be just fine."

"Batter up! We've got company." Daisy grinned at me from across the table. The woman took her job as Gatekeeper very seriously. Even from up here she'd sat where she could keep an eye on what was happening in Sanctuary, and who was coming and going.

I looked to Marcus and words fled, panic set in.

"Breathe, son. Let's go down and welcome our family home."

I nodded and stumbled between Val and Marcus down the hill into Sanctuary and met Felix on the boardwalk near the Meeting Place. He was whiter than normal, and he was pacing. Felix never paced.

"Where's Tessa?"

"Where's Kait?"

"Where are the twins?"

All three of us shot off at once. Felix gulped and led us back to the carpark where Kait sat frozen in place. Alone.

Marcus reached down and pulled her into his arms. Kait was a ghost. So, Felix filled us in.

My brain stopped functioning. I was in a void. A vacuum. No thoughts formed. No sense was made. Kait's hollow voice confirmed the worst. "They're gone." She looked to Marcus. "They took our babies." That was the last sensical word we heard from her for a while as she collapsed in Marcus's arms and Felix took over again.

"There was a checkpoint." He stopped pacing long enough to accuse each one of us. "Where are your phones? I need to be able to keep in touch with you." He turned and started pacing again. "The Gerent has set up roadblocks going in and out of Philadelphia, I mean Domination. Everyone must pass through scanners. Non-citizens— those who have bad records, or no records—are detained. Everyone else must be accounted for. Their comings and goings, and their reasons for doing so, logged." Both hands ran through his hair destroying his normally unruffled appearance.

He then looked to me. "You still have your licence? The one I organised for you?" I nodded. "You haven't had any fines, tickets, or… infringements?" I shook my head. "Praise the Light, you should be fine. I am pretty sure you will be fine. The files I had created for you, to give you a background and official status in another city apart from Gomorrah should work. I have someone working on creating an electronic history for the twins. It will take a bit of time. But I need to organise birth certificates, adoptio—"

"Felix." Val's firm but warm voice pulled him up. "Where are they?"

"I don't know. I need February and October."

We all looked around. I wasn't even aware he knew them. But that was pretty inconsequential right now. My brain was not keeping up with the information flying at me.

"We are here."

I looked around and realised everyone had come out in the expectation of welcoming Tessa, Kait and the twins home, as well as welcoming a truckload of guests from the Factory.

"Drones. Can you send one up and locate them?" He made his way through the crowd as they came forward. "They will probably still be at the checkpoint on the city's boundary on the main arterial to Laodicea. If we can locate them, we can monitor their situation. And follow them when they are moved. Also, I need help. Would you have a contact we could trust with helping me create Tessa's papers? The sooner we can get them set up, the sooner we can try to get them out. She needs to have an official birth certificate. I don't know what happened to all the records from Sodom and Gomorrah, but they are not on file. Anywhere. And I don't know how long we have. I also need to have documents created for all the children at the Factory. And their mothers. And Indy. I don't know how long we have and how far the Gerent is going to spread this poison. But Tessa and the twins first."

"What else do you know?" Val was managing the situation, as none of the rest of us were capable. Marcus was a white statue, and my brain was simply not functioning.

Felix turned and looked at her. His face completely stricken. "They will be taken to be used as servants at the palace, or fodder for The Games. We have to act now, before they are taken from their short-term holding. I have everyone on my teams working on this"—he looked to the tech twins—"but I need help." There was a crack in his façade.

They took off at a run, and with nothing else useful or productive to do, we all followed. We arrived at their workshop and already one of them had a drone in the air, its camera feeding visuals to a large screen on the desk in front of its navigator.

The other twin—whose braids were a mess because Tessa wasn't here to retie them—was at a computer, her fingers flying over the keys. "What is the name of your contact who is working on the Dark Web?" She didn't lift her eyes from the screen.

Felix didn't answer. Again, he looked around the crowd standing outside the hut. He opened and closed his mouth a few times, eyes wide, his face awash with nausea.

"Hacker handle, Felix," the short-haired one—February—offered.

Felix was on his phone madly texting. He pushed his way into the room and showed October his phone. She paused, looked at him and smiled. "It's going to be alright." Then dived back into her work.

For the first time since this hell broke out, hope started to get up off the mat. I didn't even know what they were talking about... or doing. But the looks on February's and October's faces were all that was holding me up. October pushed through the crowd and raced out the door. "Out. Everyone. Out."

February ignored her sister and asked, "Roadblock you said?"

"Yes, on the main road to Laodicea." Felix answered. He and most of the rest of us had not obeyed October and stayed crowded around, desperate and incapable.

"We're on the way. First bird's up." I heard a quiet buzz shortly before October came back into the hut and glared. We shuffled aside to allow her entry. At her computer she put on headphones and blocked us all out as she controlled and monitored the camera's view of the drone.

February had a map of the city open on her computer and Val, Marcus, Felix and I fought for a visual over her shoulder. My focus constantly flicked around all the monitors spread out over the workspace.

"This could be where they're headed." February pointed to a sports oval on the south-eastern side of the city. More screens flashed to life as one showed the ground outside their hut and Sanctuary disappearing from view at a nauseating pace. I gripped the back of her chair to stop myself falling over. "Second bird is live." She then placed a set of earphones on and manoeuvred a microphone arm in front of her mouth. Her fingers flew across the keyboard. Somehow, she was controlling the drone, following maps on a curved, three-dimensional holographic screen and having a typed conversation with someone in a text box in the top right-hand corner of the monitor closest to her.

I was immensely grateful for the cooling in the hut. Not only was summer's sun melting everything not in the shade, the computers and tech were giving off a lot of additional heat. And the stressed-out, hyperventilating bodies cramming the small space were not helping.

"This could be it." I had been watching the footage from October's drone race toward the checkpoint. My brain had been working overtime to help me understand that this was, in fact, a nightmare. It was not real. This was one of my Light dreams, and very soon I would wake up and ask myself, "What am I supposed to learn from that?"

How the drone could have got there in such a short time was beyond me. "I don't think they're there yet. I can't see them." A sporting oval with about forty people milling around zoomed into focus on October's screen. They definitely weren't sports people, and they definitely weren't training. There was a disgusting hovel of an open-roofed restroom in the centre, and guards stationed around in the stands watching over everything with rifles. Nope. Definitely not real. This was just a dream. And to make sure, I pinched myself really hard.

Then did it again as a scene from hell came to life in front of us on the screen in front of February. Armed guards, chain mesh fences, barricades and a long line of traffic snaking its way back down the highway.

"Found them," February confirmed.

Then hope took a king hit and was out for the count. Tessa's and the twins' images filled the gigantic screen as February zoomed in. Raph was in extreme distress. Riah was close to tears. Tessa was talking to a guard. He didn't respond or acknowledge her. She walked back to the twins. Embraced them both. Then set her jaw, turned around with her back to Raph. Riah did the same. They were making a shield of sorts so Raph could go to the toilet.

"Turn it off," Kait screamed from the doorway. "Don't you watch him. Turn it away." She sobbed.

The image swung so rapidly I almost vomited again. It now focused on the guards at the checkpoint. And all the demons walking through the crowd.

For the rest of the day and into the night, we kept vigil. If only we could have dropped them supplies or lifted them out of there. But with no cover at the checkpoint and those fracking spotlights on them, there was nowhere to hide. Nowhere to take cover. To get shelter. Or deliver them food… or supplies… or anything.

February and October had finally managed to evict everyone but immediate family from their hut. Then both of them worked around the clock, not lifting their heads, as they did whatever it was they had to do to make Tessa and the twins "citizens".

The drone was programmed to make regular passes over the checkpoint. Obviously, it couldn't hover in place as it would be too noticeable. To maintain constant updates on our three family members, the drones had to be switched out every few hours so that, when the time came for Tessa and the twins to be moved, there would be enough battery to follow them to wherever their next destination was. We couldn't be sure they were destined for the sporting stadium.

I must have drifted off. I woke with a start as the scent of fresh coffee came to me. Jet was carrying a tray with seven cups. He knew the drill. He wasn't to put February and October's cups—or anybody's for that matter—on their desks. They had a little side table each for drink and food. He then passed out one to Val, Felix, Kait, Marcus and me. "Any change?"

I had almost missed it. "Look. They're leaving." February stopped what she was doing and zoomed in the camera. A truck had arrived at the roadblock, and guards stood around with guns encouraging the huddle of non-citizens, including my family, to get in. I stood over February's shoulder just as the camera exploded and we lost vision. "Frack," February spat and October seethed.

"I shall cover the cost of the replacement," Felix offered.

"What? What just happened."

"They shot us down."

43

RAPHAEL: HELL IN A STADIUM

We sat in the shadows and waited by the side of the road at the checkpoint. We were not given chairs to sit on. The concrete wall was cold, and the dirt was salted with rocks. There were a few other people with us. They sat by themselves in a huddle like we did. The guards did not give us water or food. They did not let us go to the toilet. They did not speak to us or explain what was going to happen. After they had checked us over and emptied our pockets, they ignored us completely. We had nothing but our party clothes on. But poor Tessa was wearing a simple shift.

I tried really hard to hold on, but I could not. I had to go to the toilet. I waited till tears ran down my face and my insides were hurting. Tessa asked the guards on my behalf a number of times. Each one ignored her like he was deaf and did not speak our language. In the end, she, Riah and our Warrior guards made a little barrier for me, and I had to wee against the chain-mesh fence. I was so ashamed. But then Riah and Tessa had to go too. And it was so much harder for them. Out in the open, with only two human bodies to hide behind.

The other detainees who were there turned away. Like they did not want to know. Like they could make it all not real by not seeing our suffering. But then, when it was their turn, they shuffled over to

222

the same spot we had used. It seemed to be the act that tipped them into the same barrel of reality as us. Throughout the day, a few more joined our number, but no one spoke. We were all non-communicating, non-seen, non-citizens. Together, we sat in the dirt till evening when a small refrigerator truck pulled up on the road in front of us.

Without saying a word, the guards opened the back door, and used their rifles to indicate we were to get in. Tessa pulled us tight to her sides as the red haze threatened to swallow me whole. There were no windows, no seats or shelves. Just a large, thickly insulated cavern we were expected to disappear into.

All of us jumped as a shot rang out. One of the soldiers had shot something in the sky. This sparked action in one of our fellow detainees. He put up a fight and tried to make a run for it. Panic had stolen his senses and he blindly ran toward the wall of guards standing in a ring surrounding us. He was hit in the head and crumpled like a sack of potatoes. His body was thrown into the truck, where he landed in a ball after bouncing off one of the walls with an insulated thud. Then all the guards raised their rifles at us.

One by one, we climbed into the box. Tessa went first and held her hand out to help me and Riah. We sat at the opposite back corner to the unconscious man, leaving lots of room for the other five prisoners. The doors slammed shut and we were engulfed by absolute darkness. Inside my head, the red haze simmered away, bubbling and dissolving my thin façade of bravery. Was there air in here? Would we suffocate? Where were they taking us? I tried to breathe deeply and slowly, but there wasn't enough oxygen. We were going to die. This was a tomb. A silent, black, inescapable tomb.

The walls and floor vibrated around us and I could sense movement. No one said a word. Tessa's arm secured me to her side. My arm behind her clutched Riah. The crumbling precipice on which I stood was threatening to completely give way when a hiss of cold air escaped the cooling system around us. A subtle, sweet smell filled the truck and sweat prickled over my body.

The last thing I remember was hugging Tessa and Riah with all my might.

I lay on the cool, damp grass and looked into the sky. But I could not see anything apart from the high-powered lights shining down on me from huge poles. My fingers brushed over the dew and slowly I registered that I was as cold as the ground, my mouth was parched, and my shoulder hurt almost as much as the back of my hand. I tried to sit up, but it was too much of an effort. I rolled up in a ball and flopped to my side.

I was in a sporting stadium, and no matter how hard I fought to clear the fog, I could not remember why I was here and where everyone else was. I lifted my eyes to the wall of empty seats leading up to the heavens. Armed bodies patrolled the top tier. The exits—marked by fluorescent-green signs—were spaced like glowing fungi flowers in a night garden. I made a mental note to tell Riah not to eat them, they would make her sick.

Riah.

Where was she?

I tried to roll to my other side, but the pain in my arm and on my hand shocked me into full consciousness. I sat bolt upright, then waited for the world to stop spinning. Tessa sat between me and my sister, who was asleep on the grass next to her.

Black rivers leaked from Tessa's eyes, but she gave me a watery smile. Her hair was messed, with bobby-pins and knotted curls fighting for dominance in her hair.

Tessa.

Her wedding.

I tried to speak but my mouth was too dry. Tessa understood and answered for me. "I'm not sure where we are exactly. Or what has happened. But…"—she looked at the back of her hand at an ugly black mark, "we each have a number branded… tattooed on the back of our hand and, I'm not sure about you guys, but I have a small wound under my right armpit. When I woke up, there were people walking around us, checking us over for possessions. I think because we're smaller than the rest"—her eyes scanned the oval—"the anaesthetic hit harder and took longer to wear off."

As if she had been summoned by my concern, Riah stirred. Tessa leaned over and stroked her hair. "Don't touch it. It will only make it hurt more."

In a semiconscious daze, Riah had started testing the wound on the back of her right hand. I looked down at the one on my own. A raised, swollen, black number 0047 was burned into the back of my hand. I looked to Tessa.

"I'm 0046. Riah is 0048."

We all sat and stared at our tattooed hands. Scars were nothing new to me. My hands and body were covered with them. I had never had a tattoo before, though. I looked to my sister to confirm she was going to be alright. Once I was reassured of this, through the burning pain of my wound, I became blisteringly aware of my thirst. My head was still full of cotton wool, but I took the time to make an effort to take in where we were and what our situation was.

Groups of men—mainly men… I think there were a few women here as well—from where we sat, though, I couldn't see any other children—sat in clumps around the grounds. We were completely surrounded by a wall of seating, which was covered by awnings. Six huge pylons held shields of high-powered lights, casting six shadows over everything.

Dotted around the perimeter, in the stands, guards patrolled. They did not need many because there was nowhere for us to hide. There was no shelter. Just a field. In the centre was a construction. Its walls were made of fabric sheets, and they were just tall enough that an adult could not see in. There was no roof, so the guards would be able to see what was going on inside. From the smell coming from that direction, I guessed it was the toilet block.

Looking at and smelling the horror seemed to remind my bladder it was full to bursting. I was so scared. Everyone was watching us: guards, other detainees, and the demons prowling through the mix. Once Riah was sitting, I had to let them know. I could not hold much longer. "Tessa, do you think that they are the toilets?"

She grimaced and nodded. "Come on. We can do this. Remember who we are. And Whose we are."

It was then I did remember. I remembered my gift. Tentatively I laid my left hand over the back of my right.

I don't want to be selfish with the gift you have given me. But my hand and my arm really hurt. If it is something you are willing to do, could you please remove the pain and heal the wounds?

Joy sizzled in my soul as the pain dissolved. Immediately I offered the same gift to Tessa and Riah. I still felt nauseous and thirsty but at least the intense burning had subsided. It seemed, however, the use of my Badge had been a beacon, calling the Dark.

I looked to my Warrior Guard who stood with his back to me, next to Tessa's and Riah's, forming a shield against the growing numbers of the Dark's minions gathering around us. But we had no choice, we had to move, we had to break through their number. I could not hold on any longer.

Fear was like a rusty old clump of steel wool in my throat. I tried to swallow as we shakily stood up, then took Tessa's hand and, with our Guards, made our way to the stench in the middle of the oval. Within the sheets were rows of buckets. No seats, no toilet paper and no dividers. There was no privacy, just a gag-inducing reek.

In two locations near the outside of the oval were hoses for water. But there were no cups or bottles or any containers to carry or store it in. If you were thirsty you had to line up and drink from the hose. The three of us did our best to wash our hands and drink as much as we could before the people behind us lost patience.

On our way back I noticed someone sprawled on the gritty surface of the running track that circumnavigated the oval.

"Don't look." Tessa squeezed my hand till it hurt and pulled us at a trot to get back to our spot on the edge of the oval.

"What was wrong with that man?" I knew in my heart what was wrong. But I was having trouble forming the words. "Why do they leave him there?"

"He is an example. Apparently"— Tessa breathed slowly through her nose—"we are not to leave the grass."

I looked down to where we sat, right on the edge, and shuffled forward a bit more. I looked again to the stands. And the guards. And their guns.

No guards walked among the prisoners. But demons did—messengers of despair, hopelessness and fear. The first one to make its way to us sauntered past our Warriors, and tried to whisper something in my ear. Before I could make sense of what it was saying, I laid my hand on it and gave thanks to the Light that He was still with us, watching over us. Its screams drew the attention of all the other demons. They stayed away from us for a while after that.

Tessa did not let go of our hands the whole time. Neither had she stopped scanning the oval since we had woken in this hell. Even when we needed to use the toilet buckets again, we all went together, and two stood guard as the other tried to use the overflowing disgustingness. As the night progressed, I was confident of two things: there were no other children here; and we were drawing a lot of attention.

The night sky was hard to see from under the halo of blinding lights. But considering the thick darkness sneaking in through the cracks, I thought it might be late at night. It had been a very long day and Tessa was struggling to keep her eyes open. We had all been up very early at the Factory to prepare for going home to Sanctuary. But Tessa would have burned lots of energy in her excitement to see Dan again and get married.

Riah and I convinced her to lie down whilst we kept watch. It was cold and dew was thick on the grass. I was so grateful it was the middle of summer and not the heart of winter. But still, I wished I had a blanket to lay over... and under her. Especially since she was not wearing her normal clothes, but instead, a small, thin dress that was supposed to be her in-between clothes before changing into her wedding dress. I wished I had something better for her to wear. I wished I had a blanket for me and Riah. I wished we were at home.

We had decided to rotate, two on watch at all times. Except Tessa had insisted we both sleep whilst she watched over us. But finally, when she could not sit upright anymore, she relented. And that is when they came.

"Hey, guys." A group of six big men approached us. I scanned the tiered seats in the stands to see if the guards would do anything. I saw some of them look at us, but no one moved. "What you in here for?" Some of them leered at Riah. Some leered at Tessa. The leader leered at me. But a man at the back watched everyone and everything.

I swallowed and tilted my head back so I could see the man standing over me. Riah was immediately on her feet. So I stood next to her. I did not feel safe turning my back on them to check on Tessa. But I could not feel her move. Riah edged a little to my right, putting herself between Tessa and the couple of them who had fanned out. Making sure she did not cross the line on to the running track, she dropped into a defensive stance.

Oh dear, oh dear, oh dear.

I know You are with us. I know Your Guard is here. I cannot see how we may get out of this without Your direct, immediate and very real help. Please help us and keep us safe. Show me what to do and what to say. Please, please help us.

"Hello." I did not feel like extending my hand, but felt I should start off using my manners, nonetheless. Whilst I spoke, I too edged a tiny bit to my left, countering another two who had shifted position. Whilst we could not properly cover Tessa's sleeping body, I was very thankful for the demarcation of the running track at her back. "I believe we are here because we are non-citizens."

They all laughed. The man at the front spoke. "What could you two possibly have done that you needed to have your records erased? I had to pay a ransom to get mine wiped." The men behind him laughed. A few muttered their agreement.

I flicked my eyes to the man at the back who had not moved or said anything, but spoke to the mammoth in front of me. "Oh no, sir, nothing like that. We were sold to someone who brought us to this country when we were very young. I don't think he brought our records with him."

"What about her?" The man used his chin to point to Tessa. "She a slave too?"

I could feel Riah bristle. I suspect because he called us slaves. "No, sir. We are not slaves. We are free and so is… our friend." I do not know why I did not want to share Tessa's name. But it was a strong feeling, and I went with it. "She came from a city that was completely destroyed a fair way from here. I guess her records were destroyed in the fires."

They were silent for a while. I could feel the mood in the group change. I did not like the way that two of the men had not taken their eyes off Tessa. I stepped a bit closer to her and did my best to block their view.

I could sense Light building from behind me. My heart lifted. Again, I would not turn to see for certain, but I felt the Light may have sent Warriors to help us. Even though the men in front of us could not see what faced them, it gave me great courage. This time, I spoke to the man at the back. "I do not mean to be rude, but our friend is very tired, and she needs to sleep. Could you please leave now so she is not disturbed?"

Again a few chuckled. The front man looked over his shoulder to laugh with his comrades. He used the movement to disguise pulling a knife. But Riah and I both saw it, and before he had finished bringing it from its sheath on the inside of his boot, my sister pounced. She smashed both her feet into his closest knee, forcing it to buckle backwards. He dropped to the ground yelling. As he brought both hands round to hold his broken leg, Riah swooped down and grabbed the knife.

I let Riah take the lead as I took a defensive stand over Tessa's body. Both hands up. But for the first time since Sodom, both closed in fists. I did not feel we were going to survive this situation if I maintained a self-defence attitude. I had to protect Tessa and do my bit to protect myself and Riah at all costs. Val, Marcus and Kait were not coming for us this time. This time, it was only us.

The other five took a step back. They did not lend a hand to help their friend who was still rolling on the ground yelling and swearing, turning the air blue with insults. Now all five men stood with both hands in the air as they eyed Riah with a knife. And well they should. She had been trained by Val, and weapons were her native language, knives only second to her sword.

Quickly, I scanned the tiers again. Would we get in trouble from the guards for causing a scene? For hurting someone? They all watched on, none moving. But Tessa moved. Without looking at her, I tried to explain. "I am sorry you were woken up." I had to speak very loudly to be heard over the yells of the injured man. His noise had died down a bit, but he was still cussing. "We asked them to go so you would not be disturbed. But they did not leave."

Tessa's hair had reverted to its natural, wonderfully wild state after she had taken the time to remove all the pins. Dark circles shaded her dark brown eyes and smeared makeup exaggerated the weight of her exhaustion. And intense black fury flickered over her armour as she stepped past me and put her hand on Riah's shoulder, then moved over to the man writhing on the ground. "If you"—she then looked to the five men—"or your pack of dogs come anywhere near my family again, I will take great pleasure in allowing my sister to finish her work."

"You fracking lupp. I'm going to frack—"

Tessa squatted down and grabbed the man's ear lobe. He froze. She held her other hand out flat and Riah laid the knife in her palm.

Oh dear, oh dear, oh dear.

Tessa then pressed the tip of the blade into the man's groin. "I beg your pardon? Do not use that language in my, or my siblings', presence." She twisted the blade of the knife until he screamed.

Please help, please help, please help.

Eventually she released him, and he stopped yowling. Now he lay sobbing, curled in the foetal position. Tessa stood, handed the knife back to Riah—because she actually knew what to do with it—and gave her final warning. "Today is my wedding day. I was supposed to be married by now. I am very tired. I am exceedingly hungry and. I. Am. Exceptionally. Skitched off." She aimed her scowl at the man standing closest. I tapped her side and indicated the man standing at the back.

When Tessa got angry, Dan said she had a predator-bird face. She now aimed this face at the man standing at the back. The man I had felt was the leader. "May I suggest that you take your dogs with you now before we attract any more attention from the guards." She tilted her head but did not look at our growing audience. "And may I also suggest you keep your krets away from me and my family before I introduce you all to the concept of gender neutral?" She was a tiny doll with crazy hair and wild, dark eyes staring down six grown thugs.

Thank You, thank You, thank You that Tessa can be as scary as Val. And Kait. And Amina. And Daisy. Thank You that Riah is brave and quick and smart. And thank You that you are watching over us and Your Guards are around us. And thank You that Tessa is tired and very, very, cranky.

"You're alright, kid." The man at the back smiled from the eyes, not the mouth. He nodded and called his men off. "Come on, boys, let's leave the lady in peace and make sure she gets some beauty sleep." He turned around and started walking away. But he called out over his shoulder, "And someone bring Blade." At that, they all burst out laughing.

After this the men set up a camp in a semi-circle around us, a little way off, effectively setting up protection against anyone who wanted to come and challenge us. They even gave us an escort to the toilet and to get a drink. I did not trust them or like them. But it seemed neither did anyone else. For the rest of our time at the oval we were not troubled by anyone.

Thank You.

44

DANIEL: MOLTEN FURY

Using their crazy abbreviated twin-speak, which had me missing our twins even more, February and October launched another drone. All I caught were the words "stealth", "hope", and "chance". Which didn't instil confidence.

But sure enough, the drone that had been monitoring the sports stadium soon had vision of the truck. It pulled up in the mammoth carpark. This time, I actually was sick. Guards opened the doors, and all the occupants were carried out on stretchers, unconscious. They were taken into a building, and I lost what happened then when I dashed from the building and lost the contents of my stomach.

When I came back in, they were still in the rooms inside the stadium. It was over an hour later when they were stretchered out and dumped on the grass among the wildlife who had already been captured. I wanted to reach through the screen and kill the kret who went over them, checking for anything of value.

Oh, Lord. Do something. Protect them. Help us save them. Just do... something.

Even as I started petitioning the Light, Tessa's Warrior stepped forward and did something to the man being too free and easy with his hands on my unconscious fiancé. More arrows dropped from heaven and a barrier formed around them. Others were turned away, but not until after that kret had felt over her and Sariah. I saw red. I was beyond fury. I was so self-absorbed I wasn't aware what I was doing.

"Wait, Daniel. We will get them. We just need a bit more time."

Someone was speaking to me. I had to blink several times before I realised I was sitting in my car and looking for my keys, staring into the night sky. Felix stood at my window. "Please. This is hard. But we are doing what we can. We are almost there."

"Give me my fracking keys."

Felix held up his empty hands and Daisy stood behind him shaking her head. "No can do, Wild Cat. I know they're family, but if you go in there like a bat out of hell, you'll stuff up the whole plan."

"Give me my fracking keys."

"No."

Jonathan moved into view, standing between me and Daisy, with Travis, Jet, Josh, Tim and Craig around him.

A yell came from within Sanctuary. "They're waking up."

We bolted back and crowded around the screen. We could see the three of them lying in a bundle, shivering on the dew-covered grass. Tessa's shift dress was wet and dirty and far too thin and short to offer her any protection from the elements. With the intensity of the camera's focus, we could even see her shivering, blueing, goose-bumped flesh. The twins didn't look much better.

This was unreal. Surely it was a dream. How could any of this be happening? The rest of the night dissolved from unbelievable to inconceivable. None of us could comprehend what we were witness-ing. As a family we tag-teamed each other through cycles of feverish, ghoulish nightmares when dozing, and debilitating stupor when awake.

"Um… I think we've got trouble." Sweat broke out over my body as a chill swept through my heart. Exhaust fumes were billowing out of the back end of a new bus in the carpark. "I think they're heading out." There was a millisecond of a pause before all action broke out.

"Almost done," October said as she entered the hut from behind me. I hadn't even realised they weren't there. I looked to where she had been all night and her computer was flashing with numbers and symbols. "Tessa's done. The twins are just uploading now. We had to put them in obscure locations, so it looked more like a natural mistake that they didn't show up."

"Get the car, Dan." Val was on her feet and heading for the door. I had to wait till everyone had left as there was no room for me to squeeze through the stools and chairs cramped into the small space.

"I'll come as well." Felix marched ahead to rouse Arty, then stopped and spun. He called out to the twins, "Do we need you to come as well?"

The girls looked to each other, spoke silently. Then February picked up a laptop, grabbed an extra drone and followed Felix to his car.

"Wait!" Daisy was running, holding Tiger. Miriam was in her wake holding some kind of box cage. "Take him with you, he'll be needed."

Finally, we could go and get them.

45

MARCUS: RETRIEVAL

Me heart was racing ten to the gallon, but I had to keep telling me boy to slow down and back off. To try to keep it to ten over the limit. We'd not do a jot of good if we were pulled over for speeding.

"The bus is pulling out." Felix's voice came out through the speakers of the car's audio system. A chorus of whimpers, growls and groans filled the air.

"I have it on-screen, we won't lose them." February's normally monotone voice had picked up a few inflections.

"Take the next turn and head for the main arterial heading out of Philadelphia. I suspect they're heading for Ephesus." Even though Arty was expertly driving Felix's car in the lead—and Dan was following a bit too close—Felix was giving us constant instructions in case, somehow, something prised Dan's car off Felix's bumper bar.

Both cars descended into intense silence. We were all leaning forward, straining towards the speakers, desperate for them to give us hope. February's voice relayed from the car in front became our oxygen. Her words were the only thing feeding us life:

"They're on their way to a checkpoint."

"I can see them."

"I am keeping pace with their window."

"I can't stay long. I'm drawing attention."

"Riah saw me." Her voice rose with her victory. "They know we are coming."

"I'm back to eyes in the sky."

"They're slowing for the checkpoint."

We too were approaching the stop. I thought I could even see the bus ahead of us, stopped in the line of traffic. It took all I had to not bust out of the car and run, rip the doors off and get me kids.

Dan didn't let anyone get between him and Felix as the lanes merged. We were still moving but the bus had stopped. We were getting closer. I could see them. I'd bet me bibby that was their bus.

Excitement bubbled from me fingers and toes and fizzled me brain. We would have them back in no time.

"A guard is speaking with the driver."

"The bus is pulling out."

"They are being waved through."

Just as we were forced to stop in the quagmire of traffic, the bus holding three of me kids, and me heart, accelerated down the highway away from me.

An almighty roar broke from Dan as he pounded the steering wheel. We almost missed February's confirmation. "I am eyes in the sky and on their trail."

Hope didn't drain, leak or ooze out of me. It vanished in the crease of time. Instantly. Gone.

Help. Help us. Help them. Save them. Do something. Please. Just... help.

Kait was crying quietly, wrapped in Val's arms. I met me sister's eyes in the rear vision mirror, and I was as confident as sun rise was to set, there may not be death on the horizon, but there was a high chance of pain and significant discomfort for those responsible. I nodded in agreement.

"Dan." I waited till he forced his focus to me. "Breathe." I could see him holding back from launching himself across the gearstick at me. "With February's help, we will follow that bus. We will track it down, stop it before it gets to Ephesus, and we will get our family back. I need you at your best. Not only do you need to drive this car safely and not kill us all in your rage, you need to be on your best game when we get there." I pointed to the checkpoint. "The Light loves them, is watching them, and has this in His hands." I waited a pause, then repeated myself. "So, breathe."

He groaned, hit the wheel again, then brushed frustration-tears from his eyes onto his shoulder.

We then entered the worst fifteen minutes of me life as we crawled along at an incapacitated snail's pace, knowing the bus was speeding down the highway away from us.

February kept up her commentary. "They are still on the highway."

"It looks like they are heading for Ephesus."

"Good." I couldn't hold back me excitement.

"How can you say that?" Dan was ropeable. "That is the Gerent's personal playground."

"It's also the furthest city from where we are. Believe me, I've paid me dues at the Overseer's expense along these roads. They will either be slow through the winding roads of the mountains or take the longer path round the outside. Either way, we have at least three hours to catch them." For the first time since this whole debacle splattered on me happy, I felt I could exhale.

Thank you.

That didn't mean it was any easier to wait.

The sands continued to dawdle their way through the hourglass until it was our turn to face the music.

"Where have you come from?"

"Knox Hill Winery."

"Where are you going?"

"Laodicea."

"Why?"

"To visit family."

"How long will you be gone?"

"Half a day to a day at most."

"Please look into this device."

And we were on our way.

Victory's fingertips were tingling me hair roots, but inspiration of how we were going to get our kids back through the checkpoint was a dim mist at best. For now, however, the highway stretched out in front of us, calling us on. I had to keep reminding myself: one prickly hurdle at a time.

So why we were stopping again was not only beyond me comprehension, it was skitching me off royally.

"I am just releasing another drone." February's words met me unvoiced angst.

And we were off again. Arty setting a healthy clip along the quality road.

"They are ahead."

"They are slowing."

"They are pulling off the road."

Val spoke from the back seat, her voice dripping with suspicion. "What's going on?"

February answered, "We have been causing a distraction. But we had to wait until we were through the checkpoint. And on a quieter road. Thankfully, they took the mountain route."

We cruised to a stop behind the bus, and I couldn't hold me laugh in at February's "distraction". About fifty drones hovered around the bus, limiting its vision. Darting like dragonflies, being impossible targets for the guards who had disembarked to deal with the anomaly.

"Quick. Everybody out." Val was already on the tarmac, running. The two guards on the outside were so distracted by the drones, they didn't notice we were there until we were already on the crowded bus.

The driver seemed frustrated but not too put out by the whole circus. When we stormed his vehicle, he just raised his hands, indicating he was not going to die on this hill for these people. I reached over and pressed the button that shut the door behind us. "Do. Not. Open that door."

The guard with his gun drawn at the back of the bus was another matter altogether. This new obstacle, however, did not stop me sister. She marched straight up the aisle as if his weapon was inconsequential. Either side of her, the audience of other non-citizens seemed delighted by the delay. Thankfully, no one made a move to stop her, or, at this point, try to get off the bus. Seemed Val's performance was worth sticking around for.

All of a sudden, I had a flash back to the day she and Joy stormed a bus from hell to extract me and Kait. I didn't know what was going on then, but sure as a dog's leg is crooked, I did now. Before Val had a chance to explain the change in plans to the guard, Kait was on her knees, engulfing the twins. Tessa was wrapped around Dan, and I'd put myself between me family and the guard at Val's front to offer weight to her argument and another layer of bulletproof to me kids.

The soft click of the safety switch being disengaged rang clear as a bell.

Val didn't even flinch. But with congenial iron she laid out the change in plan to the young man. "Consequences."

He tilted his head. Didn't lift his eyes from the sight on the muzzle of his handgun, but she'd thrown him.

"We all have to ask ourselves what the consequences of our actions will be. For there will always be consequences." She took a step closer. "For example. On this bus you have three citizens who have been wrongly identified. We have the evidence to prove it. That is, if you had the slightest interest in looking." She took another step closer.

The guy gulped.

"The question you have to ask yourself is, what the *consequence* will be for taking three innocent children from their family." She leaned to the side so he could see our kids firmly wrapped in and around Kait and Dan—and I can tell you, right about now I was praising the Light in no uncertain terms that Tessa was so small and looking one helluva lot vulnerable. "And what will happen to you for doing so."

Even though a bystander *could* swear in court that her words weren't issued as a threat, there was no mistaking the double meaning. I suspected somewhere in the justice system a price would be paid. But right here and now, there was no doubt. I drew myself up and filled the aisle, tilted me head and made sure every ounce of me anger was pooling in me eyes.

The guy gulped again.

The rest of the prisoners on the bus sat rapt, fully engaged in the entertainment. All they were missing were the choc tops and buckets of popcorn. They knew where they were going and what awaited them. And they were in no hurry to get there.

Banging started on the door of the bus. Flicking me eyes to the side, I could see Felix in negotiation with one guard, with February's laptop in one hand. He was using the other to point to the evidence his friend had created and inserted in the system. The other guard who had been kept busy trying to evade the drones that had taken a hostile interest in him, had now realised we had invaded his territory.

Dan put Tessa down and placed himself at the front of the bus. It'd be a brave and imminently injured person who attempted to pass him.

Val continued her conversation, glossing over the threat from our family towards a bigger and more distasteful outcome. "I suspect that a member of the Gerent's Guard who made such a monumental mistake"—with raised eyebrows she indicated the other passengers on the bus who were still fully invested in the show—"might end up in The Games."

A huge bloke spoke. We'd seen him via the drone's imaging first approaching Tessa and the twins from the back of his pack, then setting up a perimeter around them throughout the night. "Might be you're right there, young lady." The fella didn't stand, didn't raise a hand, just sat, surrounded by men of the same ilk and narrowed his eyes at the guard. "Might be you're right."

The guard gulped for the third time and stepped back so his pistol could pivot between the seated threat and the one standing in front of him.

Val took another step closer. The pistol now pressed into the middle of her chest, fury pouring out of her eyes, anger dancing along her armour, and rage threaded like ice through her soft voice. "So, I suggest you think real hard about the consequences of the choice you're about to make. Because right now, I'm fighting real hard not to demonstrate the consequence of my... extreme displeasure."

The guy shook.

Pounding on the door intensified. And a voice crackled from the tech that had fallen from the guard's ear. "For frack's sake, open the fracking door, Sickle."

I'd say Sickle was stuck. To divert his attention in order to answer would lose any advantage he thought he held. He couldn't move through our group filling the aisle. And he had a bus full of hostiles surrounding him.

Val solved his problem. "Dan, open the door. Let the guard into the stairwell. February?"

"Here, Val." February's voice came from Val's back pocket.

"Call off the drones. Keep them close by. We may still need them."

"Done." As one, all the drones lifted and hovered out of sight, but still within earshot.

The front door opened, and the second guard leapt into the bus, but stopped when he met Dan on the step above him. His pistol's aim shifted from Dan, to Val, to me and back to Dan. But Val's bark halted his progress. "Consequences, Sickle."

Sickle jumped. Then tried to speak. Cleared his throat and tried again. "We've got three citizens caught up in this lot. We've got to let them off."

The guard on the step looked up at Dan and then to Sickle, then to the third guard outside who was shaking his head in resignation.

"Now." A slight tensing of muscles and movement from the passengers helped Sickle find some metal. "Move aside and let these people off the bus."

"Do it, Baines, seems he's right." The third guard who'd disengaged from Felix spoke.

"But they're tagged and bugged, sir. That's a one-way ticket."

The commanding officer tapped his right shoulder as he replied, "Well, if we need them again, we'll know where to find them, won't we. Let them off."

Baines stepped down and we all made to exit. I turned to make sure Val was on me tail and she bleeding well wasn't. What was she doing? Shaking the hand of the man from the field. Flashes of the images we'd witnessed last night had me teetering between wanting to rip the man's throat out and wanting to embrace him. I settled on the side of rational and also went to shake his hand. "Thanks for watching over me kids last night." He nodded and went to withdraw his hand, but I hung on. "But if it had gone the other way, and your dog had had his way with the blade, I would have hunted you down and made you pay like for like… with interest."

He laughed. "Message has already been received." He looked to Val. "Loud and clear." His eyes sparked in admiration for Val—physical, attitudinal, or spunk, I couldn't tell you. But somehow in this ridiculous situation, she had won herself a fan. I made sure she went before me down the aisle. I didn't want him leering over her as she shepherded our family off the bus.

We stood in a huddle, everyone in contact with everyone else, as we watched the bus disappear over the crest of the hill. Felix allowing and initiating hugs with the three released captives, especially Raph and Riah. Then he was on the phone making multiple calls updating everyone who had a vested interest.

"We shouldn't stay here too long; they might send someone, after the guards report our… departure." Val hadn't taken her eyes off the road. But eventually the pull to her retrieved family was too strong and her attention came back to us. "Before we leave though, we need to make a plan. February?"

The girl had been safely ensconced in the car, controlling the drone during our intervention, but now she was hanging back, still holding her open laptop—I suspect not wanting to intrude on our reunion. She nodded and took a few steps closer when Val addressed her.

"Do you still have a drone in the air?" She nodded. "Can you tell us if an official vehicle is approaching?" February nodded her agreement.

"Where did all those extras come from? That was fralping awesome."

"I contacted my friends and informed them of the situation." February flicked her eyes to Felix. "We have a mutual friend who I was also keeping in contact with. We formulated a plan, and they were all happy to help. You should also know that all the files have been successfully inserted into the programs. You three are now official citizens, and the twins"—her eyes looked at the two who were being passed around slowly but surely to every adult in our huddle—"are now officially your"—she nodded to me and Kait—"children. Adoption papers have been created and are now in all of your files."

Me knees buckled. Me eyes were awash with tears, and emotion carried me away to heaven. Cries of joy, whoops of excitement and yells of congratulations disappeared into a fog.

Thank you.

Little bodies slammed into me and I was in the middle of a twin sandwich. Then Kait was on the ground next to me, with her arms around the three of us. I clutched me kids and sobbed with utter relief —that they were safe, and that they were mine. Mine and Kait's. This skrat of a day had resulted in the most wonderful gift a man could ask for.

Thank you.

46

———

DANIEL: GETTING HOME

"What do we do now? How do we get them home?" I'd not let Tessa go. If someone wanted to hug her—which they all did —they had to do it whilst I maintained contact with her, trying very hard not to focus on the raised, scarred brand on the back of her hand. I'd had my turn at embracing the kids. Images of them waiting at the checkpoint. My little brother and sister... and Tessa having to go to the toilet on the side of the road. Then watching, helpless, as they slept on the cold, wet ground overnight... unconscious.... Watching as they held those thugs at bay. I'd hugged them all, too hard, too long.

"Do we just take them all back to Laodicea and keep them there?" Kait's eyes were red, her face was puffy, and her arms just weren't long enough to keep everyone close.

"Maybe we can hide them, or sneak them back in... trek across country?" Marcus was not offering much help. But I kind of got that.

"If their papers are all legitimate, why do you need to do that?" February was a bit put out.

Tessa stepped forward. "How about you ask *them* what *they* want. I mean, seriously, they are standing here, right in front of you, and I think they might have some say in what *they* want to do. And let me tell you, I am not going back to Laodicea to hide. I am not going in a trunk or footwell to hide. And I am definitely not tracking through the bush in this dress and these shoes after no sleep or food and going out of my flopping mind, to hide from the flopping guards." She'd worked herself up into a crescendo of high-octave rant. Then all the fight fled, and she slowly deflated, her bottom lip trembled and tears welled in her eyes. "I just want to go home. Eat a horse, sleep for a week, and marry Dan." Then the sobbing started.

I wrapped her in my arms and gently stroked her back as she released all of the tension and fear through tears into my chest. I may have joined her.

"Okay. So, I think these might be some options." Val's calm voice gave me some confidence someone still held a modicum of sanity. "If we drive through a checkpoint with you guys looking like you do, you will draw attention, regardless of how good your papers are. Thank you, February. Please pass on our extreme gratitude to your friends for their help. And to October, but hopefully we will be able to do that personally, soon." She squinted her eyes, and I could almost see the ideas and outcomes running through her mind. "If we go back into the city through the same checkpoint it is likely someone will recognise them from yesterday." She stopped, shook her head then addressed February again. "I know you normally do drone deliveries during the night. Is there any way we could drive to an isolated location and have food and clothes delivered?"

"Valarie?" Felix spoke up and waited until Val gave him her full attention. "We currently have two cars. I agree that we need to move from this location. Arty could find us a park... or a cafe for us to... formulate a plan. I could slip back to Sanctuary to pick up cloth—"

"Border crossings," Marcus interrupted him. "Every time we cross, we are being logged and identified. If you do too many crossings in one day, you'll draw attention."

Then I decided to throw in my two bits worth. "We told the guards we were heading to Laodicea. Could we go to the Factory. Get these guys a feed, a wash, clean clothes and some sleep. Then later tonight, just drive back through the checkpoint and see how we go?"

My idea met with silence, which was broken by February. "Traffic is approaching. I don't think it's official, but we should probably get back on the road."

I don't know about anyone else, but panic stopped my heart and I almost pushed Tessa into our car. She didn't seem to notice in her flurry of limbs to get in and lock the door. Despite all her talk of not hiding, she ducked her head down and hugged her legs.

"Let's meet up at Laodicea. February, do you mind if we take you with us for a while? I know it wasn't our original plan this morning."

The girl grinned. "I've not been to Laodicea for ages. I am happy to hang out for the day… or however long."

We'd decided not to convoy. With our family on board, I set out first, kept to the speed limit and headed back to the Factory. About ten minutes after we left, Arty would follow. Although, after we stopped at the first drive-through diner we came across, I noticed in my rear-view mirror that they'd caught up.

I knew as soon as we entered the carpark of the Factory I'd lose Tessa for a while. She'd be swept up, taken away and pampered until she was ready to sleep, so I took her scarred hand, pumped it twice and did my best to tell her everything I could through my touch until I could tell her in private.

Just as I thought it, it happened. Felix had been keeping everyone here at the Factory and at Sanctuary up to date with what was happening. As our car turned into the Factory carpark a horde vomited from Warehouse One. Both Tessa and Sariah were taken from us as they were engulfed in a sea of oestrogen. The upside was, Marcus and I were given quality time with Raph and Indy. Even Kerm and Ben came round with Kazi. The ladies had tried to take Raph from us too. But Marcus put his foot down. Vashti and Aiko weren't pleased, but when I grabbed Raph and marched him to the shower of the unit we'd been given, they backed down.

I knew I would have time with Riah later on, but for now, she was being smothered by Val and Kait. This was our time with Raph. He completely lost it when he realised we'd brought Tiger with us. And I'm not ashamed to say, after Raph was showered and dressed, fed and cleaned, I shed more than my fair share of tears at his retelling. Eventually the kid passed out, exhausted. Marcus picked up him and his cat and carried them as we went in search of the others.

Tessa was waiting for me in the room she had shared with Riah two nights previous. Sariah was passed out on her bed, Kait wrapped around her and Val sitting on the floor holding Riah's hand.

Tessa sat—her head nodding and her body wavering—on the opposite bed. When I entered the room, she turned her shoulders to me, but her eyes were closed and a smile warmed her face. "I knew you would come."

In two steps I was at her side, laid her down and crawled up behind her to hold her as she slept. Or at least I thought she was asleep. "I did try to rescue myself. To save us," she whisper-slurred.

"I know, Tessa. You were so brave. So fralking amazing."

"I just…" Tears took her.

I tried to comfort her, stroked her hair, hugged her tighter.

Marcus sat down with Raph and Tiger in his lap, his back against Tessa's bed, his legs out parallel to Val's sitting opposite him.

"You did rescue them, Tessa." Val's words were heavy with tears. "We saw on February's drone how you stood up to the guard at the checkpoint to try to help Raph. How you stood up to those men at the stadium who saw you three as an easy target." She huffed out a laugh then. Over the top of Tessa's shoulder, I saw Val lift Riah's hand and kiss her fingers.

"We saw everything. Helpless to do anything. But we saw what you did and how brave you were. Dan is right, Tessa, you were fralking amazing, and I am so unbelievably proud of the three of you right now." Her jaw was clenched, and two rivers of tears ran down her face. She didn't even try to brush them away. "Love you, kiddo, rest easy, we're here now and we'll watch over you all."

The folk at the Factory let us have our time to reconnect and attempt to recover in private. No one interrupted us except to bring bottles of water and a few sugary drinks to rehydrate the kids, and us, after all the tears.

It was dark when we finally stirred. I was aware of a hand stroking my arm, soft murmuring—and a bursting bladder. "Don't move." I leapt over Tessa and dashed from the room. After washing up and splashing water on my face, I returned to the bedroom and climbed back in behind Tessa. Everyone was awake and waiting for me.

The kids and Tessa definitely looked better. Even Kait looked like she'd actually slept, but Val and Marcus? Not so much. Might be that they were sitting on the floor, but I suspect it was more than that. I also had a feeling this was just the beginning of a new reality for us. "What's our plan?"

"We're thinking we'd give your idea a go. Have dinner with our friends, petition the Light, see if any other inspiration comes, and if not, we get back in the car and head back to Sanctuary." Val filled me in. "Felix had Arty drive February back earlier. He waited around to see everyone after we'd rested. But we've got to see if the work of our friends holds up under scrutiny sometime. Hopefully there will be less of a wait later at night to get through, and we can petition the Light that there are different guards on duty."

There was a soft knock at the door. Marcus answered, calling for them to enter. Iza stood in front of a crowd. "We heard water run through the pipes, and voices." She grinned. "Joko, Hiro and Kazi have been on guard outside your door since you went to sleep. They have been waiting for signs of life.

"Me too, Aunty Iza," Jordan piped up. He squeezed through the forest of legs and without hesitation climbed up and snuggled with Riah.

Iza laughed. "Yes, Jordan too. Even Dawn was helping. We have dinner ready when you are. Everyone is keen to see for themselves that you are well and okay." Her voice hitched and her legendary tears made a showing.

"Thank you, Iza." Val looked to the group fighting to look through the doorway. "Thank you, everyone. I don't know about the others, but I'm starving and need a coffee."

After another incredible meal of homegrown goodness and several cups of black gold—not the instant we'd had to acclimatise ourselves to at Sanctuary—we were getting itchy to get going. I needed to know if we could get through that checkpoint. Because I wanted to get on with my life with Tessa. I leaned over and whispered in her ear, "How do you feel? Are you ready to give it a go?"

"Yes, Dan, more than ready. But I don't have my dress."

I looked her over. "Can't you wear what you've got on?"

The look of horror that passed over her face had me worried.

Is she mentally damaged?

"I am not getting married in jeans, Daniel. Not after all the trouble Kerm, Iza and Carley went to, to make me a new dress." Since this was a fair bit louder than a whisper, we now had everyone's attention.

"Wait. What?" Too many things were fighting for prominence in my head. Marriage? Dress? "What?"

"Come on guys, I think it's time we made a move to see if we can get back into Philadelphia. You ready to attempt the checkpoint?" Val stood and stretched.

I flicked my head back to Tessa and raised my eyebrows in question. She smiled and nodded. The twins pushed their chairs back from the table, their bodies slumped, eyes only half open. The drag of their chair legs on the concrete made sure they had everyone's attention. We then went through the lengthy process of farewelling everyone several times over. It would be past midnight before we got back to the checkpoint. But then again, that might be a good thing.

I don't know why we made such a big deal of it. We were, hopefully, going to see them all tomorrow. At our wedding. Then, all of a sudden, I couldn't wait to get home and hurry tomorrow in. Rushing around I corralled everyone into the car, then with Tessa's hand on my thigh I drove my family back to the unknown.

47

CONTESSA: BACK ON TRACK

I couldn't keep my eyes open as we drove out of the Factory, but when I felt the car slowing, my heart kicked into hyperactivity. Sitting up straight and wiping the sleep from my eyes, I tried my best to make my hair look like it belonged to a respectable person. I looked down at what I was wearing. A neat shirt and respectable jeans. They fit well and there were no holes.

If you knew how hard it had been for me to get my hands on these, you'd realise I deserved some kind of award. I am confident there was not one pair of girls' jeans at the Factory. Seriously. No matter how hard I tried, I still couldn't get my sisters out of skirts. I swore it was going to be the bane of my existence.

Although, maybe a skirt would have helped me look more citizen-y. Were jeans good enough? "How do I look?" I asked the car in general. "Okay? Presentable? Like a citizen?"

I really did try to slow my breathing. But far. Flopping. Out. I was going to be sick. It didn't matter how many times I wiped my hands on the car-seat cover, they still came away damp.

And hot.

And cold.

And clammy.

A hand reached forward from behind me and rested on my shoulder. Kait. "It'll be okay, sweetheart. I have confidence in February and her friends. I have confidence in Felix. But above all I have confidence in the Light. Breathe easy."

"Okay. But if I have to get out of the car, I'm taking a water bottle this time. And a blanket." Then I was ridiculously furious with myself. Why wasn't I wearing a skirt? Trying to go to the toilet with no privacy in jeans would be a literal nightmare. I did not want to go through that again.

Oh. Lord. Help. Me. I should have worn a skirt.

We neared the heavily lit checkpoint. Guards stepped out of their little house and stood in front of the barrier.

Oh Lord. Oh Lord.

"Just breathe, Tessa." Dan's hand came to rest on my leg and gently squeezed it twice. I laid my hand over the top of his and realised my brand was in plain sight, and Dan had just pressed the window button! It glided down and he spoke, "Good evening."

I shoved my hand between my thighs, desperately trying to hide the evidence of my non-citizen status. The guard bent down and looked through his window and checked us out. The twins were still passed out in the very back seats. Marcus, Val and Kait sat behind us. And then there was me. The non-citizen, sitting up front in the passenger seat, branded for all the world to see.

Okay. Okay. Okay.

Breathing.

Like, this is kind of like a fight. Right?

So, water.

I can be water.

Help me be water.

I can deflect, shift, move with the eddies.

A tree. I can be a tree with my roots planted deep in You.

Help me be a tree.

The guard's bored voice broke into my meditation. "What is your purpose of coming into Domination?"

Dan answered, "We're coming home."

"Where do you live?"

"Knox Hill Winery."

"Where have you come from?"

"Laodicea."

"Look into the screen."

He did. It beeped the happy "you're a citizen" beep.

We all looked into the screen. We all received the happy "you're a citizen" beep.

I tried very, very hard to hold my relief-sobbing in until the window was up and we were on our way. But I tell you, I only made it until we were out of the bright lights and then all bets were off. I was a blithering mess. I am not ashamed to admit it. I was just. So. Flopping. Grateful.

Thank you. Thank you. Thank you.

And I think it's only fair to point out, I was not alone. I do not think there was one dry eye in the car. In fact, Dan had to pull off the road for a little bit. Just so he could get himself under control and safe enough to drive.

We'd done it. We'd made it back. We were safe. We could get married. And, well, that was pretty much the end of me. But I did pull myself together and quieten down when Val rang Felix to let him know of our… his success.

Seriously, to think where we'd be without that man. And what I'd thought of him… and how I'd misjudged him when we first met. I was ashamed.

Please help me See the heart of people, not judge them from the outside. I don't ever want to overlook such genuine beauty, such true gold, again.

Then I thought of Kari and Jason, the two I'd worked for… been enthralled by, when we'd first arrived in Laodicea. Their beauty and style had blinded me to the nastiness underneath.

Nor do I want to be fooled by a whitewashed facade. If I'm allowed to ask for a Badge, that'd be one I would love to have. Whatever you'd call it. Non-judge-y-ness? Or maybe correct-judge-y-ness?

Again, I was pulled out of my musing when we bumped into the carpark of Sanctuary. We'd made it.

"Welcome home." Daisy almost lifted me from the car. Scary much? But, seriously, I didn't know she cared. I didn't even know she noticed me. Her strong, beautifully inked arms wrapped around me and squeezed her love into me.

A whole crowd had gathered. Oh. My. Word. If I'd known they were all waiting up for us, I would have suggested we tried to get back sooner. But as tired as we all were, after Kait and Marcus put the twins to bed we all gathered at the Meeting Place so I could share our story. They could share theirs. And I could, very inadequately, and not-good-wordly, give my supreme thanks. At times I really felt a bit of Dan's vocabulary would come in handy.

After everyone had been satisfied with the telling of the story, and buckets of hot chocolate had been consumed, we were all allowed to go to bed. But not before we confirmed that tomorrow morning our guests would arrive—or attempt to do so—and we would go ahead with our ceremony.

But before we could go to bed, Val, Marcus, Travis, Daisy and Jonathan walked the perimeter to check the shield, and we all joined in giving thanks to the Light and petitioning for protection.

Then, finally, I was able to go back to the cabin I shared with Val for the last night of being a single woman. I was so flopping excited; I knew with confidence I would not sleep a wink. That was, until my head hit the pillow. Because then, I slept the sleep of the extraordinarily grateful people who had shelter, family, food and protection in the Light.

I had literally just got to sleep when someone was pulling me from my happy place, and I was not happy. Because I was warm, comfortable, safe and in my own bed. Somewhere in my consciousness I made a vow I would never leave this place again. Me and my happy place for ever. So be it.

"Tessa, your guests are here." Val launched herself backwards as I sprang out of bed.

"What? People are here? And I'm still in bed"—I looked down—"in a ratty nightie?"

"We wanted to let you sleep." Kait stood in the doorway with a groggy-looking Riah with sleep-crusty-eyes.

The kid smiled, shuffled over, and hugged me. Since our rescue I had not spent any quality time with her... or Raph. I hugged her back and pulled her over to the bed to sit with me. I looked at my two motherly-type people and felt the emotion well in my eyes.

"Don't tell me you're turning into a teary Iza. I do not think me old heart could cope with that kind of waterworks." Marcus eased past his wife as he entered my bedroom in our cabin. He was forgiven because he was carrying a tray of coffee. He put the tray down, came over and kissed the top of my head. "Love you, kiddo." He then repeated the action to Riah. "Ditto." Dwarfing us both, he sat at the end of the bed and looked at us all. I could be wrong, but I'm sure I saw an extra sheen in his eyes too.

"Do I need to, like, do something? Like, meet our guests? Or start... I don't know... making suggestions, or giving directions for this morning?" We'd never had a real plan, but whatever we did have flew out the window when the twins and I had been detained and our wedding had been railroaded.

Val chuckled. "I don't think even you could derail the freight train that is Izabel and Audette. Between the two of them, they have swept through with Marlene and Fleur and an army of Silverscales, and charmed the pants off—not literally—everyone and have complete control of the situation. Even Daisy succumbed to their charms. As we speak, everything and everyone are being organised."

"Is Raph okay this morning? Did he sleep well? Has he fought with his red haze after yesterday?" I mainly asked Riah, but the others would know equally as well.

"I am well, thank you, Tessa." Raph stood beaming from the doorway of our crowded room. I opened my arms to give him a hug but froze before he even took a step as Dan followed him in. "Are you supposed to be here?"

"Why can't I be here? Everyone else is."

"But I don't think you're supposed to see me before we get married."

"Tessa, I see you every bleeding day. The day before yesterday you were taken from me. Yesterday we turned ourselves inside out to get you back. And last night I pretty much had a coronary at the checkpoint because I was skrat-scared it was all going to happen again. Do not sit there, surrounded by our family, and tell me that I can't see you this morning. That is utter rot." He didn't freeze. Or stop moving. He just marched in, kissed my cheek and sat on my other side.

I released Raph and he straightened his growing-bean-stalk body, grinned and said, "Good morning, Tessa. We wanted to see if you were okay this morning too. Iza and Audette would not let me or Dan help, so we came here instead. Did you sleep well?"

Not for the first time I was ruing the fact I didn't have enough arms. There was just no physical way I could hug everyone. At the same time. Right now. When I needed to most of all.

We spent the next half hour or so drinking our coffee and giving thanks to the Light for keeping us safe, and bringing us home, and for our new friends, and their incredible talents and resources, and for each other... and pretty much everything. Then we all had a pretty extensive petition about the day. Mainly protection. There was no reason to expect we wouldn't be attacked. But we asked, nonetheless, that we would be safe, and the Light would be honoured on this beautiful day.

Iza and Indy with Grace in his arms came by just as we were finishing up. "Hello?" There was absolutely no room left so they stood in the doorway grinning and tearing. Iza that was—Indy was just grinning.

"Okay, everyone, time to move," Iza said. "The girls and I need Tessa and the rest of you gorgeous women. Menfolk, off you go and get ready. We will see you in an hour at the Meeting Place."

"An hour? Is that enough?" I then thought about how Indy and Iza's wedding had been interrupted before they could say their vows. "Is that too long?"

Again, Iza took control, gently pushing people from my room. "I think with all the helpers we have, it will be just enough time. Now, everybody out as Tessa gets ready for her shower."

In the week I had been at the Factory, Dan and his team had not only finished our cabin—which I could not wait to see—they'd put up the shell of another one next door to ours. The ladies transformed this hut into a gathering and final preparation station. After my shower, Iza did my hair. Nothing too flash or fancy. She'd spoken to Dan, and he'd told her how he liked it. So I wore it out in a blaze of wild, unruly abandon. Who knew? He actually *liked* my crazy hair's... craziness?

With us in the hut were Lily, Carley, Genni and Dawn. All the others were with Kait, Val and Sariah in another cabin, getting them ready. But they all disappeared behind a screen of tears as Carley held up my new dress. "A little wedding gift from Kerm, Helen, Iza and me."

It was beautiful.

Stunning.

And perfect.

Far grander and finessed, intricate and classical than I could have managed with scraps from a second-hand shop. It simply was a work of art. Surely it was too good for me... for anyone to actually climb into. But, of course, I did.

And it fit like a glove.

Off the shoulder, with soft, leafy, feather-like petals covering the corset-like bodice. The skirt flowed to the floor in an A-line of heavy fabric, and around the waist an outer skirt that fell into a train spread out. Over the whole thing were hundreds... thousands of tiny, soft, golden-hued gems of various sizes, from pinheads to the size of the stone in my ring. All in perfect tones to match my armour.

And the dress was white.

A symbol of purity.

That I was not.

My purity had been stolen from me... repeatedly... years ago by the gangs. I had since learned this was nothing out of the ordinary. It was actually quite common. All my sisters at the Factory had the same experience. Heck, even my little sister, Riah, had the same experience.

I kept running my hand over the luscious fabric, but in the end, it was too much. "I can't wear this."

"The hell you can't." Lily's protest brought me back to the moment.

"But, Lily... white?"

Iza stepped forward and embraced me. "It was His suggestion, Tessa." She stroked my cheek. "We were going to make it with fabric to match your armour. But the Light said, 'The day she accepted my invitation to be my daughter, Tessa was made new. Whole. A new creation. Her past is gone. Her future lies before her with a solid wall at her back. She will wear white.' So, we made it white." Again, she embraced me.

I guess that is what made the Light that much extra special for us girls. He cherished women. And His sons treasured women. His true sons, that was. In Him we weren't belongings or tools for pleasure... or work. We identified as... people... individuals... special... seen.

Thank you. Thank you. Just... thank you.

There was a knock at the door. "Tessa? You ready? I've been told to let you know that we're good to go. Oh. And Dan said get a wriggle on, he's waited long enough." Jet laughed from the other side of the door.

Then Craig spoke up. "He also wanted to let you know that the wall has been checked and it's strong and holding. The kids and I are patrolling the perimeter and will let you know if there is any sign of an attack from the Unseen. Also, February and October have drones in the air watching the roads for any sign of interruptions from the Seen. And Marcus said to tell you to get a move on, he's hungry and wants to get to the eating part of the ceremony before the attack comes."

I knew that wasn't Marcus's real motivation. It was just his way of saying he loved me... I think.

"One last thing before we go." Iza pulled a single, fingerless, pale glove out of her bag. "We can't remove that ugly thing"—she indicated my tattoo as she slid the skin-coloured fabric over my hand—"but we can make sure that madman has no hold on today. Neither he, his delusions, nor his ugly marks have foothold here." She then linked her silver-scaled arm in mine as my sisters preceded us down the path from the cabin, each of them robed in the most beautiful flowing versions of the original outfit Kerm and I created for them. Wrap boleros, with tulip-shaped sleeves falling over their hands, snugly fitted over white tank-tops. Huge cowls draped over their perfect faces. Long, flowing, wrap culottes gave them freedom and modesty as they moved… and fought. Each in their own Silverscale, armoured, rainbow hue.

I had always felt like a shapeless, flawed child in the presence of these hormonally modified women. Each of them had been artificially enhanced from a young age to lure men to the Temple in order to "worship" Ashera, the fertility goddess. But the only worship involved was of money and male dominance. Lily had helped me see that each woman's perfection and the scales indicating their place on the ladder of sexual proficiency was, in fact, a prison. They knew they were stunning. They knew the impact they had on men… and the women around them. They knew it was not real. It was not them. And in a show of humility, each woman covered her perfection with her cowl so that none would outshine me on my special day. It was a gift of grace. It was demonstration of sisterhood. And I was overwhelmingly touched.

At the edge of the garden we were met by all the others. Kait was wearing the most stunning turquoise dress while Val and Riah were fitted into amazingly cool pantsuits: deep green for Val and forest hues for Riah. Whoever had designed them had nailed it. Not only would Val have been exceedingly uncomfortable in a dress, it made her look both hot and classy, whilst still maintaining her kick-butt-y-ness.

Once again, there was a lot of embracing and crying and gushing over our handmade, personally styled clothes. Most of it though, of course, was over my dress. In the background, music came to us from the Meeting Place. Some of Sanctuary's community who'd been joining in on music evenings were lending their gift for the day. The sky was clear, the temperature was perfect, the garden was gorgeous, my sisters and family were stunning, and I was in an alternate universe were happiness exploded out of every molecule of creation.

"Rattle your dags, Tessa. We want to get this show on the road." Marcus was always helpful at keeping me on track.

48

DANIEL: HEADY HEIGHTS

Was she ever going to get here? Maybe she was having second thoughts. Maybe it was all too much. Maybe she'd realised that forever was a really long time and spending it with me was not such a good idea after all.

I'd run my sweaty palms down my suit pants so often I was making tracks down the seams. I turned to my crew behind me: Marcus, Raph, Indy and Felix, all wearing shmick-as suits. Indy and I were in the same ones we'd originally worn for his wedding ceremony. The one that didn't happen. He was happy to put it to good use and give the thing some happy memories.

For a guy who'd spent seven years—more than a quarter of my life —alone, I couldn't believe all the people who wanted to stand by me today. All the people I wanted to stand by me.

Thank you.

But just because these blokes were happy to be here didn't mean Tessa was. "Do you think she's changed her mind?" I asked no one in particular.

"No, lad. You know what they're like. Get all those women together with new get-ups, and it's all fuss and feathers. All eyes on each other and none to spare for the clock." Marcus shook his head and took a few steps to the side of the Meeting Place and bellowed in the general direction of where they were supposed to be gathering, "Rattle your dags, Tessa. We want to get this show on the road."

He marched back. "That should do it. Just reminded them there was something else they were supposed to be doing today other than wagging their chins."

If I didn't know him better, I'd be put out by Marcus's gruff. But I knew he was nervous… and stressed… and worried… and excited. And Kait wasn't here to help him find his grounding.

Thank the Light for Jonathan. "It's been my experience that you never want to rush a bride. She will be here when she will be here."

I scanned the Meeting Place and took the time to let it sink in. All these people were here for us. They'd taken time out of their schedules with minimal notice to be here and celebrate this day with us. Georgie and Griffin stood off to the side. Georgie, grinning like a Cheshire down the scope of his ridiculously large camera. Griff, with his permanent scowl in place, flicking his eyes over the room full of multicoloured armour, looking decidedly put out. Next to him, beaming, were Marlene and Fleur and their new friends, Helen and Kerm and an equally uncomfortable Ben.

When I remembered his eye-opener in the back of the truck on our way to confront the hordes of hell at the Temple of Ashera, I couldn't help but smile. Our three friends, Georgie, Griff and Ben, were all coming to terms with their new reality in the Light. I was so grateful they had quality men in Kerm, Felix, and Indy, to walk beside them and show them the ropes.

Jonathan tapped me on the shoulder and nodded to the far end of the Meeting Place. I gulped when I realised I was about to be confronted by *my* new reality.

We all turned to see Jordan, Hiro and Joko walking down the centre of the tent, spread out around Kazi in her wheelchair. Dawn perched on her lap. Joko carried Grace.

She was coming.

Next came two rows of Silverscales wearing their usual get-ups but different. All of them had their cowls drawn over their heads, adopting anonymity rather than revealing their usual head-turning star attraction. Each carried a small bunch of flowers. But you could have blown me over when, instead of going to stand on the "bride's side" of the front, they filed past me and each and every one of them, even Lotti—and Amina—stopped and embraced me. Some even kissed my cheek. Not one of them said a word. It was pretty powerful. Now I didn't only have sweat-streaked pants, my shoulders were soaked with tears. Theirs and mine.

Again, thank the Light for Jonathan. He passed me a hanky when, after a pause, Riah stepped into the aisle, front and centre. She locked her eyes on me, telling me she loved me, she was proud to have me as a brother, in family and in the Light. And she was super proud to stand at my left in the battle. I almost lost it at that point. But she rolled her eyes, *Get it together*. It would have been harsh if she wasn't crying herself.

Then she started coming toward me. After a few beats, though, I only had eyes for Tessa. She, too, paused at the top of the aisle flanked by Val and Kait. She didn't look at me. She looked around the group gathered. Her hand went to her mouth and Val passed her her own hanky. She dabbed her face clear, drew a deep breath, then lifted her eyes to me.

Time froze.

My heart exploded.

My brain stopped functioning.

I didn't have words, thoughts, or any rational concept for the vision that stood before me.

Marcus reached over and gently lifted my chin to stop me gaping. Tessa laughed through her tears and ran down the aisle and tried to launch herself into my arms. It was a bit tricky in her dress. I clung to her with the passion she fed into me.

Our guests laughed and gave Riah, Val and Kait time to join us at a more stately pace.

"I do believe that would be a... 'No'. I believe our... unconventional Tessa has not changed her mind, and yes, she in fact wants to marry you." Felix's commentary made me smile and got us all back on track.

Jonathan cleared his throat. "Best we get a move on, then."

But before he could say another word, the cries of, "All clear!" came from one of the kids standing on a ladder near the eastern boundary.

"All clear," Craig responded from the west.

"All clear," February called from the back of the tent. Her eyes no doubt on a laptop.

"Right then, let's get started." Everyone sat and Jonathan began. We hadn't given him any details, just that we wanted to get married. We let him take care of everything, because he was like captain-marriage-man. Being the Head Shepherd of Philadelphia, he'd done his fair share of weddings. But he was also really switched-on and knew there was tension about an attack or an interruption. So, after a quick welcome, acknowledging the distance and difficulty we'd all overcome to get to this point, he then asked if we wanted to say anything before he committed each of us to the other.

I went first. "Tessa, I love you, just as you are. Almost two years ago I told you, I want you to fly, to reach for the stars and go as far as you can. I want to be the one who helps launch you, and catch you when you land. I know you want to rescue yourself and I love that about you. But know this: when you can't, I will be waiting in the wings to do my best. Next to the Light, you are my priority. I promise you, Tessa, to always leave the light on, the key out, and the door unlocked, for you. And only you, for always.

"I don't know the first thing about marriage. All I have seen of it is Marcus and Kait. And I reckon they've got it going pretty good. So, with the Light's help, and their example, I want to give this a go with you. My best, lifelong, friend." As far as vows went, I reckon I nailed it. By the rivers running down Tessa's face and all the ladies behind her, I reckon they agreed.

But when I went to untuck my shirt to help her clean her face, Tessa growled. Predator bird made an appearance. "Don't you dare."

I laughed and pulled her tight. Noting she did, in fact, use my jacket to wipe her face. I guessed this suit was earning its worth.

Jonathan continued. "Tessa, in front of our family and friends, do you take Daniel to be your lawful, wedded husband?"

"I do."

"Tessa?" Jonathan raised his eyebrows. She looked a bit lost. "Is there something you wanted to say?"

"Oh. Yes." She turned back to me, her face blotchy and earnest. "Dan, I lov—"

"All clear."

"All clear."

"All clear."

The three cries from our lookouts came in one after the other, loud and clear.

Tessa blinked a few times, smiled then continued. "…love you. Almost two years ago, I promised that, apart from the Light, you are my number one priority. I love the real you, just as you are and will continue to love every version of you brought about through the Light's loving transformation. I promise to always come home to you, and you only. To take you with me wherever I go, if not in person, then very much in my heart. I am and will always be for you. I will be your person who chooses to stay. I am *your* home for as long as I live." Her voice faded to a whisper as her emotion took over. After a moment of warring with control she continued. "Wherever we are, wherever the Light takes us, you are *my* home. Forever."

Jonathan said, "Daniel, in front of our family and friends, do you take Tessa to be your lawful, wedded wife?"

"I do."

And that was about the end of both of us, and the rest of the crew standing around us. Even Jonathan had to take a moment.

"The rings?" Jonathan looked to the twins. Raph, standing behind me, Riah, standing by Tessa. They came forward and gave our rings to us so we could give them to each other.

"With this ring, Tessa, I take you to be my wife, my lifelong friend, forever."

"Dan, accept this ring as a symbol of my continuous love for you, my lifelong friend, as my husband."

We exchanged rings and a feeling of certainty, peace, and rightness came over me.

Jonathan continued, "By the power granted to me by the law of the land and the authority of the Light, with the greatest of pleasure and honour I pronounce, for the glory of the Light, you are both joined as one in Him, husband and wife. Let no person separate what the Light has joined this day…"

Jonathan's mouth kept moving and I suspect words came out, but he was drowned out by the roar and cheers of our family and friends. And the pounding in my head. I was kissing Tessa… my wife. And she was kissing me back.

Be at peace, My children. You are loved. Remember, despite what comes, it is well.

We pulled apart and were instantly swallowed by family and friends, hugging, kissing and crying. I was in a cloud. And not completely aware of what was going on, but came back with the cries of, "All clear."

"All clear."

"All clear."

Tessa and I were whisked away by Georgie and Griff as they set us up for photos in different locations around the property and with every conceivable arrangement and collection of family and friend groups.

I was close to losing every scrap of patience I had left. We were under Tessa's and my gum tree in the cattle paddock. Our friends and family, who had all had their turn through the photo mill, were standing in the shade of the trees nearby. Kids were running around and climbing the big old fig tree standing sentinel in the centre of the paddock.

Val, Kait, Marcus, Tessa and I were waiting for Raph, who'd had to run back to the cabin for something. Riah would not let us leave.

"I am coming, I am coming." We turned to see Raph running across the paddock carrying his drum.

I looked to Riah and questioned her with my eyes.

She grinned, and when Raph joined us, they stood together a

couple of metres away. We waited for their twin-speak to finish, then Raph addressed us. "Riah and I have a present for you. But after what happened at the Factory, we did not want to do anything to interrupt or hold up the ceremony. We decided to wait till it was over. We also wanted you to know this is our gift for you. Just from us, to just you. Our family." His eyes scanned the five of us in the shelter of the old scrappy-barked gum.

Raph sat on the ground in his flash suit and started a beat, then, as one, they both broke out into a song. Their voices meshed into a heart-breaking harmony. Obviously, they'd practised. And that fact alone was enough to bring me to tears… again. Riah had offered her voice and invited her brother to prepare this gift for us.

I was mildly aware of the others in the shade of trees nearby. But mostly I was conscious of my family… and my wife, standing around me, hugging us with their arms whilst Riah and Raph blessed us with their song. I would put money on the fact there was not one dry eye as far as their voices travelled.

They came to an end and then we waited till the last of their notes were carried away on the breeze, the moment too pure to break.

Raph sat, waiting for a response. I could see the question written all over him. Riah stared at us, then flicked her hand, *Get over it.*

And once again today, we were a family huddle swamping them both with ridiculous love.

"All clear."

"All clear."

"All clear."

"Time for lunch."

We all gathered and made our way back to the feast that had been set up in our absence. And the table of gifts that had materialised out of nowhere. The rest of the day passed in sharing a meal, conversation, memories and dreams with the family the Light had given us.

The sun dropped over the mountains, taking the warmth with it, prompting the crew from the Factory to make their farewells. Ben, Tomiko, Kazi, Kerm and Helen were next to leave and, finally,

Marlene, Fleur, Felix, Georgie and Griffin. Then in small groups Sanctuary members started heading bedward.

I looked to Tessa. She was sitting huddled between Marcus and Kait. Val was flanked by Raph and Riah.

"Thank you for an amazing day. For all the work you put into getting us to this point." I stopped and thought of my journey which started pretty much three and a half years ago. I looked to Val. "Thank you for coming for me. For Seeing me. For fighting for me." I turned to Marcus and Kait. "Thank you for putting up with me, having the patience and confidence to get me through." To the twins I said, "Raph, I know we had a tricky start, mate, but you just keep blowing my mind with your awesomeness. Riah, from the day I walked into your home you have had my heart. The both of you have done nothing but demonstrate unconditional love to a guy who was drowning and lost. Thank you."

Finally, I looked at Tessa. "For fighting with me, for me, and beside me every step of the way. For taking a chance on and loving a no-good, stinking, gutter rat. For agreeing to be my lifelong, forever friend. Thank you."

"You're getting as bad as Iza, me girl." Marcus was trying to deflect attention from his own tears by getting everyone to look at Tessa.

I held out my hand to her. "Would you like to come and see the home I built for us?"

She nodded.

"Words, Tessa." Marcus was still trying to hide his emotions.

She kissed his cheek and hugged him. Then everyone else. Finally, she came to me. "Okay."

One word.

Two syllables.

Four letters to begin the rest of our lives.

I swooped her off her feet and carried her to our cabin. But when I tried kicking the door open, it didn't budge. I'd forgotten to leave it unhitched. Shuffling Tessa so I could reach the lock with one hand, I almost dropped her.

Thankfully she saw the funny side and laughed. "Let me."

Unhooking one arm from behind my neck, she opened the door and gasped. I carried her in and placed her on the ground. With her hands on her cheeks, eyes like saucers, she looked around. "Oh, Dan, it's perfect."

Pride swelled my chest to bursting.

49

CONTESSA: JUST A GIRL

I slid to the ground wanting to be everywhere at once. I wanted to touch and feel every fabric, texture, surface. It was too much to take in.

The perfection.

The workmanship.

The art.

And all for me.

For. Me.

I couldn't stop the tears. I turned to take in the man who had made it happen. Just for me. All of it. The cabins, the boardwalks, the labour, had been of love for everyone… and the Light, I knew that. But the inspiration had been for me. This whole project was a love letter from Dan to me. My heart melted like a candle. It was now a puddle of spilled wax.

Dan removed his jacket and threw it over the back of the couch. When he saw my face, he started pulling his shirt out of his waistband and held it out to me to wipe my face.

"Don't you dare," I growled through my emotion-clogged throat.

He laughed. "You're right." Then he ripped the shirt off. I mean, seriously. Ripped the thing off. Buttons pinged onto the kitchen bench and floorboards. He then handed me the destroyed item of clothing. "You need more than a corner for this one."

Speechless. I was literally without sound, motion, or thought.

A warm chuckle rumbled from his chest, and he stepped forward and gently raised my chin with a finger. Then with the softest touch used his shirt to wipe my tears. All I could do was stare. But then all laughter evaporated, and the depth of his soul was revealed through the heat in his eyes. And I realised this, too, was a gift.

Dan was letting me in, letting me see him. This man who had spent most of his life keeping people out, was… had… is… giving me an invitation to dwell behind his wall… with him. I reached up on my toes and pulled him down to kiss him. To try, with my actions, to show him what it all meant to me. I simply didn't have the vocabulary. He was the wordsmith, not me.

I reached up under my arm and undid the zip holding everything in place. My dress pooled at my feet, and this time it was my husband who was speechless. His hungry eyes devoured my body and the gift of fancy underwear my sisters had given me. It was my turn to laugh and gently lift his dropped jaw.

Cherished.

I now knew what the word actually meant. Dan, with the greatest of care, lifted me, carried us to our bedroom, and laid me on our bed. His warmth stretched out beside me and for an eternity we just stared into each other's eyes. I had waited my whole life for this moment. To be one with my soul mate, my forever life-friend. How I wished I had not been used and abused by the rubbish in Sodom. How I desperately wished I could be whole and pure for Dan.

Maybe it was because I had let my thoughts be dragged back into the mud. Maybe it was the intimacy. Maybe it was his huge, calloused hand running down my side. Maybe it was all three, but I was snapped like a rubber band back to the hovel, the darkness and filth. The harshness, the brutality and the pain.

Would it hurt?

Would I make it through?

Would I survive?

"Hey, Tessa, sweetheart, breathe. It's okay." Dan held my face and was trying to make eye contact. His warmth brought me back to the moment.

I was an iron rod.

Rigid.

Frozen.

Sweating.

I couldn't breathe.

Dan tenderly turned me so my back was pressed into his front, and he just held me, breathed deeply and waited. "It's okay, honey, this is enough. I just want to hold you."

His breathing was deep, powerful, purposeful. In time, involuntarily, my body became attuned to his. My spine relaxed and his warmth infused my shattered brain, bringing sanity back. Memories, pain and fear worked their way out through my silent tears. And Dan just held and gently rocked me. Breathing deeply and crooning softly.

Help me... help me be brave. Help me forget. Help me move on. I know Dan. I trust him. I love him. Help me get through this nightmare. Help me show him that I love him... I trust him. Remind me I am healed. I am not that person anymore. I am new. I am cherished. I am Yours.

Grabbing my determination with a fist full of awkward, I rolled over and considered this man who lay beside me. Asleep. True to his word, it *was* enough to just hold me.

The choice was mine.

To sleep, or get over this hurdle.

Tonight.

My determination was dissolving. There was no pressure. And I was pretty tired. Seriously, who wouldn't be? We'd been through hell. We'd waited two years, what was one more night? We'd be better prepared to face this nightmare tomorrow. Exhaling all the tension, I was like a water balloon, floppy and formless with relief.

Coward.

The word came unbidden from my consciousness. It was my voice, I knew it well. With the challenge, determination flooded the gates and pushed awkward out the door. Seriously, what was I scared of? What was I? A girl…?

Actually, tonight that didn't seem to be such a bad thing. And with that, I kissed my husband with a heat that had him awake and back in the game in a fraction of a heartbeat.

50

DAISY: VILE, VILLAINOUS, VENOM

We were all still being carried along on the train of joy and celebration left over from Wild Cat and Dryad's wedding. I'd never been to a celebration that crossed over and knitted together so many cultural barriers, that blended so many expressions of humanity. *That doesn't sound right.* I mean, so many levels of the cultural spectrum? All walks of life had met on common ground in the Light, to honour life and union. These guys had been with us for almost one and half years and had proven themselves to be the real deal. I had seen them in all lights, and they were far from perfect, but they were genuine. They opened my eyes to greater dimensions of possibility in the Light.

I'd grown up in a family who were committed members of the Community. I had been taught about the Light for as long as I could remember. I was aware of wrong and right. But now I was being made aware of the truth of it. I was beginning to wonder if there was a difference between being committed to the Community and being committed to the Light. I loved the Light, but the Community? Not so much. Which had always made me feel like a leper. But now I was witnessing real Community being played out every day in front of me, on so many scapes, in many different palettes. I couldn't help but be confronted by the bigger picture. It was both frightening and liberating.

The Shepherd, Warrior, Mountain, Hot Cocoa, Nanna-May... even Tea, they all got it. They lived it. And I really thought I wanted to, too. To take that step from lingering at the lintel to fully embracing life on the other side of the doorway.

What are You calling me to? What are You calling me into? What am I supposed to do with this... thing? What do You want me to do? To be?

I was totally caught up in the kaleidoscope of concepts when someone cleared the half-eaten meal in front of me. We had gathered to share lunch in the Meeting Place. With Wild Cat and Dryad due to take off soon, we had combined a post-wedding party with a bit of a farewell. Not that they would be gone for long. A week at most. Looking at the family around the tables that'd been pulled together, elbow-buddies in the battle, I couldn't help but swell with pride, peace and purpose. There were around forty people left—seventeen families —who would never have been brought together, or even found common ground outside the Light, if not for The Quake.

Thank You.

I knew some of them from the whole Community scene, growing up when it was relatively new, in this relatively new city. It was a bit incestuous... if I can call it that. We all knew the main families, and children who grew up together generally ended up marrying and merging families. It was one of the reasons I baulked at the whole thing. But I can honestly say, I don't know how I would have ever got to know, or even wanted to spend time with most of these people, if I hadn't been thrown in with them. And my life would have been poorer for it.

What do You want from us? Is it enough to just live? To do what we're doing? To make a stand?

We were so small. So few. Against such power. And so many. We really had nothing. Except each other.

And You.

Thanks.

It was enough for now. I would work the rest out later. What I did know was that I was on clean-up duty with the kids. I looked around and noticed Raph was walking back into the Meeting Place with Ruby. Both were subdued, therefore I was on high alert.

"We have the mail," Ruby announced as she climbed into my lap. She was seven now, but still small enough to snuggle.

I looked to Raph. "What's up?"

"They are out there again. And they are saying some things that are not nice about Ruby's dad." The kid dropped the letter on the table—another one from Anonymous, one they'd both normally be jumping all over—then he dragged his feet to help out with the cleaning up.

I scooted Ruby round to give her a piggyback and together we joined the cleaning crew—today it was the kids: Phil's daughter, Jayne, Miriam's sons, Charlie, Harry and Eddie, and Josh's kids, Oliver and Lucy—to get the job done.

I tried to find the Shepherd to warn him, but he must have been out for a nap. His fatigue still wiped him out for a portion of each day.

* * *

"Overseer? Overseer? What is your response to the allegations released today?"

"Overseer? Would you like to share your side of the story?"

"Overseer, is it true you have fathered children to multiple parishioners in your Community?"

"Overseer? Is it true your daughter is not your biological child?"

Tea and I had left the kids behind and gone to investigate. A caravan of traffic had clogged our road and set up camp in our carpark. Maybe the media were in a heightened state because Lightmas was just around the bend and it was a good season for slinging mud at the Light and His people.

As soon as we—by that I mean Tea—made an appearance, the questions from the gaggle of journalists started flying. The idiots didn't even know what the Shepherd looked like. They were confusing a seventy-odd-year-old black man with a white one, thirty years his junior.

I was just so grateful that we had made it through the wedding without this madhouse-act ruining everything for them.

The catcalling was ridiculous. I wished I could deal with them the same way we dealt with the demons. Just walk straight up to them and stick them with my sword. Sadly, that was a reality that lived only in my dreams. There, I could give each of them a bone-crunching smack for their outrageous allegations and heartless slander.

The media hype had started in earnest a few days ago. The slow leak of lies had begun about a month before that—Anonymous alerted us to it in a letter. It had taken a while for the Shepherd to share the news. Of course, it was all lies, but it still made him sick. It had made us all sick.

I had to admit, he did look very different now than he had when he headed up the establishment as Overseer, or how I remembered him from when I was a teenager. And he looked crazy-different from when he'd arrived, a pale scarecrow in ill-fitting clothes. He'd filled out and muscled up since fitting in to life here. Hot Cocoa's haircut kind of made him look younger. It was getting harder to think of him as an old man. Not that he was, but to be safe, I had to try to think of him as way older—a father of teenagers. His eldest son was only thirteen or so years younger than my twenty-eight.

Old man, Daisy. The guy is a married man, with teenage sons. And an amazing little girl who owns my heart.

He is not married, Daisy.

He's a widower.

A widower for three years. And that is very different.

But too old and "corporate" for you. You made yourself a promise. Remember?

But he's not really that old. Or that corporate.

"Well, that's new." Tea tapped out his pipe on the gate post next to me.

I'd lost track and tuned out to their rants. "Which one is that?"

"The fact that our esteemed Overseer was apparently fathering children when he was in a coma."

"What do we do?" I'd asked the others to keep Ruby away from the gate so she wasn't vulnerable to the lies or caught on camera. These leeches would do anything for a story. I was grateful the Shepherd was having his afternoon nap so he wasn't exposed to this skrat.

"Luke has been filling me in with the increased hype and lies. It's getting beyond stupid."

"Is there someone we know? Or trust in the industry? Who would report our side of the story truthfully? We have to do something."

"The bull has already made a run for it, my girl. No use shutting the gate now. Anything we say will be twisted to mean something else."

"And our silence will be taken for affirmation."

Murmuring was growing to a disgruntled undertow behind me, but I didn't turn around. No way was I going to take my eyes off the intruders in front of me.

But then my heart sank, shuddered and shrank when a body walked past me and crossed the no-man's-land between the opposition and the gate. The Shepherd. He'd had enough and looked like he was going to take them on.

No way would we let him do that alone. As one, the rest of us, and by that I mean the whole community of Sanctuary, followed him out, stopping a few metres behind him. I didn't want to crowd him but wanted to demonstrate solidarity.

The media were so shocked they stood, mid-motion, frozen. Cameras poised and running. After a second, whether it was instinct or hunger, mics were up, and it was action all stations.

Jonathan spoke... projected into the frenzy, "Investigative journalism."

Nothing. The intruders all slowly looked at each other. So Jonathan repeated himself. This time, speaking to the closest camera that was filming. "Investigative journalism. Can anyone tell me what happened to it? Or perhaps you could raise your hand if you know what it means?"

Again, the parasites looked at each other then back to Jonathan, speechless.

"Has any one of you attempted investigating the claims against me?

Did any one of you bother to look into the allegations? No, of course not. If you had made an effort to contact the office of Births, Deaths, and Marriages, you would have known that on my daughter's birth certificate both Laura and I are recorded as Ruby's parents. If any of you had bothered to scroll through social media, you would have seen photos of Laura, my one and only wife, pregnant, and Ruby as a newborn, surrounded by me and her four brothers at the hospital. Yes, her hair colour is different to mine, but it is the same as her mother and one of her brothers.

"As far as sanctioning orgies in my role as Overseer? This stems purely from your warped and depraved imaginations. A 'love feast' is the celebration of the Light's love for His people... all people. And as for fathering other children in the past two years? Any one of you could have looked into it and seen that I have been in hospital, in a coma, then in assisted living. I have been under surveillance by my medical team since the day of The Quake.

"If any of you honestly believe that I have started a sex cult where I now have multiple wives and children, perhaps you should take the time to ask any of the husbands and fathers who are current—or past —residents of Sanctuary.

"As far as being a closed community, hiding from the government, any one of you could have researched and found one of the multiple people who used to come to the weekly markets held here. The only reason the gates were closed was due to the sabotage and picketing. Not because of what we do here, but because of our belief the Gerent is a man. A human being. A mortal. This is our crime. Because of this we have lost our homes, finances and freedoms, as well as family. Between The Quake and the Gerent, we have lost everything. We are here as guests of the landowner. We don't even own the land we stand on or the huts we live in.

"Here at Sanctuary, we are doing everything we can to survive, to serve the wider community and glorify the Light. That's it. We could invite you in to see for yourselves, but why should we? You are not investigative journalists in pursuit of the truth, you are parasites feeding off sensationalism. Now, as far as we can see, apart from upsetting the Gerent, we have not broken any laws. But you are all trespassing on private property. And on behalf of the owner, I am asking you to leave. You have five minutes to vacate the premises because the police are on their way and will be here in approximately four and a half minutes. The choice is yours."

And with that, he turned, winked at me, and walked past, heading back into Sanctuary. But before he made it to the gate he stopped and turned to address our trespassers again. "Oh, I almost forgot. I have been in touch with my lawyer, and if any of you choose to print, publish or produce—"

"Nice one." I couldn't help letting out my appreciation of his alliteration. *He did that for you, you know. He made an effort, despite all the skrat he's swimming through, for you.*

Oh, for freaky-freak's sake, toughen the frack up, Daisy. He is not flirting with you over alliteration. He's an old man. An old married man. Remember that. He's just... thoughtful. And old. Too old for you.

I was ashamed of my blush when he looked over his shoulder and nodded, acknowledging my compliment, then continued, "—any more lies about me, my family or the Community I live in, you will be sued for libel. Again, I would like to remind you of investigative journalism and challenge you to look up its definition." Then he walked back through the group, disappearing into the heart of Sanctuary. The rest of us closed ranks behind his back.

The crowd in front of us still hadn't moved except the few who'd had the nous to film their one and only interview with Jonathan, ex-Overseer, ex-Head Shepherd of the Community in Philadelphia. I held out my wrist and tapped my watch. And just like that, they hustled back into their cars and cleared the carpark. Jonathan's bluff had been swallowed hook, line and sinker. I don't know how much grace he'd earned us. Maybe it was just enough room to exhale before the next attack came.

51

ANONYMOUS: DONATIONS

*D*ear Brothers and Sisters,
We are not alone.

You *are not alone.*

We have friends who are not in the Light, but also not actively opposed to the Light. They have been helping to support us with Domination Tokens. Please accept this gift to help you as the city closes down around us.

I believe you are able to support yourselves to a great extent from what you produce onsite, but there are always things we need to buy from the Machine. Whether I am here or not, I will do what I can to keep sending you what I can to help. It is not much, but I petition the Light that it helps.

Anonymous

5 2

CONTESSA: FALLING DOWN THE MOUNTAIN

Neither the impending doom of the Gerent's visit, nor the ugly black tattoo on the back of my hand could begin to dent my happy bubble this morning. We sat in a world of bliss in our favourite —and what had become our regular—cafe in the city, relaxing and watching the world hurry by. We had a whole day off today, and soon would be going away for a full week for our honeymoon.

I know. Just like regular people. Lovely Felix had paid for us to have a week away in a luxury resort in Ephesus as our wedding gift. I could create and alter any clothes to make them suitable for a posh resort. But we didn't have a swimming costume. And I didn't know the first thing about making one. And didn't want to spend the next few days stressing over how to make that happen.

Dan still had some money left over from our time in Laodicea. He'd been saving up a small stash to get my ring jazzed up for the proposal, and I had earned a bit from our early days when the markets at Sanctuary still functioned. So, after coffee with my husband—yep. Hus-band—we were going shopping in a real shop, to buy real bathers. And to do some last-minute gift shopping in the Feast Day sales. Of course, we would buy things in Ephesus, but with the twins' fourteenth birthday a week after Lightmas, I was always on the lookout for something extraordinary and personal. Naturally, I had made gifts for everyone, but we wanted to make it extra special for them after what we'd just been through.

Bright lights and colours of the gods and goddesses decorated shop windows, light poles and the city gardens as people embraced the Feast Days season. It just so happened it was also the time we celebrated Lightmas, but we were a lot more subtle about it. Regardless of which god people chose to celebrate this time of the year, the different trimmings and accessories made for an interesting spectacle as I sat back and watched the world wander by from our street-side table as Mrs Dan…? "Dan?"

Eventually I called him back from whatever universe he was in, a silly grin plastered on his face—it was perfectly fair to call it silly, it matched mine. "What's your last name?"

"What?"

"Your last name. Who am I?"

"What?"

"Your. Last. Name. I'm Mrs who?"

"Oh. Sutherland." His gooey smile returned. "Mrs Sutherland. The first since Grandma."

"Can we stop by the registry and see about officially changing my name to Mrs Sutherland afterwards?"

"Let's go there first."

It's not like I didn't want to. But I also knew Dan's lack of stamina when it came to shopping. I figured maybe I could use it as a carrot at the end of the day to keep him going. "Shopping first? Please? Then registry on our way home?"

The look on his face softened my stand and I tried a compromise. "What if we leave the car here, walk to the registry office, and if there are any swimwear shops on the way there, we stop in."

His shoulders dropped and a look of relief swam across his face. "Deal."

So, with coffees finished and our plans set, we went to pay and head off on our day of bliss.

"We're not supposed to accept that anymore." The elderly lady behind the counter looked over her shoulder, then lowered her voice. "New rules. The whole city is phasing out regular money and we are supposed to use these tokens." She held up a gold-coloured coin, then spun it round and revealed it was stamped with the Gerent's face on both sides. Hetty looked down at our intertwined hands, noticed the gold band nestled next to the ring sparkling on my finger, and smiled. "This one's on the house. But see you get to the bank and exchange some money for tokens." She wrapped my fingers around the one that was in her hand. "And congratulations."

With an air of disbelief, we returned to the street and, on our phones, plotted a route via clothing stores to the registry office. I had taken Felix's advice and made a point of taking it with me wherever I went. Especially after the past week. I was learning it was actually kind of cool and could do heaps of things, like give directions. Although I must admit, everything lost a bit of its glimmer with this latest news.

"What does this mean, Dan? Doesn't our money work here anymore?"

"I don't know. We'll have to wait and see." He didn't seem to be as worried as I was and soon enough, we passed a shop selling swimwear. He grabbed my hand and pulled me in. But instead of stopping at any of the brightly decorated racks, or noticing any of the "sale" signs, he went straight to the cashier. "Do you accept this card here?" He handed the card connected to our very own special bank account to the young shop assistant.

Without speaking, she swiped it through her machine and when no beeps sounded or lights flashed, she handed it back. "No. You need to go to the bank to get your account changed to tokens. No one can do business in this city without them."

At first, I thought her emotionless, robotic response was rude. But then her words sank in, and I looked around her shop, empty of customers. I guessed it wasn't just us being caught out.

We went back out onto the street and decided to go to the registry office first, then try the bank.

"This document is not legal."

"I beg your pardon?"

The registry clerk stared back at us, impassive.

"This document is not legal." He repeated each word slowly, enunciating each syllable. Like we were idiots.

Dan joined me in the battle with the clerk to try to get some answers. "Could you please explain why it's not?"

The man heaved the heavy sigh of the put-upon and bored. He rolled his eyes between us, pursed his lips, shook his head and sighed again. Turning our wedding certificate around to face us, he pointed to Jonathan's name. "This bloke is no longer registered as a Shepherd and does not have the legal right to marry people by the law of the land in Philadelphia."

"What does that mean?" I tried not to shriek, but seriously, there are times and places for panic, and I truly felt this was one of them.

"It means"—he stared at me like I was an imbecile—"this is not a legal document. This marriage is not recognised. You are not legally married, and you have no legal basis to change your name."

Shock.

Ice-cold, immobilising shock took hold of me.

Dan too, apparently.

Neither one of us moved.

Statues.

We were statues.

"Could you please step aside, there are others waiting." The clerk's voice reached me at some level and the person behind us gently moved us out of the line. I don't know how long we stood there or how we got back to the car. I don't even know how we got back to Sanctuary in one piece. I did not remember any part of the trip.

But we made it. We sat in the car, hand in hand, and stared at the future.

Not.

Married.

We were bundled out of the car and herded into the Meeting Place. We each held a cup of coffee while Dan told everyone our news.

"I'm so sorry," Jonathan said as he paced in front of us.

Daisy scoffed. "Of all the arrogant, autocratic attitudes. How on earth can you turn this around and make it about you?"

It made me wonder why Daisy was always angry at Jonathan. He was the loveliest man. And he'd had it pretty tough. But she always had to have a dig at him. It also made me wonder why he never took offence. He always returned her digs with a smile. "I'm not responsible for the Gerent's actions. But I should have been aware that when I was kicked out of my job, they would revoke my rights and authority." He turned back to us, and his smile was a comforting blanket in this wickedly cold storm. "But my authority in the Light has not been revoked. In His eyes, and within this community, you are married." His face dropped. "Just not legally, as far as the city of Philadelphia stands."

"What does that mean?" Fear and distress drove my voice up a shrieky octave.

"Nothing, really. The state doesn't care if you are married or not. It has no bearing on your lives except for when you die, or if later down the track you decide to separate. I'm not too sure what impact it will have on the census and the Gerent's take on things, though."

Dan spoke up for both of us. "What? We've only just got married, and you're talking about us separating? Now that's a confidence boost."

Jonathan laughed. "I'm not saying you're going to separate. I'm just explaining the legalities of not being lawfully married according to the State."

"But I want to be married. I went to a lot of trouble and waited a very long time and went through an awful lot to get here so I could be married to Dan, and I jolly well want to be married." I now had everyone's attention, but from a wary, "stay away from the crazy woman" perspective.

Dan looked from me back to Jonathan. "How do we fix it?"

"Well, I am not sure how far this madness extends, but there would be nothing stopping you going to another city and booking in for a registry wedding. I'm sure Felix would know someone. They might even come here. But considering the issues arising for being in the

Light, it might be best to go straight to a Registry Office, especially since you're already married in the Light."

"Hello, Felix?" Kait was already on her phone explaining the situation. And, for the first time since we left the cafe this morning, I felt like there was some hope.

I gripped Dan's arm around my shoulders and brushed my wet cheeks with my other hand.

He leaned in and kissed the top of my head. "It's going to be alright, Tessa. You're still my wife, no matter what the city says."

"Right." Kait was off the phone, her face fierce. "Pack your bags. Felix is arranging things as we speak. You were due to leave tomorrow for your honeymoon. But go now, via Laodicea, then back to Ephesus. You can go swimwear shopping with the ladies from the Factory or when you're at the resort." She was breathing deeply and visibly, trying to stay calm. But the rage in her eyes and the light splintering her armour was making her anger pretty obvious.

Thank You for our family. Thank You again for Felix. Please make this alright. I can't believe they would do this to us. Take our marriage. And our money.

* * *

THE COMPLETE MESS the Gerent was making of our lives wasn't doing much damage to my happy bubble this morning. Sitting in a beautiful cafe in Ephesus, relaxing, and watching the world hurry by as Dan and I sat in a world of bliss. We had made it... via the Factory, an online meeting with a legal marriage celebrant, who sent us links for online forms to get my name changed, then on to our honeymoon.

Yes, just like regular people. Once again, Felix had come to the rescue and sorted everything, with the help of Marlene, and here we were. Married. I was now Mrs Tessa Sutherland.

Thank the Light we made it before a lot of the official-businessy-businesses shut down for the Feast Day holidays.

Thank You for Felix. And giving him all his money. And making him so generous. I don't want to take advantage of him, but it seems with his contacts and finances, he always has what we need. But I know You give it all to him... not that he doesn't work hard for it, I know he does. And he's paid a price for it, I know he has. But the outcome of all of that is, he is there to throw us a lifeline and I just want to say thank You. It's reassuring to know You love all people, not just the down and outers like Dan and me. Not that I'd ever call Val a down and outer, but You know wha—

"Tessa?" Dan shook my arm. "I said, do you want to go check out the beach?"

"Again? This will be your third time today."

"What? You don't love the beach? I can't believe how frolping big... and powerful... and loud... and amazing it is. Had you ever seen the ocean before?" He was like a kid in a candy store. How could I possibly deny him a trip across the road to walk along the beach again.

"No, Dan, I hadn't ever seen the beach before. And yes, I would love to go check it out again."

"Cool." He stood but looked at me sideways from under his eyelashes. "You gonna wear your swimmers again?"

"Right, I get it. It's the *beach* you want to see again, huh?"

"Can't blame a guy if he wants to have his cake and eat it too." His grin melted my heart because it was genuine. The guy actually loved me. He was genuinely turned on by my stick figure and wild hair. "But to be honest, I get to see you in your swimmers every day for the rest of my life. But the beach? I don't know when we'll be back again."

I stood, took my overdress off, wrapped my sarong around my waist, wrestled most of my unruly hair up under my broad-brimmed hat, then held out my hand.

Dinner in the restaurant was perfect. I had just finished the most scrummy dessert. I leaned back and sipped my chamomile tea. The atmosphere was relaxed, dimly lit, quiet and perfect. I couldn't really see much of the other diners, but I looked around and considered all the people here. "It's hard to think this is some people's normal."

Dan, sitting to my right, leaned back in his chair and took my hand. He did that a lot. I don't think he even knew he was doing it. I'd noticed since the wedding, he seemed to think he could, or should. I don't know, but I liked it. "Do you want it to be ours?"

Well, you could have knocked me over with a serviette. "What?"

"Is that what you want?"

"What?"

"Seriously, Tessa. As soon as we stepped away from Sanctuary, the heat died. It was like the final months at the Factory, after the battle. The way we do life is not the way normal people live their lives. I'm just asking what you want."

"You'd leave Sanctuary? Our family? If I said that's what I wanted?"

He took a very long time to answer. I began to fret, but worked hard at my cucumber disguise. "Well, I will admit that when I committed myself to you before we went and took the Temple of Ashera dow—"

"Hang on a minute, you didn't propose till after."

"Yeah, but I committed myself to you the night Indy left. Anyway, stop interrupting. When I committed myself to you—regardless of when that was—we were both in the Light, fighting for the Light, being guided by the Light and I thought that's where our future lay. I still feel that very strongly. But I know it's not most people's normal. This is normal. But, if you changed your mind and said you wanted normal, well, we'd have to figure out what that looked like." He tried to look relaxed. He leaned back and very subtly rolled his shoulders and wore a calm mask. But I had known him long enough to see the tension. The fear.

I put him out of his misery. "Dan." I waited until I had his full attention. "What part of me... of my life is, or has ever been, normal? I kind of think the concept is so alien to me that if we tried it, I might be allergic. There is no way I could step out of our lane into this one permanently. Every so often, to take a breath might be nice, but long term?" I couldn't hold back my chuckle. "I think it'd be the end of me."

His head dropped and eyes closed. He breathed deeply through his nose then looked at me with dark, dark eyes. A cold shiver sparked my synapses. "You finished here? I'm thinking I'm ready for bed."

53

ANONYMOUS: DEPARTURE

Dear Brothers and Sisters,

The time has come for us to leave. We have heard the city gates are being closed, with no one to enter or leave prior to the Gerent's arrival. We have done what we can to support you from the outside, but now we must flee.

Once again, please accept our few remaining tokens to help you in whatever way they can.

May the Light continue to guide, strengthen and protect you,

Anonymous

54

DANIEL: REVELATION

"I love you, Tessa, with all my heart. You know I do. So, when I say this I want you to hear me and what I'm saying, not what you think you're hearing."

She looked up at me from behind the fancy phone Felix had given her. Just like he had given all of us. She tilted her head and a furrow formed in her forehead.

Before she could get too worried, I raced on. "If you take one more photo of me, or video me doing something completely random, like cleaning my teeth, or drinking my coffee, or leaning on the railing, I am going to go stark raving mad. I love that you love taking photos, but please, give me a break."

Her face softened and she dropped her hands, taking the camera away from her face. "But Daniel, our family want to see what we're up to and since you won't take any photos, I have to."

"But we've come away to spend some time alone, to get to know each other without Val, Marcus and Kait breathing down our necks. When you take all these photos, it feels like you're reporting on... everything... on us... me."

"But I am." Again, she tilted her head. "I'm letting them know what we're up to and what we're doing, and how we're going."

"One week, Tessa. We've been gone for one week. You went away for a week before we got married and we survived. That's what made it so great when we caught up—we could tell each other what we did. When we saw each other. With words. Face to face."

"But look at what happened then. We got taken away and I didn't know if we would ever come back, and I was so worried. But now, we can keep our family updated and they know, not only that we are having a good time, but that we're okay."

Our week was coming to an end, and it was pretty obvious Tessa felt the same way I did. Even though she was in touch with everyone— Kait and Iza especially—every day, it was time to go home. Abbot used to remind us it was important to make time to celebrate and give thanks to the Light for our victories. In three days, we would get to do this on the Lightmas Feast Day among friends and family.

The irony was not lost on me. A guy who had been a self-professed loner, who'd worked hard for most of his life to keep people out, had become a part of a family, and I missed them. And not only them, but the others at Sanctuary as well. Mind you, that did not mean I felt the need to be reported on every day… every hour of the day… in every pose.

It was great being away, but we couldn't help worrying when we started reading all the slurs against Jonathan in the papers. We'd wanted to come home early, but Kait had told us to stay in Ephesus. It was being handled. And true enough, the next day, all stories were withdrawn. One paper printed a small apology on page ten, but apart from that it was like it never happened.

Regardless, one thing I'd learned growing up in my family—which was just my mum and me—was that mud sticks. They may have withdrawn it all, someone may have apologised, but the damage was done. Jonathan would forever be known as the guy who robbed the Community, started a cult and fathered multiple children to young, single women. Ruby's parentage would always be questioned by a percentage of the population. They had done their job well.

We sat on the verandah of our apartment. The sky was a moody grey with swirls of black and blue. Rain was coming in over the sea;

curtains of grey washed the view away. It was the perfect weather to match my heart. I looked back at Tessa, and she had respected my plea and put her phone away. Now she was curled up on the couch next to me, tucked up in a throw rug, buried deep in a book I had bought earlier from a charity shop. The book I hadn't had a chance to start yet. One finger absently stroked the raised scar of the branded tattoo on the back of her hand.

"We should make the most of our time left, Tessa. Do you want to go back to the beach?"

"Huh?"

"Beach. You want to go?"

She looked up, out, and back to me. Eyes wide, face screwed up. "Um, no. But you go. I know you've only been three times today and if you don't hurry, you'll get wet."

Another irony. That a guy who grew up in a city, the desert on one side, mountains on the other, would have such an affinity for the beach. Maybe it was the dreams. Since the Warrior dude from Laodicea told me to remember by dreams, I had been really focused on recalling them. One of the weird ones, where nothing violent happens, takes place on a beach. I'm standing looking out over the water from the vantage point of a sand dune. I'd had the dream so often I felt like I was literally... physically at the beach.

Not only did I love the ruggedness and the wildness and the uncontainable vastness and power of it, I loved the smell, the taste of it. When a gale blew and I couldn't hear anything apart from the rushing of the wind and the pounding of the waves, it reminded me that I was insignificant. But the dream had taught me that I belonged to something outside of myself. It was here, walking along the wet sand, waves beating and pulling at my feet, that I was reminded that alone I was like a twig. Yet in the Light, I was in the care of the One who controlled the sea.

And that is why I could never leave my family. Even though things were about to get really tough. The battle was going to get savage... again. I couldn't not go back. And that was also part of what I loved about Tessa. That she understood. She felt the same. We weren't just on the same team, our hearts beat with the one passion. I knew that the path the Light had us on with our family was not the norm—even for others in the Light—but it was our purpose and, because of that, it was my joy.

But enough of that, it was time. Tonight was our last night before packing up and heading back. I was going to make the most of it and spoil my wife with a nice meal and a movie before going back to the constraints of our normal.

My hair was stiff from the sea wind, my skin coated with salt, and my feet like ice from hosing them off at the resort's back entrance when the first drops of the storm hit. I decided to use the stairs and give myself a workout racing up to our floor. I burst through the door and stopped dead when I saw Tessa's face. She held both our phones and, instead of speaking, held them both out to me. Confused and not knowing what to make of it, I took mine.

> Kait: DO NOT COME HOME. The battle has started, and the city is in lockdown. You won't be able to get in. We love you. Petition the Light for us. Go to the Factory. We've told Felix. We love you. Stay safe. Please, please, please, DO NOT COME HOME.

55

KAITLYN: THE TIGHTENING NOOSE

"The power's been cut." Jet came racing back down the hill from the house. We'd had our suspicions and sent him up to check. It was the only building not running completely on solar. Thankfully, the guys had insisted on hooking the bore water up to solar, as well as everything else in Sanctuary, so as to cut the burden of Mary's bills. Now, however, when the city wanted to punish us by taking our electricity, it had little to no effect.

Of course, there were many more ways in which they could hurt us. And the rest of the city. Felix had phoned us to let us know the city gates were now officially shut. Apparently, the Gerent was in town to do his rounds of his people and he didn't want any troublemakers escaping. Overnight, at midnight I believe, the barricades went up and all those who were out couldn't come back in, and none whom were in could escape.

Please let Anonymous and their crew be safe. Please let them have got out.

The noose was well and truly closing and our fate was about to be revealed. I was just so grateful the families with vulnerable members had been able to flee earlier. Of course, Mary would never leave. And we had our kids here with Ruby. There were Josh's kids and Jayne, Phil's daughter, who were all younger than ours, but their fathers had decided to trust the Light and their future at Sanctuary. As had Caspian and Indrila who remained with us with Cyan, who was now eighteen months old.

Watch over them and keep them safe.

And even though it broke my heart to be separated, I was grateful Tessa and Dan were away and safe as well. They had been having such a lovely time. They'd had a chance to experience a week of respite, away from the intensity of the front line.

Guard them, protect them and bless them. Please.

We had no idea what was in store. We had, and did, face Other warfare every day. Major battles were becoming more frequent.

Out of all of us at Sanctuary, Val was the only one who had come across opposition from rulers in the past. From the turmoil of that context she met and rescued Abbot. It had become illegal to be a Shepherd of the Light in his home of Zoar. His Community turned against him and sentenced him to death by hanging. It was to happen in his own home grotto where he'd lived a monastic life. But Val had waltzed down there by the river and explained that there'd be an alternate ending to their story. And so there had.

For the rest of us, it was all new. And unknown. And all the more terrifying.

I don't know why it should be this way, but I felt safe having Raph and Riah nearby and—within reason—in Unseen warfare. But political? Worldly? Cultural battle? No way. I trusted the Light with my own and their lives. But part of me—which occupied a significant percentage—wanted them gone. Away from here. Far, far away. I wanted them wrapped up and sent off and kept safe, and sound and... safe. But in two weeks they would turn fourteen. They were not babies any longer. They were their own people, who had to make decisions for themselves... within reason, of course. They had already proven themselves on the battlefield, time and time again. I trusted them. I trusted the training they had received. I trusted the Light. But it didn't help the worry.

I don't even know what to ask for. I am so scared for my children. Oh God. Please. Just please protect them. And don't let me hinder them, get in the way of their need to grow up and experience You and Your saving, delivering power. I want the world for them, but I also want them safe.

It had only been seven hours since the roads were blocked, two hours since the city's satellites and phone networks were taken offline, and one hour since the power went off. But minute by minute the crowd of demons on our perimeter grew. Our multi-hued shield wall still stood. Our extra Guards still remained at attention on the outer rim of our shields. We each were still accompanied every second of every day by our personal Warriors, but the oppression of the enemy was suffocating.

For the past week it had been too distracting to keep watch whilst working to keep fed, let alone try to get any quality sleep at night. We were all exhausted and strained to breaking all the time. So, Val had divided our community into three teams, and we moved into life on rotation. Family groups were joined and then divided up so there was at least one adult on each shift, petitioning the Light and maintaining the shield behind their own and their neighbour's cabin. 8 pm to 4 am, 4 am to 12 pm, 12 pm to 8 pm, people rolled through life ensuring that at all times groups were either sleeping, working or posted as lookouts, petitioning the Light on every point of our boundary, every tick of the clock.

At each change of shift, we met at the Meeting Place as a whole and gave thanks to the Light and petitioned Him. It was the only time we got to see all of our family and touch base with how everyone was travelling and pass on any happenings of the shift.

But now that the enemy had upped the heat, the pressure in our little cooker was intensifying. We had no contact with the outside world. Even February and October were being targeted. Hackers were trying to break into their system. I had no idea what they were doing or how they were being stifled, but I was aware they were doing an awful lot of work and not a lot of sleeping.

Thank you for these girls and what they are doing for us. Give them wisdom and the ability to outwit their opponents.

* * *

THREE DAYS. For three days nothing happened. Except that the enemy grew in numbers. They gathered on our boundaries. When we looked out now, all we could see was the demonic, covering every piece of ground. We were literally an island of Light in a sea of Darkness. But for three days, nothing happened, and it was exhausting. Those who were on duty petitioning the Light kept watch on the perimeter. Waiting. Alarms ready to sound.

And so, as Lightmas dawned, it happened.

"Batter up!" Daisy's clear call from the gate had us all on alert and the kids running to each cabin where someone slept, bringing all of Sanctuary to attention.

"They're coming in from every side." February backed up Daisy with intel from the drone.

All of us working in the garden downed tools and ran to see what we were in for.

Oh, dear Lord, save us.

56

MARCUS: ONSLAUGHT

Raph and Riah came bowling into our cabin and climbed over themselves to wake me. I was so tired I'd been out like a light the instant me head hit the pillow a mere moment ago. But I was also keyed as a piano, so the moment they entered the cabin I was on me feet, sword drawn in a defensive stance ready to take on the enemy, even if I didn't know where I was or what day of the week we were up to.

We'd been showering before bed and sleeping in our clothes so as to be ready at a moment's notice. And I guess that's what this was. Notice.

"Dad, quick. They are coming."

I was pulled up by the sledgehammer Raph just swung into me chest.

Dad?

Both kids just stood there. Looking. Waiting. Edgy and bouncing on their toes.

Dad?

I swallowed the beautifully wrapped box stuck in me throat as it pushed tears out me eyes. "Dad?"

Both kids dropped their eyes, and a tiny turn had them closer and slightly turned into the other. It was instinctive from years of self-preservation and protection against rejection from adults. I didn't care, it just made it easier to drop to me knees and embrace them both. Burying me head into their joined shoulders, I tried to share me love through me hug.

"Come on, Bear, what's the hold u—" Kait burst into the room with her sword drawn. "What's going on?" First, she was worried. Then when there was no harm, she was edgy as a broken mirror. With her sword as a pointer, she very clearly told me what I should be doing and where I should be. And even though it was nice that I was taking time out to hug the kids, now was not really the time as the gates of hell had been opened and we were on the verge of the zombie apocalypse, so could I please get my butt out of this cabin and take my place on the front line.

And no, she didn't take a breath.

We all looked at her standing there in a blaze of green glory and smiled. "Yes, Mum," Raph answered her.

"Mum?" This pulled her up short and after a beat, her eyes were awash and her lip trembled.

I allowed her exactly thirty seconds to do as I had done—embrace our kids—then reminded her of the zombie apocalypse.

We ran to the border overlooking the plain to the west where most people had gathered, and I pulled up short. I'd had the 4 am to 12 noon sleep rotation, but I could tell instantly that I'd managed maybe thirty minutes sleep. The sun hadn't fully risen yet, but even so, there was enough light to see the horror unfolding before us.

Kait hadn't been joking when she'd used "zombie apocalypse" to describe the situation. On every side, demons were clearing to make passageways for their followers... Hosts. Puppets under the thrall of the Dark marched like zombies towards us. In the past, we'd faced one at a time and it was nothing to swipe an Unseen blade through them to "wake" them. They'd been as happy as larks in mud, but easy enough to deal with and send them on their way, essentially unharmed.

But here we were faced with at least a hundred. And with only thirty-seven members of Sanctuary—eight of whom were kids, too young to wield a sword, and we were short Dan and Tessa—we were outnumbered far too many to one. And that was just the human side of things. Previously, the Hosts hadn't fought back. Like lambs to the slaughter, they'd just let us cut them down. Surely, they were a diversionary tactic. But still, we couldn't lay down the welcome mat for them into our home. To our kids.

"Jonathan," Val barked. Not to be rude... *maybe* not to be rude, but I suspect more to get everyone's attention. She was in battle mode now, laser focused and single minded. "Would you petition the Light for us all before we begin"—she looked from me brother to the hills on the other side of the plain—"quickly?"

"Light of our lives and love of our hearts, guide, protect and strengthen us in the battle. May our blades be sharp, our armour be thick and our wills be yours."

"Thank you. Raph, Riah." Val had our full attention again, calling for our kids. "Please accompany Mary to the Meeting Place and watch over the children." Since Tessa and Dan weren't here, Riah would be on guard with Raph. Mary was a fierce warrior, her armour and weapons testimony to her life in and love of the Light. But she was as fast as a wet wig. Truth be, Riah would be first line of defence for the lot of them, Raph second and Mary third. Our job was to keep the Seen away from them and let them deal with the Unseen the Light allowed to approach. This was the only thing that settled me metal. They were experienced fighting the Dark, and the Light was filtering what came through.

Val, Kait and I each gave them a quick hug, kissed them both and sent them off to guard Ruby, Cyan, Jayne, Lucy and Oliver. Oliver would be a good backup for them. He was a few months older than the twins but still too inexperienced and a liability. Lucy at twelve with the help of Jayne, who was eleven, would be useful watching over Ruby, Cyan, Pod and Tiger.

The rest of us knew the drill. We would each stand with our cabins at our backs and fight the enemy in front of us for all we were worth. Val walked the perimeter with February, who had vision via her drone of the enemy's activities in our immediate surroundings. The west that opened to the fields, and beyond them to densely forested hills, was where most of the attack was coming from. Mary's house was to the east of our enclave, and the enemy lines here were thin. Thank the Light, folks like Mr Berry, Miriam and Dori had their cabins that side. They were capable but would not face the full force of the enemy's attack.

The south held the cattle paddocks behind the laundry and the old communal washrooms and toilets. Here, too, the enemy was light on the ground. Many of the Dark's minions had set themselves up at the north—in the carpark nearest Daisy's and Travis's cabins—but most came from the open fields behind our cabins. Val encouraged every member, reminding them of tactics, and would lend a hand when fighting got too hot. The girls—February and October—rigged up a simple communications port in each section of Sanctuary, and through February's laptop, Val could give commands and updates to everyone or specific groups.

Val also had access to October's intel via February. The twins had drones in flight watching the wider perimeter and the entrance roads leading to Sanctuary, monitoring both Other and Seen intruders.

Val was the general manipulating the troops and I trusted her one hundred percent. "Hosts approaching." Her voice was loud and clear through the portable Bluetooth speaker placed on the roof of Dan and Tessa's cabin. But we didn't really need her to tell us what was directly in front and centre. Now all the Hosts had made their way through the enemy's ranks, they stood two to three deep around us—close enough for me to see death pooling in their vacant eyes.

Our Guards, bolstered by extra members, stood as an additional layer outside our shield wall. Out of everyone in this sick scenario, I would hate to be these guys the most. We had a barrier between us and our opposition, and our first battle was against mindless, relatively harmless Hosts. But nothing stood between our Guards and endless ranks of demons. I remembered the final battle in Laodicea when the Eagle Riders and Chariot Drivers joined the foot soldiers.

Today I hoped like a kid on Lightmas eve this same crew were ready and waiting as backup in the wings.

I pumped Kait's hand twice and then stood ready. It was weird not having Val with us, it would change the way we fought, but you can bet your bippy we'd be none the less effective.

At fifty metres out, as one, the Hosts came to a standstill. A hush fell over the occupied hectares behind them. Millions of demonic beasts turned their undivided attention to us. Millions upon millions of red eyes burning with hatred looked to us. Hungry for our defeat, they salivated. We were all stretched as taut as a bowstring. Then, as one, the Hosts screamed and ran. Behind them the demonic roared, chasing their puppets through our barrier of Light, whipping them into a frenzy. Every cavity in me body echoed with the demonic cry. Our Guards let the Hosts past but closed ranks on the enemy.

I recognised a couple of faces from those who had come before, but they were all screwed up in rage, pain and madness as they broke through the barrier and threw themselves onto our blades and made their attempt to break past.

Thankfully we weren't the only line of defence. Those who made it past us—purely by force of numbers—had to contend with the next line of defence. On the other side of the cabins, on the boardwalk circumnavigating the outer rim of the veggie garden, Jet, Craig and Kelly, with Cara's three sons, were waiting to stop any who tried to get through to the Meeting Place where Riah stood watch with Raph and Mary. Gemma volunteered to stand guard at October's door while the girl watched over us all.

The enemy had done their job well. The first wave was not danger-ous, but they were a pain in the buttooshie and as welcome as briars in me underwear. We had to cut them free of the binds to their Dark drivers, then deal with a crowd of humans underfoot: angry, anti and abusive. Daisy stepped up alongside Val, Kait and me, and we showed them the way out—with extreme prejudice. In doing this, we were forced to abandon our posts, deflect attention from our part of the shield and take our eyes off the battlefield. But we couldn't continue to fight the hordes at our front door whilst we had Hosts in the house.

They were not keen to leave and tried to wreak as much havoc as they could on the way out. We called in reinforcements. Jet and his crew helped herd, push, threaten and kick the intruders out. But before we could lock the gate, Ruby's scream brought us all running.

Snakes. Huge, black, insubstantial snakes were making their way through the camp. Just the sight of them drained me energy. With the action and our attention elsewhere, they had breached the walls. Our Guards still fought the enemy in hand-to-hand on the field just beyond our shields, but we were now confronted by the curses and spells of the Dark's disciples inside our home, once again.

"To the children." Val's bellow echoed around the camp as it rang out from every speaker placed on cabin roofs and other places around Sanctuary, but loud and clear from the woman beside me.

Raph, Riah, Oliver and Mary stood around a table on which Ruby, Jayne and Lucy, holding a crying Cyan, stood. All the snakes had made a B-line to our kids. Again, I was aware that our perimeter was barely manned, and the inner circle was left trying to evict the last of the Hosts. But right in front of me, Raph and Riah were doing their best to stare down and fight off the biggest, ugliest, abominations I had ever seen.

I'd suggest me sister was a tad frustrated she was not staring down the enemy on the front line. Or could be she was just hungry for a knife-free fight. But most likely it was because it was our kids. Me sister Val went fully berserk, running in, jumping over, through and between the nest of ugly to get to Raph and Riah. I am sure she was glad to get to Ruby, Mary and the girls as well. But in her wake, all that was left were hacked up pieces of dissolving, nasty muck.

She turned to face the perimeter and released a bellow of savage rage, the likes of which I'd not heard or witnessed from her before. Her armour was flaming deep, dark indigo, flickering with lightning. Her sword was pure light, and her eyes were pools of fury.

I had a sense we could possibly cast her adrift into the sea of enemy right now and none could stand in her path. But still, as always, despite her rage and frustration at being pinned down—and I suspect not having Dan and Tessa safe in her sights—she was, pure and simple, a bleeding battle hog.

Me mutter had her turning her attention on me. Not me desired outcome, mind you. But it did bring her down from the ledge. She grinned. "Keep up, old man." Still mad as a wet cat, she ran her hands over the kids to make sure they were unharmed, left Jonathan, Daisy and Jet to check the others, then carved a path back to the battlefield.

Which was just in time, because the yells and cries of distress informed us the walls had been breached. I only had time to yell instructions to Jonathan and Daisy, "Take over the watch," before following me sister into the maws of hell flooding Sanctuary, with me wife at me side.

57

DAISY: HERO STATUS

Okay, so previously I had admiration for Warrior. She kind of scared me but inspired me to step up into my roll of Gate Keeper and guardian of the Light. It was a good thing to be inspired to be more than what you were, to step deeper into the best you could be. But this was a whole new level.

Jonathan and I tried to keep the watch, but we just didn't have the people power to plug the gaps in the wall. As much as I hated it, I had to leave the twins, the Colt and Filly, in charge of relaying the information. Our Guards were doing their bit to sandbag the waves of Darkness pawing over themselves to get to us.

I had to admit, each time I looked up and saw the horizon blacked out with our opposition, my part of the wall faltered. How could I maintain faith in the Light when the odds were stacked so high against us?

I was beat. I could hardly see from the rivers of sweat that blinded and stung my eyes. My determination to keep going was warring with the fatigue that threatened to consume my will. We'd been at it most of this stinking-hot, never-ending nightmare of a day. The sun had moved from our backs and now beat down on the crown of my head. I feared it would only be moments before it would blind us to the relentless enemy in front of us. My fingers were locked around my blade and my calf muscles had started screaming in cramps about an hour ago. We'd had to abandon Jet and his crew to watch the kids, so the Shepherd, Tea and I could lend a hand on the wall.

I tried to pretend to be angry when Jet, Craig and Kelly took their places in the line, and Charlie, Eddie and Harry made a stand next to their mum, Cara, who was fighting alongside Callum and Phil. Neither could I pretend to be angry when—shielded by the Filly—the Colt and Oliver did the rounds with some salty, sweet power-drinks. The Colt, quickly laying hands on everyone he could as he passed, sent bursts of energy and healing into them. The Filly, I knew, was pulsing out waves of Peace. It was the only thing that kept us going.

I just kept petitioning the Light that the kids were safe, the line would hold and the Shepherd could keep going. When Sariah and Raphael did their rounds, this all seemed possible. But as they disappeared down the line, my peace and hope faded with them. Normally, the Shepherd needed a nap every few hours, and today we'd been going since 4 am. We had now breached afternoon and I was flagging. He must have dug into resources well beyond my understanding and pay grade.

We had little choice though. We were fighting for our home, our kids… our lives. When you're literally up against a wall, with nowhere to go… and everything to lose… it's amazing what resources you can unearth. There was no falling back. There was no cavalry. We were it, and this was life or death.

Please give us a reprieve. Help us somehow.

I snuck a glance to my left where a clearing was slowly widening in a circle of burned, smouldering grass, pushing into enemy territory. Demon bodies lay in slowly dissolving piles in ever-increasing circles around Warrior, the Mountain, and Hot Chilli. But it was almost impossible to force my eyes away from Warrior.

It was like all sanity and sense had left her. Or maybe her battle-lust simply pushed her rational, calm side out of the ring. The woman was all instinct and machine, salivating for the fight. I took my hat off to the other two who fought beside her. They knew her and her moves. Completely holding their own, they watched her back and sides, slaying the enemy who came too close or looked to halt her killing spree. All the while causing their own significant dent in the pack around them. The three stood where no mere mortal had the sense to—each in their own sphere of influence, aware of, yet not interfering with or getting in the way of the other. Tirelessly they held back the tide. And I wish I could tell you that was the end of it. But, with the size and sheer force of the enemy, our shield was failing, left, right and centre.

"Daisy." The Shepherd lurched to one side and, without any finesse or style, intercepted a sword swing to my head. My heart seized then ran ten to the dozen. *Get back in the game, Daisy. Toughen the frack up. You are needed. Grow up and get on with it.* I gave myself a good mental shake and focused on the enemy in front of me. Now was not the time to watch a master class. It was a time for hack and slash.

Please help. I don't know how much longer I can keep this up.

"Incoming, incoming." The Colt ran behind us, his voice yelling into the mic attached to his earpiece. His warning echoed around the camp from the speakers still functioning around Sanctuary rooftops.

And again, the wall faltered. We just couldn't do this.

Please, please help us. You can change this; You can save us. Please help.

58

CONTESSA: GAME CHANGER

"Tell me again, whose plan this was?" If you had told me last week—on my honeymoon—that I would have received the opportunity to crawl through the bush in the middle of the night, in "adventure gear", as my Lightmas treat, I would have laughed.

Snorted even.

I mean, seriously, adventure gear?

But I must admit, Marlene was carrying it off like you wouldn't believe. I had never seen the woman in shoes with less than three-inch heels, and here she was, tramping like a champion in boots, cammo pants and a thick drill shirt. Whilst looking amazing.

"Tessa. Head in the game… honey." Dan tried to dampen the bark with the endearment, but couldn't he see? I was trying to do everything I possibly could to keep my head *out* of the game and not think about what my family was suffering right now. Or if my family was still alive right now. No. Instead, I would consider the outfit choices of my companions and rate their effectiveness for comfort, movability, and style. Like Fleur. The woman was a petite, like me, and she—

"Tessa." This time Dan was gentler with his approach, and quietly took me off to the side, away from our group who were finding a comfortable place to take a five-minute break. "Sweetheart. I know you're worried and so am I. But this is our mission, and we are leading our friends into an unknown, possibly one-way trip, to chaos. And I need your attention on the tech."

His face was drawn and pale. The late morning light revealed dark circles and deep worry lines—even if I hadn't known for a fact that for the past three days he hadn't slept well. Neither of us had. Since receiving that horror message from Kait: "Don't come home." Like we wouldn't. Like we would tuck ourselves away from the battle and let our family fight without us.

But it had taken too many days to organise ourselves. To find out what was happening, with total tech blackout. Getting any information out of Philadelphia—no, I absolutely would not call it Domination—such a stupid name—was impossible.

We'd holed up at the Factory in Laodicea and made plans. I totally understood Indy's rage before going into battle to get Iza and Amber back from the Temple of Ashera. But he only had to wait forty minutes.

We'd had to wait three days.

Three.

Days.

After contacting Felix's friend, Maurice—who was the tech genius behind getting "good citizen" papers sorted for the twins and me—we had a bit of an idea that the Gerent had shut down Philadelphia, cut all contact with the city and planned to go in-person to flush out the insurgents... us. Except we weren't there. Yet.

We then had to get equipment: good walking boots and heavy-duty clothes to protect us from the wildlife, whilst keeping us cool enough not to cook during our endless trek—in summer—with supplies: high energy snack bars and water packs—then walk through the night, across country—the long way through the flopping mountain range to the south—to sneak across the city line and into the hills across the plain west of Sanctuary.

Of course, as soon as the rest of our family from Laodicea heard what was going on, they were falling over themselves to get their own pair of walking boots and water packs to join us. It was heartening.

And worrying. Thankfully, Indy convinced Iza to stay home to care for Grace and keep the Factory operating, whilst petitioning the Light for us around the clock.

We weren't alone. Dan and I didn't have to break through the enemy lines by ourselves. But the danger was very real, because it wasn't just the Unseen we were up against. It was the ruling power of our nation.

And when I say "just the Unseen", don't get me wrong. I knew how dangerous the Dark was and how he influenced every aspect of the world we lived in. But mostly, in the past, we'd been fighting one front: the Others. This time it was going to be Seen and Unseen. And as always there were no guarantees.

So we had travelled through the night and, after a quick break for breakfast, we'd hiked through the morning until we stood at the base of the hill to the west of Sanctuary. Dan had signalled a halt and a break to have something to eat for a light, early-lunch, and drink. We wouldn't be stopping again until we were with our friends in Sanctuary, or dead…

Amina was looking so good in her gear. Cammo suited her. Even though she was still scary, she had always been impress—

"Tessa?"

I wrapped my arms around my husband and hugged him so hard my arms hurt. I wanted him to be safe. And not die. I wanted all my family safe. And our friends. "Please be careful. Please be safe. I love you."

He held me for a minute. "Are you having second thoughts? Do you want to stay here?"

"Are you serious right now? Of course I don't want to stay. How could you possibly say that? Our family is over that hill, and they need us…" The smirk on his face pulled me up short. So, I hit him.

"That's my girl. Head in the game." He pulled me in gently and kissed my head. "These people need us to do our job. You and I know what's likely to be at the top of the hill. We've been here before and know who's up there and most likely what they're up to. We need to stop them, disable them, try not to permanently damage them, then swim through the ocean of hell on the other side. I can't do that if you're not where you're supposed to be: by my side with your head in the game, and eyes on the Light." His eyes softened. "Don't leave me, Tessa. Stay with me."

I pumped his hand twice. "Always and forever."

Please help me help him. Please give us strength and courage for what lies over that hill. Help me keep my eyes on You and not be distracted by the enemy. You are stronger and meaner and tougher and scarier and more awesome than everything they have. Thanks that I got to see Your epicness at the battle of Laodicea. I know You have that up Your sleeve and any time You want You can draw the ranks?... squadrons?... units? of Warriors card. So, thanks, and please help me do what I have to do, so everyone else can do what they have to do. So that we can get in there and then deal with whatever comes next.

I reached up onto my toes, wrapped my arms around Dan's neck and pulled him down and kissed him soundly.

"Whilst I am... elated that you two have managed to... align your vision for how we may proceed, I do think the time is upon us to take the next step. Maurice has just informed me that the battle on the other side of the hill has begun, and the first wave has been sent in."

"Skrat." Dan straightened but didn't take his arm from around my waist. "Thanks, Felix." We rejoined the group. "Everyone know your role? At the top of this hill we are very likely to come across the same group, or similar group of people who were responsible for setting demonic snakes... or curses... or whatever the hell those things were, against Sanctuary, two months ago—we have no idea of how ma—"

"Maurice suggests about twenty."

"Thanks, Felix. Twenty humans. They follow the Dark, they will be backed up and protected by demons, but they are mortal. Hopefully, with their attention on their work, and their guards entertained by the show, we might be able to sneak up on them. Even if we can't, our Guards will help."

I looked around our group, as did everyone else, and made eye contact with our Unseen companions. At this point in time, we still only each had the one.

Dan continued, "Once we've taken the hill, we will leave Kerm, Helen, Lily, Shauna and Carley to cover us, petitioning the Light, and to keep us up to speed with eyes from their vantage point via two-way. Seems the satellites and phone towers are still out. We will petition the Light for more Guards on you and to keep you safe." The five of them nodded in return. "Then under the cover and protection of our Guard, the rest of us will fight our way through the enemy to get to the walls of Sanctuary. Felix, Marlene and Fleur, right flank. Audette, Amina and Vashti, left flank. Indy, you're with Tessa and me.

"However, when we get to the top, everyone keep your eyes peeled. You will all be in the mix, and you will all come under attack. We are outnumbered: our fifteen to their twenty. But we are trained, equipped and prepared. And we are in the Light. We hold the advantage. Any questions?"

No one said a word. We had petitioned the Light during the three days we were waiting. And solidly this night, before we left. We knew that everyone at the Factory was doing the same without ceasing as we progressed. And so, for now, there was nothing else to do but follow the plan. It was a good plan. Well, better than no plan. And it was time to go.

In the quiet heat of the midday sun, we silently formed single file and made our way up the western side of the hill. We were covered by the trees and greenery. But this also slowed us down a bit. There was no path for Dan to follow, but our goal was up the hill. So that's where he went, constantly looking for the best path to lead us… as quietly as possible… to our first real obstacle. I was warm from the hike but was grateful I had kept my gloves on. Iza had gifted me with a bag of fingerless, skin coloured gloves, knowing how I felt. Now, wherever I went, I always had several pairs with me. They made my hands a bit sweaty, but they protected my palms from the rocks and rough bark as I did my best to follow in Dan's footsteps. They also kept that disgusting brand-tattoo from my mind. The number—0046—permanently scarred my peripheral vision. Hence the gloves. In summer.

Our Guard had doubled in number and forged ahead of us as we climbed the hill. They were busily engaging their opposites, before—

but not too much earlier than—we had the opportunity to get a good look at ours.

Yuck.

Just yuck.

I had thought adventure gear was unattractive. But compared to these guys, it was like formal wear.

The human followers of the Dark were wearing armour made from skeletons.

Demonic skeletons.

With rotting flesh growing out from the bones.

But as if that wasn't enough, the flesh merged and pulsed in and out of their own flesh.

It was disgusting, it was like the people themselves were living, rotting corpses.

And they stank.

Actually, I'm not sure if they stank, in truth. Or if that was just what my eyes were taking in, and I was imagining the stench. Anyway, the whole thing was repulsive. And not only because of the skeleton-armour that encased them; their weapons were just plain distasteful. In the middle of a clearing was a huge stone coated in both dark-dried and fresh-flowing blood from the carcass of some poor, innocent creature. But the whole effect was topped off by insanity. Their intel was as good as ours, and they were waiting for us. When we breached the ridge of the hill, as one they all came at us, screaming and wailing, hissing and spitting.

The size of the group—closer to thirty than twenty—plus the over-whelming grotesqueness put us on the back foot. But we had been training in the Light and fighting these battles longer than these guys had. Or at least I liked to think so. It gave me a little bit more confidence to front up to this vomit-inducing horror.

Instinctively, we fell into formation: Felix and his crew on the right flank, Vashti and her group on the left. Indy dropped back to fight beside Lily and Carley, leaving Kerm, Helen and Shauna to form the final pod of three. And I fought alongside Dan.

To be honest, I wasn't upset. I'd much rather be a pair than team up with an unknown when the heat was on. If we couldn't have Sariah with us, I'd rather not have anyone. Indy had been training with his crew almost two years now, and he knew them better than we did.

But I had to admit, Dan kinda freaked me out. It was like he'd zoned out and gone to another place. He started fighting with different tactics, almost like he was fighting with a different weapon, but it was effective. He barged to the centre of the clearing and all the enemy focused on him.

I gave him plenty of room… we all did. Moving to the outer edges, the others mopped up the wounded and cleaned up those who decided they didn't want to play anymore. I watched Dan's back, knowing him well enough to stay clear of his weapon. He was lethally effective. But make no mistake, I would have a serious "chat" with him about this when it was all over. I was not the slightest bit impressed he changed his style and plans, mid-battle, without letting me know.

But that could wait. For now, the issue was, what did we do with the bodies? Yeah, I know that doesn't sound good, but a positive was they were all still alive… well, I thought they were. Surely, they were? We had used weapons of Light. And as far as I was aware, weapons of Light had never actually killed anyone… human. But, maybe, having the Darkness that had been a significant part of them—feeding them, sustaining them, and driving them for so long—torn out of them, was too much of a shock? Best case scenario was they were unconscious. And we wanted them to stay that way. Out of the action until we had done what we needed to do without them interfering. Indy brought zip ties over to the group and, under the close watch of our Guards, he handed them out and we secured the hands—behind their backs—and feet of everyone there.

We then dragged—tried to drag—the thirty or so bodies into the shade of the trees around the clearing. We didn't want them visible from the air. But they were too heavy. So, Lily, Carley and I just rolled them. We weren't too gentle, but they hadn't been very nice, so I didn't feel too bad. The others joined in and we left Dan, Indy, Amina and Kerm to stack them neatly.

By the end of the operation, I was even less gentle and not feeling one iota of compassion. Not only had these people opened themselves to the Dark, attacked us for living in the Light, and made our difficult situation worse, they were taking precious time away from our mission.

As much as I resented them and what they had done, not-harming them and keeping them sheltered was the right thing to do. Which was confirmed when the Light sent extra Guards to watch over them when we asked Him. Now we were confident that the group we left behind would be safe as they focused on petitioning the Light on our behalf as we went on.

I stretched my back and went to my pack to have a big drink of water, allowing my gaze to take in the scene over the brow of the hill that awaited us. I couldn't help my distress escaping, like a whispering pressure valve. "Oh, dear Lord. We're doomed. Doomed before we even begin."

59

DANIEL: BREAKTHROUGH

Just before we headed out, we heard more disciples of the Dark...
Hosts? breaking through the bush around the clearing. They
were going to have to pass by the pile of their comrades. Good.
But not so good was the fact that we would then have more of the
enemy at our backs when we set off down to Sanctuary.

I signalled to our group of five petitioners, who were making
themselves a comfortable camp with a view of the slope and field
between us and Sanctuary. They and the rest of us did our best to melt
into the bush around the edges of the clearing. We would have the
intruders covered. We would have to trust our Guards to take care of
the gaps.

I flicked my eyes around the glade and was proud of the way our
group had worked as a unit. We were exhausted from the night hike,
the mountain climb, battle and the clean-up. I couldn't help but be
frustrated by this added hold-up, but knew the Light was all over the
situation. He was taking care of Sanctuary, and He would take care of
us. I crouched down beside Tessa in the shrubs and waited. Her body
was a tense rock. She wouldn't make it to the next round if she didn't
relax. "Breathe, honey."

She turned and glared at me, the predator bird giving me a lecture via angry eye twitching. I ducked down super quick, pecked her lips in a brief kiss, then tilted my head back towards the clearing. It was enough to take her mind off the imminent danger and inhale some air.

We heard them before we saw them. "Check this out. Looks like someone's already done our work for us."

Confusion caused me to almost drop my sword. We all remained hidden and on alert as we watched three people—two blokes and a woman—emerge, weary and on guard.

I swore under my breath as Felix stood and made his way to meet the newcomers, sheathing his sword.

"Felix?" One of the men. Fit, middle-aged and wearing pale-blue armour.

"Al? What an… auspicious and timely meeting."

As soon as my brain acknowledged their armour I stood and followed in Felix's wake. The rest of our crew did likewise.

The bloke Felix had addressed as Al looked around the group, the woman with him as confused as we were.

Felix spoke into the void. "Luke. It is wonderful to see you again."

Travis's son, Luke, beamed and strode forward to shake Felix's hand. "What are you guys up to?"

The woman stayed silent, eyeing our group. She was as tall as the guy named Al, which was tall for a chick. And she was scary classy. Her hair was cut in sharp angles to match her cheek bones. She walked like she owned the ground under her, the bush around her and the air she breathed. But she must have been one of the good guys cause she was fully encased in armour like a deep red wine. Seems none of us were ready yet to break out the introductions.

But Felix was doing a good job as intermediary. He swept his arm to incorporate the square kilometres of demons we were about to swim through. "We thought we might pay our friends at Sanctuary a visit to offer them… encouragement, and an extra blade or two."

The woman burst out laughing. "Now, that seems to be my kind of odds. Pleased to meet you all, I'm Cissa. And I am very glad to have bumped into you after you took care of this lot"—her eyes flicked to the laid-out Hosts—"and before you took on that lot. Care if we jump aboard?"

I couldn't hold back my guffaw in the face of the sheer ridiculousness of it all. Here we were, fourteen of us from the Factory—five of whom were staying behind, on the hill—and three of them, to add a sum total of twelve blades against... millions. But I had to admit, having their company bolstered my confidence to barely registering.

I marched forward and hastily did the rounds, introducing my crew to theirs and explaining what we had in mind. We didn't have a lot of time, we were desperate to get to our friends, but also not particularly keen to set off through the mire to get there. So, we spent a few moments petitioning the Light for confirmation that we were on the right track and not a suicide mission, asking that he kept mainlining the wisdom, stamina and courage, and perhaps a miracle or a dozen along the way might be possible as well?

With no further excuse to delay, and a desperate pull to help our friends, as a group we breached the hill and considered the insanity we were about to attempt. The sun cast short shadows in front of us and gave us a clear and honest view of the enemy on the plain below. Currently their focus was drawn to the swamped island that was our home.

Tessa pumped my hand twice, then took her sword in a double-handed grip. With her eyes straight ahead, she gave me a very clear message. "You were successful in the clearing, taking out the enemy. I am so very proud of you." She turned to look at me with a tilted head. "But, if you *ever* do that to me again: shunt me into the unknown, in the battle, while you take off on some random, dream-induced field trip"—the cobra head-wobble made an appearance topped off by predator-bird eyes—"I will personally skin you alive."

"Noted."

Felix gave a polite cough indicating they were ready. He, Marlene, Audette and Fleur stood in a semicircle around us. I felt the presence of the others behind them. And all of them were looking to me to lead.

So, appears You planned for these other guys to join us. And since none of them are stepping up with any suggestions, I guess it's back to Plan A: Get through the mob and help out when we get there. If this is wrong, please stop me. If this is right, please show me how the heck that's going to happen.

We were all forced to take a step back as arrows from the heavens pierced the atmosphere and Warriors of Light formed a thick barrier around us. Not only was I coming to accept divine intervention when we needed it most, I was almost giddy with the relief of it.

Our personal Guards stood within the circle of their comrades. The newly formed angelic shield, seven rows thick facing the plains below, parted and a Warrior approached. She was over seven foot tall, dressed in golden armour like all the rest, but her bearing indicated she was the leader of this group. With steely, unfathomable eyes, she regarded me. Under her scrutiny I felt like a toddler with a toy sword playing at dress-ups and had a lot of trouble staying on my feet. Instinctively I wanted to drop to my knees... to lie prostrate before her. Instead, I just shook like a leaf and tried to remember what Val had done when this had happened in Laodicea. And Sodom. She had nodded. So, I did too.

The Warrior nodded back. "Well met, Daniel. I can see you have been remembering your dreams." She glanced at the clearing where I'd kind of gone a bit battle crazy remembering my "horse" dream. Then she flicked her eyes to Sanctuary, where I instinctively knew she was referring to the shield wall. "There is more to come."

Great. "Any hints about what I'm supposed to do?"

She nodded... and winked. *Did she just wink at me?* It was fleeting and then, before I could shut my mouth, I was staring at her back. She raised her sword and spoke in a language I could not understand.

During our interaction, I had not noticed that most if not all the demons on the fields below us had turned to face us. Until now.

Framicking great.

The lead chick... girl... woman... Warrior hefted her kick-butt sword to the sky—I suspected this was our signal—made a bone-jarring battle cry, and then we were off. I didn't have a moment to think about the others. All I had room for was gratitude I had kept up my running.

By my guesstimation, it was just over two kilometres from the bottom of the mountain to the outer perimeter of Sanctuary. Our guard shielded us and split the enemy as if parting a frozen sea with a heated icebreaker... at neck-breaking speeds. I was aware things were going on around us, but we were well and truly shielded by the thick wall of Warriors. These guys were high, wide and fearsome and taking care of business for us. I devoted all my attention to not tripping and making sure Tessa was keeping up. She was. As was everyone.

Later, I would conclude the Light had interrupted the laws of nature in some way whilst we were shielded within the Warriors' formation. There was no way all of us could have travelled that far, that fast, without being totally winded and useless when we arrived at our destination.

On our way through the blurring horde, I had flashbacks to our first entry into Laodicea. Seriously, was that three and a half years ago? Tessa, Val and I had been riding in the back of Old Faithful. The sun had just set and both sides of the highway were banked with an endless ocean of the demonic in all their hideous rank and file. Our Guard had done some crazy skrat back then to shield us and get us in safely. We could hardly see anything because we were looking out into the dimming light, peeking out the side windows in the back of the truck.

This time, we were on foot. And in the heat and heart of a battle. But again, we didn't see much action.

That was about to change.

As we approached the shield-wall of Sanctuary, the front Warriors flanked to the side, giving us a clear run into our home ground. My first reaction had been to run in and embrace everyone and make sure they were all okay. But it only took a fraction of a second to see that they weren't. They were flagging. Fast.

The shield wall had been breached in several sections. And even though we had travelled till late morning, and been waylaid for longer than I'd have liked, the Chief Warrior had indicated these guys had been hard at it, slogging away in the battle since first light. We instinctively spread out to relieve the burden and cover the gaps. If it had been any less dire, I would have taken the time to enjoy the shocked faces.

As soon as we breached the wall I yelled for Sariah. She flew to us, and without hesitation took her place by my side as we turned to face the tide forcing its way through the gap behind Tessa and my cabin.

Once enough members of Sanctuary could step back from the fighting and see that reinforcements had arrived, it enabled them to get a better perspective and get back to fixing the wall. Our little group surging through the sea of Darkness had been twelve against thousands which, outside the Light, was incomprehensible. Here in Sanctuary, they had only been twenty-seven against an uncountable enemy. But our twelve, added to their number, was enough to allow hope to break through the Darkness.

Until it was snuffed out.

60

DANIEL: THE REMEMBERING

Remember your dream.

We were on the outside of the wall, protecting the opening and fighting to keep the enemy away until others could mend the gaps. I was fresh. Adrenaline pumped through my veins, and I was ten-foot tall and bulletproof.

Remember your dream.

Again, the voice invaded my confidence and I stumbled. Wave upon wave of memory, of visuals, smells and sounds assaulted my consciousness. My blade dropped into the dust because I needed both hands to hang onto my head. I lost track of what was happening around me in Philadelphia as I was instantly transported back to the hell-house of my dreams.

There is a group of people with me, and we all stand frozen, waiting in speechless terror. Waiting for the final light of the day to be extinguished, and along with it, the warmth and security it brings. Paralysed in mind and body, I can smell our collective fear as it thickens in the evening breeze. I think the scent of our despair calls them. There is no room for rational thought or reasoning. We have nowhere to go, we have nowhere to hide. We have no way to fight them and no way to protect ourselves. Once again, like every other night, we are to be the offering.

All eyes are trained on the house opposite and the high, chain-wire fence that surrounds it. Why it's there, I have no idea. It doesn't keep them in. Every night they come and, like impotent slabs of meat on a plate, we wait to be taken.

The hour has come. The nest spews forth its vile occupants. They fly, crawl or amble over and through the fence into our house, through the window where we stand watching. For all of us, hope was a mist that had been burned away long ago by repetitive slaughter. Most run screaming. Some just open themselves, gibbering and slobbering in gormless surrender. I fight and desperately cling to the remnants of my defiance and resolve, so that these, too, don't abandon me.

I run. Silent, trying to grab the kids, herd the ones who are still thinking, who haven't given up. I try to hide. I try to save as many as I can. But it doesn't work. It never does. We are always taken. We are always butchered. Sometimes I'm lucky and I go first. Other times they make me watch whilst they tear apart and gorge themselves on the others.

I wake up. And then, the next night, it happens. All. Over. Again.

But after I come to the Light, it is different. I have a plan. I know I can do something. We don't have to just sit and wait for the inevitable slaughter and defeat. We can fight them.

The first couple of times, I try to hide from them, outside the house so it looks empty when they arrive. But they find us.

The next time I get everyone to run, to get away from the house. We don't have to stay like dinner on a plate. But they catch us.

The next time I make weapons and hand them out. Some of us stand up to them and fight them. We can grow claws of our own. But they beat us.

The last time I have this dream, I realise I don't have to let them in. I have been looking at it the wrong way all along. I have been a victim waiting for punishment or... disaster to happen. Even when I tried fighting back, I was still looking at it from the perspective of a victim, letting these creatures into my territory.

But I have the authority to keep them out. They don't have to come into my house, they don't have to come in and destroy us if I don't let them.

Then I realise what the fence is for.

The last time I have this dream I watch at the window, eager for the sun to go down. Ready for the battle to begin. This time I am terrified and excited at the same time. People come away from the window and stand behind me. They are scared, jittery. Nerves are raw, and everyone is on edge. I feel it at my back like a wave pushing me to the edge of the window and holding me there as the twilight makes way for the night.

And then they come.

But this time I watch as, in slow motion, everything moves silently through the thickest molasses. Momentarily I forget my purpose, transfixed by their retarded movement. As they near the fence I snap back to attention and roar, the tension added with my fear amplifies like a cannon. "No! You will not pass!"

They stop. They scream. Back to normal speed. Back to normal volume. The noise is deafening. But they don't go past the fence. They can't go past the fence. They buck and tear at it, they fight each other and screech. Intense hatred, all directed at me, but they can't get to me. It's hard to put into words just what it is like, but I am shocked... stunned... overwhelmed with relief and surging with the satisfaction of victory.

The fence... our shield.

I shook my head and looked up. Tessa and Sariah stood over me, fighting. Our Guards stood out from them, filtering the numbers targeting me—the weak link. Lurching to my feet I yelled, "Everyone, back inside the wall. Now." I had to call several times to be heard over the roar and clash of the battle. Then I sent Raph and Oliver to relay the message: "Strengthen the wall from the inside. Pull everyone in."

We had been going about it the wrong way. We were outside,

guarding the gaps, as those on the inside worked on repairs. It was only the smallest nuance, but a world of difference.

We were fighting a fight we didn't have to fight. Wasting energy. Allowing the enemy to beat us down, which continued to weaken our wall. We had a part to play in this battle, but the war belonged to the Light. In a blink of an eye, He could finish this, just like he did in Laodicea.

He didn't need us outside, He needed us behind His wall, under His wing.

Everyone filtered back inside. Those of us who still had the energy covered the retreat. Val, Marcus and Kait, still outside, drew the focus of the horde like moths to a flame. Extra Warriors went to them. There was no way I was going to try to interrupt Val's battle rage. I would leave that to those more immortal than me.

"Get everyone to meet here." I indicated the clearing we'd retreated to, directly behind Val, Kait and Marcus's stand; the rainbow wall stood between us, thin and wavering. All the kids raced to follow my orders.

Just before I explained, doubt ran roughshod over my revelation. What if I was wrong?

Please let this be right.

I didn't dawdle. My parental-like people were still outside the wall, the only humans standing between the ocean of evil and us. They were causing enough distraction and entertainment for the enemy to give us a splinter of reprieve.

I addressed the remnants of Sanctuary. "We are safe in the Light. Sanctuary is His home, where He resides, where He is worshipped. This is sacred ground." I had everyone's attention. "He alone, singularly, is greater than all of them out there." Some nodded, others gripped their swords tighter. "In His name we have the right to banish them from this place. His place. Are we in agreement?"

As one, everyone either nodded, grunted or affirmed, "Yes."

"Together, we have lived in His presence, for His glory, under His banner. So, let's, together, with a united voice, proclaim his glory and rightful kingship." Energy buzzed, eyes burned and muscles flexed.

As one, we turned to face the solid, glowing multi-hued wall and I roared, "You shall not pass."

Silence flew out like shockwaves over the spawn of hell. In its wake a voice, sharp and deadly as a double-edged sword, snapped us back to the present—Sariah. Just as there had to have been some Unseen amplification behind my declaration, so too my sister's song pierced the atmosphere surrounding us—from the mountains, across the plains and reverberating through the enemy lines. Sariah lifted her face to the heavens and sang to the Light's glory. Whilst it didn't knock me for a six like the first time I heard her sing in the battle back in Sodom, it still knocked my socks off and rocked me to my core.

After a moment of awed silence, the rest of us followed her lead and lifted our voices in defiance of the enemy to glorify the Light. Our wall exploded with power, the full spectrum of His Light refracted into every hue, tone and colour representing the diversity of His people and the brilliance of His creation.

The horde was forced back. The first wave fell in the initial blast of Light and the rest turned and ran. We had secured the wall. The enemy once again was locked out. The Light's Warriors stood in rings around us, reinforcing our defence. Nothing was getting in here for a while.

But we kind of had to get the message through to Val, who was still wrapped in the throes of her berserker rage, chasing down those in retreat.

In the end, the job was given to the Warriors to create a barrier around her and send the three of them in. And I was very happy it was Val's Guard who led that crew. I was no way brave enough to tell that girl it was time to come in from warring.

The head Warrior who had orchestrated our run into Sanctuary stood toe to toe with Val and yelled in her face, "Stand down, Mighty Warrior. It is time to rest your blade."

Val shook her head and came back to her senses. Marcus and Kait collapsed where they stood, and Val wavered on her feet, too jolly stubborn to fall over. All of us raced out and escorted... carried them in. We definitely weren't out of the woods, but hopefully we had time to breathe before the bell for the next round sounded.

"Batter up!" February's voice crackled across the speakers set up around Sanctuary's rooftops. "We have incoming. Military. And lots of them." Moments later we heard the roar of the trucks and saw the plumes of dust the convoy was creating.

61

JONATHAN: AND SO IT ENDS

I raced to embrace Al, Cissa and Luke. "Run. Go back the way you came, and hide. They don't know you're here."

"We'll keep you posted and support you as we can." Al embraced me again. "Shall we take Ruby?"

I looked to the dust plumes coming closer. Then to Daisy who held my girl. It was the hardest decision I had ever had to make. "Yes. Take her and run. Hide. Keep her safe. I will contact you when it's clear."

But my daughter had other plans. She screamed and clung to Daisy. I was literally torn in two. We didn't have time. But my dear friends had to get away. "Go. I will send her shortly. But you three must get away before you are identified."

"I'm not going. I'm staying with Dad." Luke crossed his arms and made a stand.

"Fine. That's fine. You two, please, just go. Keep helping us from the outside."

My best friend gaped. "You knew?"

"Of course I knew you were Anonymous. I recognised your writing. Now run. Cissa, take him now."

She ducked down, kissed my cheek, then took her husband's hand

and dragged him away via the back fence leading to the yards and paddocks behind Sanctuary.

I turned to face my people. They were completely spent. Val, Marcus and Kait could barely form a conscious word, but the warning another attack was coming had roused them. Tessa, Dan, and the folk they brought with them from Laodicea were not in much better condition. None of us were.

Our exhausted bodies were being hauled back from the promise of rest. We had to think. To act.

"What do we do, Bear?" I spun to see Kait clutching her kids, her face stricken. "They have to go too." Marcus looked from his wife to his kids, then to me. Torn. We were all absolutely paralysed by fear for our kids.

What do we do?

Holding hands, Dan and Tessa stepped forward. "We'll take them. We know the way."

With a fierce embrace, I hauled Ruby out of Daisy's arms and kissed her. "I love you. Go now with Raph and stay safe." I looked to Daisy and tried to give her the same message without using words. "Take her and run. Take the same path the others used to come in. Go now. Find help in Laodicea. Keep her safe. And you. You have to be safe."

Daisy just stood still, shaking her head. "I can't leave you. I can't leave Sanctuary. This is my home. I helped build it and defend it and I will not abandon it."

I looked around. Indrila and Caspian were weeping over Cyan who was confused and fussing in her mother's arms. Phil was pushing his daughter, Jayne, towards Tessa. His plea to his daughter that she should run came out choked: "Help with Cyan. She knows you."

After a panicked muddle of frantic hugs, Dan peeled a sobbing Ruby from my arms and grabbed Riah's hand. Tessa, ushering Raph in front of her, held Cyan, and with Jayne at her side, they all bolted for the back border of our home. If we knew they were safe, we could stand our ground. We knew fighting the Unseen was part of our everyday life. But taking on the Seen was something altogether different.

Already my heart was shattered. I had done what I could to save my girl, but it tore me in two.

Watch over her. Watch over them all.

It was all I had time to think before the snake of trucks pulled into our carpark and blocked the entrance and most of the street. The back of one troop carrier was thrown open and six soldiers unloaded a ridiculously ostentatious throne. A red carpet was rolled out, a dais laid. The throne placed in its centre. Then a shade shelter was secured. I was sad the process didn't take longer, thereby giving our kids a better chance to get away. Once everything was set, the back door of a pretentious, oversized, overlong, black car opened, and the Gerent emerged. He marched over to the throne. Two soldiers held out a thick sable cloak for him to put on, before he climbed the stairs and took his place. Once he was seated, another soldier placed a ridiculous crown on his head.

"It has taken me a while to get here, but now that I am, I would like for you to send out your leader."

No one moved. Whilst we were prepared to die for what we believed, none of us were too keen to run into our death.

"Send the leader of your community out now, to bow before me and acknowledge me as your god."

Still, none of us moved.

The Gerent flicked his hand and another soldier stepped up, holding a device. "They are making a break toward the hills at the back of the compound. All three of them are together."

"Excellent. Bring them back." His voice was calm and reasonable whilst his eyes were mad and murderous.

My will and hope were shattered. I was a deflated, shredded balloon. The only thing keeping me on my feet had been the hope that Ruby would be safe. I turned away from my family and vomited the remnants of the meagre food I'd scavenged today. The fence post at the front gate was the only thing keeping me on my feet. I was dimly aware of the moans and quiet cries of my family behind me.

* * *

HYSTERICAL SCREAMS HAD me back at attention. The Gerent nodded his head and from behind us, Dan stumbled with blood streaming from the side of his head. Tessa's eye was swelling shut and she was cradling an arm. And all of our children were gagged. Jayne held Cyan, who wasn't moving. They were herded along by soldiers prodding them in the back with rifles.

"Did you think I would let my little pets run away? You forget, I own you. You are my subjects, my possessions." Very quietly, the Gerent repeated himself with a caveat. "Send out your leader now or for every minute you keep me waiting, I will kill one of these. Starting with the youngest."

Jayne was thrust forward, desperately clinging to Cyan. She fell to her knees but refused to let go of the toddler. She teetered and tried to stop herself from falling. The best she could do was roll to her side, doing her best to protect her charge. Riah and Raph raced to help her, but they too were knocked over as punishment for helping, falling awkwardly due to their tied hands.

Phil bellowed and had to be restrained by Josh and Callum. Indrila and Caspian were openly weeping. Kait, Marcus and Val were white with rage. I turned to face my family, caressed Daisy's cheek and tried to tell her everything I needed to say with my eyes in the five seconds I had before I needed to go.

But just as I turned to exchange my life for our children, Mary came by and grabbed my hand. "You always were a good boy, Jonathan. Never quite understanding the truth of it, but a good boy, none the less. You see, this is *my* home. *I* am the head of this family." She smiled at all of us. "You, my boy, are the heart. And it is high time you learned your place." She took Daisy's frozen face in her hands and kissed her cheek. She embraced Jet, then turned to leave us. But I had to grip the fence post harder as I almost fell. Travis stepped out of the shadows and looked to the crowd behind him. When he found what he was looking for, he nodded. "You know I love you and am very proud. Keep to the Light, my boy." A groan broke from the gathering as Travis held out his bent arm and said to Mary, "May I have this dance, my friend?"

She looked up to his eyes and smiled. "Indeed, it is a beautiful day to dance in the Light." And together, slowly, they made their way out to stand trial before the Gerent.

He lifted his eyes to mock us. "And what kind of people are you, that you would hide behind the old and frail?"

"Listen here, young man. Watch who you are calling old and frail. You might have an army behind you, but I am in the Light. *You* are not overpowering us. *We* have deigned to meet with you. You, *child*," she put such judgement and shame in the word, even the Gerent flinched at her accusation, "are not, nor ever will be, or could be, a god. Quake before me, mortal, for I represent the God of creation, the Lord of lords and the King of kings. I pity you in the darkness that surrounds you. Your judgement day is coming, but today, for me, is the victory. I stand here in the Light, ready to receive my gift of life. Ready to lose all to gain Him and glory for his name."

"What on earth are you talking about? You deranged, senile old bat. Bow before me and acknowledge me as your god."

"I will never bow before any other than the Light. He is my God. He is the Truth. But I petition the Light on your behalf that your eyes are opened, and you see the Truth before the judgement day finds you."

"I am your judgement, woman. I will take your life if you do not bow before me." The Gerent's rage had him standing on the edge of the dais.

Mary looked even smaller than she was as she stood defiantly against our earthly ruler. "You cannot take from me what I freely give."

"Make her submit." The order was screamed as soldiers stepped in and knocked Mary's knees out from under her. She fell to the ground and couldn't stifle her cry. Travis dropped to his knees, not before the Gerent, but to help Mary right herself. We all just hugged each other tighter and wept.

Help her please. Keep her strong and faithful. Help us all stay strong and faithful.

The Gerent's rage was palpable. He snatched the pistol out of his offsider's hand, and with a deafening crack that echoed through the valley around us, Mary's body crumpled into Travis. He was knocked to the ground from the impact. For a moment I thought he, too, had been killed. But very slowly he rolled out from under her dead weight. With his head bowed he righted Mary's body as much as he could on the ground beside him. He stroked her face, unaware that he was coated in her life blood. He then, very slowly, straightened and stood to face the Gerent.

"Now you," the Gerent screamed. "Get back down on the ground. Bend the knee or die."

"Well, here's the thing, sir, I can't do that."

The Gerent nodded and Travis's knees were knocked out. I'm confident he knew it was coming, but there was no way he was going to his knees willingly.

Behind me I heard Luke groan.

"Submit." The scream echoed across the fields around us.

Travis righted himself so we could see his profile. He was, to the very last, doing all he could to encourage us. He lifted his face to heaven, smiled then looked to the Gerent and simply said, "No."

The Gerent nodded to the men either side of him. One held him whilst the other kicked him in the stomach.

"Acknowledge I am your god."

Through gritted teeth, Travis murmured, "No."

Spittle flew from the Gerent's twisted mouth. His skin was mottled red, purple and white. I stood pinning Daisy and Jet to my sides. Both gripped me so hard; the pain was the only thing keeping me from imploding. All of us, as one, were weeping, petitioning the Light and standing proud of who we were and Whose we were. If this was our lot, we would gladly accept.

Just please don't make our children suffer for long. For Travis and for them... for all of us, please, make it quick.

The Gerent stormed down off his dais and punched Travis in the side of the head. My brother's body flew sideways into the guard at his left. His cry was absorbed by our own. The guards roughly returned him to an upright position and lifted his head by a handful of hair. The Gerent stood over Travis and screamed in his face, "I am your god. Submit."

A quiet but defiant whisper, "No," was the last we heard from our beloved brother.

The Gerent screamed then punched him again, and again and again. Travis's body lay inert in the dirt at the Gerent's feet. Blood dripping from the psycho's fists. But that wasn't enough. He then pulled out his revolver and emptied a clip into Travis's lifeless body. "I am a god. The only god. There is no other god but me. And you will. All. Submit and worship me. And me alone."

At this last declaration from the enraged madman, seven arrows from the heavens pierced the air and formed a circle of Warriors around the Gerent. Even though he could not See, even he could sense something was happening. He froze, tilted his head and, with wild eyes, looked around him.

The lead Warrior of the seven allowed the psychotic ruler a moment of Sight. I imagined that, right now, the Gerent would have preferred ignorance. "You have overstepped your bounds. Let this be a warning to you."

Shaking my head like a wet dog, I tried to clear my vision and refocus—just in time to see the Warrior remove his hand from the Gerent's abdomen. With a high-pitched wail, the madman who had wreaked havoc in Sanctuary dropped to the ground, screaming. The pain released in his cries was unbearable. Thankfully it must have been too much for him to remain conscious, for the noise shut off as suddenly as it had begun.

Aides ran to his side, deemed he still lived, and ferried him away, presumably to hospital. It would be better if it were the morgue, but for now we would take what we could get.

Why didn't You take him? Why did you let him live? Forgive me. First, thank You for saving us. Thank You for saving my girl... girls... our children and for protecting Sanctuary.

Then it hit me like a sledgehammer, Travis and Mary were gone.

"Take courage." The lead Warrior spoke as two others helped Mary and Travis to stand. Yep, you heard me. Stand.

My eyes streamed with tears and again I had to pinch myself for clarity. Their bodies still lay in the dirt, their blood seeping out, being drunk by the thirsty soil. But in the Unseen, Travis and Mary stood, returned to their prime, acknowledging each other with beaming joy glowing off their perfect armour. The other Warriors gently and reverently unbuckled and released them from their life-shields, and the six escorted our loved ones away.

The lead Warrior faced us. "For now, take time to recover. The war is not over, but today's battle is won. You have time to mourn, rejoice, consolidate and prepare. There is more on the horizon, but enjoy this small window of peace."

And he was gone.

62

MARCUS: CLOSURE

We slept the sleep of the dead, exhausted and grieving. Our camp was shell-shocked, with hearts teetering between careening off in celebration of our eleventh-hour rescue, and being trampled underfoot at our devastating loss. None of the kids could move a muscle without at least one parent fussing and feathering about. But the children didn't care, notice or want it any other way.

We all needed everyone in line of sight at all times. The trauma had us chained in a gang and floundering in thin air. Not only had we lost two key figures central to our home, I was cast adrift with no purpose to pour myself into. Here and now I was about as useful as a blank flag on a still night. The battle was over. The work here done.

Truth be, looking backward through the looking glass, we should be grateful that the war came knocking at our front door. It had woken the members who'd just been going through the motions. It had birthed… tattooed… reality onto their lives and pinned their eyelids open to The Way of it. They had now been pulled—holus bolus—through the doorway. The fight was real, and the choice had to be made. Prefer life here and now, like the High Council, and receive death. Accept death daily, like Mary and Travis, and be granted life.

The Way of the Light truly was top side down and inside out to the world we lived in.

Anonymous, Al—who had not followed his friend's instructions to leave the city... for the second time—informed us that despite the Gerent's illness, his wishes had been carried out by his overzealous Second. The last four members of the High Council who had advocated bending the knee had been rounded up and express-delivered to The Games. Even though they had sold their souls, it wasn't enough. They were being held personally responsible, accountable and punishable on behalf of those who chose to defy the Gerent's demands. Like dust in a tornedo, they'd not stood a chance—the Gerent's people guaranteed it, not even taking the time to microchip or tattoo.

However, on a deeper level of depravity, considering the Gerent's dire need for new kidneys, each victim of The Games was kept alive long enough to become an organ donor for the many waiting for a chance of renewed life. It was seen as an act of benevolence from a gracious ruler-god, giving life and "saving the sick" as well as entertaining the masses and handling crime.

Why didn't You destroy his diseased heart instead of his kidneys? Why did You let him live? What purpose does he serve? What good can come of this man's dark rule?

It just added another weight to our grief and ripped any false facade away from our lives. The threat was real. But if we stepped out from under the protection of the Light, we were without hope. We could not trust the Gerent to hold to any promise. We could not trust any but those closest in the Light.

"Come on, Bear, it's time." Kait stood in front of me. Sitting on our bed in me Sunday best, one shoe on, the other hanging from me hand. The bodies had been cleaned and dressed, the holes dug—me hands bore witness to the labour of breaking through the hardened soil— around the tree roots to a depth of six foot. Their markers would forever stand sentinel in the back paddock overlooking the Fields of Victory, as they'd now been named.

I looked into her eyes. Me pain was mirrored and returned with love. Either side of her stood me kids, Raphael and Sariah. Both still bruised and battered, tattooed and scarred. Audette had informed us, one of her surgeons had tried to perform a mercy operation to remove the microchip of an escapee. After scanning, the device was located, attached to the victim's heart. Next, when the doctor attempted keyhole surgery to remove it, the tracer emitted a toxin that killed the patient within moments. She contacted us immediately and made us promise, until we had confirmation from her, we were not to attempt to remove the device. She would do all she could to learn more, but until then, three of me kids were vulnerable, traceable and on the Gerent's radar.

This was just another cloud darkening our victory and dampening the reprieve. I couldn't help the tears and gut-wrenching pain slicing through me at the memory of them standing captured, bound, gagged… and beaten. I dropped me head into me hands and wept. It could have been them. *Thank you, for all I'm worth, it wasn't them.*

The bed sank as each sat beside me and hugged me something fierce. Kait knelt in front of me and cradled me head. The sound of sniffing had me looking to the door. Me other two kids, Daniel and Contessa, stood there. Dan still bruised and battered, Tessa's good arm around him holding him steady. He still struggled from headaches and concussion. Tessa's other arm was bound in a sling. But they were alive. And they were here. Wiser, worse for wear, but among us.

Behind them, rivers escaping her eyes, Val stood aloof. Doing her best to hold it together. I groaned and slowly removed myself to the doorway and gently embraced the two.

Through the tidal wave of emotion, I tried to speak. But nothing came out. A squeak, a grunt. Until, "So brave. So grateful. So…" But that was the end of me. After gently embracing the two I lifted me head and wiped me face on me shoulder and opened me arms to me sister. She came and let me hold her as she released the same fears we were all battling with.

That's the trouble when you open yourself to love. As soon as it gets past your defences, the waves… tides… vastness of it drowns you. You're powerless against the inevitable pain and debilitating loss.

Me family knew me. They knew they were me weakness; without them I was nothing. They were allowing me the time and space to reassure myself that they were okay. Hurt and scarred, but alive.

After a family-scrum hug, it was Val who got us all back on track. "Time to head out and pay our respects to the fallen, give thanks for those who survived, and honour the Light for His faithfulness."

We took a few extra moments to wash our faces and rehydrate, and I finally got round to putting me other boot on.

Nature was doing her best to applaud our fallen. Soft white clouds dragged themselves across a piercing blue sky. The cattle grazed on the hills of lush green pasture. A gentle summer breeze hummed through the leaves of the old gum as we stood within its shade and farewelled our brother and sister, who to many had been mother and father.

In me heart I knew this was a time of celebration, but looking at Jet, Daisy and Luke, it was hard to feel the joy. The warmth of family from far and near did help. All and sundry from the Factory in Laodicea were here. Cissa and Al. Colleagues of Luke's from the hospital. And a number from the Community had quietly snuck in, unsure as to what their welcome would be, to bear witness. It really was a testimony to just how much Mary and Travis were loved.

Full respect to me brother Jonathan for remembering the members of the High Council, the first victims of The Games in Philadelphia. As much as they had been a significant pain in the buttooshie, Dennis, Rebecca, Niccola and Stuart weren't bad people, they were just scared.

Justly so, as it turned out. Witnesses said they never stood a chance, not even raising a finger in defence of their lives. Shepherd-less sheep... lambs... to the slaughter. The threat was real, and the danger was great.

The Gerent had thrown the gauntlet at our feet and, in the Light, we accepted his challenge. We all had targets on our foreheads, and me kids had trackers attached to their hearts. Now was not the time for doubting the power of the Light, it was time to stand firm and trust His eye was on me lambs.

The Gerent's second had "negotiated" with the Community here in the city, enabling them to continue in their "good ministry to the people". But the new Overseer was one of the Gerent's men. They were allowed to go about their business and daily lives, but the warning was constant, the eyes everywhere and the ears to every square inch of ground. However, here at Sanctuary, the Light had stationed a legion of His Warriors, five deep around our perimeter. And with the confrontation up close and personal in his memory, the Gerent was choosing to turn a blind eye and deaf ear to us… for now.

The mounds of dirt covering Mary and Travis's earthly bodies were buried under mountains of flowers and tributes. Each person was offered the opportunity to share memories, stories and blessings shared with our fallen loved ones. Jonathan led petitions to the Light that we might learn, remember and be encouraged by the witness of our brother and sister. And then, all those with a musical bone in their body offered their Badge, leading us in a time of singing and praise.

In the hush that fell after the ceremony, it was hard to pull ourselves away. But then out of the blue, Cyan started giggling. She was in Indrila's arms and pointing back to Sanctuary. We all turned to look at Tiger, chasing Pod in circles before the cat scampered up a tree and teased the dog.

Her giggles were the key that unlocked the emotion, and a slow chuckle broke into a hearty laugh. "Nanna-May always said Tiger was going to get the better of that pup one day." Jet, firmly tucked under Jonathan's arm, led us back to the Meeting Place where we sat and broke bread together, sharing fond and hilarious memories of Travis and Mary in a belated, subdued Lightmas lunch.

After the meal Jonathan read the letters that accompanied Mary's will.

* * *

Now listen up you lot, I know you are going to be sad.

So, stop it.

It is I who am sad for you.

I am free. I am with my love, in the Light, whilst you remain.

Have your time of grief and move on. Life is too short to be tied up in tears.

My dearest Jet, I love you and am immensely proud of you. Obviously, I have left you everything I own. All my assets, treasures and finances. However, you are too young to have the wisdom to make the most of these things. Daisy and Jonathan are trustees of my estate until you are of age—unless you already are. Learn from them and Travis. He's a good egg and can teach you lots.

My dear little Ruby, thank you for allowing me the joy of being in your world and blessing me with your youth and enthusiasm for life. The world thought you were being cared for by us, but it was you who were invigorating and sparking new life in us. You will always have a place in the house at the top of the hill. It is your home too. Don't ask me to figure out the logistics, I'm old and tired. I will leave that for the young and creative. But be assured, I claim you as one of mine and this gives me great pride and joy.

Travis, you old coot. You have been my elbow buddy for decades. It has been an honour to serve beside you and to call you both friend and brother. I suspect I shall get to heaven's gates before you, so I wanted you to know you are both an inspiration and challenge to me to keep my eyes on the Light, and my hands in the world. Thank you, old friend, for far too much that can't be written here.

Daisy, my girl. Open your eyes and heart and jolly well get over your-self. Your father was a hard man. Not at all a good model. Look around you and see. See the heart. Receive the love. Share your weak-ness. It will only make you stronger. Stay strong in the Light. Continue to open your arms to the poor and extend your hands to the needy. You are seen. You are loved. You are not alone.

* * *

Jonathan, you were always a good boy. Thank you. Thank you for always taking the time to listen to this old girl—Mad Mary—and see my truth underneath. For taking the time to see the heart of those around you. Your time is coming. Your battle will only intensify and become more difficult. Gather around you those whom you trust. Let her in. She will guard your heart, stand by your side and watch your back. She is fierce, she is loyal, and she needs you.

* * *

About Sanctuary. It is my desire that our extended family always have the bottom paddock for whomever needs… sanctuary. Let it remain a place of safety, of refuge and respite from the world at large. Please. It has given me such joy knowing that the Light has allowed us to host such a wonderfully talented, unique and interesting group of people. Let it remain a place of exploration, discovery and creativity in the Light.

* * *

My family, it has been my greatest pleasure to know you and to share my final years and home with you. Celebrate this victory and rest in the knowledge that He is greater than all the world can throw at us. I look forward to the day we meet again.

* * *

THERE WAS NOT a dry eye or downcast soul in the Meeting Place. How she did it, I'd not figured out. But from that moment on, our sadness started the gruelling trek from all-consuming, to a shadow that would take a permanent residence.

We knew we had a short time of reprieve as the Gerent waited in hospital for his kidney transplant, and then recovered. We also learned that his Second was just as savage, but not quite as driven. We needed to make plans for the short-and long-term future. We had to ensure the safety of our family in the Light and make preparations for the next wave of torturous hell that lurked just over the horizon.

EPILOGUE

DANIEL: CLOSURE AND OPENINGS

I loved the plan. The plan was good and being part of the plan was even better. But sometimes it sucked. Like now. Two months out from Defeat the Deranged Delusional Guy Day—3D Day—and I was still seeing stars. And not the good type. The hit up-side my head still had my ears ringing and my eyes fighting to work in tandem. Especially when I tried to read. Audette had told me I had to "give it time" and eventually all would align, and I would be "right as rain". But the headaches, inability to escape into a good book, and the hangover from my latest dream was a cocktail that was literally doing my head in.

But good news was, we were moving out. I mean, I had grown to love Philly, and no doubt our family walls had stretched to include this lot of loons at Sanctuary. But I was getting itchy feet. As was Marcus... and Val... and everyone. Our job here was done and we'd recovered... kind of. The mop-up was finished, and we were now mostly spending our time coming up with creative ways to twiddle our thumbs.

The roar of laughter from the crowd gathered in the Meeting Place was the proof in the pudding. Word had spread, like dye in a fishbowl, that I couldn't read. I mean, I could read, but not right now. So Kait—

with a bit of help from Mr Berry—had organised the kids to read some of my favourite books in the evenings. To start with, the older ones just narrated. Not to be left out, the crazier of the younger ones, led by my little sister, started enacting the scenes. It turned out to be so popular, the adults were falling over themselves to be part of the act.

I couldn't complain. The effect was hilarious and enough to raise my spirits. But tonight, all I could raise was a smile. I was still wiped from the delivery of our new assignment in Sardis via a dream: "Enlighten the Seeing Blind Man". What kind of convoluted craziness was that? It was worse than "Find the Black and White Girl", the message that had started our wild goose chase in Laodicea.

But "not complaining", remember? I loved the plan; the plan was good and being part of the plan was even better. And I would keep repeating that truth to myself as long as it took to remind myself that the choppy water I sailed in these days—in the Light—was far better than the boiling pitch I was drowning in—in the Dark—previously.

The headaches would pass, my eyesight would align, the Light would continue to kick butt, and my wife—I couldn't hold back the grin at that thought—was my forever-friend and home. But the instant cessation of the "Read to Dan" madness pulled me out of my bliss bubble.

Pod's barking at an intruder... I mean, guest—I still had trouble changing my mindset—pulled us up short. Shadows approached the Meeting Place and all us adults stood as one, formed a fence between the newcomers and our kids, and came very close to drawing arms. I guess I wasn't the only one having trouble changing my attitude.

Our guests, not only arriving under the cover of darkness, also wore baggy clothes and hoods. They pulled up short at our... welcome, for want of a better word.

Daisy, as per usual, was the first to engage. "Why are you here? What do you want?"

The three visitors looked around the group, at each other, then one stepped forward, dropping his hood. "We're sorry to interrupt your evening. We have come to request an audience with Jonathan... our Overseer."

At this, I noticed I wasn't alone when I moved to place myself between my brother and the intruders. The barrier protecting the children became a wall to enclose Jonathan. Daisy went so far as to draw her sword. It wasn't too big a deal, though—these guys were in armour, so it was more for show. If she had pulled her knife, I probably would have drawn mine to back her up.

A wry chuckle from the back of our group broke the tension. "It's alright, everyone. Stand down. I am not that weak that I can't greet our guests. Good evening, Sean. What brings you to *Sanctuary?*" Jonathan put extra emphasis on that last word.

Message received. Well, by everyone except Daisy; she did not sheath her sword. "Not too sure about that, Shep. You missed your nap this afternoon." The bite in her snark, however, was dampened when, as Jonathan manoeuvred his way to the front of the group, he squeezed her hand. And she didn't let it go. As Jonathan moved to address our visitors, he had to take Daisy with him. With her sword still in her free hand.

With wild eyes considering Jonathan's—human—guard, the spokesperson stuttered his message. "Th-thank you for seeing us." His eyes darted over his shoulders, checking his backup was still present. "We have come to ask you if you would consider returning to your position as Head Shepherd and Overseer of the Philadelphian Community?"

Daisy's scoff interrupted Jonathan's response. He side-eyed her, then answered. "We have been led to believe the Gerent has installed his own man in that position. Surely you can understand the position that puts me in."

A woman stepped forward and took over. "Forgive us, Overseer. What Sean forgot to lead with was..."—a wry smile broke out over her face—"a request for forgiveness. We have seen the error of our ways and our significant mistake in aligning ourselves with the State. We see that this is not the way of the Light at this time, in this place. We were wrong, we have petitioned the Light for His forgiveness." She lifted her arms to indicate the vibrancy of her blue-green armour which gave witness to the Light's grace. "And now we are here asking you for yours." She dropped her eyes to the ground and shook her head. "We have wronged you and our brothers and sisters by not standing strong when we chose to hide within the Darkness."

Jonathan reached his free hand out and laid it on the woman's shoulder. "Leah, be at peace. All of you, be at peace." Jonathan made a point of looking them over. "It is obvious the Light has welcomed you back, so how could I not practise my gift of forgiveness too. We are living in troubled times, and it takes its toll. But I am glad to see you are all well?"

The three nodded.

"Well, that's just fine and… freaky… fantastic. But you expect him to stand up against the Gerent, again, and take on the whole of the freaky man's army, just so he can be sent to The Games, and you can run and hide, again? I don't think so." Oh, dear lord, Daisy had adopted the cobra head-wobble. With her armour on fire, sword in hand and light flashing off all the silver clips in her flaming red hair, she caused all three to take a step back. So, these folk weren't just penitent, they were wise, too. Noted.

Thankfully, the ever-present smile in Jonathan's eyes brought her back down a notch. "It's okay, Daisy, let's hear them out."

"Thank you, Overseer," Leah continued. "We have heard of the site on the hill to the west of Sanctuary where the Dark's followers set up camp to attack not only Sanctuary, but the wider Community as well. We have been on a pilgrimage throughout the city and its boundaries, petitioning the Light for His cleansing, His presence and to break any of the Dark's strongholds. We believe this would be a good place to use for our meetings." Leah's confidence had returned and her enthusiasm was making a show. It opened the doorway for her other companion to speak up.

"It's perfect. They would never look to find us there. And if they did, there are so many escape routes leading into the bush and, from there, multiple hideouts. We could meet on irregular nights at irregular times and continue to be the Light's representatives in this place.

The three of us, and some others, will continue to go to the Gerent's Community meetings, so we can keep an ear to the ground and make it look like we're submittin—"

"Like you did last time?"

"Enough, Daisy. Let Cal speak." Jonathan's gentle but firm reprimand had her retreating.

The guy's response was subdued. "She's right, though. We did submit last time. And for that, the Gerent has allowed us to keep our "Shepherd" status. Maybe it will make it easier for the Gerent's men to believe it's in still our nature this time round. We could use it to our advantage."

Sean spoke up. "We don't want to make the same mistake again. We are in the Light, we trust in Him and want to be true to Him and Him alone. Will you forgive us and lead us again?"

The night stopped in that moment. Hung in the balance. Even Daisy held her breath and her tongue. But there was no disguising the fear and... excitement? bursting from her insides-out. What would he do?

The fire that blazed from Jonathan's armour was a bit of a give-away, but if anyone was in doubt, the spark in his eye and the extra few inches to his stance were pretty convincing evidence of his thinking. Looked like the Philly Community were about to be born again... underground.

AFTERWORD

A NOTE TO MY READERS

Thank you so much for joining me on the fourth leg (four! Can you believe it??) of this adventure into the Light. I hope you have enjoyed this new chapter in the lives of those encased in the Armour of Light, and have been encouraged by their victories and gracious with their failings.

If you have enjoyed this book, please consider leaving a review. It would inspire others to pick it up, as well as encourage me to write some more. Although, that's not too hard to do.

To keep up to date with more books in the series and other news, sign up to my newsletter at donitabundy.com

Donita Bundy

HUMBLE INSURRECTION PLAYLIST

Humble Insurrection Theme: Children Come Running – *The Dust of Men*
   Daisy: Sparrow – *Branches*
   Jonathan: Before I Go – *Guy Sebastian*
   Mary's song: Three Little Birds – *Branches*
   Kaitlyn: Baby Hold On – *Liz Vice*
   Marcus: Banks – *Needtobreathe*
   Sariah: Hold My Hand – *Future of Forestry*
   Raphael: With Love and Compassion – *Sam Levin*
   Valarie: I Won't Back Down – *The Goo Goo Dolls*
   Daniel: Life is Good – *The Hunts*
   Contessa: Sweet Ever After – *Ellie Holcomb*
   Family: Ring the Bells – *Johnnyswim*

ACKNOWLEDGMENTS

To my family and support crew, thank you and a special call out to the following:

First and foremost, I would like to thank my mum without whose help and support this book would not have seen the light of day.

Belinda Pollard, my friend, sister-in-arms, and editor, whose wisdom, life experience and oodles of patience helped me cross number four off the list.

Alix Kwan, the most amazing proofreader of all time, thank you for carving time out of your very busy life to help continue the dream. Your work ensures we can let the story have its head and not be held hostage by typos.

Ella Green, Lee Cawthray (supplier of chocolate) and Rev. Loretta Tyler-Moss, the mighty three and the most wonderful cheer squad in the history of the universe. Ever.

My Beta Reader Crew, who fronted up for another round of wading through the outworking of my—at times—chaotic mind, ensuring order in the lives of those who live within these pages.

•Ella Green

•Lee Cawthray

•Belinda Pollard

•Bethanie McKenna

Dr Rob Elliott (Medical Specialist) and his wife Ruth (ex-nurse). Thank you again for being so generous with your medical knowledge and understanding of hospital best practice. If there are any discrepancies between what I have written and real-life situations, it is due purely to me taking my creative licence too far. It is not in any way due to the excellent information I received from these wonderful people.

Helen Briffa, PA to Assistant Bishop Cam Venables, Bishop for the West, for taking time out of her *very* busy schedule to help me understand the *incredibly* busy schedule of an "Overseer".

The Somerset Writers Group; a more diverse, caring, supportive crew of creative geniuses would be hard to find.

My family at our own Soteria House; for your constant prayers, support and encouragement, thank you.

And finally, and most importantly, I give thanks to the Light, whose story I believe this is. Whilst it is told through the lens of my life experiences, it continues to be inspired, carried and created in His strength alone. My prayer remains, dear reader, that you find inspiration, challenge and encouragement to keep journeying the incredible adventure in, and with, the Light.

ABOUT THE AUTHOR

Donita Bundy lives in the Somerset Shire (Queensland, not England) with her husband, two boys, her socially inappropriate cat and irrepressible red dog. She loves creating images with words and, when she's not writing, her camera. Eating chocolate, hanging out with the wallabies and walking the aforementioned red dog are a close second.

To connect, follow her blog, listen to the podcast, check out the gallery or just keep up to date with what's going on, go to her website and sign up to the newsletter at

donitabundy.com

ARMOUR OF LIGHT SERIES

BOOK 1: DANGEROUS SALVATION

What if your saviour was more dangerous than your enemy?

Lonely and living on the streets, forced to steal clothes to survive another bitter winter, Daniel has an encounter that turns his world upside-down. Confronted by two strangers who tell him things about himself that no human could possibly know, Daniel is offered a choice: to stay where he is and face the dangers of the street, or accept the invitation of a warm bed, a family... and to join their war. Can he trust the safety this "family" appears to offer? Or will he give in to the temptations of the Dark Lord? He must make a decision. Fast.

ISBN: Print: 978-0-6487423-0-8

Ebook: 978-0-6487823-1-5

BOOK 2: BLINDING REVELATION

What if the Unseen was more blinding than the Seen?

The crew have survived the chaos and hardships of Sodom to arrive in Laodicea's lap of luxury. A city ahead of its time: beautiful, pristine and enemy-free. It is the perfect place to rest, recover and regroup. But all is not what it seems. Something sinister lurks beneath the sterile exterior of the golden city. How will the refugees from Sodom adjust to life in this foreign city? With no common enemy to fight, what will hold them together? Is this place heaven on earth, or is it the threshold of hell?

ISBN: Print: 978-0-6487823-3-9

Ebook: 978-0-6487823-4-6

BOOK 3: BROKEN RESTORATION

What if complete restoration requires absolute brokenness?

Evicted from the luxury and freed from the restrictions of Laodicea's Community of Light, the crew find themselves homeless and without prospect. Stumbling upon old family and new friends at an abandoned factory, the Light's purpose for them is gradually revealed. But surely they have misinterpreted His plan? Are they up to the challenge? Will their personal stumbling blocks be too great to overcome? Is the Dark too insidious and ingrained in Laodicea to be defeated?

ISBN: Print: 978-0-6487823-6-0

Ebook: 978-0-6487823-7-7